Mercy Among the Children

Mercy Among the Children

a novel

DAVID ADAMS RICHARDS

Arcade Publishing · New York

FIRST U.S. EDITION 2001

Originally published in Canada by Doubleday Canada, a division of
Random House of Canada Limited.

Library of Congress Cataloging-in-Publication Data

    Richards, David Adams.
        Mercy among the children : a novel / David Adams Richards.
        —1st U.S. edition
          p. cm.
        ISBN 1-55970-586-8
        I. Title.

        PR9199.3.R465 M47 2001
        813'.54—dc21   2001022671

Published in the United States by Arcade Publishing, Inc., New York
Distributed by Time Warner Trade Publishing

Visit our Web site at www.arcadepub.com

10 9 8 7 6 5 4 3 2 1

EB

PRINTED IN THE UNITED STATES OF AMERICA

To Robert Couture

Mercy Among the Children

PROLOGUE

Terrieux lived in a small apartment on the fourth floor of a rooming house in the south end of Saint John, New Brunswick. One day in November of 1997 a man was waiting for him in the entranceway. His name was Lyle Henderson. He had a watchful look — the kind that came, Terrieux suspected, from being big when young and having had bigger, older boys and men challenge him; or perhaps from being an adult to children when he was no more than a child himself.

He was about twenty-five, dressed in a white winter coat, blue sports jacket, and a pair of blue dress pants. He wore a ring on the index finger of his right hand, which could be used in any street fight and added to his appearance of a tavern bouncer.

Terrieux's place was away from the city centre, among the newly renovated waterfront buildings and down a half-hidden alleyway, in an area that smelled of the docks and Irving pulp mill. There was a smell of diesel, and a shapeless conglomerate of depressed buildings and houses that ran off around a corner, where there was posted a Pepsi sign over an old convenience store, faded cigarette advertisements, and a newer advertisement for sanitary napkins. The door was open and cold air hung at the entrance.

Terrieux had retired as a police officer years ago, to join the Canadian navy. He had been a naval officer for some seven years. Then, feeling betrayed in a way by Canada, or by the failure of his marriage that came about because of his position, he had resigned and drifted to the States, where he had worked in New Orleans on the docks and in the Gulf of Mexico on an oil rig. He was heavy-set and strong enough that neither the work nor the rough life bothered him.

He knew how to handle himself, something that showed on his face, the expression of which was an unapprehensive certainty in himself.

But, feeling displaced, he had come back to the Maritimes, with short stops in Virginia and Maryland, in 1995. His wife had gone years before, and was remarried to an accountant with W.P. and Maine. He sometimes saw her again and even now he felt a resentment from her that he would give anything to overcome. It was the sad look of a woman of forty-nine who had in her life dreams unfulfilled, and would blame forever her first love for this.

Now at fifty-seven he stood between fathers and their children, parolees and the parole board, a buffer between out-of-fashion men and those who wished to change the life of those men. He knew the men, because he was one of them. He knew the lives they led, lives no better or worse than others he had dealt with. And he was cynical of change in a way most intelligent people tend to be. That is, he was not cynical of change so much as cynical of those who would in fashion conscience alone commit themselves to it.

Lyle Henderson had a story to tell, perhaps about this very thing, and he was hoping Terrieux would listen. This was not an unusual request from the men that Terrieux knew, but was unusual for a boy of Lyle's age and demeanour. The demeanour was something seen only in youth, a kind of hopefulness in spite of it all. In spite of the blast of misfortune that would crumble lives to powder. It seemed as if Lyle understood this, without benefit of much in his life. Perhaps while standing here in the doorway of the Empire Hotel he understood how much the man he was talking to had himself suffered. Perhaps they were reflections of each other, in youth and middle age, a mirror into the past and future of rural men caught in the world's great new web.

Terrieux nodded, smiled, and invited Lyle upstairs.

Down below as they climbed toward the third landing they could see traffic and hear students getting on a bus to the university. The walls of the old wooden house, inside and out, were grey, with paint from a job done eleven years before. After a time they came to Terrieux's small apartment at the back of the house.

In the yellow rooms with a portable television, a couch, and a few chairs scattered about the kitchen, Lyle's face suddenly had a tenderness. To Terrieux it seemed a face that said it probably deserved much more tenderness than it had ever received and had given more also. Saying, even more, that tenderness was a commodity of valiant people. This is what Terrieux understood by Lyle's look, which was almost, somehow, entirely compassionate.

"Did you ever hear of a man named Mat Pit — ?" Lyle said, taking a deep breath. Or perhaps he took the breath just before he had asked (which would, Terrieux knew, give a different *reason* for his breath).

"No," Terrieux said, "I don't think so."

"He was my neighbour," Lyle said, "when my brother and sister and I were growing up in our house in the Stumps."

"I know where that is," Terrieux said quickly.

The Stumps was a tract of land in northeastern New Brunswick, along the great Miramichi River, which flowed out of the heavy forests into the Northumberland Strait, north of the western tip of Prince Edward Island. The Stumps was part of the vast and stunted spruce and brilliant-coloured hardwood that shadowed the salmon-teeming river as it widened into the Miramichi Bay. It had been settled first by Micmac Indians and then by displaced French, who hid during the British expulsion of the Acadians in 1756. The Irish — like Henderson — came half a century later, for some reason still loyal to a British crown that had pissed in their face. They worked the woods and cut the timber, and towns grew up along the great river that ran south and east almost to the top of the state of Maine. Its people were fiery, rough, and not without brilliance. It was the river where Terrieux had been a police officer years and years ago, when he himself was not only Lyle's age but in height and colour looked exceptionally like that young man.

For a moment Lyle stared out at the old wooden docks of this largest industrial city in New Brunswick, part of the receding empire of British North America, quickly being swallowed whole by the more vigorous and certain empire to the south, so that the very name

Empire Hotel took on a splendid quaintness for the detached, very unsplendid building in the fog.

"You were a police officer?" Lyle said.

"For six years."

"It is a very strange thing — all that has happened since then — you know — with *him*."

"Oh — with who?" Terrieux smiled.

"I do not blame you," Lyle said. "But if every moment and movement is in some way accounted for, no one knows what *not* killing someone sometimes does."

"And who did I *not* kill?" Terrieux said, smiling cautiously, and glancing at the boy's belt for a weapon while deciding which chair to thrust at the boy's head — if required.

There was still the scent of the fire that burned a building across the street a few weeks ago. A certain smell of ash in the cold air.

The boy (for this is how Terrieux thought of most under thirty) thought for another second, and reached into one of his pockets. He laid a picture on the table.

"It's — this," he continued, his voice shaking just a little. "I am thinking — looking at this man, who I grew up beside — what would have happened had things been slightly different. If on that night long ago when he fell through the ice — on the east side of Arron Brook Pool — a place I have lain my coyote traps — and shot a bull moose with a nineteen-point rack — you let him sink. I never suspected that that man I sometimes shared my thoughts with could already have been buried if, well — not for you. And I know the peril you put him in that night by chasing him made you give up police work. For another moment he might well have drowned at sixteen. You see, he has taken advantage of us both."

Lyle whispered this last phrase as Terrieux took the picture. Terrieux held the photograph out and looked at it. His eyes were going, and he took from his pocket bifocals and put them on cautiously, looked at Lyle and then at the picture again.

The man in the photo was wearing a jean jacket, with his hair combed back, his eyes like burning beads, and Terrieux quickly formed a mental picture of the sheer agony Mathew Pit must have caused others and himself. *Must* being the word, since this young man was here with this picture, and not a soft young man either but a young man whose blow-by-blow encounter with life was etched upon his still young face.

So certainly Mat Pit had caused him — something.

Terrieux had had a few run-ins with this man in the picture. He had taken him to court twice; both times the boy was let go. And finally he had saved Mat's life one late March night about 1964. Mathew had tried to cross the brook to escape Terrieux and had fallen through. The water beneath the rotted ice was deep and swift, but Mathew was not at all penitent. In fact he had tried to make it out himself and for the longest time refused entreaty from Terrieux to give him his hand. Terrieux suspected him of much but could prove little.

What made him give up police work was how he had almost, *almost* caused this Mathew Pit's death. Or how the media *said* he did. How they complained that Terrieux "over-reacted" and that he had harassed this child many times before. When a suspension came because of this, Terrieux gave up police work.

He remembered Mathew Pit when he stared at his eyes and blond hair. He remembered that he had a sister, and a young brother. Something was wrong with the brother. Mentally retarded, as they said then. The brother, Trenton, did not grow above four foot nine.

It was all a long time ago.

"He was different than any other young fellow — more certain of himself, more dangerous because of this," Terrieux said.

"Yes," Lyle said. He kept staring at Terrieux. "He — from a certain perspective — ruled our road and took that precious air from every-one else's dreams."

Terrieux flipped the picture in his fingers and handed it back.

"I am thinking what if you *had* failed to rescue him?"

"I almost didn't. I lost him for a while. Then I could hear some-one scraping away at the ground. It was Mat Pit trying to claw himself out of the brook. I went down with a stick and inched out so I could grab him. He hesitated a long while — but finally he gave me his arm."

"I had to come and see you — and tell you what happened after you pulled him out of that brook. I want to tell you what happens in life, if you don't mind."

"Ah," Terrieux said. "I who know nothing of what happens in life?"

"Well — that's not what I mean, of course," Lyle said unapologetically.

Terrieux did not respond. And then something happened to rankle him even more. The boy, Lyle Henderson, took out a giant notepad, filled from front to back with notes and quotations, and flipping to some folded newspaper articles said:

"It was the Age of Aquarius — is that what gave rise to the Pits of the world?" He smiled, a little eagerly, as if growing familiar too soon, which is a trait that Maritimers have, so used they are to everyone being a neighbour if not a friend.

"Perhaps it was." Terrieux smiled.

At this moment the boy seemed nothing much more than a tavern thug, and Terrieux was disappointed that his past could be delved into by anyone so easily.

Terrieux picked up the photo and looked at it once again. Then handed it back again. Lyle smiled again.

When Lyle smiled his face changed just slightly to one that had appropriated enough pain to last a lifetime. It was a face that still, however, registered hope; a hope with an internal stop gap.

Here Lyle looked at his notes again — pages and pages of quotations and arrows. "Everything I relate is true. It is what I have witnessed and what has been told to me — the conversations of others even when I was not present are very near to being exactly what they were, told to me by those who remembered them first-hand, or talked to someone who knew. It has taken me almost seven years to piece together what it was all about, and I want to set it before you now. Maybe you can write about it, as a former policeman, just for interest sake, and maybe you can expose the Mat Pits of the world."

Lyle lighted another cigarette and looked out the window at the Church of the Redeemer, settled under the cold black Maritime day.

Terrieux nodded his assent, and Lyle began.

MERCY

ONE

The small Catholic churches here are all the same, white clapboard drenched with snow or blistering under a northern sun, their interiors smelling of confessionals and pale statues of the Madonna. Our mother, Elly Henderson, took us to them all along our tract of road — thinking that solace would come.

In November the lights shone after seven o'clock on the stained-glass windows. The windows show the crucifixion or one of the saints praying. The hills where those saints lived and dropped their blood look soft, distant and blue; the roads wind like purple ribbons toward the Mount of Olives. It is all so different from *real* nature with its roaring waters over valleys of harsh timber where I tore an inch and a half of skin from my calves. Or Miramichi bogs of cedar and tamarack and the pungent smell of wet moosehide as the wounded moose still bellows in dark wood. I often wanted to enter the world of the stained glass — to find myself walking along the purple road, with the Mount of Olives behind me. I suppose because I wanted to be good, and my mother wanted goodness for me. I wanted too to escape the obligation I had toward my own destiny, my family, my sister and brother who were more real to me than a herd of saints.

My father's name was Sydney Henderson. He was born in a shack off Highway 11, a highway only Maritimers could know — a strip of asphalt through stunted trees and wild dead fields against the edge of a cold sky.

He did poorly in school but at church became the ward of Father Porier. He was given the job of washing Porier's car and cleaning his house. He was an altar boy who served mass every winter morning at seven. He did this for three years, from the age of eight to eleven.

Then one day there was a falling-out, an "incident," and Father Porier's Pontiac never again came down the lane to deliver him home, nor did Father ever again trudge off to the rectory to clean the priest's boots. Nor did he know that his own father would take the priest's side and beat him one Sunday in front of most of the parishioners on the church steps. This became Father's first disobedience, not against anything but the structure of things. I have come to learn, however, that this is not at all a common disobedience.

Back then, harsh physical labour seemed the only thing generations of Canadians like my grandfather considered work. So by thirteen my father wore boots and checked jackets, and quit school to work in the woods, in obligation to his father. He would spend days with little to comfort him. He was to need this strength, a strength of character, later on. He had big hands like a pulpcutter, wore thick glasses, and his hair was short, shaved up the side of his head like a zek in some Russian prison camp.

He worked crossing back and forth over that bleak highway every day; when the June sky was black with no-see-ums, or all winter when the horse dung froze as it hit the ground. He was allergic to horses, yet at five in the morning had to bring the old yellow mare to the front of the barn — a mare denied oats and better off dead.

My grandfather bought a television in 1962, and during the last few years of his life would stare at it all evening, asking Sydney questions about the world far away. The light of the television brought into that dark little house programs like *The Honeymooners, The Big Valley, Have Gun Will Travel,* and *The Untouchables;* and glowed beyond the silent window into the yard, a yard filled with desolate chips of wood.

My grandfather Roy Henderson would ask Dad why people would act in a movie if they knew they were going to be shot. He would not be completely convinced by my father's explanation about movie scripts and actors, and became more disheartened and dangerous the clearer the explanation was.

"But they die — I seen them."

"No they don't, Dad."

"Ha — lot you know, Syd — lot you know — I seen blood, and blood don't lie, boy — blood don't lie. And if ya think blood lies I'll smash yer mouth, what I'll do."

As a teen my father sat in this TV-lightened world; a shack in the heat of July watching flies orbit in the half dark. He hid there because his father tormented him in front of kids his own age.

I have learned that because of this torment, Father became a drunk by the age of fifteen.

People did not know (and what would it matter if they had known?) that by the time he was fifteen, my father had read and could quote Stendhal and Proust. But he was trapped in a world of his own father's fortune, and our own fortune became indelibly linked to it as well.

In the summer of 1964 my grandfather was asked by his employer, Leo Alphonse McVicer, to take two Americans fishing for salmon at the forks at Arron Brook. Roy did not want to go; first, because it was late in the year and the water low, and secondly, because if they did not get a fish he might be blamed. Still, he was obligated.

"Get them a fish," Leo said, rooting in the bowl of his pipe with a small knife and looking up with customary curtness. Roy nodded, as always, with customary willingness. He took the men this certain hot day in August to a stretch of the river at the mouth of the brook, where the fish were pooled. He took his boy, Sydney, with him, to help pole the canoe up river and make the men comfortable. Then in the heat of midday, he sent Sydney north in the canoe to scout other pools for fish while he spent his time rigging the lines and listening to the men as they spoke about places as diverse as Oregon and Honolulu, while being polite enough to have no opinion when they spoke of the quality of Leo McVicer's wood and his mill.

Sydney poled back down river later that afternoon, looking in the water, and saying the fish had gone far up but that four salmon rested here, taking the oxygen from the cool spring, lying aside the boulders at the upper edge of the rip.

These men were important. They had been instrumental in help-ing Leo McVicer and Leo wanted to amuse them the way Maritimers do — by pretending a rustic innocence under obligation to *real* human beings who have travelled from *real* places to be entertained.

So after three hours, Roy whispered to my father: "It would be better for Leo if they caught something — if they are here to help finance the new barker for his mill."

And with those words, and with his shirt covered in patches of sweat and dust, and with his neck wrinkled in red folds from a life under lash to sun and snow, with his blackened teeth crooked and broken, show-ing the smile not of a man but of a tobacco-plug-chewing child, and with all the fiery sinewy muscles of his long body, he set in motion the brutal rural destiny of our family. Asking one of the men to give him a rod, he tied a three-pronged jig hook to it, had Sydney pole above them and then drift silently down through the pool without pole in the water, to point out where the salmon were lying. He threw the jig where the pool joined the spring and jerked upwards. All of a sudden the line began to sing, and away ran the fifteen-pound salmon jigged in the belly. After twenty-five minutes he hauled the spent cock fish in, killed it, and hooked another. The Americans were laughing, patting Roy on his bony back, not knowing what Sydney and Roy and the wardens watching them knew — that this exercise was illegal. The wardens watching stepped out, confiscated the rods, and seized the men's brand-new Chevrolet truck.

Leo McVicer heard of this at seven o'clock, when he got back from the mill. He paced all night in quiet almost completive fury. My grandfather went back to work early that Monday, willing to explain. But Leo fired him on the spot, even though Roy had sought to please him. For that I was to learn was Leo McVicer. Never minding either that the great Leo McVicer had often poached salmon for New Brunswick cabinet members and the occasional senator from Maine who partied at his house. This of course my grandfather did not know. He was kept from knowledge of the decisions of his great friend, as he was kept out of the dark rooms of his gigantic house.

To be fired after years of faith and work broke him, and he sat, as my own father once said, "like some poor sad rustic angel confined to hell."

Still, there was a chance — if only one — to work his way back into the fold. That summer Leo's men were unsatisfied and twice threatened a wildcat walkout. Finally McVicer beat them to it, and locked the sawmill's gate.

For the next two weeks things existed at a simmer between Leo and his men. They milled about the yard like atoms bouncing off each other, collecting and separating, collecting again, in pools of dusty, loitering brown-shirted figures, caught up at times in wild gestures, at other times almost grief-strickenly subdued. And within these two states there was talk of sabotage and revenge. No trucks or wood moved on or off McVicer property, and they stood firm when a welders' supply truck tried to enter, howling to each other and holding it back with their bodies, knowing little in life except what bodies were for, to be bent and shoved and twisted and gone against. At the end, the welders' truck was defeated. With a jubilant shout from the men into the empty September heat, the driver turned back and a lone truck of herbicide was left unloaded in the yard.

Finally Roy Henderson asked my father's advice. What could he do to make things better for Leo, and regain his job?

There was one thing my father advised: "Go to the men." My father at fourteen stated, "Convince them to end their walkout." He added that Leo would be grateful — the contracts filled, the herbicide unloaded, and Roy would be considered instrumental in this.

Roy headed into the woods on a warm September afternoon, with the pungent smell of spruce trees waving in the last of the summer heat. Just before he arrived onsite three men cut the locks to the gate. They stormed the truck and rolled the hundred barrels of herbicide off it, busted the barrels open with axes, and dumped them all, along with forty barrels of pesticide from the warehouse, into the upper edges of Little Arron Brook. The new barker was sabotaged, a flare was lighted to engage the men in more hellery, and a fire raged.

All of this was documented by a local reporter. A picture was taken that day long ago. Unfortunately, standing on the hulking ruin of smouldering machinery, a half-crazed drunken smile on his face, was my grandfather. It made the front pages of the provincial papers. He had not exactly done what my father had advised him to. In fact he looked like a vigilante from the deep south stomping the ruins of innocence. It was how *they* wanted him to look.

I have this picture still. As faded as it might be, the image is strikingly familiar, savage and gleeful, as if in one moment of wilful revenge Roy had forgotten the reason for his journey that afternoon.

Grandfather told Dad that he had tried to stop, not start, the conflagration. But his picture, even faded to yellow in an old archival room, shows him a rather willing participant in the mayhem. As if his grin leering from a newspaper at me, a grandson he never knew, was his only moment of bright majesty, caught in the splendid orb of a flashbulb, which signalled our doom for the next thirty years.

All others there that day got away when the police arrived but grandfather, too drunk to run, fell from the machine he was prancing on, and crawled on his knees to the police car to sleep.

The fire burned eleven hundred acres of Leo McVicer's prime soft timber land; timber subcontracted to the large paper mill. After my grandfather's picture was published, this fire became known locally as the "Henderson horror."

"Roy is bad — his son is mad," the saying rose from the lips of everyone.

Meanwhile Roy Henderson, illiterate and frightened of people who weren't illiterate, had to go to court and pay a lawyer to defend him on both counts; that is, of poaching and the destruction of the barker. My father described Roy as he stood in court in a grey serge suit. He had lost his beloved television. He was confronted by a menacing prosecutor. He shook and cried. He was sentenced to three years. People teased him on the way out of court.

Sydney, at fourteen, would make him biscuits and hitchhike to Dorchester to visit. But Roy, who had never been in jail in his life, refused to eat.

"Tell Leo I will not eat unless he forgives me," he said, sniffing, and sitting with his hands on his knees. His hair was turning grey and grey hair stuck out of his ears; his eyes were as deep set, his brow as wide, as some rustic prophet. But Sydney knew he was no prophet. He gave Sydney this message, as the sunlight came in on his prison trousers:

"Tell him that my life is in his hands — and then see what he has to say. Tell him that the biscuits are hard now, and gettin' harder. Go on, fella — get goin' —"

My father left the prison, in his old red coat and torn gumboots, and ran all the way to Moncton — thirty-seven miles. He caught the train, went to Leo — not to the house, but to the office in McVicer's store that had served our community for years. The store was a monument to the class of people it served, where calendars of halter-topped blonde and blue-eyed girls shining Fords with Turtle Wax were hidden by Leo under the counter, and where diversified products were unknown but Humphrey work pants and boots, and corduroys for children, were sold, along with erasers and scribblers and pencils for school.

"I just lost me a hundred-thousand-dollar barker — and a million-dollar lot," Leo said, without looking at Dad but looking through some invoices of clothing that he believed he had not ordered. "Now I have to clean up the barrels that got into the brook," Leo said, flipping the pages. "Everyone —" flip, "the Sheppards —" flip, "the Pits —" flip, "the Poriers —" flip, flip, "and everyone else said it was yer dad — *yer* dad and no other dad — and what do you want me to do?"

"Go visit him so he'll eat."

"Go visit him and cheer him up so he'll eat a good breakfast — well, damn him."

My father went back to jail to see his dad. It was close to Christmas and snow had fallen and covered the cities and towns, the long raw southern New Brunswick hills were slick with ice.

My father pitied Roy yet could do nothing to rouse him. At first Roy did not believe that Leo, whom he had known since he was sixteen, wouldn't come to see him. He stood with his hands on the bars of the holding cell they had brought him to, looking out expectantly, like a child. He addressed his own child as if he was another species, a strange creature that one day had appeared in his little cabin, someone Roy himself never knew what to do with. And that is why often as not he addressed Sydney as "fella."

"Yer saying he won't come to see me, fella."

"That's what I'm saying, Dad. I'm saying that he won't come to see you."

"Let's just get this straight — not that he's busy and might come to see me some other time — or something like that there?"

"He won't come, Dad."

Roy's look was one of incomprehensible vacancy, as if from some faraway land he was listening to some strange music. Then his eyes caught his son's and became cognizant of what had been said, and perhaps also for the very first time who his son was, and what grace his son held. And realizing this he was shocked, and broken even more.

"Well I pity him then — for doin' that — is all I can say," Roy whispered. And he refused on principle — perhaps the only one he had left (and to prove, just once, grandeur to his son) — to eat.

A few weeks later, ill with pneumonia, Roy Henderson was taken to hospital on the Miramichi. He died there, and was buried in an old graveyard downriver, leaving my father alone.

I always said *I* would have done more. But my father felt he had done what he could. He never left his father alone. He walked 230 miles of road, appealing to McVicer to forgive. He fasted as his father did. He broke his fast only to take communion. He remained with his father to the end, even though it was a solitary vigil. But he would never seek revenge. Revenge, my father believed in his fertile brilliance, was anathema to justice.

After Roy's death Dad lived a primitive life, for what contact would he have with others? He would be teased whenever he went out to a dance; girls would string him along as a joke. He began to drink every day whatever he could find; to forget, as Sam Johnson has said, and

I once found underlined in a book my father owned, "the pain of being a man."

The pain of being a man, or simply being cold or wet or tired. The old barn was long gone. His house was built of plywood and tarpaper. Its walls were insulated by cardboard boxes. It was fifteen by twelve and sixteen feet high — so it looked like a shoebox standing on end. That is something that I like to remember. Most of his life was lived principally here.

He lived three years alone hiding from people who might do something *for* him — I mean send him to foster care. But no one expressed any concern whatsoever on his behalf. Except for one man: Jay Beard, who lived in a trailer up on the main road and hired Dad to cut wood. At one time Dad got a job (as illegal as it must have been) planting dynamite to blow boulders at a construction site. He was not afraid and he was also nimble. He earned what was a good deal of money for him, and with it he bought both his mother's and father's graves their stones.

At eighteen he was coming home from a long hot day in a lobster boat on the bay, where he worked helping bait traps. His skin was burned by the sun and saltwater and his hands were blistered by the rope and the traps. But that day he met Jay Beard, who was selling off many of his books, books Jay had inherited from his dead brother and had himself never read. Beard was actually looking for my father to sell these books to. My father bought three hundred paperbacks and old faded hardcovers, the whole lot for twenty dollars, and brought them home by wheelbarrow.

Then in early fall of that same year Sydney, who in reading these books had given up drink, went to Chatham to see a professor about the chance at a university education. The professor, David Scone, a man who had gone to the University of Toronto, disliked the Maritimes while believing he knew of its difficulties and great diversity. Looking at my father sitting in his old bib overalls and heavy woollen shirt proved what he felt. And he commented that it might be better for Dad to find a trade. This was not at all contradictory to Dr. Scone's sense of himself as a champion of people just like Father. In fact, being a champion of them meant, in his mind, he knew them well enough to judge them. And something he saw in my father displeased him.

"Yes, I know you have come here with your heart set on a lofty education — but look in another direction. A carpenter — how is that? — you seem like a man who would know angles." And then he whispered, as people do who want to show how lightly they take themselves, "It would not be as difficult for you as some things in here, philosophy and theology and all of that —"

Scone smiled, with a degree of naive self-infatuation seen only in those with an academic education, shook his head at the silliness of academia, while knowing that his tenure was secure and every thought he had ever had was manifested as safe by someone else before him. My father never had such a luxury. There was a time my father would have been beaten by his own father if it was known that he read. Knowing this, tell me the courage of Dr. David Scone.

My father said that being a carpenter might be nice and he liked carpentry but that he liked books more. Outside, the huge Irish Catholic church rested against the horizon, the sun gleaming from its vast windows and its cavernous opened doors; its steps swept clean, its roof reflecting the stains of sunlight, while on the faraway hills across the river the trees held the first sweet tinges of autumn.

"Well, then — you want to be a scholar, do you. So what books have you read, Sydney? Mystery — science fiction — Ray *Bradbury* — well, there's nothing wrong with that at all, is there?" He smiled. My father was about to answer. Dr. Scone was about to listen but he was called away by the head of the department, a rather rotund priest with thick downy cheeks and a bald spot on the top of his head. Father stood and nodded at Scone as he left. Then he walked home from Saint Michael's University and sat in his kitchen. He did not know how to go about qualifying for university. It had taken him five weeks to find the courage to do what he had done. Now he felt that the man had condescended to him. What surprised him was the fact that an educated man would *ever* do this. He had been innocent enough to assume that the educated had excised all prejudice from themselves and would never delight in injury to others — that is, he believed that they had easily attained the goal he himself was struggling toward. He did not know that this goal — which he considered the one truthful goal man should strive toward — was often not even considered a goal by others, educated or not.

He had by that evening discovered his gross miscalculation. He was angry and decided to write a letter, and sat down in the kitchen and started to write to this professor, in pencil on an old lined sheet. But when the words came he realized a crime had taken place. (This is how he later described it to my mother.) The crime was that he had set out in a letter to injure someone else. He was ashamed of himself for this and burned the letter in the stove, sank on his bed with his face to the wall.

Later I came to hate that he did not send it, but it was noble. And what was most noble about it was that it would never be known as such. Nor did that in itself alleviate his suffering over what the professor had said, or his memory of the professor's self-infatuated smile when he said it. That is, like most spoken injuries, Father had to sample it not only at the time it had taken place but for days and even weeks after, and again each time this well-known professor was interviewed in the paper about Maritime disparage or his lifelong fight on behalf of First Nations rights. (Which became a lifelong fight at the same time it became a lifelong fight among his intellectual class, most of them ensconced in universities far away from any native man or woman.)

The fact that my father not only was a part of the demographic this professor was supposedly expert upon but had worked since he was a boy, and had his own ideas from years of violence and privation, made the sting ever sharper and fresher each time he heard Dr. David Scone lauded for his *utter decency* by our many gifted announcers on the CBC.

Yet by his honour — my father's honour — he could and did say nothing. Even when Dr. David Scone tried to influence my mother against him.

I know now it was because of an incident that happened when my father was a child of twelve. One day he and another boy were shovelling snow from the slanted church roof. The boy had robbed Dad's molasses sandwich and Dad pushed him. The boy fell fifty feet, and lay on his back, blood coming from his nose and snow wisping down over his face.

My father, perched high upon the roof next to the base of the steeple, was certain the boy had died. He did not believe in anything, had hated the priest after that certain incident, that falling-out I mentioned. But still he whispered that if the boy lived he would never raise his hand or his voice to another soul, that he would attend church every day. *Every damn day.* What is astounding is, as soon as he made this horrible pact, the boy stood up, wiped his face, laughed at him, and walked away. That boy was Connie Devlin.

I don't believe Devlin was ever hurt. I believe my father only thought he was. The bloody nose came when the boy fell, but was nothing to be upset over, and the boy liked the attention that happens when people think you are dead. I told my father this when I heard of his pact years later. I said, "Dad, you never touched the boy — so therefore God tricked you into this masochistic devotion. God has made you His slave because of your unnatural self-condemnation."

My father never answered; he just turned and walked away.

Connie Devlin was to plague Father all his life. And it was from that day forward my father's true life started. After that day, things happened *to* his life that showed, or proved to him at least, other forces.

What my father believed from the time his own father died was this: whatever pact you make with God, God *will* honour. You may not think He does, but then do you really know the pact you have actually made? Understand the pact you have made, and you will understand how God honours it.

TWO

My mother, Elly, was an orphan girl brought up by a distant relative, Gordon Brown, originally from Charlo.

My mom was reported to have had two siblings adopted by other families in other places. This fact, the fact that by her own family she was left in an orphanage, and then taken to the home of Gordon Brown, had a profound effect upon her. It made her solitary as a child, and nervous. She had many rituals to keep herself safe, because she felt anyone could come and take her away, and felt also that anyone had power to do what they wanted with her life. She therefore went to church every day, praying to God, and hoped for miracles in finding her siblings and her mom and dad, whom she never stopped looking for. She was considered odd by the people — even by her adopted parents and her stepbrother, Hanny Brown; pitied and looked upon with sadness as a very unclever girl. Worse for her social welfare, she saw miracles — in trees, in flowers, in insects in the field, especially butterflies, in cow's milk, in sugar, in clouds of rain, in dust, in snow, and in the thousands of sweet midnight stars.

"Why would there not be?" she once told my sister, Autumn Lynn.

But others of course tormented her continuously about this. No one considered her bright, and she left school at sixteen, her second year in grade eight, hoping for a life in the convent. Two years passed where my mother did chores for neighbours, babysat, and attended church. Then her friend Diedre Whyne — a girl who had a much more affluent family, who was sharp and gifted, had taken two years in one at school on two different occasions — took Mom under her wing, finding a job for her in Millbank, away from the prying eyes of the nuns at the Sisters of Charity. Thinking of the circumstances, who among us would have done differently?

In Millbank, still considering the convent, Mother met my father, when he was about nineteen or twenty. They met at the community picnic, where she was working the tables and he was helping hitch on.

To hitch on a load at a horsehaul — where a two-horse team proves its strength by hauling sleds with incredibly heavy loads — is extremely dangerous. Some men won't do it with their own teams because the horses are so hyped on tea they bolt as soon as they hear the clink of the hook being snapped to the sled. A man has to jump out of the way in a split second or be run over. However, my father earned extra money to buy more books, and if he was not oblivious to the danger, without conceit he was not concerned by it.

The last day of that particular long-forgotten horsehaul, the horses and even the horse owners now long dead, held in a large field near the main river, Sydney went to the huge canvas army tent for water. My mother was working the table just inside, which looked exactly the same as the outside except the grass blades were covered, and saw Father approaching. The old cook rushed to her side and forbade her to talk to him, for he was a danger to people.

This woman arranged a date for my mother with her nephew Mathew Pit, home from Ontario, where he had spent two months in the Don Jail. This date was arranged and Mathew picked Mother up that evening at her rooming house and drove to the sand pile, a kind of lovers' lane without the lane, near McVicer's sawmill.

He had asked his younger sister, earlier in the evening how he should behave, and how he should approach this great chance. Cynthia had smiled and in a moment of sisterly diplomacy that would be for years captured in his mind, and now years and years later in mine, said: "Give it to her."

Mathew parked, revved the engine, and, reaching over, put Mother's white bucket seat in the reclining position, so that she was no longer staring out the windshield but staring at the spotted ceiling. He opened a quart bottle of beer for her to drink, plunking it down between her legs. All about them the half-burned acres of land sat mute and secluded in midsummer and the old sawmill looked melancholy with its main building sunken and its huge gate rusted and locked. It reminded one of years of mind-numbing work, of cold and heat and a degree of futility seen in deserted overgrown places where life once flourished.

"McVicer has a million dollars and not one friend," Mathew said with country cynicism. "That's not how I'm going to turn out — here for a good time not a long time, I say —"

My mother said nothing, for McVicer had once visited her and had given her an apple, and an orange one Christmas day and a sock with a barley toy and nuts.

For twenty minutes or more not another word was spoken, and Mother's thoughts might have been as flat, her face may have been as uncommunicative as Joseph Conrad's Captain McWhirr, the hero of "Typhoon," who wrote to his parents, when a very young seaman, that his ship one Christmas day "fell in with some icebergs."

Certainly Mother must have felt that she had fallen in with some icebergs, and she was unresponsive, as he now and again reached over to keep the bottle between her legs upright.

Finally Mathew finished his own quart of beer; he did not hurry it, and supposed this is what my mother was eagerly waiting for him to do — finish. Then, with her still staring at the ceiling, and the quart bottle still plunked on an angle between her legs, he took off his shirt and showed her the two eagle tattoos on his biceps. Then he put his hands under her dress. Suddenly, after being dormant as a turnip for almost a half hour, she gave a screech.

"What the Jesus is wrong!" he said, as shocked at her screech as she herself was. "What did you think was going to happen here? For Christ sake — this is a date, ain't it?"

Mother got out of the car and walked back and forth in the evening drizzle as he followed her, snapping gum, with his hands in his pockets and a beer bottle dangling from his right hand, blackflies circling his broad blond head. Her arms were folded the way country girls do, her lips were pursed, as she walked back and forth trying to avoid him. Finally she went to a set of barrels and kneeled behind them.

"Please, Mr. Pit, thank you for the wonderful time but I would like to go home," she said.

He smashed his bottle in anger and upset the barrel she was hiding behind. "Get up outta that," he said as if hurrying a draft horse out of a cedar swamp. "This is the same stuff they use in Vietnam — to flush out the gooks."

"Yes — that is very nice thank you very much — Mr. Pit sir I would like to go home —"

"Go home now? We just got here!"

"Yes please Mr. Pit sir thank you very much." She kept her head down and her eyes closed as she spoke. She had been told not to sass her betters, never to think she was smart, and always to mind her manners. All of these recommendations from the Office of the Mother Superior, at the convent of the Sisters of Charity, she was trying hard to remember. She was told this more than others because she was a child without a father, and without a name. A few nuns as unclever as she had rapped her knuckles raw trying to make her remember the five points of obeisance to the Lord and to her betters, and told her she could not be a nun if she was a nuisance.

But she felt, and quite rightly, that Mathew was close to hitting her. If he had hit her, Mother would have only lowered her head and whispered that she was sorry. He yelled that she didn't understand what a good time meant, and she nodded and with head bowed walked behind him back to the car.

"I should leave you here," he said. "Bears and bugs to eat you — pussy and all. How would you like that?"

She did not know what he meant. She looked about her feet to see if there was a kitten.

"Please Mr. Pit I want to go home."

"You want me to drive you home?"

"Yes sir Mr. Pit."

"Give me a kiss and I'll drive you."

She turned and began to walk, head down, along the old derelict road toward the highway. He drove behind her, honking the horn.

"Yer some dumb to give up losin' yer cherry to a man like me — tell you that!" he said, his head out the window and his hand on the horn.

Finally, at the highway, she was persuaded to take a drive. She got into the back seat and sat like a child, her eyes closed, her lips recounting a decade of the beads.

Mathew phoned her six times in the next four days to ask her out again, telling her they would go to a different place. She was going to tell him she had mumps — but since she did not want to lie she told him that she "once" had mumps.

"It's that good-for-nothing Sydney Henderson," Mathew told her. "He has you braindead. He's almost like a devil the books I heard he reads and everythin' else!"

Her spurning made Mathew wretched. It was a wrong that went beyond all others. For how could Sydney Henderson — Sydney Henderson, the boy whose father tormented him in front of them, so everyone had howled in laughter, the boy Mathew had slapped at school trying to make cry (Sydney didn't) — have caught Elly's eye? How could God allow this to happen? Mathew did not know. He only knew he would break this spell.

By sudden inspiration Father was asked to a beach party by Cynthia, Mathew Pit's younger sister. She had been in trouble many times (once for biting a bride's ear), and already her face had a chameleon-like changeability seen in those who have studied social opportunity more than they have studied themselves — a beautiful face, no doubt, wanton at times, at times hilarious, but always resolute, fixed on purpose beyond her present state, which was rural poor.

For Mathew's sake Cynthia would break the attraction between Mother and Father. In the lazy heat of her upstairs room, beyond earshot of their mother, Mat lectured her on what she might do.

"I'm not going to do it with him — I won't go that far. He'll get a hand on it but nothin' else."

"I'm not asking you to do no more," Mathew said with a kind of anger he almost always felt. Then something else happened, again by afterthought. He had had on his person for a month, given to him by Danny Sheppard — for the purpose of giving it to Elly — a tab of blotter acid. He had forgotten about it. Now he gave Cynthia the tab, to spike my father's Coke. Cynthia took the blotter acid and put it in the back pocket of her tight terrycloth shorts, without comment. This was at ten past six on a Friday evening; their large old house, with its two gables, its front door facing the back yard, smelled of stale summer heat, peeled and poled wood, and fried cod, lingering from the kitchen up the dark, forbidding stairs.

My father drank a Coke at ten that evening. By this time Cynthia, bored with his conversation to her about Matthew Arnold (who wouldn't be at a beach party), had drifted away to one of the Sheppard boys — Danny. But Father in drinking this acid did not act out and become violent or paranoid as Mathew had hoped. Instead he walked all the way to Millbank and woke my mother by throwing pebbles at the window of Kay O'Brien's house next door.

"Sir, you have the wrong house," my mother said after watching him for ten minutes and deciding it must be her he was after. "You must throw your pebbles over here!"

"Why didn't you read my notes?" he said, throwing the last white pebble into her room.

My mother could barely read, and did not wish to tell him this, for the nuns had broken the skin of her knuckles many times with the rap of a pointer. Always, to her, letters had appeared backwards and upside down.

"I have no care for notes from big important people, and I think you are being some darn forward," she said hesitantly. "Besides, I am getting married."

"To who?" he asked, deflated.

"To Jesus Christ," she said.

"Maybe I can talk you out of it."

"Don't be improper."

"I see some angels near you."

"You are being funny at the Lord's expense," Mother said piously.

But to Father the vision was accurate. The night was drowned by soft and splendid moonlight, moonlight in every direction. It had formed a gliding path on the water from the east to his feet beneath him. It was as if he could walk on this moonbeam, see for miles, and not bother touching the ground. It was as if my mother was standing naked, with angels on her right and left shoulders.

"I walked up here because some force propelled me to — last night I never would have been so bold — I see you like this and I want to marry you."

"Go home, please —" she said. But she did not want him to go anywhere.

"Say you will marry me or I won't leave."

"Go home and I will think about it. You're Sydney Henderson, right?"

"I was when I started up here —"

"Go home — tomorrow you will know my answer."

The next day my mother, Elly, went to see my father, Sydney, in a dry, yellow hayfield near Arron Brook. He watched her walking toward him wearing a light cotton dress and a pair of sneakers. She walked up to him, all the while speaking to men he was haying with. Then stopping before him, she took his large face in her hands and kissed him to the great merriment and cheers of all the others. So I was told. It was here Dad saw my mom as a simple human being, good though she may be. He did not see the angels ever again. He saw her as beautiful — but simply a woman, whose breath when she kissed him smelled of the radish she had been eating.

Still they were seen together as two youngsters, without money or hope for a future, backward and living precariously with no indication that they could ever better themselves.

Many people said they were grossly mismatched. The Poriers, the Pits. McVicer himself. And McVicer had the Whynes invite Mom on a blueberry-picking excursion to Wisard Point. The Whynes were as prominent as the McVicers. Prof. David Scone was a friend of Diedre, and took an interest in Elly. Scone and Diedre were both very radical, and Elly was so shy she had a hard time looking at them directly. She also felt that there was a conspiratorial feel to the trip, to where Elly was positioned in the car, to who offered her water, to the questions asked her about Syd.

Dr. David Scone sat with her for a long time patting her hand with his but looking stern and irritated, as if some great weight was now upon his shoulders, some grave social duty (not realizing of course that it was the simple vulgarity of matchmaking). It was of course an age much like this age, when people conspired to look good more than be good. When they got to the blueberry field, Diedre picked beside her, and talked a long time about how David Scone held kind feelings for and was intent upon helping the poor of the Maritimes. He was Diedre's companion; platonic (it would seem). Professor Scone was most concerned with the plight of rural women, who had never been taken seriously. Now it was time that they were. (Dr. Scone seemed to have himself just discovered this, as if writers like Brontë or Hardy had not.) My mother said that would certainly be nice, to be taken seriously — especially in serious matters.

David Scone had black hair that curled over his ears. He was tall and thin, his arms were thin and weak looking. His black silky beard covered a milk white face. But Mom did not at all like the way he looked at her, which was with a steady haughty glance, as if everything she had ever done had been told to him by someone else.

I believe she recognized in Professor Scone the baffled pity and subtle condescension a man of education often has for others, and which others had held toward *her* all her life, a trait more mocking than considerate and known by the poor or the "disenfranchised" in a second. Also there may have been a certain hope involved. This could be sensed in the late-summer air and the wide expanse of trees where an old bear came out to gorge herself on berries not far from them. That is, the new world had caught Mother up in its snare every bit as pernicious as the nun's pointer falling on her small white hands. Yes, they told her, she would have a great life without my father, but that she must be bold, inventive, and lie to get rid of him. To Diedre he was a physical monstrosity.

"God, whatever will you do?" Diedre had asked Mother that

afternoon; and then she whispered: "David Scone is divorced and does like you very much, can't you tell? He also is a *professor!* — a professor showing interest in you — my dear —"

"I thought he was *your* boyfriend," Mother whispered back, trying to show interest out of politeness.

Diedre looked at her strangely and then smiled. "I do not have *boyfriends*, love."

"But I love Sydney," Mother said. There was a pause. Mother heard a grasshopper tick in the grass beside her bowl of blueberries, and stood and moved five paces away. Diedre followed and kneeled beside her once again. It was as if — and Mother sensed this — my father's feelings for her did not matter, that they believed Sydney had a calculating mind from which they would free her.

"Can Sydney after all his trouble learn about love?" Diedre whispered finally. My mother had been waiting for the shoe to drop. For all her young life, shoe dropping, reprimand coming, chores given were the things she knew about.

"If he had to learn it I would not seek it," Mother replied, still whispering, which showed in a truly elemental way that she would always match wits.

Within five minutes, a sharper, colder, and more longing wind came from the bay, and reminded one of autumn coming on.

"I will name one of my children Autumn," Mother said, "for the wind has informed me I will have a daughter." And again she stood and walked five paces. Again Deidre followed and plopped her bowl beside Mother's.

"So, Missy, did the wind inform you if that would be your fifteenth or sixteenth child?"

Late that evening, when she came back to her rooming house, a two-storey white building with a large enclosed veranda, and saw Sydney waiting for her on the steps, with battered boots on his feet, his hands bruised from work, his body aching from piling lumber at $1.65 an hour, she realized how much she did love him.

Diedre told my mother she could have a job in Fredericton far away from Sydney Henderson and my mother should count herself lucky. My mother did try to feel lucky, but could not. The road, the little leaves on the trees — all of this, the dusty quality of the clouds, all these *miracles* she would miss if she went away.

So that Sunday, three days after their blueberry-picking excursion and a day before she was supposed to go to Fredericton, Mom telephoned Diedre from her rooming house and said she could not possibly take this job.

"He's bullying you — he talked you out of it, hasn't he?" Diedre said. "Has he hit you or something?"

My mother whispered that this was not true, but she was crying so much the answer seemed a lie.

"I love you," Diedre said. "You will not ruin your life — I want to take care of you — but at times you are infuriatingly ungrateful. Think of *his* attitude toward you — and think of David Scone's attitude and how he cares so —"

"Does he care for all women, this Dr. David Scone from the university?"

"I can tell you all women," Diedre said excitedly.

"But then why did he fight with his ex-wife?" Elly whispered, tears running down her cheeks. "That is no way to honour someone. Sydney has not fought with me — and we believe the same things —"

"Don't be childish. David Scone's relations with his ex-wife is a private matter, and we are not discussing David Scone's attitudes but Sydney Henderson's attitudes toward you —"

"But," my mother whispered, "what are your attitudes toward Sydney?"

Diedre said that if Mother continued to speak like that she would just hang up on her and let her live with Sydney in a shack and see what would happen. So my mother, used to being bullied so that her fingers were arthritic by being rapped, said nothing else. Then Diedre, placated by my mother's silence, spoke:

"Just go over for a year — you will meet *real* people. I love you more than anyone does — but — let's just say this: Dr. David Scone knows something about this man — Sydney." Here she became short of breath, as people do when they wish to relay information that they fear might not be readily accepted. "Sydney went over to the office one day and tried to bully David into getting him enrolled. He did — with big plans about this and that. But David was not bullied and soon got rid of him! Take this job we have offered — it is your only chance! God — you're a child. Babies and diapers to that man — who as you know has been implicated in all kinds of things!"

My mother, staring at the dresser as Diedre spoke, saw the white stone Father had thrown into the room, and swayed by this, whispered, "Goodbye," hung up, and with a cardboard suitcase, and the white stone safely in her pocket, made her way to Dad's property.

THREE

Mother had never seen my father's house, for he was ashamed of it. It was the house we, the children, would grow up in. It was, even by Mom's standards, a living proof of destitution. The first day she saw it, she told us, she stared at its yellow and red front, its tarpapered sides, its long tin stovepipe, before she entered in. Perhaps she was thinking she might turn around and walk all the way to Tabusintac and never see him again.

Across Arron Brook and beyond the dark spruce trees, on that day, as on all days, sat the Pit residence. The Pits' and my father's houses were the only two on this entire stretch.

She entered the house, for the door was left open. The table was metal, as were the two kitchen chairs. There was a cot in the corner near the wood stove, and books over the floor, books of every size, books on every subject, history, philosophy and geography, novels. Books that he had collected from the time he was fifteen when he had gotten his first paycheque, working in a batch house in the woods. And books now collecting dust, long ago pored over. Hemingway, Voltaire, Conrad, George Eliot, and a hundred other authors sat within her reach.

It had turned cold with an east wind. The stove was out, and she could see her breath. On the back wall the paper was peeling, the side of one wall had a huge water stain, the kitchen window lay jammed, and beyond this was the moan of the wind in the trees. Far away was the roof of Rudy Bellanger's house, Leo McVicer's son-in-law. He had married Gladys McVicer, the spoiled eccentric daughter of Leo, the year before, in a wedding with five hundred guests, including the premier and a senator from Maine.

My mother set her things down and began to scrub.

The place was almost clean by the time Father got home that night.

"Elly," he said, "you didn't have to do this. Why aren't you at the boarding house?"

"They were about to kick me out," she said. "I wouldn't take a job in Fredericton —" She looked at him, and realized how foreign he looked to her at that moment, coming from the woods, with his chainsaw, his back covered in drizzle and wood chips and sweat, his eyes ablaze from expended energy and glowing from the wildness of where he worked and the danger of it besides.

"Oh," he said. "I guess you are stuck with me."

"You have a lot of books," she said, looking about the dismal place, dismal in the way the cold enters a small place in the middle of a bog.

"It's what I have spent my money on," he said almost apologetically, because he didn't want her of all people to think of it as an affectation. "I never read a book until I was fourteen — I taught myself how to read — no one taught me — but as you can see I've made up for it." He paused, looking at her worried and tired face. "And you know what I have found out in books?" He smiled.

"No," Elly said.

He sat beside her. Outside, the air was bleak and thick with the monotony of rain, and they smelled northern fall above the tin roof, the quiet scent of autumn hunger. A moose bird flitted in the drizzle from a spruce's dark bottom branch and hopped to his old tin barrel in the evening.

"I will say this once, and not to demean all the good they have tried to do for you. But I have found out, even before the death of my father, that no one can do an injury to you without doing an injury to themselves." The wind and rain battered the eaves of the shoebox-shaped house, as if to mock him.

"Those who scorn you taunt only themselves — I knew this without reading one word; because in reading one is reminded of the truth man is given at birth — by man I mean man and woman. My father never had to read a book to feel ashamed after he hit my mother or me.

"When I was younger I drank a lot — very much — and when I was drunk I did and said silly things. One was pushing a boy from a roof — oh yes, I was drinking even then. I don't intend to drink anymore — but I wanted to tell you that — so you would know — I have to be vigilant in that regard. But it has caused my other regards."

She looked at him, bewildered. He smiled, and filled a pot with water for tea, walking about in large untied miner's boots.

"They put you out of a boarding house —" he continued. "Well, they have demeaned themselves. The nuns bullied you as a little girl and you washed floors for them, peeled potatoes, and went to mass every morning. I know the nuns. But now your friend Diedre has harmed you and yet speaks about a future society in which no harm will happen. I have heard her speak. Last year I went to a lecture she gave. Well, they are fine people. But they have never lived one night like either you or I. Yet do they have one bit more?"

"Perhaps they have more certainty in themselves," Mother answered.

"A certainty when wrong is still wrong," Father said. "Connie Devlin is certain I caused all his problems all my life. He plans to destroy me because I pushed him from a roof in anger. I know this."

He paused again, and scratched his head, and tried to think of what to say to convince her.

"The problem today is between two groups of people," he said as

he stirred the pot for tea. "One group believes the world must change
— and David Scone and Diedre might wish to *use* you to prove it.
There is a second group, the group that you and I belong to. The
group that says that in man's heart is the only truth that matters. You
cannot change a constant by changing how rules might be applied
to this constant. Someday Diedre will see you are closer to the truth
than she is, but it will be a long struggle."

Mother nodded quickly, as if she hoped he would end his reflection
because she did not understand it; and she had never seen this side of
him. She lowered her eyes and breathed heavily and sighed.

"I will stay here," she said, "and we will be married — and what
happens will happen, for or against us doesn't matter now."

FOUR

My parents moved into that house across the lower flat scrub beyond
Arron Brook from Mathew and Cynthia Pit.

A year after Dad and Mom were married, Diedre Whyne came to
visit. Just as she had predicted, my mother was pregnant. And she
looked about the terrible little place with a certain recrimination. God,
what poverty — she had never seen it before. And again I add, who can
blame her for her reaction, here in such a place at such a moment?

She came to the point. Cynthia Pit had met with Diedre, who now
worked for the Department of Social Services. Cynthia was very upset,
told Diedre she was pregnant — just as my mother was — and that
Sydney was the father. Cynthia said she had gone to Sydney to ask for
some financial support, and Syd had rebuked and struck her. It was,
Diedre suggested, an awful situation, worse because of its sordid rural
implications. My father said nothing.

Diedre had come to suggest a solution. My father would have a blood test as soon as the child was born and clear the matter. If he was the father, Diedre would see that the marriage done in haste was annulled, and Elly could still go to Fredericton and take that job.

Sydney looked at Diedre and said kindly he would not take any blood test.

"And why not?" Diedre asked, tapping a notebook on her knee. "What have you to fear?"

"Nothing. But it will cast hilarity on Cynthia if it is done and shame on the child. I will not participate in the shame of one and the ridicule of another for my own welfare in a community that has had no use for me from the time I myself was born, has called me simple-minded and my father mad, at the request of a woman who suspects me of beating my wife and hopes for the failure of my marriage."

Diedre thought this false heroics, and a grand wily scheme to escape responsibility. She turned at the door, and with it opened said: "Now Elly, your last chance — I will wait fifteen minutes."

She waited, but Mom never left the house.

The night of Cynthia's child's birth there was a heavy snowfall, pleasant but with a numbing cold. There were no cars moving on our highway; the grader had not plowed. Christmas was soon to arrive and people were stuck in town.

Cynthia was in labour so Mother, eight months' pregnant with me, and Father crossed the inlet on snowshoes to help her.

Mathew, drunk for days, lay belly down on the couch. Now and then he would get up and drink from a bottle of wine. There was no one else in the house except Trenton Pit, the young retarded brother. My father once commented that the place was in a shambles. The old woman had gone at noon for the doctor and hadn't returned. Cynthia was herself drunk. Christmas lights shone in the dark by the bed where the twenty-year-old woman lay. The string of lights had been plugged into a small wall socket and left to twinkle in obscurity as the radio played country tunes.

"It'll be drunk when she calves," Mathew said, leaning over and leering at my mother.

All his life my father felt ashamed when he heard men blaspheme pregnancy. He had seen much of the drunken terror of men, ridiculing women when they were pregnant.

"It's no use to be boisterous now — you should be calm," he said.

Now that the blizzard had swept in from the bay the last traces of streetlights were blotted out. No doctor would make it in this storm. My mother boiled water and my father prepared as best he could to deliver the child.

At nine o'clock on the night of Christmas Eve the child was born. It was a girl. It remained still, a strange grey colour, the umbilical cord about its neck. Mathew inspected it as one might inspect a carburetor — that is, with a good deal of curiosity.

He then covered the infant in the Christmas lights that lay on the floor. They twinkled over the child's grey naked body. Cynthia lay still. The moon came out and shone on her naked pelvis and legs.

Mathew picked it up, still covered in lights, and tossed the child up and down in the air, trying to revive her.

Father took the child, and breathing into her mouth tried to revive her. He held its nose, counted and breathed softly, and then massaged its chest.

The moon was now full on the sparkling white snow, and all the land was bathed in peace. The infant child was grey the colour of the faroff moonlit snow.

I was born January of 1970.

Autumn, my albino sister, was born a year later.

FIVE

In the seventies Dad could get no work, and so went smelt fishing in the winter. I would walk beside him and watch him haul his nets up through the great blue ice. We would leave the smelts to freeze in the sparkling air, which always made them taste much better. Far away on the ice were other fishermen's sheds, and the glare made my eyes water, and sometimes the wind would smell of beans at five o'clock on a Saturday night.

On Saturday Mom would wax the floor, and the smell would loiter in the air and in the shadows from the lingering sun. And Autumn and I would put on our woollen socks after supper; Dad would put on an old Elvis Presley record and Autumn and I would dance across the floor until it was shiny and smooth. Sometimes Mom had me as her puck and Dad had Autumn as his, and they would heave us across the slippery floor toward the opposition's goal. We would slide like mannequins and crash into each other like shuffleboard stones, while outside and overhead beyond our music the cold night blossomed in winter's crystal silence.

Everything went fairly well until the winter my father was accused of stealing a box of smelts.

Connie Devlin had his nets down below my father on a flat stretch. My father had the better stretch. At dark, just when the twilight flushed across the ice and wind began to moan through the trees, my father would come off the ice, hauling his wooden box of smelts by a rope through his frozen and cracked leather mittens. Connie had a habit of not checking his nets, and my father, who I think always felt responsible for Connie, worried about the smelts.

It sounds ridiculous, two men with nothing at all fighting over a miserable nothing at all on a flat of ice in the middle of our great bay. Oh, our bay in the winter — how many memories it brings; ice breakers and seagulls and purple-tinted sky.

Yet the smelt fight reminds me strangely of *Down and Out in Paris and London,* in the hostel where two desperate men are fighting over the one pair of clothes because one wears them to panhandle in the day and the other at night. I *know* those men in my blood. But you see — my father did not want to fight over a box of smelts.

"I will make it up to you," he said to Connie.

I know now, as I should have then, that my father never stole as much as a matchbox in his life, but they were stolen. By who — well, Mathew Pit and the Sheppard brothers, Danny and Bennie, very likely. Bennie who wore a leather jacket with studs up the arms.

What I had not seen until this time is how we were marked. Oh, I had seen some derision against my father at a horsehaul or church picnic. Yet by the time she was five Autumn knew of it more than I. She was aware of how people looked at her at church — a place I soon hated, with people (all of them) I soon despised. She was the mark that showed who we were as a family, because she was an albino — precisely because of this. And she was to feel this too deeply all her life.

Men can grow up on my river, or in my province or anywhere, and see nothing of violence or anger. There is as much rich or middle class here as anywhere — I have dealt with them. But if you are born in a shack near someone who wants your land, dislikes your presence, covets your wife, is angered by your marriage, you are in a part of the world millions and millions see and have no course to redress.

I want to tell you something that is important in understanding my father and our relationship with both Connie and Mathew. I now believe Father knew who took the smelts but on principle would not say. More important, Connie Devlin knew who took the smelts as well, but was loath to jeopardize his relations with the Pits. If on their bad side they could make life terrible for him, just as they had at times for my father. Besides, the Pits were Connie's first cousins. Connie had to blame someone so the Pits would not suspect he suspected them. He blamed the man the Pits disliked.

This is how things are done when you are afraid. Connie goes to Mathew Pit, cap in hand (figuratively speaking), and asks him what he should do.

"Hell, get the cops after the son of a bitch," Mathew said, sniffing as he tore the backbone from a smelt. "They are always after me no matter what I do! — can't shit and they be after me. It's time we showed them what's what!"

"You think I should?"

"Course."

"And if I have problems with that son of a bitch will you back me? — he already throwed me down from a roof and left me fer dead."

"Course," Mathew sniffed.

Now I wish to tell you that the decrees against my father were not constant, or even at that time inevitable — many months could go by without one. I am telling you of the occasions that I remember. I also remember walks in the woods, and picnics and fishing trips up Arron Brook in the spring where Dad would speak about poetry and Walt Whitman and Thoreau; yet what I say here is something to measure my father by — he did not know that he, and not Thoreau, was the real article, or that his civil disobedience went to the very soul of man.

Still by that decree, Constable Morris came to our house. It was a day in late February; the snow smelled of dirt, and the trees were coated in grey ice. It was bitter cold at the door and Morris stood in a mist of damp air. He stepped inside and looked at our small surroundings. He was the authority come to show us who we were and to keep us in our place. (I remember feeling this even then.) If he told my father we were all fined a thousand dollars my mother and father would have believed him. My father did not understand what the courts did. Not in *that* way. (I use his gullibility to explain his greatness.)

Connie had telephoned the police for years over things — he was an old hand at being a snitch. Say Jay Beard played his guitar on Sunday, the cops would be phoned, or if a grader was parked near his property over the weekend, or a property stake was removed. That is meaningless trifles. Now it was a box of smelts.

Morris was laughing about the smelts. But when he came in he stopped laughing. He glanced at my mother and was transfixed.

At her *beauty*. I could tell this though I was only eight years old. She was so beautiful. He could not take his eyes off her. He instantly saw how ordinary my father looked compared to whom he was married to, and it surprised him. I see his face suddenly beet red, and then somewhat accusatory when looking upon my dad and the surroundings he had offered my mom.

I believe Morris's anger with my father started at that very moment. He tried to deal with the matter objectively, but his eyes kept coming back to this woman sitting in the corner with a little albino child on her knee. As for Elly, her skin was pale, her eyes soft blue, her hair auburn that fell like cinnamon ringlets about her ears, while her smile when it came lightened man's burden.

Who would *not* want to take my mother away from such a sentence? My fight against the condescension and the scorn my father suffered started at that moment. I was just not aware of it then.

"Now Sydney," Morris said, taking out his notebook, "where are those smelts? Come on, you have some smelts, boy?" He no more than glanced at me, and then over at my mother again.

"I have smelts," my father said, looking at Connie.

"Well then —" Morris said, smiling at my mother, "what does your wife Elly say of all this roaring and ranting? Come on, give the poor woman a break — give those smelts back to this man, will you now, Sydney, like a good fellow — and I'll give you a break here. You don't want to go to court over a box of smelts, do you, wasting a judge's valuable time?"

"No," Sydney said, blushing.

"No," my mother whispered, lowering her head.

"Well there now —" Morris tapped his notebook in his hand, waited for my mother to look at him, and then decided, and it was a decision that would carry a heavy consequence against us, that he could curry a certain favour with my mother, not if he believed Dad innocent, but if he *suspected* him. That is, he could influence Mother to be well disposed to him, Constable Morris, if my father had taken the miserable box of smelts and he showed leniency in that regard.

All this time Connie Devlin stared over Morris's shoulder first at Morris's notebook and then up at my father, his boots covered in mud and a look of startled self-righteousness on his still obsequious face.

I glared at him, seeing him as an enemy of my blood for the very first time. Morris got Dad to promise to replace the box of smelts before the season was over, and to shake Connie's hand. At first Connie said he wouldn't shake the hand of a coward, but Morris made them do so.

Morris smiled. "Now Connie, we'll get those smelts back to you and we will forget all about this — it's hard enough having to patrol this area without having to deal with smelts." He looked at mother, and his face actually registered pain that he would have to leave her presence. I understood this feeling from other men who had seen her. She was that beautiful. Then, with Connie Devlin behind him, Morris walked back to his patrol car.

All was silent in our house for over five minutes. I looked at Autumn and she looked at me with a sad face. People were now entering our childhood world and seeing Autumn as an oddity. And she was now, for almost the first time, realizing she was different. And no one in the whole wide world could help her with this; and when she looked my way, for help, as she did that very moment and many moments later on, I could give her none.

On occasion people had walked up the shore in the summer when they were having parties and taking the well-worn path into the timber, would sometimes drunkenly tumble upon my sister sitting in the trees beyond our house, combing the hair of one of her dolls. Once when they did, I heard them shriek and begin laughing as they ran back down the path in skirts and high heels.

"There's an albino back there! Jesus Christ, where are we — the Ozarks?"

My mother looked at me now and sighed.

"That's a police officer?" she said finally, as if a question.

"Yes —" My father nodded. They were again silent for another five minutes. The wind began to pick up in the trees. My mother had baked a cake, and had made molasses cookies for us, but now our feast was ruined and none of us knew what to do.

"He is still a nice man for all of that," Elly said.

"Yes, he is," Father agreed.

"Do you think I should have offered him tea?" Elly said, smoothing her dress with her hands.

"I don't know," Father said. His lips moved and he spoke under his breath calculating how much money a box of smelts would cost us.

"Well," he said finally, "A box of smelts is nothing — and you can help me too, can't you, Lyle — we'll make a challenge of it and have it back to Connie by tomorrow." He looked over at me, picked up Autumn and put her on his knee.

I told him I didn't want to help him, nor did I think it fair to have to go out in the morning and collect a box of smelts when everyone knew Mathew Pit had stolen them.

"Son, people have treated me unfair most of my life. To beg a truth in front of them is unconscionable, because truth gives them a respect they might not deserve. Besides, to think that they will have a better opinion of me for doing so is unwise. I didn't take those smelts. I know this, and Connie knows this. He knows who did, but he is afraid. Mathew Pit is crazy, and people know this. My greater plan now is to get the smelts and give them away and then someday it'll turn around. I know you are only young but what I tell you is true."

And he smiled at me, and smoothed Autumn's white hair. Her eyes were pink and she wore pink glasses, rendered blind without them. She needed new glasses too, but we could not afford them. Once she was stumbling along a ditch without her glasses and being teased by some children as I walked home from fishing trout. I had to take her by the hand so she could find her way. Her dress was white, as were her stockings; but her stockings and her panties were often worn with age.

Thinking of this, I challenged my father for the first time.

44

"What about the time — people said that to Autumn — and you know what I mean — and they laughed at Mommie that day. I don't want people laughing at Mommie when she went to the store."

I was breathing heavily and I was staring at the wall. My arms were folded in a childish tantrum.

"It doesn't matter," Father said.

"But maybe it matters to Mommie," I shouted.

"Oh no," Elly said, smiling slightly and looking at my father.

The next day we got Devlin a box of smelts. I remember Father froze his right hand doing so. We brought them to him in the afternoon. Devlin went about his house working and not acknowledging that we were there. His house was much nicer than my father's, with an attached garage and a flower garden — covered in winter of course. He had gotten most of this because of money his father had left him.

"Mr. Devlin, sir," my father said, though he had known him since he was seven.

No answer.

"Mr. Devlin — here are your smelts."

Devlin looked over without comment.

"Do you want us to leave them here or to take them inside the garage?"

Connie pointed to a spot and said nothing more — as if he had been deeply affected by my father's dishonesty, a person whom he had once considered his friend.

On the way back down our lane in the setting sun, I told my father I would pay him back.

"No," my father said. "It is never a matter of paying people back. It always causes you more sorrow in the end."

I went home — went back to school. Smelt season soon ended, and not another smelt did I eat.

SIX

At Christmas I became aware, long before Autumn did, of our essential poverty. I knew of it by the time I was eight. Perhaps even before that. I caught it as one catches a warning wind on the south side of a fish shanty on the open ice. You know, in your most secret heart, the full force of that wind is just around the corner, but you stick to the side where there is sun, hoping the wind doesn't find you out.

We were one of the fifteen families in our parish given a charity box by the church. But Father insisted on earning ours. So he and I would go each December 22 in the frozen afternoon and help in the church basement to fill those cardboard boxes and wrap children's presents.

We worked alongside members of the parish who were much better off than we, as we wrapped presents and boxed turkeys and cranberry sauce for those in the community much like ourselves.

The Poriers — a family of lower-middle-class duty and some acquired vanity — were always there. Penny Porier was a little older than I was. Dressed in a white rabbit coat, with a white fur hat and muff and white leotards, she entered my life smelling of peppermint and tied up with a Christmas bow one December afternoon when I was eight or nine; to me the embodiment of perfection. Just as was her house, and her father's car, and the small bicycle with the horn that her brother, Griffin, had. I coveted that bicycle — I dreamed of it day and night, I took walks past their house to see it, even though Griffin would never let me on it. But once — once I touched it as he rode by.

I know Penny's father — Leo's foreman and the priest's brother, Abby Porier — liked others to see how busy he was; and he liked my father (whom he had competed with at horsehaulings as a boy) to know that no one had more responsibility than he himself. He was a stocky man with a bull neck and the proud look given to certain kinds of limited men who believe they earned whatever they received. It makes them prosaic, fearful of exhilaration or exuberance and stingy with their children even if they do not mean to be. To him, his paycheque and his Christmas bonus were a bestowal from no one and nothing but his own hard work and worth. He believed that it could never with one swipe of dismissal be taken away.

He liked the idea that I would watch everything he did, from cleaning his truck windows to tying his boots. I could not help doing so. Griffin told me his father got calls from McVicer, sometimes at three in the morning.

Griffin had driven in a backhoe. His father cherished Leo's trust — it was like currency, really. And Penny and Griffin knew this, and both were self-assured because of it. Penny wore a Christmas ribbon in her hair. But what I did not know was that I wore Griffin's old pants. He had sworn not to tell, but Penny knew.

That year I remember someone asked what I was going to get for Christmas. Penny looked at me and my face froze. I looked at Griffin and he smiled when I said: "I'm going to get a bike like Griffin — just like that one there."

"Syd, your boy is going to get a bike?" Abby asked nonchalantly across the half-dozen tables. The air had the particular scent of cement basements, of dust and old wax, and a certain futility contained within it. Abby waited for Father to speak and peeked at his daughter. Griffin, his head down, kept nudging Penny. This ashamed and infuriated me. But I could say nothing.

My father wore an ancient tie clip glimmering in the basement. He looked up at me, his face wan and tired from a life of work, as if to say (although I did not know it then), "This is your cross to bear, son."

Abby was called immediately after this moment to take a call from Leo McVicer. So Father kept working with his head down packing turkeys and toys. Griffin glanced at me once more, his neck pinched in his white shirt by his small green tie with a reindeer on the front. After ten minutes Abby came back, rubbed his coarse unshaved face, and said he had to leave.

"Griffin," he said, "don't you say nothin' — 'bout what I spoke about."

Griffin gave me a look of accepting pity and tired superiority. I did not understand that my clothes were what he was looking at.

December 24 we went out late in the afternoon to deliver these boxes with Father Porier. If it was not Christmas Eve it would have been only another grey and lonely winter day. But Christmas Eve makes everything special for children. We delivered the boxes up and down the shore road, and I remember the sound of snow falling on each cardboard box of groceries.

The boxes were piled in the back seat and in the trunk. Each box had a present for each child of each house, had a twelve-pound turkey donated by McVicer himself, had preserves and nuts and dark fruitcake from McVicer's own store, and barley toy candy and candy canes for the children.

Most of the houses were off the unpaved shore road, and every house was easy to deliver to except the Voteurs'. That day their father was waiting for us, with a shovel, the crotch of his pants torn out, and wind blowing chimney smoke far up over his head. He did not want a box for himself. He was drunk and was sitting on the porch step awaiting us. At five foot five and 125 pounds, he had the unfortunate name of Samson. The Sheppards were his cousins and the year before had ordered his family to move. Samson and his wife and children had just gotten back in. It was the last house before the reserve.

The bay had made ice, and the waves had frozen in midair. Glassy twilight came with the smell of smoke.

Samson sat here at four o'clock in this waning light of a bitter December afternoon. Seeing the crotch out of his suit pants, his face covered in small pricks of greying beard, I had my first glimpse — my first real glimpse — of a poverty of spirit, and I associated it in my young mind with Abby Porier, with his suit pants too tight.

I knew something about the Voteurs. I knew Cheryl, who was in my class. I knew they had a son, Darren, who was Autumn's age. I knew Diedre Whyne had come to them with the police one October night and the social services had filed a motion against the parents and wanted to bring Cheryl and her sister, Monica, to Covenant House, which Diedre ran for abused girls.

I looked at their wet shingled house smelling of pulp and darkness and the sad scent of smoke, like eggs on raw air. In the house the children looked raggedly from the single-pane windows. You could spy one, if you looked, at every window looking out at us. Cheryl, Monica, and Darren.

Worse than the dark unattended house having no decorations for Christmas, the children had placed one light behind the curtain, and a plastic Santa Claus was stuck to the window of the front door. Their door faced the bay, but like so many rural houses of the poor they were surrounded by land and owned no property, had the bay in front of them and never had a boat.

"Maybe you should take this box in, Sydney," Father Porier said. There was a moment of silence. I wanted to yell to my Dad not to do it. Then Father sighed, looked over his shoulder, and told me to hand him the box from the back seat with the large boxed doll. Taking the box he got out of the car.

"I'll kill you," the man said.

Never minding this threat, my father walked across the smoke-scented yard as snow began to fall in dreary flakes over the old peaked roof.

Samson stood, raising his shovel as my father walked up the slippery steps, and started to move the handle back and forth four or five inches, as if taking aim with a baseball bat. I thought of the stations of the cross on the church windows as I stared at my father's dark hair and thin neck. If Samson swung he would split my father's head wide open.

"Here Comes Santa" was on the car radio and perhaps, who knows, on the radio inside the forlorn little house.

I suppose at that moment I was too amazed to think of my father as courageous.

The man held the shovel. "Take yer head off," he said as he braced himself.

My father stopped, looked at him, and then continued up the cinder-covered icy steps, duty bound to deliver the damn box of groceries so we could get ours. Father was now at a height where the shovel would cut his head off at the neck, and then a moment later split his skull like a sawdust ball. But still he walked. Samson shouted, backed up, screamed. Still Father moved toward that tiny audience of dejected little faces, a strange Santa Claus bearing gifts.

Then Father stopped before Samson and waited. One moment, then two, then three passed. Suddenly the old spade shovel dropped. Voteur began to cry, and I could see his children watching this horrible Christmas special.

"You don't know what it's like to be taken advantage of, I can't get any money," Samson said. "I don't want to beg — I was a good man once. I had job at McVicer — till the fires."

"I know," my father answered. "That's why I brought you your groceries. I want to tell your children that these are groceries that came to them because of who you are and what you have done for them. It's Christmas — for the children," my father whispered.

Voteur gave a look, as if his face had crumbled, not by the harsh terrible words he had heard against him all his life and the mocking of his size, but by simple compassion. Dad patted Voteur roughly on the shoulder, handed him a package of Player's cigarettes (cigarettes that my father only smoked at Christmas), and went into the house.

Finally, after I'd been chewing the same stick of gum for three hours, we went back to the vestry and Father and I both kneeled for the priest's blessing. Porier gave as usual a rather tawdry and lackadaisical blessing, then, wiping his nose, set the church bells to ring automatically for Midnight Mass and told us to get our box.

We went to the basement. To the surprise of us both there was no box left. We searched the basement for a box marked Henderson, but there wasn't one. So we trudged up to the vestry again, but Porier had left us to go to dinner with his brother Abby, without knowing of this omission.

We went out and up the old Church Lane. The snow was falling and the night was raw. In the distance, on land owned by McVicer and fronting the very back end of McVicer's old sawmill, sat Porier's house. It was a small wooden house with a peaked front roof, and pointed edges where the snow wisped. The oil barrel was covered in snow, and on the roof a Santa Claus was sitting in his sled waving in majesty at the world. I noticed the fir tree softly glowing in the window, all the lights alighting the eaves and the snow as it continued to drop lazily down. From their house came unusually noble music. But I shook with cold all the way home. My nose ran and my cough was continuous and harsh. I saw Penny Porier glide by the window in a white nightgown as my father and I walked by. It was almost as if, if I could ever touch her, just once, I'd be saved.

SEVEN

That night we walked to Midnight Mass. The stars were so brilliant, and little Autumn said she knew where Orion was. Since I didn't I told her she was correct.

After mass, after all the singing, after communion where everyone praised baby Jesus, and a little child was baptised, after this we set out for home over the ice-chipped roadway. There was snow hanging from the trees, the road was pitch black, and we could hear a singing in the distance.

Mother was telling us how we someday would go to Saint John on the bus and how she had been planning this for my summer holiday. Of course she told us this every Christmas, and every year it would be a year later.

Everything was calm, and Mom walked with her arm in Dad's as Autumn, her whiteness having a ruddy health, and I walked first ahead of them and then trailed behind. After a time I realized that some men had come out of the woods to walk behind us. Dad told me not to turn around. One of the men told my mother he had long wanted to haul her dress up and see if he could put something better than "a al-bino" up her pussy. My father simply said:

"Boys, go home."

The men looked at him and burst out laughing. His suit was fifteen years old, shiny on the knees, and his old coat pockets torn. He wore an imitation red carnation that Autumn had won for him at the fish tank at the children's Christmas party two days before. Behind us the sky was black. I could see my breath as I stared at my broken boots and I kept hoping someone would come up the lane to stop these men. They knocked my father down.

When he fell to the ground his carnation came off. He went to pick it up, and the third man stepped on it as the other two kicked him. I hated them, and I ran through snow swirling in the black wind to try and help, but my father held me back. In doing so he could not protect himself from being pummelled and cutting his hands on the ice.

I'm sure my father knew who they were, but he didn't want me to know — for knowledge leads to sin. Even if they did not have their faces hidden, the road was pitch dark — not a light shone.

"I told you I'd get you back," one of them kept saying. I can hear him today, a raspy singsong voice. "And now I'm getting you back."

"Take the children home, Elly," my father said, the damned barley toys he had bought for us, for an after-mass treat, falling from his pockets.

Autumn was hysterical and kept clutching my arm, and I was scared, especially when I looked at Autumn's face.

Finally car lights turned onto the frozen lane, and the men were gone in a second. Jay Beard had come back to get his guitar, which he had forgotten after singing at the church. He helped my father to his feet. Then he took time to drive us home.

"I forgot my carnation," Dad said. "It fell on the road."

"I'll go get it," Jay said. "If you go they might be back — them being roaring Christmas drunk is all — they won't bother you again tonight if you stay here with Elly. It's just drunkenness making them shine."

It was the first time I became aware of our true isolation. That my mother could be discussed like she had been. I wanted my father to say, "I will go with you and get them," but he only nodded. For the first time, more even than the work with the Christmas boxes, I realized there was a poverty in us that had nothing to do with dirt.

As I became older I would know any child of poverty, a smell like dark storm and milk. I would smell it in cities not only here but in Europe, and I would realize that all of them in a sense were a part of my blood.

Now it lingered beyond us in the sweet frozen darkness of the poor. There was in this poverty a scent of holy water my mother used to sprinkle on Autumn's dresses, for she cherished this little albino girl.

When Mother got out of the car she thanked Jay and modestly smoothed her dress over her exposed legs. I was suddenly informed of myself as a child of privation and disgrace. Just like the Voteurs. Cheryl Voteur and not Penny Porier was *my* kind. I had only thought I was different from her blunt knowing little face.

My father took off his shirt and sat at the kitchen table near the Christmas tree we had decorated with such passion. For the next few days he couldn't bring himself to read.

It's hard to think of that little house then. We did not have much. We had a radio, where Autumn and I would listen to a station in Boston — disco music was big. We watched television. Autumn read voraciously and would entertain us with her one-woman plays, and Mom made taffy. But my father was known as the Henderson boy who had helped cause the fire at McVicer's Works and so was out of work. He refused welfare.

I wanted to telephone the police. My father thought about it and said, "Let it go — for now." I was furious with him the next day because he hadn't fought. Every time he looked at me I put my head down. After a while I forgot about it. But one day, perhaps because of shame, or maybe just because I had grown, I met Dad walking across

Highway 11 as he went home from an afternoon job helping shovel snow from the doors of a pig farm. He stopped and waited, smiling at me. I pretended I didn't see him. For the first time I did not run to catch up, and for the first time I never took his offered hand.

EIGHT

Leo McVicer. The very name personified Chatham. His very suit pants personified struggle up the ladder, from pauper to prince. The great dark high-ceiling buildings of orphanages and tenements, the cement steps covered with wet snow. His childhood of pain and loneliness had made him idiosyncratic.

He was a Catholic Chathamer from the hill, a scrappy red-haired youngster with a fierce face and darting blue eyes who would chase the rich children (those who were Protestant) into Queen Square and beat them for the fun of it. He was a bully and a torment and a sneak and a ruffian and a son of a bitch. He had liked that.

When he was nineteen, just before he went overseas, he boxed as a featherweight, calling himself the Chatham Flash. There was a picture of him in a black T-shirt and trunks, with small six-ounce black gloves, on the upstairs wall in his house. His white, short, and uniform arms belied his powerful punch. It would be little problem for him to knock out a man twice his size. He knew this. Of course he had changed and grown out of it. He had gone to war, and he was in Company B of the North Shore Regiment, and he had faced fire and he had faced death and he had faced isolation and danger.

After the war he saw opportunity in owning the land. He bought it all out from under Roy Henderson, who ended up working for him. Leo knew work and he knew men who worked, he knew horses and tractors and how to take advantage of men to keep them honest and get the best from them.

My grandfather lived on a piece of land given to him by Leo. And that small bit of land was ours.

When I was twelve, in 1982, Mr. McVicer called Mathew Pit and Father to the office in his house, made them shake hands, and hired Mathew and Dad to clean his old sawmill, to shovel the grounds, to dump bulldog lime in the tailings pond and anywhere around the perimeter, and to haul the barrels of herbicide to an incinerator in Edmundston. He helped them start a well-digging business.

People said that this was because of Autumn, because of the snip of hair Mr. Gerald Dove had taken years before.

Sometime in 1977, Gerald Dove, a young man with receding red hair and a moustache, had come to visit, asking Sydney about the fire my grandfather started. He sat across the table from us, his eyes glowing brighter the moment he unsnapped his leather briefcase with his thin white fingers. We all watched him breathlessly as he produced a tape recorder and a questionnaire.

Dove asked if we had any trouble with our water, or was there any sickness in our family. He spoke to my father about other places — problems in Wyoming and Michigan that were very similar. He told Father that McVicer wanted him to discover the extent of the problem for possible restitution. My father said nothing to this at all.

Dove spoke about the circumference of the burn and the late rebirth of the hardwood ridge along the Point Road, which showed a certain dwarfism due to toxic properties, not all, he said, coming from McVicer's Works. But there was a prevalence of toxicity in certain molecular structures dumped throughout the sixties from the mill into the tailings pond that ran directly into Arron Brook and into the groundwater thirty families relied upon. He said that McVicer would soon take action because of his findings. He spoke of the nitrogen oxide core samples he had taken on wetlands above our own house the winter before and how they tested a certain amount of carcinogen.

"Tell me," Dove asked, "are there any incidents of diarrhea or stomach sickness?" Mother said she felt well, generally, and the water was okay.

After the interview Dove and my father went out to the mill ground for two hours, and as Father walked about the ground, Gerald Dove took notes, measured off certain things with giant steps, and scooped up samples of dirt.

When he came back to our house, he collected a sample of water. Then he snipped a bit of Autumn's stark white hair and put it in his pocket, but he didn't smile or say thank you. Then he shook my father's hand as an afterthought and walked away. I stared at the place where Autumn's hair had been snipped until I could no longer tell where the snip was.

Now, because of the snip of Autumn's hair, Gerald Dove had done five years of tests. Although these tests were inconclusive, people were saying McVicer owed us money.

Dad told me that Dove was McVicer's nephew (not really a nephew — he was a protégé who was called that) and originally wanted to defend McVicer's environmental legacy because Leo had taken care of him as a boy. Dove had worked at the mill in the summers and after winning a Rhodes scholarship, got his doctorate in what was called environmental biology.

Dove and Leo's daughter, Gladys, had fallen in love as teenagers. Leo was given to acting rashly to protect her, and so disallowed them to see each other. This was the reason Gladys, who was a year or so older than Mom, had married Rudy Bellanger.

Still, Leo had brought Dove back to help him out of a controversy with the environmental agency. And after all, Dove owed him. And like everything in Leo McVicer's life there was a moment when he would collect what he was owed.

Now, after five years of exhausting tests, Dove had changed his mind. He wanted Leo to pay all the families fifty thousand dollars apiece. I asked my father one night, after we had come home from fishing and were sitting out back, if he had heard of this. I was very excited about it, and supposed he would be as well.

"Oh yes, I have heard of it."

"Well — do you want to get money? It might be a lot of money."

"No," Father said, looking at me and spitting on a whetstone to sharpen his axe. I stared at the side of his head in astonishment. It was a cool night in June and damp could be felt in the trees and grasses. I could not believe Dad would not want money.

"No matter how much?" I asked. I could smell my father's dark skin and woollen sweater covered with spruce, saw his tanned leathery skin, his huge hands, and trembled in anguish.

"No matter," Father said. "It was not McVicer's fault — he had no more knowledge of it than anyone else. We all used that herbicide — not only McVicer. My father had his own barrels to use on our lane, so who's to say it is McVicer's fault? The world has gone on — that's all that can be said."

So instead of suing McVicer he and Mathew Pit went to see him the next afternoon. McVicer helped my father and Mathew start a well-digging business. Initially this business was profitable. Yet came a certain problem with the drill bits, and after a while the company went bankrupt. McVicer took it over, dug two more community wells, and sold it. But I know McVicer had done what he had set out to do. He had brought father and Pit temporarily to his side, and prevented, he hoped, litigation.

The pouring of bulldog lime as a purifying agent about the mill ground and hill beyond went on into July of that year. My mother helped Dad with this, and came home with burns as large as dollar pieces on her skin from wheelbarrowing the lime, which got between her toes and fingers. There are no burns worse, I can tell you.

It was shortly after that Leo McVicer himself came to the house to visit, bringing us a large assortment of cookies and teas from his store. My mom had just had another miscarriage; her third or fourth.

Leo asked Mother how she was. He was dressed in a three-piece suit, with a golden watch chain hooked to the inside pocket of his vest. He looked at the thin walls of our house, and was concerned about the centre pole in our main room. He knocked on it and pushed it as he looked at me, as if I had anything to do with it. He picked up Autumn and smiled at her. He felt her shoulder bones and her feet. He shook his head. We all looked at him in astonishment, as the little Voteur girls had looked at me from the window.

He was by far the richest, most important, most charismatic man to have ever entered our house, and here he was, pouring my mother tea, handing cookies to Autumn and me off one of Mom's plates, talking about people we all knew, as if we were all *friends*.

He went and sat beside Elly and took her hand.

"I will start building a bridge sometime soon," he said, "and put a highway through. It will swing north — where the mill once was — all of that will be road — highway. It will put a stop to this nonsense about the bad molecules in the soil. I will hire Sydney. Elly, you are a friend of Diedre and have done no harm to me. So Sydney will have a job if he wants. It will mean you can leave this old shack — and find another one bigger and better."

With this he bit a cookie carefully, and listened to the great wind from the bay tossing against the branches of the trees. Both Autumn and I watched him chew the cookie, I suppose trying to determine if he, a millionaire, ate like other people. He then asked me had I ever boxed.

"No," I replied.

"Would you like to?"

"No," I replied.

"You are a strong youngster — nothing wrong with your bones, is there?" he asked.

"No," I said.

He never took his glinting blue eyes off me, and I became more uncomfortable the more he spoke. It didn't matter his size, or what people had called him. Inside he was a conqueror.

Then he asked Mother, in a long roundabout way, to work as a domestic in his house. The work would be steady and not hard. She would be paid well. She would not be bothered with cold or wind, or bulldog lime. When he said this he picked up her left foot and looked at it. Then he told her he had a salve he would bring to help heal her burns, burns that had turned her foot both red and black. Father, who bathed it for her at night, called it the Stendhal foot.

"I love the name Autumn," McVicer declared. "What are you going to be when you grow up?"

"I am going to be a writer," Autumn said, still hiding behind her mom.

"A writer," he said.

My mother, thinking this answer presumptuous, smiled awkwardly.

"Like Zane Grey? Well, as long as you don't write about me," Leo said, chuckling.

I stared at his large brown hands, his white starched shirt cuffs pulled down over his wrists. I looked at his silver cufflinks. There was a rumour this man had killed an opponent in the ring when he was nineteen. I knew he could easily have done it.

Leo then looked at me, as if he realized what I was thinking. He put a hand-rolled cigarette in his mouth and nodded. He told me that he had followed the lightweight Roberto Duran for many years. Now, after the "no mas" fight against Sugar Ray Leonard, he was saddened. He smiled, alone in his thoughts.

"Someday you will box," he said, pointing his finger at me in mischief. "You don't want to. Well, neither did I. I didn't want to fight — no, at first I ran. But like me you won't have any choice. You have no choice, do you? Already you have to protect this girl here — this Autumn — and as she gets older the more you will have to — I know it won't be easy for you — life is never easy for McVicers or Hendersons. It wasn't meant to be easy — but grab life by the throat like a scrapping dog — and when it throws you on your back never hesitate to fight dirty, because it won't fight clean with you."

With his eyes burrowing into me, I nodded neither one way nor the other and glanced at my mom. Here, then, was a man much different from Dad. I think I was instantly in love with him.

NINE

My mother went to work in Leo's drab masculine three-storey brick house out on the bay, with its yard filled with alders and gardens and secret alcoves.

Leo's son-in-law, Rudy Bellanger, had the responsibility of driving my mother to and from her job. It has taken me almost ten years to discover, down to the very conversations, what happened between them at this time.

After a cool June, the summer days were humid, and each morning she would wait for Rudy at the top of our lane by our small twisted mailbox that would go months without its flag up. Sometimes I walked up the lane with her for company and sat beside this mailbox.

"It's not any of my business," Rudy said to my mom one day, after I left her. "I don't know anything about Sydney, but he's not much of a provider for you and the children, living in that spruce bog of yours — must be something — in the summer the mosquitoes and blackflies — you can't sit outside. Really — with your looks, he's not the man for you — is he? Think of that little boy there — what's his name — Lyle — just looks like a scarecrow — you don't want that, do you?"

He smiled and touched her cheek quickly and gently. My mother did not know what to say. She did not know what everyone else knew about Rudy.

The next day Rudy bought her a cassette so she could listen to music as she worked. She told him she had never been to a rock concert.

"I still go to them all," he said, walking in his high-heel boots about her ironing board as she ironed McVicer's shirts. "I can take you to one," he said. He put his hand lightly on her back and took it away.

That day he seemed to be upset with his wife, Gladys, over something.

Then the next day he showed Mom a wad of twenties, held by a tie clip. "See that clip," he said. "Yeah — you see it, don't you — *gold*."

My mother was embarrassed by this, and said nothing about it to father or me.

Rudy was a friend of Mathew Pit, and Mat would tease him about her. Rudy's fifteen-room brick house stood out on a promontory over the bay and like everything else in his life it was owned by Leo McVicer. He resented this, and had plans to use his father-in-law's influence to make his own way in the world of Liberal party politics. Mathew and Cynthia monitored these plans of his with great sympathy and understanding. He was forever driving Gladys to and fro, but she gave him no affection whatsoever.

One morning in August of 1982, a month or so after Mom started work, Rudy asked her to go to lunch with him at Polly's Restaurant. When Mom said she didn't have the money, he simply laughed, took her by the arm, and walked her to the car.

Polly's was an unruly place where people drank away the afternoons. My father himself would not go in there, given the temptation he felt when it came to drink. Rudy, however, was comfortable here, and spoke in a self-pitying way about his wife.

"I'm a full-blooded Canadian man, left alone," he said with great piety. "She can't even get out of a chair without help now — it's just terrible."

"I could go and sit with her if she doesn't have many friends," Mother said.

Rudy tipped a glass of rye and water, bit on an ice cube, and looked at her.

"Why don't you drink your gin?" he said.

"I — don't drink very much," she answered.

"Why, just because yer husband can't handle it?" Then, seeing he had alarmed her, he smiled. "Well — what I really want you to do is to come with me to the Bob Seger concert in Montreal — if you want to see a concert, I hate to travel there alone — we could get a room — you know, hotel room — you could tell your husband you have to visit some people for the weekend — I'd tell Gladys — oh, something —"

"Bob Seger. Who is he?"

"Ha!" Rudy exclaimed as he chewed his ice and looked quickly around. "I'll have to teach you."

She stumbled over her order, trying to decide what she might afford, staring now and again at the glasses of gin he put in front of her. He then told her he had gotten away with some big deals in his life. But Mom didn't understand about big deals.

Nor did she want to go to lunch at Polly's Restaurant, where men cursed, and where my father was the butt of jokes.

After work she would have trouble eating supper. And I remember her making us dinner and shaking, staring at her plate and pushing it aside.

Then the days became shorter, and fall changed the colour of the leaves, and the leaves died, and fell, and soon I could see the frozen brook through the bare branches and notice the ice along the riverbank as snow started to fall. My father had started work on the bridge, and worked ten-hour shifts. All of this made Autumn and me very happy — because for the first time we felt ordinary. Once I thought I saw Penny Porier smile at me — I was almost sure of it.

Elly was determined that we would go on vacation the next summer and spoke to us about it often. By November she had some money saved. We were going to go to Saint John; to the art gallery and museum. She revealed her plan to Mr. Bellanger at lunch one day.

"Oh yes," Mom said, "next summer — we will take the bus to Saint John — I haven't been there before —"

"I suppose big spenders like you have a luxury suite," Rudy said.

She tried to make lighthearted conversation as they drove back to McVicer's house, but he said nothing. She felt guilty for bragging.

After she got home that night she went over the brochures she had collected, calculating what we might or might not be able to afford. I know now she wanted to give up her position. She did not want to let Mr. McVicer down, yet she believed Mr. Bellanger thought she was being ungrateful.

She did not see him for a while. Then one day a week or so later he went to the McVicer house. The stones and pebbles on the long cold drive were muted and there was a vague smell of burning branches. In the fields behind his old barn were traces of the snow falling hard from the raw sky. Rudy saw my mother bringing in some bedsheets at the clothesline.

"Look at this," he said, holding up two plane tickets. "See?"

My mother looked at them.

"I'm — sorry — I don't know what they are."

"The tickets for me and you to Montreal — like I told you — I go to them all — you'll get to see a real city." He tapped the tickets and looked up at her with a strange smile, a smile that said he knew he was using deceit and could not help it.

"You come with me — see how the other half lives, eh?"

She shook her head, and he lingered in silence with the smell of autumn snow in the air. Finally he went away, slapping the tickets at the wind.

The next day there was a dusting of snow on the lane. Rudy came to the house in early afternoon and entered the side door near the back stairs.

He took off his black pointed cowboy boots, straightened his socks, and went inside. With his boots off he was one half inch shorter than my mother, but weighed eighty pounds more. He wore red pants with a wide belt, and a blue shirt with a pink tie.

My mother was vacuuming the den and was startled by him. She told him that if he needed to talk to Mr. McVicer he would have to wait, for Leo had gone on his annual hunting trip.

Mother smiled. "Maybe you could come back Saturday."

"Maybe," Rudy said. "You don't have a drink for an old friend, do you?"

"Oh no — I'm sorry."

Mom stopped vacuuming as he came toward her, and tried to think of something lighthearted and kind to say. He walked straight to her — and touched her cheek.

When he touched her cheek in the room filled with the drab

furniture of the generations gone by and the bits of squalid light that lay against the rear window, she backed away, tripped on the vacuum. Her skirt came up to her waist, and her panties were visible.

He pulled her to her feet, and he felt under her panties and fumbled his hand against her crotch hair, trying to penetrate with his finger. His eyes were closed, but when he opened them he saw that hers were terrified.

"I have to go home —" she cried, "I do — I want to go home — I have to, please, Mr. Bellanger — please sir — you do not understand — I love Sydney, please sir — I have hurt myself."

"How can you love Sydney?" he said. "I mean — you wanted this —"

He realized she was mortified, but he couldn't stop, because her legs were moving against him. And quite unexpectedly, he shuddered against her right leg.

The air had the faint smell of cleaning detergent. She looked so small, terrified, and countrylike. Not the kind of person he had imagined going to Montreal with, as he had when he walked to the house.

She went to a chair and sat down, with her eyes cast toward the rug, some blood behind her ear. The worst object of indictment against him was her brown paper lunch bag that she had not yet opened, sitting on the dining-room table.

"You better not tell," he said.

He pulled his boots on the wrong feet and fled the house. He staggered down the drive where he had walked in sweet anticipation a few minutes before.

He leaned against a spruce tree and tried to think. He knew if she told he would be fired, Gladys would leave him, and he would be left with nothing.

Now he smelled her sex on his fingers and felt the blood drain from his face.

He ran back to the store like a child.

He went into the store and closed the green door blind, locked the door, and in the back, near a barrel of McIntosh apples, began to shake.

He hadn't intended this at all. But hadn't she led him on? Yes —

for why would she go to Polly's with him? And how many people he knew saw her there? And how many drinks did he buy her? And how many men had she led on at Polly's as well? They had all looked at her — she wanted them too. He could have witnesses lined up — he would need help! And wasn't her husband a worthless example of a human being, robbing and setting fires (oh, he remembered that)! The two of them were, really. And their children, who he had seen at church; one a saucy-faced boy, the other a scrawny pink-eyed albino! Yes — they were depraved, ignorant people who did such ignorant things, everyone knew!

No — his story would have to be that she tried something and he had told her he was married; that she then laughed in his face — and then demanded money! Yes — demanded money!

The phone rang in Rudy Bellanger's house the next morning at eight-fifteen. His wife answered.

"It's Daddy," she said.

When he came to the phone he was trying to think of how he could extricate himself from this terrible feeling, as much as from the situation itself.

"How did you make out hunting — you get a deer?" Rudy asked.

"Rudy, what happened here?" Leo said, calm. "Were you in the house —?"

"I — don't know —"

There was a long pause.

"Well, damnit, were you in the house or not?"

"No — of course not."

"Was anyone hanging around the house?"

"Just Elly — maybe Sydney — I don't know."

"Well there you go — we were robbed of five hundred dollars — right from the drawer upstairs. So that's why."

"What's why?" Rudy asked.

"That's why Elly phoned in sick, Rudy, and said she wanted to quit.

65

Get down here — I want to decide how I'm going to handle this. I mean, she must have been put up to it — by *him*, damnit — I've treated them decently — more than that — *fuck*."

He banged down the receiver in Rudy's ear, but Rudy's hand hung on to his phone, because he had never heard Leo say that word.

TEN

My mother heard about the robbery just after noon hour and went to see my father on the bridge. It was a black, cold day. The snow had balked in the morning, but now it seemed certain to snow in the afternoon. Clouds hung over the woods, and the road already glittered with hoarfrost. All was silent, as it is in the country in late fall.

She looked ashamed, made attempts to look into Dad's eyes but could not.

"What's wrong?" he asked.

"Mr. McVicer's house has been robbed of money. Mr. McVicer phoned."

"You weren't at work?"

"No — I didn't go to work today."

"Why?"

Mother looked at him quickly and said nothing. Then she looked toward the flat ice just skimming the river. "I felt bad," she said.

"What's wrong?" Sydney bit his huge leather mitten off and then felt her cheek. His glasses were fogged, and at the best of times he could hardly see things close up. She grabbed his hand and kissed it and smiled.

"I'm sorry," she said.

"Why — what has happened?"

"I must go to Mr. McVicer's house — will you come with me? — I don't want to go there alone."

"Certainly. We'll go now." And he took off his safety helmet and told an already irascible Mr. Porier where he was going.

They started walking to the southeast, turning down an old chip-sealed road toward the shore as tiny dartlike snowflakes fell out of the winter sky and numbed their faces. A huge buck, whose doe had been shot by Mathew Pit two days before, stood far up the dirt side road, watching them. Autumn followed them at a distance, but they told her to go home and wait. She watched them walk together toward our destiny.

The bay was not yet frozen, yet most of the properties, being summer cottages, were boarded for the winter, and the bushes entwined in burlap sacks. Wind whined through the trees along the shore road and up in the old man's yard, while the long narrow drive glistened with black ice. As Elly got closer she took ever smaller steps.

"What's wrong?" Sydney asked again.

"I don't know if I can do it — go see Mr. McVicer."

My mother trembled. Smoke came from the chimney on the east side of the house and broke and scattered, and small rotted leaves twirled into the air from time to time, like a dance of lost children.

"Please take my hand," she said.

"Elly," my father whispered, "what have you done? Did you take some money?"

Elly, a blue tam pulled down to her forehead, hiding her eyes, looked at Sydney as if she was questioning his question. She pushed her hat up and sniffed, and shook her head mournfully, as if she was about to cry.

"I took no money," she said.

He took her hand and they went to the door.

My mother had thought about this all morning. She had not had much luck in her life.

If she spoke of yesterday's incident, Rudy would deny it, and there was a good chance McVicer would think it nothing more than a ruse to cover what she had actually done, which was take his money from the upstairs drawer.

Of course she had taken nothing. What held more power over her lack of resolve was the fact that Sydney was even more gullible than she. So she had never told him about her progressively uncomfortable conversations or how Rudy disliked him; how he had subtly mocked Sydney in front of the people at Polly's because Sydney would be ashamed if he knew. And she did not want him to be ashamed. My dad would never ask for help, but he was enormously grateful to both McVicer and Rudy.

Because of this my mother had lied, had told Sydney that Rudy was interested in him and impressed that he read books and wanted to go to university. To change this story now would seem opportunistic because of the theft. Every moment she had failed to speak the truth, to save my father's feelings, went against her now, when truth spoken sooner might have saved her from this accusation.

To explain anything about her meeting with Rudy, and Rudy's assault, would seem nothing more than a face-saving alibi. Worse, an alibi that hurt and damaged the reputation of a man Sydney believed was being kind to them. A man who was married to poor sick Gladys, and lived in a fifteen-room house.

So it was clear: she should have told Sydney the night before. When he had kissed her at supper he knew something was wrong and had asked her what was the matter. But she was too humiliated to tell him.

Now the robbery fit like a key into tumblers in some terrible Pandora's box, and prodded by her silence made her, by everything she had done or refused to say since five-thirty the day before, culpable.

When my parents got to the house Rudy was sitting in the den. He wore his gold cufflinks and watch, his small sapphire ring. His fingers were short and white, his fingernails clean and manicured.

He glanced at my mother, smiled piteously, and glanced away. For her part, her eyes were downcast, her tam still on her head, half covering her eyes, and her small nose was reddened from the walk. She kept admonishing herself for having gone to Polly's Restaurant.

When McVicer looked at her, her smile hopelessly affirmed her guilty state. His eyes were penetrating. He had been a decorated officer in the Second World War.

Tossing some piled-up mail aside, Leo asked them what had happened to his money in the drawer. To show how important this was, he had not changed his clothes. He still wore his hunting boots, hunting vest, and humphrey pants, dotted with specks of blood.

The old house took on various shades of light as the wind blew, and seemed to Elly to smell of guns and fly rods and rubber boots.

"Where's the money?" Leo asked.

"I don't know," my mother said, looking at the floor — a floor she had been vacuuming when last in the house. She looked at the creases the vacuum cleaner had made. At the midpoint in the rug was the very spot the vacuum cleaner had been turned off. After Rudy left yesterday she had gone into the washroom for a second, washed the blood away, had come out, in a daze, and couldn't finish the vacuuming. Thinking of this, she glanced Rudy's way and saw that he was looking at that exact same spot on the rug. Their eyes met and she looked quickly at the floor again.

Although Leo cared for her, he was more than willing to admit a disappointment in trusting her. He had known her family well. Her adoptive father, old Mr. Brown, was a humpback whose shirts were bought at his store. Each year her mother picked fiddleheads and strawberries and he allowed her to pick them on his property.

Finally he turned away from Mom and rubbed his hands together. "You can't tell me what you did with the five hundred dollars," Leo said.

"No," my mother whispered, shaking her head. Her legs trembled. She was going to say "No, because I didn't take it," but she'd already said she hadn't taken it.

"It wouldn't be nice for a married woman to have to talk to the police, would it."

"No," my mother whispered, looking up quickly, tears flooding her eyes.

"Nor would it be too nice if I fired Sydney — well, why shouldn't I?"

Leo said in his strong river accent, which always comes to people here in the midst of deep emotion.

But by now my mother couldn't speak. She only shook in spasms, her left foot leaning on her right foot, a stance she had had since a child, whenever people at the orphanage were angry at her.

"Tell them you didn't do it," Sydney said.

Still she only cried, because of the kindness Leo and Sydney were trying to show her. Sometimes in the afternoon Leo had told her to stop working and sit with him and drink a cup of tea. He would talk about his wife, of how she had to go to the hospital, of how the world was changing and men acting like women and women acting like men.

Now she felt she had betrayed him and those nice cups of tea. A stern and practical old man, but one who nonetheless cared very much for her. Sydney was laughed at by Mathew Pit, tormented by Mathew's sister, Cynthia, and Elly had tried to protect him by telling him that Rudy was impressed by him. It may have been the worst miscalculation of her life.

Leo spun around to Sydney. "Perhaps you did it for her — yesterday about five o'clock?"

"Oh no," my mother said, trying to wipe her eyes. "No," she said. "He didn't — he couldn't — he never could — I did."

Sydney said nothing. The wind blew fiercely.

"You did?" Rudy said, astonished.

"I — I don't know if I did or didn't," Mother said.

"I — could have you prosecuted. One phone call." Leo paused. "But you have children — it's the children I think of — not you. Sydney, I will not take Elly's money — but you will work on the bridge until you pay the five hundred back — you will pay it back. You have been a problem on this road before, Sydney — stole money from the church — and boxes of smelts and blamed it on others — and said things about people when they tried to help you. Well — and Ms. Whyne — Elly — Diedre Whyne, do you remember her? She advised you not to go off marrying Sydney. How do I know? I know because I am a friend of her father — she is my goddaughter — she cared *that* much for you — she wanted you to go off to school, didn't she, and get an education — she tried very hard with you —"

My mother nodded hopelessly.

"But you didn't go off to school, you got married to Sydney — now look at the trouble you're in — you never took advice — we knew you were slow — at church — we knew, we helped you — let you do things for the Catholic Women's League and help at the picnics — we all liked you. Oh, I sometimes think Ms. Whyne has very hard ideas — but her father is a friend and I trust her. Has she asked to see you recently? Last week didn't she want to talk to you?"

Again mother nodded.

"But you're frightened of her. Why?"

My mother did not speak.

"Sydney is telling you not to see her — isn't he, because she is a social worker and ready to take care of you?"

Leo McVicer said this without having the least understanding of social workers. He simply felt that Whyne was the nice young woman who at times came down to Christmas dinner and played the piano, and now and again played bridge with him and Gladys. She was a woman who was being useful to society, protecting people like Elly Henderson from themselves, which he felt was what women were supposed to do.

"I think you put her up to this, Sydney — didn't you! You believe you deserve this money — because of Roy — or perhaps what Gerald Dove has said about your daughter — and the supposed bad molecules?"

"That is not true," my father said.

There was a long silence.

"Go — before I decide to turn you in," Leo said, gesturing at nothing.

"I'm sorry," my mother said, "I am — Mr. McVicer — I —"

"What?" Leo said.

"I didn't get the upstairs hallway done."

"Go!" Leo roared. "Both of you go!" He roared so loud Rudy himself shook.

They left and cut across the dark fields north toward the road, in silence holding hands. When they got to the road my mother stopped, stood still against an aged rotted spruce stump, and said out of the cold gloom of a November afternoon, "I did not steal."

My father sighed.

"I know you did not steal," he said, stuttering. "I know they think you did. I know Diedre will once again begin to assess us. That doesn't matter. The only thing that bothers me is the poor old man." He looked at her kindly.

My mother nodded. In the last ten years Diedre had done everything she could to pry my mother away from Sydney. That my mother would not look upon her views as the right views, as the sound and practical views, poisoned the relationship.

Elly thought all of this in a second — how Diedre would use this to hurt her.

"Don't worry — truth will out," Sydney said.

They continued their walk, not understanding how evil and darkness attach themselves to the good or great to destroy their will to live.

"Why would she rob me, Rudy — why?" Leo asked. He turned sideways in his seat as he spoke, but just for a second and then straightened again. Then he turned sideways to listen to Rudy's answer, staring at him sharply and straightened once more.

"I don't know," Rudy said.

"If she wanted the money, if she needed the money, she could have come to me —"

Rudy nodded.

He looked at Leo and was frightened. He was frightened of his temper, his well-known reputation for never giving in to those he suspected.

"But they think I am terrible — so they'd rather steal from me than ask me a favour. How well did you know her?"

"Oh, not well at all."

"Did you think that she was like this? Capable of anything like this?" He turned sideways to listen, and waited with a prolonged stare.

"I didn't think she was like that."

"No, no," the old man said, drumming his fingers on the armrest. "She didn't seem so to me either."

There was a long, uncomfortable silence.

"Everyone is turning against me, that's what I think," he said finally.

"No, Leo — that's not true —"

But Leo could only think of all of his friends who were now dead, and of how little friendship he had left. He himself had never robbed a soul, had in fact done the opposite. Except that now he was being accused of careless disregard for his workers' health twenty years before. It stung him deeply, for he had as yet found no way to fight against it. Or no way to fight against Gerald Dove, whom he had hired just for the purpose of this fight. Dove, whom he had taken from the orphanage on a whim and kept as his own son.

"Dove has gone bonkers, you think?" he asked. "Power hungry, you think? Trying to destroy the man who made him, you think?"

"I think so," Rudy admitted, relieved that the subject for now was changed.

"Yes — a little education. You know, Rudy, I could have chose anyone — from a number of boys at that orphanage. Careless disregard," he said. "Am I a man of careless disregard?"

"Of course not."

"I certainly am *not*," he wagered, as if trying to provoke an argument.

Nothing made him more furious than to think that *these* men, *these* grown men, men *he trusted*, who used those chemicals to keep down budworm disease and clear roads — when everyone else was doing the *same*, back in the sixties — would stop using these chemicals the exact moment everyone else did, and charge that *he*, Leo McVicer, was guilty of knowing what they themselves, and even scientists, did not!

"Yes," he said, glaring at Rudy, when he thought of it. "Many a lad turned against me bought their homes with money they earned from me, paid their stinking mortgages from my chequebook —"

"I know," Rudy said.

"They aren't men. They all have the blood of pigeons," Leo said.

Six years before, Leo had donated eighty thousand dollars to the university so the citizens could keep the university here on the river. Yet this very night, at the university, in that very wing McVicer himself had paid for, Dove was conducting an environmental study of his groundwater.

And Leo was now being accused in the paper, a man with grade five education accused of being an elitist and *against* the working man, by Prof. David Scone, who had met the working class, not by calluses on his hands, but by reading Engels and Marx. Leo did not understand this at all.

Leo thought that bringing Gerald Dove back would accomplish three things. First, the accusations against him by the Environmental Protection Agency would be proven false. Second, Gerald would see Gladys, and see what folly their childhood love was. And finally, that Gerald Dove sooner or later would come to work for him on a permanent basis.

None of it had happened. The accusations were as damning as ever. Gladys only remembered the wound in her heart when Gerald Dove went away, and Gerald Dove looked upon his daughter as he had when he was a boy. Instead of Dove coming to work for him they now could not stand the sight of one another. This was the first time Leo had failed so utterly in his calculations.

Leo remembered carrying Gerald Dove in his arms over the swinging bridge on the Norwest Miramichi and looking into the child's windblown red hair; and it seemed that on that bright sunlit day in 1953 he should have been warned.

"A molecule," McVicer said now, looking at the most recent article in the paper against his company and tossing it aside.

It was a molecule, unseen in the winter cold and summer heat, unseen when children went sliding on the great dark hills, unseen when my mother poured bulldog lime, unseen on the forest floor near the great barren pools. Some people never felt the effects, but others — well, others' immune systems were destroyed. And others were born with feeble hearts or lungs, and some with no pigment to their skin.

"How can I fight them?" Leo asked, for the first time in his life uncertain. "How can I fight Gerald Dove if I care for him — or Elly if I care for her?"

"I don't know," Rudy said, close to tears.

"I know nothing about molecules," McVicer continued. "I remember when I was a young boy hearing that there was such things as molecules, and I tried to collect the smallest piece of sand I could to find one." He shook his head. "But I never did."

"I know," Rudy said.

"And now Elly — stole my five hundred dollars," Leo said.

Rudy asked if he could leave.

Leo McVicer stood, lit his pipe, and felt in his pocket Elly's dress tag, which he had found on the floor, as he watched Rudy drive away.

ELEVEN

At eight-twenty on the morning of December 8 my mother, sending Autumn and me off to school, had come face to face with the cheapness of a sexual misdeed, and could tell no one about it.

She went for a walk. She realized she was two months' pregnant, and so often her pregnancies had failed. (There were twins stillborn after Autumn, and a miscarriage.) The sunlight blinded her eyes, the autumn sky was blue, and the snowdrifts from the night before had turned into small glaring and crusted waves in the field beyond. On the river the ice was blue, and she remembered how she had walked on the ice last year with Sydney, when he went to set his smelt nets, and how glimmers of light had spiralled down like the fingertips of stars deep into the world beneath their feet. Bubbles of air lay trapped under that ice, on each side of those brilliant shafts of sunlight. And Sydney told her that the day, and those bubbles of air and those wonderful fingers of starlight, were there just for her. The wind, just as today, blew recklessly over it. Over time, she remembered, clouds had formed in the sky, and the sun became dimmer. Beyond them lay Northumberland Strait as it flooded toward the North Atlantic, beyond Prince Edward Island.

She thought of this and was suddenly happy with her lot. For as Sydney told her, no one owned the ice, or the sunlight spiralling down into it, or any other sunlight, nor crisp autumn days, and no one had authority over her enjoyment of the world. That was given to her by something — *someone* else. He told her that when he was a boy he had become convinced that nothing man did or said mattered *until* this was understood.

Elly walked away from our small dilapidated house and toward the church lane a few miles away.

She stood with her back against the wind, or sometimes walked with her face into it, until finally, with her feet numb, she accepted a drive from Hanny Brown to the turnoff of Saint Paul's. Hanny had been like an older brother to her when she lived with his father and mother, and he looked at her the same way now. Often when he had a chance he would slip five dollars into her pocket, and every fall he came to our house with dresses for Autumn Lynn.

Elly walked the lane to Saint Paul's. The trees waved, got smaller and more crooked, the closer she came to the bay, and the wind turned more bitter against her face. She went into the church, which always to me smelled of heavy oak and the forgiveness of sins. She blessed herself and kneeled, and looked at the porcelain Christ, with his sides bloodied just as they always were, and remembered how she had cut herself when she had fallen over the vacuum cord. It was awful for Mr. McVicer to think this untruth about her. And what if he told the police — or what if Diedre found out? Diedre, whom she had once hugged and sent messages to they called "butterfly kisses"?

How she had loved that little girl with the blonde hair and small mouth with its self-delighted smile.

What had changed between them was simply a lived life. She now prayed for her *siblings* wherever they may be. She thought that if she ever found them — and here she would daydream — they would cherish each other and Elly would no longer have to be frightened that her children were going to be taken away (which is what Diedre told her might happen).

She sat in the pew. Had fourteen years gone since her marriage? She and Sydney, once filled with hope, still clung to nothing. And yet had they both loved me, and little Autumn Lynn, for that long? And had she not taken her luck for granted? That Autumn was an albino — did that matter so much? She was still a wise and beautiful child.

Then she remembered how Sydney had corrected Dr. David Scone, at Mr. McVicer's house — a few months before the robbery.

Scone had looked at the birds in the trees flying about the property on a windy summer afternoon, and had quoted a line from a poem he attributed to Byron, and Sydney said:

"I'm sorry, but I think it is one of Keats's sonnets."

The professor eagerly maintained that he could tell the difference between Byron and Keats and laughed. Sydney nodded and said not a word more. But Elly knew the professor had quoted this line to impress her and had been furious to be shown up by a simpleton.

Yet for Sydney none of this mattered. Mom had asked him later that night where the line was from. He told her to go to his *Poems of Keats*, to look at page 111, and at line seven — and there, exactly there, was the line.

"Why didn't you say anything?" she said.

"Oh, because he seemed so certain," Sydney answered, "and I hurt his feelings — I don't want to do that. Besides, he has done nothing in his life he is proud of — he doesn't want to be stuck at Saint Michael's University — he's tried for years to escape from here — and most of all he believes he knows more than I do."

Elly left the church and walked up the side road, and met my father. She told him that she was sad, and was worried about their trip — not for her, but for the children.

"We have never been on a trip," she said. "We have allowed our children to miss so much."

"I promise to do better. I will plan the trip for next summer — I promise," he answered.

She smiled valiantly and said nothing. She stared past him, her eyes dry.

"What is it?" he asked.

She told him that she was pregnant again and was worried about a miscarriage, and about their situation.

"We will make do with that too," he said.

Then she told him what Diedre Whyne had advised her a week ago.

"She suggested that I have a procedure and then I would be free of it, and think of my own self."

"Ah — yes," he said. "Many people do that now — abortion."

"Abortion," my mother said, and she burst out laughing, for honest to God I don't think she had heard that word before in her life.

Long after my mother was asleep that night my father remained awake. He paced and he thought, and the night was wild, and he was alone. I could see his light on in the room as I tried to work on my homework. I was hoping to sneak Dad's old rifle out the next day and hunt, and I had torn out an advertisement for a knife, and I kept this under my pillow or in my back pocket.

Of course because of my mother (or I blamed it on her) we said the rosary every night. Tonight we had prayed that she wouldn't get sick with this pregnancy, and that no harm would come to Autumn Lynn. We prayed for my father, that he keep his job, and that Leo's money be found.

I lay in my bed under the slanted walls of my small room, which was built at the back corner of our shoebox, and listened to my father and imagined what he was thinking.

Like most men who have had little happiness, my father had expected this newfound happiness, the one he had taken in his job, not to last. And he was right. It was an awful situation for him and Mom. Three nights before, every one of our dreams seemed possible.

He felt he should resign right away. But he could not. Then he decided that if he proved himself at work — worked as hard as he could, worked until he puked — McVicer might finally see that he had erred.

Still he felt that the love he had for my mother, and the love she bore him and the children, was always under assault. So he was alone with his thoughts because I was not old enough to understand them or to help alleviate them.

He had never told my mother but he had heard all about Polly's Restaurant; that men had teased him about her just as boys teased Autumn and me at school. Even Cynthia had come to him last summer, the day after he had corrected Professor Scone, and asked him to a dance at the new community centre. I was with him and I remember what she said. He told her he could not go, and she winked.

"Oh, when are you going to smarten up and get out and have fun? I bet Elly does." She sighed. "Down at Polly's Restaurant each and every day with Rudy Bellanger — I wonder what they get up to in his car along those lonely roads?"

My father had given me a wretched, courageous look and said nothing.

"Why, God, do you allow this to happen?" he now said. I heard him faintly speak this line from my bed. It never bothered me. For I knew my father and I knew he spoke like this. But if he ever got an answer from God or anyone else, he did not say so to me. When I talked to God I did not ask why things happened — I accused him of what was happening — that was the essential difference between father and me.

He looked at my mother sleeping as the wind howled. Her small arms were outside the blankets. Her face was pensive, and now and then she tossed. Thinking he would wake her, he stopped pacing and he sat down.

He and Elly had passed each other many times in the summer, in those fields when he was a child baling hay for her adopted father and she picking strawberries. They had even stood beside one another in church, and had not known it.

That is, he had not met her until it was ordained. This is what he knew in his soul and this is what he told me many times.

To have another child now might be unwise. It would not be difficult to stop it; there were those around who would do it, and offer a benevolent service, especially to a child *like us*. I mean that's part of it although they would never say so. My mother and father's dreams were always dispensable to certain people, who for some reason believed that they themselves and their own dreams were indispensable.

Yet a different moral problem had confounded my father for the past week. It was something no one else who worked on the bridge would have troubled themselves with, yet to my father it was the only thing a man of conscience *should* worry about.

Connie Devlin had been fired for incompetence. He was accused of being drunk on the job. He had come to Sydney seven days before begging him to intercede with the boss. He said that being fired meant it would be difficult to get his unemployment and it was near Christmas.

Because Sydney was trusted, some men asked him to arbitrate on their behalf. Devlin coming to him was not unusual. They relied on him, and they teased him. All mocking is a form of fear. Those who are most mocked are generally most feared. My father was mocked all of his life.

He thought about what he should do. The next day, he went to the office and pleaded Connie Devlin's case.

Porier was a man who lived by McVicer's rules. He had built his house on McVicer property, shopped at McVicer's store, took a loan out for a car with McVicer's blessing. Porier was not at all a big man — but he had a bull-like neck and thick arms — and his two children, Griffin the boy and Penny, were looked upon by him and his arrogant wife as being far superior to other children.

Connie Devlin as night watchman carried a time clock that had to be punched at intervals of one half hour. During the night previous to his being fired the clock was missing seven punches. Thus three and one half hours had gone by when Connie wasn't cognitive enough to punch the clock.

Sydney argued that Connie should be given the benefit of the doubt and Leo not finding out would be the best course.

"Perhaps it's like he says — the clock is broken," Sydney said.

Porier did not want Leo to know how good a worker my father actually was. He was jealous of him. He was worried that Sydney might use this firing as leverage; and he was very worried about Sydney's capabilities with the men themselves. "The men don't appreciate what you do for them," Porier said.

Sydney said that it did not matter what the men thought.

"I hate gullible people — they are a burden to everyone," Porier said. He sniffed and hauled out a map of the river, for no other reason except to prove to Sydney how busy he was. On the desk was a picture of his children, and one of Gladys Bellanger holding Penny in her arms. She was Penny's godmother.

It was cold outside, and cement mixed with mud covered the whole acre where the trucks were parked, and the sky was like a blue stone. The yard was grey and barren. Small trees bent over the cliffs along the water, the same stifled colour as the muddied concrete.

The bridge had inched out and out into the river, and they were sinking the support shafts. Porier was extremely pressed by his work, and had disdain for anyone interrupting him.

Now he glanced up from his map.

"Devlin would never do this for you," Porier said, shaking his head in time to: "Devlin would not he would not he would not."

My father again nodded, and said that this was probably true but if he took his cue from Mr. Devlin he would never have told the truth in his life. He smiled at this, because it was said good-heartedly.

Then my father said: "If you give him his job back, I will do an extra shift as watchman. That would very likely relieve your suspicions."

Finally Porier, without moving, but throwing a pencil the length of the trailer, said he would give Connie Devlin another chance. His face was dark and riveted with anger, his neck swelling with muscles, his fingers blunt and thick. His anger was always like a passion coming over him. He waved his hand in dismissal and added if even one half hour was missed Connie would be fired and, he added, like the afterthought of a general who sends people to their death, so would Sydney Henderson. And if Leo did not like it, he himself would quit and he could get his son-in-law to finish the bridge.

Moreover my father would not become work foreman at this time, as Porier was planning, which meant no forty-dollar-a week raise.

Later that morning, a week before the robbery, Sydney went to Connie's home. When he told Connie the conditions, Connie stared at him and said in astonishment: "You didn't do that for me?"

"Of course," Sydney said.

"Why?" Connie said, and he looked around at no one in particular as if wanting to relay to someone his feelings of astonishment.

"I don't think you being fired over one incident was fair," Sydney said.

"Fair," Connie said, mulling over the word, and licking his lips together. "My, my."

Tonight, a week later, as Elly slept, Sydney pressed his hands together like a child forming a church steeple and remembered the weak expression on Connie's face when he had said "My, my." He had taken two shifts as watchman for no pay. Connie had not once thanked him.

Elly was pregnant again, we were growing older, and here he was still living in a shack. He knew the world Elly had come from. But he had not improved it much. Diedre Whyne of course was right, and this was part of the reason his soul was inconsolable. If they took the child away things would be better. As far as finite things went, Ms. Whyne was right. But of course Elly and he would not do that. *Could* not.

What about the car he had just promised her, which she had told Autumn and me? All his life my father had witnessed men who had had better luck and had gained much more than he, some through deceit and treachery. But there was nothing to be gained in worrying about them.

"It will happen as it is supposed to," Father muttered that night. Although saying this was no comfort at all. Suddenly Devlin's smile pressed a heavy weight on my father's heart, just as Prof. David Scone's dismissal did years before. He reached forward and stroked Elly's hair. Then he kneeled and prayed. Why did a grown man do this on his knees in his underwear? I do not know. I have never been able to understand why.

I have always known my father believed in the necessity of a stoic life, and still and all hoped with stoicism for some proof of life being worthwhile.

Wind wailed against our house, and it was dark up on the highway. Now and again a tractor-trailer with a load of peat moss would grind along the road, stopping to turn toward the detour and the old bridge farther along the river, and the lights would catch our upstairs window, and show Father pale and almost naked. Yet no matter how thin my father looked, he was strong and impenetrably faced the cold and snow. He would work and had worked in below-zero all day in a sweater without a coat. Ice and snow was his world. The fire of ice; the sweet blue orb of snow.

TWELVE

When Rudy Bellanger went to Mathew Pit late the afternoon after his incident with Elly, shaken and white, with a story about how my mother had tricked him by showing him her panties then refusing to comply, and would certainly tell Leo that he had assaulted her, Mathew looked unimpressed. He had always felt she was like that: a bitch from the village of Tabusintac who milked cows as a little girl, went to church, and kept a crucifix under her pillow. And now was married to a simpleton who read books and talked in riddles. These antics were nothing. Mathew said he knew all about women like her, and he banged a bottle of rum down heavily on the table as if to prove it.

Mathew said he had himself dated her and had long known the girl. Rudy's fault, Mathew advised, lay in his good nature and his kindness, and his general decency. Mathew sniffed and folded his arms and tapped his boots on the linoleum floor. But now it was time to get tough, Mathew said. Rudy shuddered when he looked at Mathew Pit's face.

"How are we going to get tough?" Rudy whispered.

"If that's the kind of woman she is — we can get her back soon 'nough," he said, in a raspy tired voice.

The air was dulled by the smell of burning wood and autumn air coming through the front window onto the dust-covered sill of Pit's old house.

For seven years Mathew felt himself best friends with Rudy Bellanger, whom he called Banger, and had done everything he could to be entitled to something when the old man died. His biggest mistake, however, was at certain times to trust Rudy with information. Last year, he had advised Rudy about the property where the highway would go, and was exasperated when Rudy told his wife, who immediately informed her father. Leo then bought that sliver of property for himself, making another thirty thousand dollars profit. Mathew, who never had the front money to buy it, had informed Rudy because he wanted a split.

"You stupid no-nut bastard — you don't do that," he had said. "You keep these things quiet," he said, pinching Rudy's cheek and pretending it was a joke. But his smile, showing white even teeth, was angry. "The goddamn McVicers get everything — everything all the time — this shoulda' been for you — the Whynes and McVicer share this whole area and we is nothin' but peasants."

Still, Mathew was not about to see anything else go up in smoke because a bored wife flashed her crotch hair. He knew how Leo liked this woman, and was of course aware of her good looks. For the last few months he was wanting to discredit her not only for his own vainglory but because being a realist (and knowing Rudy's weakness with Cynthia) he could sense that something would happen that might jeopardize his friend. He had warned Rudy to stay away from Elly on four different occasions, but the last thing Rudy understood was himself.

Mathew was more angry with my father, whom he had always considered slow and dumb. (He did hear that Sydney had read Tolstoy and Conrad, but what did that matter?) How could Sydney have set this all up, he thought.

Mathew Pit believed people viewed the world as he himself viewed the world. And Mathew was totally unaware of how far his imagined plans had gone, over the last few years, and unaware of how dependent he was upon plans to secure Rudy's trust and receive recompense for this trust. When he was drunk Rudy often said they would be partners as soon as the old man died.

But because of this incident with a woman Mathew himself was still sometimes enamoured of, Mathew's house of cards was beginning to implode without anything being realized.

Mathew had looked at Rudy that late afternoon, a stained bolt-shaped ring on his index finger and a cigarillo in his mouth. Behind his head under the dreary window a calendar with a picture of a half-naked woman was grimed with thumbprints.

"Don't worry, we'll take care of that girl," Mathew said, snapping a bit of leather shoelace with his heavy hands.

Mathew talked in a whisper. His eyes glanced to his left and then his right, and he went back to repairing a snowshoe, tying it off as conscientiously as an artist.

When Rudy left Leo McVicer's that afternoon, a half hour after my parents had, he was well aware of what had really happened. Mathew had robbed the house.

Rudy had been appalled by the look of Elly, and he could not justify destroying the young woman's life. He drove to Mathew Pit's after he left Leo's, determined to get the money back, to cut all his ties with Cynthia.

Mathew shook his head and yelled something indiscernible to Trenton's dog, then kicked at it. He did this to further his control over Rudy Bellanger. What infuriated Rudy about this was that he sensed in Mathew's movement how much Mathew knew about him, and disliked about him.

"You can't do anything else to her — this must be the last thing — she is just a poor woman — they have nothing," Rudy advised Mathew Pit. "I don't mind getting rid of them, as you say, but I don't like cheating old Leo in order to do it."

That is, Rudy said what weak people always say to prove they are of one and the same mind with others. Of course he minded getting rid of my mother. It was the only thing he minded more than cheating old Leo. Besides, he felt Leo had cheated him, and was at the bottom of his heart somewhat happy.

But by his own weakness all this had happened. Now he said:

"I need the money back."

Mathew laughed. "The hell you do. I'm the one got you outta this scrape — you are the one, my boy, who loused up my deal with the land north of the river — I bet Leo thanked you for reminding him there was one sliver of land he didn't control."

"I know — he was wrong — but you can't keep the five hundred," Rudy implored.

"I'm going to keep it till after Christmas — by then everything will have blowed over." Mathew spoke with calm assurance and had the studious look of a man who is used to holding others' feet to the fire.

Rudy could do nothing but say he would go see the police if this continued.

"Police — police, is it! Leo would want that — he'd welcome it." Mathew gazed at Rudy with eyes that were unfocussed and unnerving. There was a bit of blond whiskers on his upper lip and chin. He wore a jean jacket and heavy work boots covered in mud. His blond hair was slicked back in the ducktail he always wore, even though the fashion had long ago changed.

Mathew thought anyone who dressed differently was a faggot. He did not know how else to describe his anger and frustration when he saw them. The boys looked like girls and yet condescended to him because of their education. And if he was anti-intellectual (as Leo McVicer was), he had a right to be, by birth. All his life *they* in some way or the other had spit in his face, and those whom he had trusted after three years away at university looked upon him with dismissive conceit. But when their cars or motorboats were broken they came to him.

Their treasure was education, which he did not understand, and so he (and his sister, Cynthia) teamed with Rudy as a business partner not because Mathew knew business but because it didn't threaten or hurt him. In this maze of confusion he had of late suspected Sydney Henderson of being one of them, the intellectuals, one of those who with half a chance would dismiss his entire life. So it was not important if Sydney or his wife got blamed for anything. He would blame them for anything he chose. He had dated her and *she* had scorned *him*. Worse, Sydney had a job on the bridge. The bridge was a large project, part of the project that would create the new highway through land Mathew had instructed Rudy to buy. It would have meant over a year of high wages.

Mathew had spoken about sabotaging it. He was now set on this course.

"I don't know about their concrete — and part of that last span is buckled," Mathew had said the week before. "What if I took a piece of dynamite — then look out, eh?"

"Connie Devlin is the watchman," Cynthia had told him. "He will come back to haunt you if you do it."

Cynthia was beautiful — and more ruthless than her brother. Nevertheless, Mathew was prepared to go ahead with his sabotage on the bridge. He felt that it might help Rudy with his problems if he could cast doubt on the worth of the foreman, Abby Porier.

Now he stared at Rudy Bellanger wearing his suit and gold cufflinks and said: "How much that cost ya?"

Rudy didn't answer. His face turned red, and he fidgeted and asked for water. Mathew poured him a glass.

Rudy finished his water in a gulp and asked for more.

Then Mathew smiled kindly at Rudy again.

Rudy wanted to build a marina to cater to the dozens of new pleasure boats and sailboats on the river. Rudy had planned this marina for ten years, secretly for the first seven. One night, drinking with Mathew, he had told him his plan. Pit's eyes widened as Rudy took a paper napkin and drew his plans on it, showing the sports bar, the upstairs lounge, the deck lounge. It was very much a replica of a marina he had seen in Halifax. He said he could easily get a grant from the Atlantic Provinces Business Bureau because he knew three people on the committee.

Rudy believed his planned takeover was moral, very moral, until the robbery. For thirteen years, since the day of his marriage, it was *his* store, and *his* property. Now, because of Elly, everything had hit a snag. His whole life seemed nothing more than a house of cards imploding. He was the last one who would be able to complain about any moral snag now.

Though Rudy had not been involved in the robbery, how could he not say he knew who had? And more to the point, how could he not pretend it was Elly and Sydney to save himself?

There is no worse flaw in man's character than that of wanting to belong.

Rudy believed he needed men like Mathew Pit. Men like Mathew Pit had no structure, nor needed any. They had no class affiliation and needed none. Mathew was by trade a mechanic but he could be anything. He did not need a business structure, as businessmen like Rudy needed. He only needed a scheme, and that scheme was more important than any office or committee boardroom. People like Mathew would know what it was like to sell shoelaces fifteen for two dollars, or how to make two million in a week. It depended only upon the scheme. Mathew had his scheme, and that involved sooner or later moving to Ontario with a lot of money (that he would get from Rudy) and buying a fishing and hunting lodge in the north. He had told no one this.

Far from being a throwback to another time, as anyone looking at Mathew Pit might think, he and his sister were the new ruthless entrepreneurs. They would listen with almost stupefied inattention to the words "ethics" or "moral responsibility" — but they both knew fierce loyalty and hatreds. Sometimes they could be burned at the stake before giving up a friend. But they also both knew, especially Cynthia, how to use friends, and how to give them up in a heartbeat.

Here in a hallway of Pit's old house, the walls crowded with pictures of old men and horses, Rudy could see into the far back room when Cynthia came downstairs after her shower. He had succumbed to her advances, right under his wife's nose, and he had promised himself he would never do that again. She was beautiful, with dark hair and eyes, but was far less genteel than Elly.

Of course at this moment he was through with all his philandering and had decided wild horses wouldn't be able to haul him back; that he would never get into trouble again, or cause anyone any more grief.

Now, as Rudy sat before him, Mathew looked genuinely concerned.

"What is there to worry about? Didn't I do as you asked?"

Rudy had never asked Mathew to do anything, let alone rob the house. But Rudy convinced himself it might have happened that way because the alternative was just too hard to accept — that Mathew respected him so little he would do whatever he wanted.

Rudy told Mathew that this was a terrible thing. And what he wanted more than anything else was to be reassured that Mathew, his partner, knew that this was a terrible thing.

"Look," Mathew whispered, "I had to take care of Sydney when he was a kid — because he was always being smashed about, and I never got no credit for it neither, nor do I want none. That damn house he lives in, three rooms, no heat in the winter, and you couldn't sit in it in the summer for the smell of human piss. It ain't much better now — he still owes me money from the business, he cheated me, he lied about us." He waited for this revelation to take effect. Then he continued in a soft whisper.

"And think of what will happen — she'll just try to hang on to you — that's the kind she is, Tabusintac bitch, and that's not right, get rid of the both of them. Somewhere in the future is your money, so think — don't let a bitch who's not gettin' it at home between you and your dreams. I won't touch the money — and when everything will have calmed down — later on — next summer when things with me and you are going better I'll just slip the money back into the store — no one will be out anything. Whole thing will be forgot."

"I don't know," Rudy said. "I feel bad — for the two of them — and their kids. I know how Autumn is laughed at — once I got angry at people for it."

"Listen," Mathew whispered, "Sydney is a troublemaker. Get that through yer head. I had to bail him out a dozen times and finally I just give up. You ask Connie Devlin. Pushed him off a roof fer god sake — the boy's not got all his load — and here I have a retarded brother livin' next to him — I almost cry to think of it."

Then he got up and squeezed Rudy's shoulder, and Rudy nodded and smiled.

As he spoke Mathew remembered his humiliation at not getting on the bridge when Sydney had. And as for Rudy — well, Rudy decided, as others sometimes had, that it was in his best interest to invest in a lie, a complete fabrication when it concerned my mother and father. He did not contemplate at that moment how large the lie would grow, or what dimension the monster would finally take, and who all it would swallow; nor that in the end others he did not know as anything but children would have to turn in the dark and combat this monster with courage he himself never needed to have.

But more important, he knew that my father was a greater man than Mathew Pit. Yet what he did now was say to himself: "Who am I to know who is a good man and who isn't — in this day and age, with cocaine and all the rest?"

He thought of Sydney; how he, Rudy, believed him, just the morning before the assault on Elly, to be superior to him. And how he had used this notion of superiority to play havoc with his wife. He thought of Diedre Whyne, who, feeling herself superior to Elly, had once spoken candidly about Elly needing her tubes tied.

Still hadn't he himself profited from people's opinions of Elly, from her beauty (since the intolerant nuns until now a mark against her) and her gentleness (considered from the days of the nuns to be stupidity)? Yes, hadn't he profited from the liberal idea that she was not enlightened — and hadn't this "energized" his feelings toward her?

Rudy had argued against Elly needing her tubes tied, and Ms. Whyne had put him in his place. But actually Ms. Whyne's opinion allowed a licence when it came to my mother that was surreptitiously attached to the very fabric of Rudy's disagreement with her. It became clear to any person willing to think it through that those who were trying to *help* her, as Ms. Whyne was, and those who would *use* her, as Rudy had, were essentially the same type of person; both felt superior to her, and felt their humanity not only superior but different in kind from hers.

He had not seen this until now.

He, Rudy Bellanger, had in effect cast Elly and Sydney away as thieves; and worse, both of them went away without a sound of protest. Worse, Elly admitted to the theft to protect her husband. Moreover, he saw how this lie against them was not considered important by Mathew Pit, who sat in the heat of the kitchen with his large red arms, and his tattoos visible.

Now Rudy, knowing everything, and understanding it all, was willing at that moment to let my parents suffer. Moreover, he could not take back what he had said, or confess what he had done. His father-in-law may have forgiven him before, but he would not now. Now every day that passed made it worse than the day before.

Therefore, though he thought it was only my mother and father, and by proxy their children, who had been cast out, by this casting out Rudy's own Golgotha was now beginning. He had to keep it away by whatever means he could, if not for himself, then for Gladys, whom he loved. Oh yes — that was the real tragedy — his love for her; even though he was bossed around by both her and her father, even though whenever Gladys got angry she would yell: "I will leave you without a cent, Frenchman!"

He still loved her.

He looked at Mathew. "You aren't really going to sabotage the bridge?" Rudy asked, smiling.

"What do you think?" Mathew said, quietly.

"On my honour I'd have to tell," Rudy said.

"On your honour — your honour? You know all those rumours about you — if one got back to yer wife — and her sick — why should I protect you?"

"I don't want you to talk about Gladys like that."

"Of course not," Mathew said quickly, with feigned respect. "But think what will happen if the bridge is sabotaged — no more Porier. It will help you when it comes time for our — *your* — marina. Then you will hire me as your foreman — and I will do a better job than anyone. If the bridge goes they will have to point the finger at someone — Sydney, say — then we are really in the clear for ever and ever! No one would accuse you of anything after that! I don't mean to get you scared — but just to let you know our bind is not over — not right yet. Before you came to me yesterday I didn't consider doing the bridge a smart move. But now I see it is our only option. We got to do things now fast — set the snare — because already Sydney has gone up to the cops."

"He has?"

"Well — think! For cripes sake — what would *you* have done if yer wife was accused?"

"I'd go to the cops."

"There —" Mathew sniffed. "So now is the time to do something else — *to make sure* — that's all I am attempting to do, make sure — for *yer* sake, not mine! I never give a damn for myself. Set the snare now — set it now. Who is on the bridge all the time doing all the shit jobs? Sydney. Well, maybe he got tired of doing them — maybe he wanted to get back at Leo — I think that's probably how it is! After the sabotage Leo has no one to turn to — Porier is fired — you come in, straighten this business out — what more could a person ask? You hire me as foreman as I say! All of a sudden Sydney goes to jail, and Elly begins to see you for who you *really* are — Gladys is still your wife — and she is a good woman — but look who you will have on the side."

Rudy drank more water. He knew that if at any time until his life was over Mathew Pit found him disposable, the loyalty he believed he had built up would dissipate in a whiff of blue autumn sky. And he also knew this conversation was absolute proof of it. This in fact was what Mathew was telling him. Mathew's talk was always underscored with *conditions* that made people as diverse as Rudy and the Sheppard brothers fear him. There was no mention of blackmail, but Rudy had put his trust in a man who had no real feelings toward him. And this was the story of Rudy's life, because he was a weak man who allowed others to dictate to him what life should be. The bridge would be sabotaged to keep Rudy in line as much as anything. So who really was the snare being set for?

"I don't care what happens to the bridge — but if it goes down, there will be hell to pay," he said as gruffly as he could, hoping that this comment alone would be enough to dissuade Mathew.

"Oh, that's what makes it fun," Mathew said, his light blue eyes unnerving.

Rudy stood, put on his white down winter coat that gave his face the youthful appearance of a red-cheeked teenager, and headed for the door, with the salt-and-pepper hat on his head. Lights shone out on the snowbanks and made everything warm, and from behind him there was the odour of gin, which Cynthia loved, and marijuana, on which Mathew planned to spend the five hundred dollars after Christmas.

Mathew followed him, begging him to stay (for he was worried about what Rudy might do or say), and at the last minute called for Cynthia. She came into the kitchen just in time.

"Rudy," Cynthia said. She waved a tiny bag of cocaine.

Rudy sheepishly climbed the outdoor steps again, almost slipping on the black ice. He pretended he was angry and had business on his mind, and did not want to see her. He pretended (as he had with my mother) that he was important but did not know he was important.

He pretended that he could resist her. Yet in the light her legs were bare. She was wearing a pink nightie and smelled of bath oil. She looked hurt when he told her he wasn't going to stay. But when she turned away, he lifted her nightie. Except for bikini panties she was naked underneath.

"Oh, you always do this," she said, quickly running her tongue over her teeth, and pressing her body against his.

He tried to turn away, but her words made that impossible. Cynthia kissed him with her tongue, opened her eyes while his were still closed, glanced at her brother, and winked.

THIRTEEN

After Rudy went home Mathew left the old house. In the dark with its two pointed gables the house looked sinister, desolate as it was, and far away from town. The fire that my grandfather and later my father were blamed for had caused a black veil of trees and uprooted stumps, and dark-watered ditches surrounded them.

People would pass this house on the way to other jurisdictions and other lives. Linguistic professors from the university in Fredericton would not know that Cynthia could do a crossword puzzle in ten minutes; nor computer analysts know that Mathew knew the size of every truck and car engine by the sound of a one-second rev of that engine. That did not matter to people passing by a house with junked cars and cannibalized engines in the back yard.

The world was fast moving on, and from these autumn skies Mathew and Cynthia saw the new information age staggering the previous ages into submission. Once or twice in their lives people from Mathew's background would have a moment where they would prick the national consciousness; they would be interviewed and condescended to, with such gaiety of dismissal it wasn't even registered by our more educated countrymen. Overall, men like Mathew were laughed at, ridiculed or feared most of their lives. If there was bigotry against First Nations they were accused of it (even though he had worked with First Nations men and women far more than those professors or writers who would accuse him). If there was intolerance they were accused, even though he had worked on roads and shared his bread with black men from Africville. Chauvinism they were accused of, even though he thought of Cynthia as his superior.

The world had gone on, and had been parcelled into manageable concerns; and this world left him and his sister out. Well, in some way it still allowed for his sister, for her gender demanded it. But he knew that now, at thirty-three years of age, time was falling away from him. If there was no money soon, he would have to go back on welfare. He hated and no longer wanted that. Just once he too would like to have people notice him. And Rudy was his key. He could do the bridge not to positively influence Leo about Rudy, but to keep Rudy, whom he was sure would someday be wealthy, under his thumb. This was his intention, and Rudy had seen it in a second. But somewhere in his heart Mathew knew he was making a mistake.

He turned with purpose and crossed the road into the dark freezing autumn wood. He walked along a worn path — worn by children, and by himself and Sydney and Connie when they were children, and by their parents when they were children — and down a slope. In the black night where others would lose their way his direction was sure and his strides bold and purposeful. His arms and legs were thick, his back broad and strong.

He stopped. There was something walking up the path, in a sway-backed meandering way. As Mathew stood still watching it the bear moved, groggy with a year's supply of fat for the winter. He waited for the bear, who had not seen him — for he had nowhere to run, and he wouldn't turn his back on it. Just when the bear got close it stopped dead, sniffed the air, and at the same moment Mathew threw out his right hand and hit the bear on the snout with a crash. The bear bleated rushing into the trees, and Mathew lighted a cigarette and continued on. They were so poor in the mid-fifties his father would kill a bear each fall, grind the meat, boil the bones for stew and the fat for soap; this is what Mathew remembered of his childhood — the old house smelling of bear fat dripping into soap, and bear stew on his plate for supper. He had never feared a bear after that. He had, however, always feared his father.

Mathew turned into Connie Devlin's lane at two o'clock in the morning after Leo had sent my mother and father from his house. He entered through the back door, by the small, well-kept kitchen, opening the lock with a Buck knife, and walked into Devlin's bedroom and woke him up with a shove.

"You want to help me out of a scrape," he said, "and get back at Sydney Henderson once and for all?"

Connie opened his eyes slowly, without fear, looked at his wristwatch, and rubbed his nose quickly. His face was beet red, like a baby having eaten jam, and he sat up.

"What kind of scrape — ?"

"I want to knock the span down — it has to be replaced anyway. Sydney will get blamed — it won't take too much starch out of it — just seven or eight feet — the place you guys are worried about. They have a abutment to keep things off it — I think driving the company half-ton ahead onto it should do the trick."

"Why would he want to knock the bridge down? Why would I do that? I don't understand."

"I swear there'll be big money in it for us — it's gotta go — the span's gotta go."

"Who's paying you to do this?"

Mathew thought for a moment. "Rudy Bellanger will pay us — if it's done right —"

"But that's his own company."

"That's what makes it legal."

Connie said he had just gotten rehired after a dispute and didn't want to chance anything. He did not tell Mathew that Sydney had gotten him rehired under stringent conditions.

"It is a awful case," Mathew said. "Sydney was just caught stealing a bunch of money from Leo —"

"God, where? At the bridge?"

"No — at the house — Elly did it."

"Elly!"

"I think so — but they will try to blame it on you — just as always."

Connie looked at him curiously. "Me — ?"

"Well, I can't be sure — but we'll do something very big," Mathew said. "It's a shot into the future for us both. You just help me with the span —" He produced a stick of dynamite he had had in his possession for a long time. "Just let part of a span fall into the river — and Rudy will pay us four thousand apiece."

"Four thousand apiece?"

"Yes — four thousand apiece. It'll be good for Rudy — Rudy needs our help — we love Rudy, you and I."

"Love Rudy?"

"Well, I've always had affection for Rudy — I don't know about you."

"Sure," Connie Devlin said, and wiggling his toes in his big red socks (he always slept with socks on like he had as a child because of cold toes) sneezed and coughed. He said sure, because he didn't want to chance what would happen if he said no. He was Mathew's first cousin. He had usually been in on things of this sort, in one fashion or another. Just by Mathew's face, he knew Elly had done no such thing as rob the house. Mathew had.

And this showed the difference between Mathew and his two friends. Connie had as much on Mathew as Mathew ever had on Rudy Bellanger. But what Connie knew kept him both faithful and silent; what Mathew knew about Rudy kept him arrogant and dangerous.

Connie Devlin listened to these plans. He would turn out the lights the night Mathew drove the truck across the abutment and threw the dynamite. Mathew knew nothing about explosives, but he knew Sydney did. It would be considered Sydney's fault. Everything would work from that.

Cynthia had disapproved of the robbery because everything

Mathew had done so far had failed. Then tonight, before Rudy visited, she told him that he soon better prove that he could do things right or she would think of him as others did.

"And how is that — how do others think of me?"

"Well — a bigmouth blowhard," she said, "but underneath — a gutless fool."

His eyes jumped slightly when he looked at her. Still, had she not said this to him, he would never have rethought the dynamite or the bridge.

Now he left Connie and started his trek toward home.

Cynthia had been envious of the rich and powerful she saw as a child. Politicians and mavericks from all walks of life, some who owned cottages along the bay shore. Families from places like Montreal and Oshawa, Ottawa and Toronto. People so adept at dismissing these wide-eyed children in those small fishing houses. She wanted more than anything to be like them.

Mathew was her sole resource, but her mind was brilliant enough to see avenues where Mathew did not go. Right to McVicer himself, if need be.

She did not know that her remarks about Mathew had caused a change in him — and that he would take a chance on the bridge just for hellery.

It was on her part a rather significant mistake.

FOURTEEN

As news of the robbery spread, my father was looked upon with more suspicion, and men stayed away from him. A week or so after Connie Devlin was allowed back onsite I took Dad's dinner to him, carrying it as if I was a waiter, in joy that I had something to deliver my dad.

My father came to meet me, patted my head, and went to sit with Connie to eat his lunch. Devlin turned and said loudly:

"I ain't no robber rubberhead — go sit yerself somewhere else before ya contamp-inate me with yer robber germs —"

He got a great laugh out of this, which is what he was hoping for. I trembled with rage. My father sat with his eyes down the longest time, and then looked over at me.

"Get along to school, son," he said.

Autumn and I did not know about the robbery until we heard about it at school. And my first reaction was how ordinary it was for *us* to be blamed for this.

I always wore a tie to school — it was as if my mother wanted to isolate me even more. A tie, a heavy white shirt, old suit pants, and black shoes. Autumn always wore a dress, white stockings, and a pair of black patent leather shoes that had once belonged to Mother herself. Her eyes were red, her eyelashes thin and weak. One day after she was teased she whispered in my ear:

"I will someday have eyes to stare the world in the face — and my eyes, Lyle dear — well, my eyes will be Autumn blue."

Still, we were dressed the way my mother believed children should be dressed to go out. It was genteelly countrified. That I did not know how to throw a punch to protect us made it dangerous. The boys of my youth valiantly tried to get me to fight — two or three of them at a time, calling me "little Lord Fauntleroy."

Autumn stood behind me when they teased her. Did I hit them back? No — because my father had drilled into me the vanity and falseness of violence. So I turned away ashamed, and endured with my sister the callous and chronic idiocy of others. My mother was called a thief, and then a whore. They told me she drank gin at Polly's and had her panties taken off by Rudy Bellanger.

Across the brook the days got shorter and the wind blew the substance of hard snow over the tufts of hard broken fields. I would go home and stare at my mother in strange agony. I could not ask her if this was true.

I was usually up before breakfast because I would stoke the stove, or sometimes Autumn and I would be sent out to meet the milk truck at the top of the lane. Autumn did well in school and I did not. Nor did I do that well in sports. But I did do well in the woods. Already I had explored the woods and surrounding area, and I had seen where the salmon would run close to shore on their journey into our waters.

I saw some danger in the woods. I knew what it was like to get turned around and lost. Usually as the cold days came and the snow fell I planned for trips to snare rabbits and trap mink — things I could sell for some extra money. I did not want the money for myself. I was saving to buy Autumn contacts to make her eyes the blue she desired. I could find mink tracks, and rabbit, of course, and was beginning to notice coyote tracks as they came into our area. The coyotes here were almost the size of wolves, mating as they did with wild or running dogs.

I wore a heavy coat, a hunting vest, and lined boots, and spent my afternoons away from everyone, and could run comfortably and break a trail on snowshoes.

Trenton, Mathew's young brother, was almost nineteen but looked like a child. He wandered about the bridge worksite, and went there — in spite of people telling him to stay away — to collect nails and loose cement, putty and wire. Not only my father but Porier had to help him across the road because of the transport trucks turning toward the detour. The snow fell often that year and he was in danger of being injured.

The old woman was too tired to bother following him, as she once did, and though she sometimes kept him inside, he had enough wits to get out by himself. But my father's concern hit a snag with Mathew, who said he didn't want my father in his yard. Perhaps Mathew feared Trenton divulging something — it is only a guess. Still, Sydney started walking Trenton home. The Pits did not like this. Mathew came outside one night and told my father not to bring the boy home again. I was with them.

"But I don't mind doing it," Sydney said.

"Don't matter — stay away from the boy — stay away from him — you hear — I don't want him with you!"

"It's just that the bridge —" my father started to explain.

"The bridge," Mat piped up. "All as we hear day and night is goddamn heavy equipment on that bridge — it shouldn't be built here at all — it's all just political — we didn't have a say and don't have a cent from it. And yer as much a part of it — ya poisoned my chances at a job — yer not going to be playing about with this youngster —"

Trenton wandered to the site the next day. So Sydney decided to have a conversation with the old woman, Alvina Pit, without Mathew being there. He went across Arron Brook to the Pit house after supper on December 18, 1982. White smoke drifted out of their chimney, and fresh raw snow sat upon the aging stumps behind the house, while a glow from outside Christmas lights lighted the sky farther down the snowy road.

Alvina was outside decorating the tree. In her look, the small blunt nose, the eyes a little close together, her soft lips, my father could see Cynthia in thirty years.

Alvina looked at him the way she had been taught to, as if his rationale, since too obscure for most people, was trickery, as Mathew had warned her it would be. She was like many unthinking women who bowed to their sons.

"I think I should keep an eye on Trenton," he said. "Because once he gets out of sight of Mat and you he is on his own."

"I look out for him all he needs," she said swiftly, because she wanted him to know he was one of the people Mat and she would protect her son from. She knew all about how he humiliated Mathew. Mathew told her.

My father stared at her old coat and frayed scarf and watched her work. There was a wisping sound of snow at the back of their house, the sky had darkened, and wind had blackened the old iced-over sawhorses in the corner of the yard. Sydney looked at the upstairs window when a light went on, and saw Cynthia in the hallway.

"You don't have to run after him —" Sydney said. "I don't mind bringing him back."

"He is our responsibility, thank you very much — you don't seem to have done much for your own!" She did not look at him as she worked, but looked at the spruce tree she was trying to pin Christmas lights to.

Alvina felt justified in mistrusting him — a grown man who was mocked by the community for being odd, and was considered strange. Strange in Alvina's mind meant only one thing, though she would never say this aloud.

Grabbing my father by the coat, as if this was the way to make herself heard, she said Trenton's life was in God's hands. Trenton, she maintained, was a child of her old age, and therefore God had been wise enough to make him how he was. He brought joy to everyone.

Trenton huddled in an old man's overalls and bib beside her as Sydney took out the candy cane he had brought and handed it to him.

Alvina continued, "God has every hair on Trenton's head numbered in his great mind." (She repeated just what Father Porier had told her.)

Sydney nodded. "I know he does, Alvina. But what does that matter if tomorrow night he is killed on the bridge!"

This statement frightened her. "If you go near him again I will get the police!" She walked away across the frost-bulked yard, her heavy black-seamed nylons dragging at her ankles.

Trenton turned and ran, his back bent and his legs flaying like a daddy longlegs, a candy cane in his mitten.

Dad came back home, and told us what was said, almost word for word. So, like other conversations I have heard second-hand, I have committed them to memory and now relate them to you. Sydney told my mother he was wrong in what he had just said; and it was said in a rash way to convince her.

"I shouldn't have tried to frighten her," he said. "It all came about because of Mathew's damn stubbornness."

"If there is a safety concern Porier should go to her, not you," I said.

But Porier was infuriatingly conceited, Father said. Someone being injured would mean little to him; not because Porier was bad, but because he had warnings posted about the weak span, and had an abutment in front of it.

Sydney asked my mother if he should phone Alvina and apologize.

My mother sighed. "Just leave it be," she said. "It is up to them. And Lyle is right, Porier should go over. Hopefully everything will turn out for the best."

My father then spoke, softly, as if to himself. I was sitting near him, and saw his hands tremble as he talked. He said he had no knowledge of why he was abused as a boy, why he was born in such poverty, why he had faced what he had, when others who wrote for the paper and became members of the Legislature had never seen a day like he.

"But remember," he said aloud, "we still have our faith in God that everything will turn out."

"Why?" I said angrily. "The old priest didn't even give us a Christmas box."

"Son, a priest is not the Church, and the Church is not the faith," Father answered.

He then told us that in order to run away from his life, he had read. And in his readings he realized that he was to suffer for some reason.

"Remember Cynthia's stillborn child," Mother said, "and how Mathew spoke about you then — he will say it again if he can."

"Leopards don't change their spots," I said. "The father of that baby was Danny Sheppard, everyone knows — and they blamed you for a long time!"

My father nodded and said nothing more.

FIFTEEN

The next day was his last day of work at the site. We knew he would be let go after the holiday. The only thing he had managed to do was to keep Devlin in work while he himself was to be fired. This irony must have pleased Mathew.

Dad got up particularly early, and did not eat breakfast. They would have to rope off the third span, which had buckled along the side. This day has replayed itself in my mind for years.

My father left for work at seven and worked the whole day and came back home about five-thirty. At six-thirty the telephone rang, and Mrs. Pit asked if Trenton was there.

"No, he is not," Sydney said.

"You don't have him — and are keeping him from me?"

"Of course not."

"Please, is this a joke? Cynthia thinks you are keeping him on us for some reason. That you think we are bad people or are hiding the boy — for — for some purpose."

"Mrs. Pit, tell Cynthia I wouldn't do such a thing — I *couldn't* do such a thing."

It was bitterly cold. My father put on a worker's jumpsuit and left the house to search for the boy. I went with him to the inlet. He never spoke to me. I felt his anxiety as we walked.

There were gentle shrouds of snow falling from small fir trees in back of our house. From the far side of the inlet we could see the waving flashlight beams of people in panic, Cynthia and others, and hear the faint hollering of the old woman — a woman Sydney had never really spoken to until the day before, and a family he had never truly known.

They were searching the shoreline but were frightened to go onto the newly formed ice. (Trenton had gone onto the ice two or three times before.) My father was frightened as well, and perhaps he was very frightened, but decided someone had to go.

I told him that I was lighter and I could go. (I had always wanted to prove I was as brave as he was.)

"No," he said sternly.

The ice was as bottled and grey as the back of a nurse shark and my father soon disappeared in the darkness. He walked toward the strait calling Trenton's name. But after a time he saw the open water, and felt the frozen wind, and turned back, heart sinking, and thinking of the bridge, just at the time he heard a thud, like snow falling from a great height, and he felt the ice shift under his boots.

My father ran to the bridge. He arrived twenty minutes later and shone his light along the yard, by the cranes, and down along the shore. The security lights had not been turned on; the whole structure was silent and forbidding. He went to the power house and tried to turn on the lights, and could not get in. He went back to the spans and stood where yellow cranes and tractors sat blanketed in snow.

He was about to turn his light out when he saw a form lying to the left of the last span, on the ice. And what was worse, a section of that span had let go. Rebar jutted out like spikes into the night, and eight feet of the span itself was gone. Just as father had feared. Teetering off the broken span was the company truck.

By the time my father reached the boy, Mrs. Pit had arrived. She wore boots over woollen stockings, and her woollen coat had a pink housedress button sewn on its neck. The wind wailed, and in the dark, clouds could be seen sweeping the sky above them.

Her rosary dangled in her hands as other men arrived and brought the boy's broken body up.

"Trent," she said, in a whisper, fearful of waking him. She kept walking about him, as if inspecting a strange sweet flower, breathing on her folded hands where the rosary dangled. Now and again she would bend over and touch him, touch the Saint Christopher medal on his neck; making sure he wasn't an apparition. Snowflakes fell on her bare head and covered his thin bare legs.

"You told me this would happen—" Alvina said suddenly to Sydney.

"You pushed him down — you told me you knew what would happen to him today — you said he would be dead and he was!"

Sydney, too stunned to speak, looked at her, and then at Mathew and Cynthia.

At the very moment my father looked up, Elly came running out of the darkness, and her face came toward him with the expression people have when late for an appointment. She wavered and stood still, like a post being put into place.

The body didn't move except for the hair being blown by the wind. The hair that, as Alvina had said just the day before, Christ had counted and knew. Cynthia glared at my father for so many reasons. No one knows why a woman as beautiful and as free as she was attracted to my father. But she had been for a number of years.

"You — you pushed him down," Alvina said again. "You drove that truck — you brought him here in that truck for something terrible, and when he didn't want to you pushed him!"

However much Alvina, Cynthia, or my mother wanted my father to speak now, my father could not. He simply stared at them. He respected the old woman in her moment of trial, and did not want to trifle with her feelings by contradicting her accusation so soon after her shock. He felt others would *know* it was said in *shock*. He stood silently in the freezing air. From the corner of the bridge Leo McVicer glared at him. His bridge, his crowning achievement — all gone in a thud of snow.

He said, absolutely calmly, "What in Christ was that truck doing out there, Sydney? There was nothing supposed to be out there." He turned and went home.

Finally paramedics came. They gathered up the body and moved away.

Worse for us all was the money. Trenton had the money that had been robbed from old Leo's house stuffed in his pockets.

Of course, Leo McVicer believed Sydney took the money; that's why he was letting him go after Christmas. Though he entertained a thought of someone else robbing him, he now no longer could, because in his mind both events fed off each another. He telephoned the police the next day and told Constable Morris his suspicions. He wanted to help the police — but he also wanted his money back. The question floating in the air was this: Why would the money be in Trenton's possession? This is what Leo himself addressed to Constable Morris, and Morris, fed information since the time Father was accused of stealing the box of smelts, retaliated against my father — set up a scenario against him, judged him without any evidence. But that everything *fit* seemed incontestable — the threat to Alvina, the truck to whisk the boy away, the money to give the child for a sexual favour (the whole five hundred dollars for a sexual favour given to a retarded boy, that in itself is perverse), and the child's death. The more information that came to him, the more Morris made it fit.

Besides, his feelings for my mother's suffering were kindled anew, and flared in a romantic way as he remembered her in our little house. This was part of the grand labyrinth my father had to traverse — and he had no string to follow even if he managed to slay the bull.

When I heard what they thought my father had done, when I remembered how Mother sent me to him with his lunches, when I remembered his years of suffering, my scorn was for every man or woman who had ever trampled my parents down — and no scorn burned brighter.

"Man can overcome any fate by scorn," Albert Camus said in his essay on the myth of Sisyphus. Perhaps I was thinking of my father as Sisyphus. His plight seemed the embodiment of some great callous stupidity, comic in its futility. Yet there was something else, held off until now, until this moment. It was my first unmasked *contempt* for propriety.

It was the propriety of the event that I was actually reacting against and ultimately challenging. This is what made me renegade.

At Gratton's funeral home a few miles down our old highway on that Tuesday afternoon there was a lineup of people waiting to pay their respects. The graders were out plowing the road down to the bone. Men and women, simple good-hearted working people, bright and filled with love — people one should never have to explain away — stood in line to pay their respects to that child who had walked among us with his dog, Scupper, and run in fields hidden from the highway.

His funeral was paid for by Leo McVicer.

Part of this outpouring came because Trenton was a retarded child who had died such an unfortunate death, and any community would have reacted the same. And part of this mourning was a spontaneous outpouring that comes when the family who has suffered such a loss has already had an unlucky life. These good-hearted people needed to be there for this troubled Pit family, to prove that they stood shoulder to shoulder in such a horrendous loss and that past deeds, mistakes, or feelings toward Cynthia and Mathew Pit meant little or nothing compared to grace and love.

A rumour that last summer my father had taken Trenton to the drive-in theatre in Bushville was rampant.

Father Porier did two services and two high masses for the repose of the soul of Trenton Pit.

A picture of Trenton holding Scupper — who since his death walked to the bridge every evening searching for his master — was carried on the front page of not only the local but the provincial paper. There was a picture of the collapsed span, the unlucky company truck my father had supposedly driven, and the dog at the bridge sitting in the snow.

People said my father went to the bridge in the truck because he would be safe from spying eyes — but God had judged him and had collapsed the span. When a rumour surfaced that dynamite had been thrown at the span it seemed also knitted into my father's plans. He was to be let go, so he threw the dynamite in retaliation.

Trenton's mother spoke of finding Trenton's hockey cards neatly lined up on his dresser that night before they went to search for him, and a prayer for the protection of children on his bedstand that Father Porier himself had blessed.

The lineup grew longer.

Of course Father's innocence afforded him nothing. This is the torment I have carried with me. From the time of thirteen I have thought only revenge. I have thought only revenge.

The funeral was attended by seven hundred people, and dignitaries — mayors from the four largest towns on the river, our member of Parliament, and others.

The day after the funeral there was another article in the paper showing the procession. I have carried it in my wallet for fourteen years. I have wanted to understand it. I have sat near streams when I was alone fishing as a child, and I have looked at it. I have seen it grow yellow with age, and still it incorporates the strange giddy pain of our family. And I have yet to understand it. But I see in it the pedestrian moral high-mindedness of accusation unaccompanied by the search for truth.

This is an article of expediency, and it comes from our river, and doesn't even mask its gloating outrage.

SIXTEEN

I now know Trenton found this money and took it back to Sydney, for he had overheard Sydney's name mentioned by Rudy and Mathew. The money had been hidden in the same hole behind the couch where Trenton would hide his plastic soldiers and his candy. When he reached in to hide the candy cane Sydney had given him that night, he realized what money it must be. So he would give it back to Sydney. The Christmas candy cane my father carried in his hand on that dark night he spoke to Alvina was his and Trenton's vial of poison, the paper discharging the sentence of death and ostracism. I had handed the candy cane to my father in a thoughtless moment, as a goodwill gesture from my family to the Pits, and told him to take it to the boy.

Trenton picked the money up and did not know where else to take it. The money was stuffed in his pocket, with his glasses. All that day Mrs. Pit, fearful of something happening to her child after the strange conversation she had had with my father, would not let Trenton out of the house. She telephoned Father Porier and he instructed her to say the rosary and bless the child with holy water. She did this, and as always prayed for the intercession of the Virgin. And then finally at five in the evening fell asleep in her rocking chair in the small room off the kitchen. She often fell asleep there because of heat from the stove. Trenton was sitting in the dark, looking at the soft blue and green lights on the Christmas tree.

It was dark when Trenton managed to get the door opened. The snow had frozen at the end of the wood and up against the boughs being used to bank the house — a tradition throughout our rural Maritimes. The snow piked over the paddock fence, and was seen in patches between the trees. The moon was out over the great water. Our twisting road was silent, the flares were set up as warnings at the end of the bridge, burning away in a smudge drifting to the sky. Trenton expects to see my father, because all he knows is that my father works on the bridge. He steps onto the gravel road being engineered, and walks toward the troubled span. The watchman is not there to stop him, the lights are off. Worse, Mathew had just parked a thousand-pound truck on a weak span. The sabotage collapses it at the moment Trenton is walking toward the truck. At first there is just a slight groan and then a loud swish, and a section of concrete span collapses with a small blast of dynamite. Mathew sees the body fall while the truck remains caught up on the steel beams above. He thinks to himself it must be Connie Devlin who is falling.

When they find the boy, Mathew knows exactly where the money came from, yet cannot say. He did not know his plan would work so well. This is what secretly terrifies him — the damage he alone managed to do.

The day of the funeral, at home, sitting with his mother, he is awakened by his own culpability. Now for the sake of appearances he will seek revenge on someone else for his own crime. He will kill Sydney Henderson. He *has* to!

He cries over the dead boy, not only in love but because he fears he will be caught. But he is not caught. He isn't even suspected.

Another scenario is envisioned. My father sabotaged the span because he was not given the job of foreman like he had been promised, and was to be fired after Christmas. The night before, he had threatened to take the child away because he was *infatuated* with him. He had even bragged that he knew what would happen to the boy that very day. And didn't it happen! How brave he was to kill an innocent retarded child. And was this the first Pit child he had killed? No — for hadn't he tried his handwork with the Pits before, when he helped deliver Cynthia's child?

One person is sought out as a reliable witness — Connie Devlin. And what does Connie say? Nothing — yet. He is waiting to see what will happen and what is planned. He is ingeniously quiet for the moment. If it looks like Mathew will be caught he will side with Sydney. But if it is Sydney who is suspected, he will be compelled to come forward.

Ms. Whyne is furious at my father. She *knew* this would happen. Hadn't she predicted it?

"People like poor Elly Henderson should be aggressively informed about their options when it comes to having children — here she is pregnant once more to that hideous man —" she says. "When there are other options — is our world so backward as to not see what must be done for her?"

Everyone agrees with this completely. The shack we live in, with its small clumsily fitting tin pipe, seems foreboding, and Autumn, beautiful clever Autumn to me, once so special, is now with her snow-white hair and skin considered a sign of my father's rural depravities. The idea of the carcinogen in the soil is forgotten. Our house is framed in the local paper just after the funeral. God, it looked sad.

Those men my father had done favours for, filled out application forms for, helped with their unemployment benefits, forgot him and remembered only a man who read strange books. They crowded together, I am sorry for saying this, like the gutless pukes men tend to be.

It is now January. There is going to be an inquest. Those police officers and prosecutors tell my father that if he gives himself up they will not charge my mother with the robbery of the McVicer house.

"You don't want your next child to be born in jail," they say. "Or your children to be taken away."

Nowhere to turn, they go to Connie Devlin. My mother convinces my father to do this. She is certain that those he helped most would now have to help him. A certain willingness of people to trade upon the lines of common human decency. Besides, she is only human, and doesn't want her child to be born in a jail or Autumn, especially Autumn, to be taken away.

That day, with all the work on the bridge halted, Connie sits at the table in his kitchen, his head down, his eyes cast upon the floor, his thin stringy hair neatly combed over his balding head. He listens to the radio, the country and western station from Fredericton, smoking an Export cigarette and tapping his beige cowboy boots. My father asks him to help. Connie glances at Elly, exhaling smoke.

"I have no idea what I could do," Connie says finally, "to save you."

"You know he helped you," Mother says.

Connie says nothing for a long time. Then he shrugs, as if this is not a subject to discuss amongst gentlemen.

"So," he says, "I didn't know he were like that?"

"Like what?" Elly smiles.

"I just didn't know he were like that with little boys," Connie says, sniffing proudly. "I mean, I heard things 'bout it — but I was too good a person myself to believe it —" he adds, astonished at his own goodness.

My father accepts this insult in silence and, his voice still even, asks: "Connie — did you see anyone at the bridge any time of night besides — well, besides the boy — who would have been silly enough to drive that truck onto that weak span? Who left those floodlights off?"

Connie, tapping his cowboy boots on the linoleum floor, shakes his head, as if the question itself is a monstrous insult and his integrity is at stake. The last of the winter sun has left gold streaks across the snow and along the kitchen window, and gold dust from the sun filters into my mother's auburn hair as she stands in her orange winter jacket and boots. Here is where you see my mother as a child even though she is thirty-two. They could hear a grader on the highway. The bright windows of Connie's house rattled.

"I can tell 'em only what I know — that I haven't seen nothing at all," Connie says. "Except you." He smiles solemnly at this, and the curl of hair at the front of his head, with his enormous red face, makes him look like a baby in a crib.

The air in the house is warm, and Connie's work mittens hang over the radiator in the living-room corner, and his work socks padded at the heels and toes hang over a chair in the kitchen. Again he glances up and then glances away.

The next day Father got the first of the letters:

"Eye for eye — your oldest child will die."

Perhaps they should have been more careful about who they targeted.

The note was written as everyone says and no one believes actually is. It was written from letters taken from those articles in the paper and pasted to a typewriter sheet. There was a warning for my mother pasted at the bottom of the page: "I will get the cunt too."

It was the first time I had ever heard that word, yet I understood exactly what it meant. My father had no intention of showing the notes to Mother. But she discovered them. I remember my parents at this time — when I was thirteen. For the last few months, because of their jobs, they had been trying to enter the world — they would tell each other about music, and fashion, not because they wanted so much to keep up, but because neither had ever been involved in the great world beyond their doors before.

They set out in mid-afternoon to the police station with the letters. The road had a glare upon it; the day was silent. A few school buses sat in parking lots waiting for students to get out of class. The wires above them hummed in the wind. And my mother kept up the pretense that everything was all right. She asked my father questions about books, because this is what she knew he wanted her to be interested in. She wondered what it would have been like to have graduated. She took my father's hand as she spoke.

Her life had taken a dramatic turn without benefit of education, and she now must protect my father and her children, who were all as confused about the great world as she.

That is how I remember them, on a day six months before Percy was born, walking hand in hand the eight miles to the police station, assuring each other that their lives would be like the lives of other people, while the substance of snow blew about them, from their feet to their chests, in small, twisting eddies, and left their boot prints on the road, obliterated before dark. And they were making this trek for our benefit — because you see it was the children who had been threatened.

Why did they walk? Oh, irony for a man who was supposed to have driven a truck onto a span to sabotage his life's work — my father had never learned to drive. But by the time they found that out, what would it matter?

SEVENTEEN

My father walked beside Mother telling her that these letters were "just the ticket" to relieve them of their burden of culpability. My mother said nothing. Perhaps she knew there was nothing to say or perhaps she understood what my father had neglected to tell us about his life — that there was and always would be a blunder concerning him, which he himself never seemed to care about, but which he may have entertained a small idea that his family might care about. They huddled together as they walked, and the closer they came to town the colder the day became. It turned bitter with squalls of rinsed rainbow light that comes with wind between faroff brick buildings and can be remembered by anyone who has lived in the north as a child.

They kept their faces away from the snow, so as to be able to breathe, yet were blinded by the glare from the sun. They walked the entire distance.

My mother still talked as if our trip was an event not only natural but soon to take place, and as if the event now taking place was not only unnatural but something that could happen to anyone.

She felt things would turn out if only they said and did the *polite* things. In all my wondering about this moment in my parents' lives, I can think of no better word to use. My father's one unshakable belief was that people could do him no harm if he did no harm himself. He had not hired a lawyer, made not one statement to refute a soul, not even that he could not drive, and in the end handed my mother the letters with stoic majesty. I think over his life, by turns elated and dejected, and realize that so many of his finest moments were lost to the great swarm of mankind — he never made an entrance on the large stage. Yet in so many ways no moment was wasted, and no man was essentially greater.

Mother put the letters in her purse. Her small rustic propriety would now face the propriety of an organized body of law and principle that weighed and meted out justice as if justice was truth. My mother believed — in her heart and soul — that mercy was truth.

They arrived and sat in the office, and waited for Constable Morris. He had interviewed both my father and me, and at one point I remembered a kind of muted dull fury when he looked at Sydney that left me cold. What, I thought, did this man think of us?

Then, with a sense of dignity and duty that comes from some people who have never had much to do with learning, my mother, Elly McGowan Henderson (for this is what she was called in the paper), took the letters out of her purse and handed them to the young officer.

"And what's this?"

"These came to us," she said. "In the mail."

The officer took a letter and held it over his head to view it in the light through the window blind. He then flipped the notepaper back and forth rapidly as if it were wet. Then, holding it up again, he looked over the top of the page at my father.

"Pasted?" Morris asked with a look of stunned inquiry.

"Yes," my mother answered. There was a brief pause. Again he looked at my father, but this time he smiled knowingly.

"Sydney, you did a fine job pasting this — is this to throw us off the scent?" Morris laughed out loud, perhaps because he believed he'd made a witticism; that is, the scent of my father.

"I got it in the mail."

"Got it in the mail?"

Sydney nodded at the duplicity, not of his but of the officer's tone. Unfortunately the nod, and the polite smile behind it, made him look dishonest. Morris had, we were to find out, a copious amount of information on Sydney that came from neighbours of ours, all willing to help the police. How he had looked at their young child funny, how he had once eagerly volunteered to help with a children's camp, and a teenage retreat.

There was silence. The wind rattled the blank windows, and one could imagine the snow blowing across the wide field and buffeting clotheslines. The officer was short, thick set, with somewhat larger teeth than normal. He looked over at my mother not for an explanation so much as for a complicity of sentiment with *him*.

"Of course it was mailed to him," my mother said with a somehow heroic tone. She looked at Sydney quickly and took his hand. Sydney only nodded.

The constable put his glasses on, made a face as if his nose was itchy, and said: "How can you be sure he has not made all of this up? — he has made up things before — haven't you, Syd — made up things before — little things — big things — money and robbery — robbing the poor box at Father Porier's church — you got a good kick in the bum for that, didn't you — lighting a fire at McVicer's mill — you got away with that, didn't you, Syd? The box of smelts? Hmm? It's all catching up to you now — lies and deception, deception and forgery?"

"I have never in my life heard him exaggerate or tell a lie," my mother whispered.

The officer's face went blank. An uneducated woman, the woman Diedre Whyne had phoned him about, saying that he, Constable Morris, must be willing to take the initiative in her case, sitting in a heavy old coat, with her face reddened from frost in the mid-afternoon room (her cold face added in some way to her being suspect), had told him that he was not only mistaken but presumptuous.

I know there are all levels of rich and poor in our society, and Mother and Father were very near our bottom rung. Morris was determined to be looked *up to* by Elly. This was a secret not even admitted to himself.

Besides, the idea itself was infectious. The idea that my father, living in a shack, was an oddball, and peculiar enough to do something heinous to a child. A *fell* man — a barbarous man. That was part of it. It was in fact essential to it. Not essential to the crime but to the outrage over the crime. My father understood this, I am sure — but he did not fight it. People would believe what they would believe, and nothing more.

Constable Morris took a different tack. He stared at my mother with newfound assumption. Perhaps *she* had mailed the letters. She denied this by complete and utter silence, a silence I have noticed in my life that the poor and mistreated have often had. When the silence became intolerable the officer smiled and shook his head, as if my mother's moral superiority was nothing but a ruse he easily saw through.

He was not a bad man, Officer Morris. He was, simply speaking, a stupid man — although stupidity and cruelness of heart enter the door hand in hand. In fact Officer Morris believed he was *winning* this confrontation. And he was pleased by his own sense of rueful-ness. And he felt *progressive* for his ability to take them on.

But suddenly he stopped for lunch. He sat at the desk drinking coffee and eating a tossed salad and a chicken sandwich on home-made bread. My father and mother, unaccustomed to the ways of the police (or anyone else), stayed where they were, not looking at one another. Now and then Morris unfolded a napkin, wiped his mouth, folded the napkin again, and set it back beside his fork. Then, finish-ing his coffee, and looking into the cup, he continued.

"I've been thinking — what can be made of the letters?"

He held the letters in his hand and looked at Mom, stifling a belch. At first he complimented Mother on her loyalty. Not one woman in a hundred as good looking as she would be so loyal to a man like Syd. Then he put the letters down with a firm hand, and asked, while patting his hand over them, did she have any love for humanity in her? He again looked at my father and said, loudly, as thoughtless people do when speaking to those they think beneath them: "That's humanity, Sydney — it means humankind, the human race. Sydney, I'm asking your girlfriend if she has any feelings for it — being attached to you — that's why the question is asked."

Sydney nodded, holding his hat with the faded fur earflaps in his hand and looking about the room as if expecting someone else to be there. Then he looked back at the officer and adjusted his glasses.

"Yes," he said. "Humanity."

"I suppose you want our protection?"

Again there was silence. My mother waited for an assault upon them by lowering her head just slightly — not in fear but in shame for other people.

Constable Morris stood over them, looking down at my mother, with her pale face, blue eyes, and chestnut curls. Her day had begun at seven in the morning, heating water on a stove to bathe, because we had no hot water tank, and using the kitchen chairs to iron her maternity frock so she would be presentable to *him*. Now, in silence, obdurate and proud, the wind blowing across the desolate fields between the landscaped houses of town, creating those soft fleeting rainbows, she fumbled with her fingers, and said nothing.

I can only tell you that I wish I had been there at that moment, no matter if I was thirteen. I would have struck him because of his rudeness.

Another officer came into the room and said that if they wished to file a complaint he would be willing to type it up. But there was no suspect, and any of dozens upon dozens of people might have mailed this. Nor were my mother and father above suspicion. And perhaps Sydney liked all the attention. Morris glared at him, as the other officer said he knew people who did things for attention, set grass fires, and pull fire alarms — perhaps this letter-writing scheme was an attention-getting device.

"You like this, don't you, Sydney —" Morris piped up, "like this part of it — you're not caught yet — but still the paper is writing about you. They say you are something of a philosopher — and like poetry — quote me a poem, Syd — quote me even one line of a poem — I bet you could not — spit it out — one damn line of any poem from anywhere at any moment that was ever written. Come now — you must know one — do you know one?"

"As flies to wanton boys, are we to the gods;/They kill us for their sport," Sydney said, staring almost in shame at the constable.

My mother listened to this and her lips tightened. Constable Morris turned his swivel chair away, and leaned back, stretching with midday fatigue.

"Do you want to make a formal complaint?" the other officer asked more kindly.

My mother said, "No thank you, sir." Her lips trembled. My father was again utterly silent. Ever since he was a boy and beaten he was silent in the face of adversity. He was silent in school when people gathered about him at recess, and he was silent now.

"You're dumb, aren't you, Syd?" Morris said. "You knock up a little girl like Elly here — a sweet girl from the boonies who's never met a real man, or been to a party or had a date, or taken a trip — you are her first — first to touch her — I know you, Syd — then you keep her in a prison for fourteen years, knock her up three or four times — use her to rob Leo McVicer who likes her and refuses to press charges, refuses even to fire you until Christmas is over only because of your children. Then you take that money from her, frighten an old woman, use a stick of dynamite you had on you for years, and entice her retarded boy to the bridge, you even bragged you would do so saying you knew more than God. A heathen, eh, Syd, and this poor woman is in your clutches, because she's never felt a real man between her legs —"

Then, swivelling around to face them, he added: "I know real men who would love to get to know you, Elly — you could go back to school — on to university — get a student loan — now is your chance — I've talked to Dr. David Scone about you — imagine, a man like that — a man who would have nothing to do with Sydney yet is interested in you! Stay here, Elly, turn evidence for us and he will never bother you again. You and your children will be taken care of — I'll see to it, and you'll be enrolled in university." He stood to walk away, and then turned abruptly again, and with great almost mindless fury added:

"You like picking on women, Syd, and old men — do you? — come from the Bartibog in some shack, do you? — eat moose meat, do you? — perhaps you thought the old lady would give you money, did you? — and perhaps poor Trenton tried to run away from you, and you lured him to his death. That made you feel powerful, did it? Well, do you want to step outside, I'll take my uniform off and you can have a go at a real man — see how you measure up — oh yes, look at your face — I'd love to wipe that smirk from it. So you want to come outside and fight me?"

Again my father said nothing.

Then the second constable brought Morris another coffee. Officer Morris, his face beet red, sat down, looked through a file, sipped on his coffee, and after a minute or two looked up startled, as someone will when they wish to acknowledge to everyone concerned their willingness to dismiss you out of hand.

My mother stood, black purse in hand, with my father. My father simply said, "Thank you now."

My mother asked for the letters back.

"The letters will remain with me," Morris said, taking another sip of coffee.

My mother stared at the dismal day. How was she to repair her life if it could be mocked so easily? She felt a deep, immense loneliness and love for my father that went beyond loyalty — she felt their love was meant to be, in some way, when the atoms in their blood coursed through the endless stars in the endless beginning of the night.

"Thank you, sir," she said again, "but I don't want the letters misplaced. They are proof of my husband's grave innocence." *Grave* was without a doubt the word to use, but she did not know at that moment why she had used it — it had tumbled from her tongue. It tumbled from her tongue like a word from a slip of a girl in some pasture downriver on some May afternoon, like the word *circumnavigate* had come from her lips one day when she was ten and in love with Diedre Whyne and the world.

The constable looked at her.

"His grave innocence," my mother whispered again, blushing.

"Please," the constable said, waving his hand at her histrionics.

My mother stared at him, unsure what else he could possibly do to them that showed his utter disdain.

Sydney looked at her and said: "We must go — there is nothing more to do."

"Yes," she said, and they left the shelter of the station.

They started their trek home again, this time with the raw wind behind them. Sydney took off his ragged blue scarf and gave it to Mother, and she put it around her face. She had planned that after everything had been cleared up she would take Sydney for a treat at the restaurant.

Now this hope seemed a vague and distant thought born out of another age. Now again she was worried about her pregnancy and desperately afraid of losing another child.

If only she had not taken the job at McVicer's house — if only she had not felt sorry for the old man. If only she had not gone to Polly's Restaurant for hamburgers, or if only Sydney had not gone over to Alvina Pit. For some reason she felt them both culpable. But worse, in the wind, the blast of cold that penetrated her coat and sweater, she felt that no one in the universe cared for her husband or her children except her.

She asked him if he wanted something to eat.

"No, I'm fine," he said.

"Sydney — you need something to eat — you have not eaten in two days. I have five dollars." She went into a corner store and bought him a carton of milk and a sandwich.

"What do you think — will anyone help?" Sydney asked when she came out.

"No, they will not help."

He nodded and looked sideways a second.

"I know," he said. "They will not help — we have been for some unknown reason, Elly, thrust strangely into hell." He smiled and touched her face tenderly.

My mother looked very pale — my mother was always pale, as pale as a sweet autumn sky. Her lips trembled.

"But it doesn't matter," he said. "Sometimes at the worst time something happens to make things all well again. Sometimes when I am out smelt fishing, just when it looks as if it will never brighten up, the sky clears, the ice turns a dazzling blue, and rays from the sun drop down onto our shoulders."

They stood a moment longer while he opened the carton and looked into it, seeing in his periphery vision small and changeable whirlwinds of snow over the street beyond them, and the day darkening over the stolid bare houses.

"I guess you have been let down by me — I am not very good at the world — in all my life I have not been. I don't know why. It is a trait I have had. I come to people believing not that they don't know things but that they do, and will, because they do, agree with what I know.

Then when I find out I have been very mistaken about them, I become silent. I thought this would clear a path. I am not very bright."

"Oh, Syd," she said. She smiled and tears flooded her eyes.

They turned along the road together.

EIGHTEEN

For a week or so after, Mom stayed in bed, because she was afraid to start bleeding and lose yet another child. The doctor was angry with her for being pregnant and having walked to Newcastle; and the one time she went to see him, he admonished her when he examined her.

No one spoke to Autumn or me at school, but the activity about us caused increasing anxiety, especially on Autumn's part.

We went with other people to the great churches to pray — to pray that Mom would have her baby — for she had asked us to go. For the first time I remembered my father did not go to church. I found out he had been refused communion when he stood in line. He could have had mine. I did not want or need it to be saved from these people. I sat in the pew and stared at the gold chalice that Father Porier held in his white liver-spotted hands, with his white linen hankerchief stuffed into his sleeve and the light lingering on the stony altar, and hated him, for my father's sake; for my father refused to hate.

It is strange, the thing people most value about themselves they will lose sooner or later. My father during this time lost the church. It crumbled beneath him and left him alone in the air. And how he needed it now, with an inquest coming. He sat at home reading, not the things written against him or Mom, but reading the *Meditations* of Marcus Aurelius. I saw the Penguin edition of that small book in his back pocket for days. And I remember thinking that professors teaching it at Saint Michael's or at the University of Toronto hadn't the same need of it.

Often I saw Rudy Bellanger at church at the masses given for the soul of Trenton Pit, wearing his Knights of Columbus uniform and blessing himself and receiving communion. The Knights went on parade, and he stood with his father-in-law, Leo McVicer. Leo McVicer was secretly blamed by some for having hired Sydney in the first place, and Leo knew this. So he acted.

He threw a benefit at the community centre for the children — it was called "The Healing of the Children." It came in January on a Saturday when the sky was purple with cold and ice lay ten feet thick in our bay.

Everyone got a toy. There was a hot dog eating contest and Rudy wore a chef's hat and boiled hot dogs in a giant pot. There were cookies and cakes from the store, and a stereo system set up for music that the children skated to at the outdoor rink. Constable Morris was there, letting the children sit in his patrol car.

Mother begged us to go.

"You are children too," she said. "Why would they not know this?"

So with trepidation we headed out in the raw afternoon. But I was too smart to show myself. Instead Autumn and I, hand in hand, watched the festivities from the field beyond the community centre. We stood hand in hand because I knew that when we were noticed we'd be chased by the other kids. And that is what happened. Griffin Porier saw us, and with his friends tried to cut us off from our house. I was so scared and I ran so fast I ended up dragging poor little Autumn like a rag doll behind me. But we made it across Arron Brook, to our yard, with a whistle of rocks coming behind.

The Pits were usually in attendance at mass, for Alvina insisted that Mathew take her so she could be seen receiving the Blessed Sacrament. It gave Mathew a certain grace, as a worldly, hard-bitten man who had had his share of difficulty now humble enough to be seen attending to his mother and to Christ Jesus. And for Cynthia as well, long considered a seducer of young men, to be seated in the pew with black skirt and gloves. There was talk of her first child, who would if she had lived, have been my age.

Alvina stumbled forward — never standing at the altar but kneeling silently, with hands folded, and closed eyes damp with tears. Watching her — with Cynthia helping her back and forth to her seat — there came the rather pleasant thought associated with early death.

I was sent as a representative of the family, an emissary not made welcome. People stared at me as I genuflected and stared harder at me if I took communion. So in spite of my mother's request, I did not take communion after a while. Anyone can be made to feel a hypocrite, but I, wrestling at the time with the very *idea* of a God, considered my own self ludicrous. One day a man put his hand on my shoulder as I walked up the lane. He smiled at me and said it would have been better if I had been stillborn and Cynthia's child had lived. He walked on, still smiling. I never forgot the feel of his wrinkled leather work glove on my shoulder. He was Danny Sheppard, purported to have been that child's father, and one of the most desperate men on the river.

At one particular mass said by Father Porier both Rudy and Mathew Pit were in attendance, although they did not acknowledge one another. Porier walked to the podium and said:

"I have asked God for those who are responsible for this poor child's death to be here today — for they have insulted their own human dignity. I do not see them in attendance, but Christ has not given up on them."

After mass that day, Rudy went to see his father-in-law and had tea. He had joined the Knights of Columbus because he needed to prove to Leo McVicer that he was a moral man — he had joined it on Leo McVicer's insistence. But now everything had fallen apart. His life was in tatters, and he didn't hear a word old Leo said.

He went to see Mathew that night, when the others were in bed.

"I am upset too," Mathew told him.

"Well, it's just that *we* know where the money came from, don't we," Rudy whispered. "I mean, *we* know you were setting out to do what happened. It is a betrayal of everything I — and you too, Mathew — stand for —" Rudy smiled timidly. "I know I told you on one occasion that I would like something to happen to the bridge just so Porier wouldn't always have the upper hand. Still, I wanted nothing like *this* to happen. It is very bad for Elly and Sydney to have to deal with this. And their children — they are being tormented at school — it was hard enough for them before — you know, with she an albino, and the family so poor. Isn't there anything we can do to get them off? Say you take some of my money and we find it — and say it was a mistake — then I say I mistakenly misplaced the money — Elly is off the hook and the case against Sydney will be rethought. I mean, is that a good idea or not?"

"You are trying to give me away — to get yourself clear!"

"No, no — I'm just —"

"You are ready to blabbermouth all over town!"

"No — I'm not —"

But Mathew's look was one of utter self-preservation. Suddenly Rudy realized that this man would kill him if need be. Mathew by now had convinced himself — for the sake of convincing Cynthia and his mother — that he had nothing at all to do with any of this. His mother and his sister looked upon Mathew as the spokesperson for the family, and he had been quoted in the paper saying that the moment he saw the body of Trenton was the moment his own life ceased to be important. To say this to the press and then to be found guilty would be harsh indeed.

Rudy slunk away and said nothing more. He went home but could not bear to look at his wife when she spoke of putting Sydney and Elly in jail. For she was a woman who had no understanding of the world — and putting people in jail was a fine thing for her to want. Knowing about Rudy's infatuation with my mother, she had envied Elly.

"Will you stop that singing!" he shouted as she took hot rolls from the oven. "It's a young mother's life."

"Oh," Gladys said, turning. Unknown to Rudy, she had fallen two days before with a weak spell. "I didn't know you felt so *strongly* about Elly," she said.

"Don't be silly." He quickly chewed on some ice he took from his glass of rye. "She's just a poor woman married to a goodfornothing goddamn idiot. They live in a shack, for Christ sake — they'll be forced off our river soon enough!"

"Yes," she said, eyeing him quickly and then staring straight ahead and breathing quickly through her nose. "Silly me."

NINETEEN

The inquest began in February, with a Sheriff Bulgar and the chief coroner in charge. It gathered a great deal of interest around the province and as far away as the state of Maine.

Every day I read the paper hoping to see the words: "Mistake — Sydney Henderson a hero." But that did not happen. Three times over the course of those weeks a picture of Autumn walking along the shore road appeared.

And this is what I found out reading the paper:

The prosecution wanted to prove my father was negligent and overbearing and perpetrated a crime to cover up a misdeed. The case against my father rested on the assumption that he had deliberately driven the half-ton onto the weakened span. That he did this with full knowledge that the span would collapse. That he was enraged he was being fired after the holidays because he was caught in a theft. They wanted to charge my father with second-degree murder. Every family vied for every smidgen of information, and Constable Morris, Connie Devlin, and Autumn Henderson became household names.

The coroner had gone down to look at the bridge, and estimated the distance the boy fell, the time of day, and how far the warning flares were from the abutment and the abutment from the weak span, and what damage the dynamite did. And more essentially, where the truck was parked at the time of the disaster.

The sheriff had measurements taken, and wanted to know if Connie Devlin was on his rounds. Connie said he was of course on his rounds, but that he would speak only at the inquest. The sheriff confiscated the time clock.

The sheriff wanted to know why the floodlights were turned off, and if the generators themselves were faulty. All of this was fine, but in essence had nothing at all to do with my father, whom I knew had been at home that night eating his supper.

Our lawyer, Isabel Young, was thin with dark hair. My father had thought it was not necessary to bother a lawyer, and he had sat in court by himself for the first three days. It was my mother who went to her, by taxicab, and asked her to help.

Elly took out our vacation money and placed it on the lawyer's table, crumbled ones, twos, and fives.

Isabel Young smiled, and said she would not need that. But she told my mother things would get very rough. People were talking of a vendetta, and Cynthia Pit was bent on retaliation. Besides, Diedre Whyne, whom Isabel had fought in court before, was trying to get the children placed in foster care, as Diedre said, "Once and for all."

This would be a huge case for Diedre, and the children's plight at the house would be used. Isabel knew this, and said she had long fought Diedre Whyne. Mother looked at her. She might have replied that she too had long fought this woman, although she had not wanted to.

Then Isabel told my mother she would do her best. "Of course he is not guilty," Isabel Young said.

"He isn't?" Elly said, strangely alarmed that another person would say this.

———

Constable Morris was a witness for the prosecution. He stated that the boy had been dead well over an hour before the police were informed, and probably had lain there alive.

Morris spoke about how callous my father was when he came to the police station, and how Elly seemed to be mesmerized by him when he quoted a poem that, as Morris said, didn't even *rhyme*. The courthouse crowd was amused, and giggled and turned their eyes on Sydney.

Then Leo McVicer was on the stand for two days, informing the court about his business, the tender he received for the construction of the bridge, and the fact that he was one of the river's most well known and respected employers. There was talk about his mill, and the idea that a toxin had gotten into the groundwater, and how he had managed to have Mathew and Sydney dig new wells because of this, because he was a conscientious benefactor.

He spoke about the robbery. He looked straight at my mother as he said: "I don't at all know about Sydney. I knew his father — he was a hard case. But Elly tried to bring up her children; they had very little — the arse was out of the boy's pants on more than one occasion — and on occasions I went over to Abby Porier's and got his son Griffin's hand-me-downs — and I would bring the box over to Elly — half the time the young lad Lyle was wearing Griffin's clothes."

His voice and his presence carried a good deal of weight, and one could tell he was shaken by the affair. But he was never as shaken as I to find out that I wore the hand-me-down clothes of the brother of Penny Porier.

Leo was asked by my father's lawyer what his estate might be worth.

"Three million — four million — five — I don't know."

"So you are very well-to-do and very well known."

"Perhaps."

"And you go on hunting trips and that is well known as well?"

"Perhaps —"

"There has been acrimony against you — you closed your mill with one phone call some years ago — and put two hundred men out of work. Someone then sabotaged your yard by fire."

"That was years and years ago. And Sydney's father — yes, he was accused of it."

"Is there anyone else who may have robbed you — or want to sabotage the bridge because they felt you had done them injury — anyone else at all?"

Leo shrugged. "Maybe. But offhand — well, I can think of no one who had the chance as much as Sydney did — and the motive."

During the next day's session there was a statement by one of the labourers, given during cross-examination by the defence, about the distance of the flares from the abutment. This labourer said that he was unhappy working near that span because it had buckled. That not only he but Sydney and Porier were also worried about this, and had blocked this span off. That driving a truck onto it was suicidal.

This did not actually help my father but put on record that he was one of the few who had said he knew what might happen if a truck was placed on the span.

Therefore the evidence of the night watchman became imperative. Where was he and what had he seen? The whole river wanted to know. Sheriff Bulgar knew the night watchman was supposed to have been making his rounds near the abutment at six-thirty — the time the truck, and the young boy, fell. Bolts along the steel span had been cut. Who cut them? The person who sabotaged the span, or people trying to relieve pressure on the buckled steel?

Other things, like dynamite, may have caused damage to the structure. This left Leo McVicer open to the possibility of a horrendous lawsuit if Sydney was not charged.

This is the case twenty-nine-year-old year old Isabel Young brought forward. Her contention was that the crime was one of a negligence far beyond my father's scope.

By the second week of the inquest my father could not go to or from the courthouse without being heckled and threatened by our concerned townspeople. My father almost begged for death. I know that now. He walked past those who would want him killed. He was never frightened to die and never made one attempt to protect himself. My mother prayed to Saint Jude, and felt that was why he was spared. I do not believe in Saint Jude. Yet I have no other answers.

My mother could not let Father go to court alone, so she forced herself to get up and dress in the cold dawn, and made her way by his side. Soon Jay Beard was driving them to and from the court.

The days were short, and lights in the courthouse were on all afternoon. By three o'clock it looked almost like night. Across from the courthouse the windows of the brick school were just as bleak, grey snow was piled across the open field, and schoolkids gathered to gawk.

My father's lawyer privately asked my mother what she knew of Sydney. And though my mother thought she knew everything there was to know, his lawyer had gathered facts that were news to her. His school years were a dismal collection of torment, where he would hide in the ditches rather than face the boys waiting for him. He had been beaten by his father whenever he tried to protect his mother from assault. There was always wine at the house. He suffered from ringworm and dysentery. But the worst revelation was almost comic, as they sometimes are when you build up to them.

He had been shot by a .22-calibre 410-gauge over-and-under rifle when he was a child of twelve. The bullet that entered him had caused appendix attacks ever since. The lawyer had a picture of Sydney lying inside an oxygen tent.

This is what kept him in the hospital where he had taught himself to read. It was after his mother's death, which he thought he was partially responsible for, that he became withdrawn and reclusive.

Elly did not know any of this, but she knew now what the laceration on his stomach was from.

"Well then," Isabel Young said, "don't tell him you do know."

On February 7 Mother and Father left the courtroom about four in the afternoon and were driven to our lane by Jay Beard. When they got home our own lane was dark and a snow fell over the frozen mud heaves. Deer had yarded here and you could see them grazing on what was left of the buds of frozen maples. Autumn and I were staying at Mother's aunt's down near Barryville.

Mom and Dad walked along the lane in silence until they came to the house with the tarpaper flapping in the night. A squall of snow was moving across the bay.

Just as they got to the door, it opened. Out walked Mathew Pit and stood before them in the eerie snow-soaked yellow light from the porch. He stood before them only that indiscernible jiffy, yet his eyes had a look of triumph; and this look, the impetuous self-delighted look that opponents who are most ignorant of you often carry, came as he brushed by them and disappeared into the frozen tragic dark.

Mathew felt a pressure to act, not to save his family honour, but to save himself from his own guilt. Every day about this time — after dark fell on the snow — there was a moment when the death of the boy was truly unbearable for Mathew. Because he knew exactly — and he and Rudy Bellanger and Connie Devlin were the only three — how it had really happened. How the boy had lain there; how he lifted his arm as if to plead for help. And what had happened, and the memory of the boy falling through the air, was seared into Mathew's mind like a brand on a heifer. But each day falseness grabbed him, hugged him, and kept him in its swell.

Now going to our house he had found a book. And the book was the thing — for those most susceptible to scorn are learned men fallen.

That night, crazed with anger that Sydney would not admit to what he had done, Mathew had come into my father's yard to confront him, to beat sense into him. It seemed that my father, though he was innocent, should be morally bound to confess, because all the river believed him guilty. Mathew came to press upon Dad his own disgust; but Dad was gone, the house was opened, and inside, he had found a book.

He found a book from the new world Scott Fitzgerald in glory once saw from his room in Paris, but now from some further age, a book that enlivened us with the possibility of everything *except* redemption. A book that swept its wings through the corridors of hell and enjoyed what it found. Mathew had found a book on the shelf that proved about my father all he wished to.

Mathew left Mother and Father standing in the petrified silence. He walked across the frozen ice threaded with snow and made it out to the community centre.

Here people were listening to Waylon Jennings' music and playing cards. Mathew entered with windswept eyes and a golden chain on his neck. He walked in and put the book, my father's book, on the centre table.

"Read this filth," he said. "This is what I found — just read the filthy bastard's book."

"Where did you find it?" Connie Devlin asked.

"At his house."

Cynthia looked at him, picked up the book, and when Polly herself went to take a look, Mathew brought the entire group to silence by saying:

"I wouldn't be lookin' at no such filthy filth, Polly — not like that there —"

"I have a thing or two to say when I come forward," Connie Devlin said, sniffing hard and shaking his head. Finally he had decided which side he would be on. He gave in to his old enduring weakness, to be like others and to take his chances later. Now he could tell the story Mathew had invented. The self-inflicted ruse was that he had made up his own mind to tell the truth *in spite* of his longstanding friendship with Sydney Henderson; and this is what others believed.

"Nothin' hurts me more than this here," Connie said. "He got me back on the bridge — but *now* I know why — it was to turn my back the other way when he done his dirty work — to keep silent when the generator was broke and the bolts all snapped off. Well, I can keep silent about a lot — not that."

"Yer just doin' right," someone said, "just doin' right."

Now people tried to comfort Mathew because of the terrible book, and he flinched in self-righteousness and drank his beer, looking at them with a self-infatuated pain, an opiate that all clung to.

He realized that as the victim of a tragedy — the tragedy of his own making — he had a new and an indefinable power. This became more evident when my aunt — an aunt I almost never saw — timidly approached Mathew and asked to shake his hand, asking forgiveness for "that side of my family."

Aunt Edna, after ignoring us for fourteen years, was fired with an Episcopalian sense of duty, a zeal sublime in her raw cheeks and tooth-pick-thin body, filling her time between sessions in court with gossiping about Sydney's father. She was driven to a kind of eroticism by the sudden grip of local fame. And now she wanted more than anything to be seen with Mathew. He nodded at her glumly and said, "It ain't yer fault, Edna — me and mine has no cause to row with you."

Then they hugged and others nodded their approval.

Mathew at thirty-three was like a restless young god, not so much of Olympus but of some strange underworld, where one boy's death and another man's agony kept him glowing under a false sun — like a light falling from the street into an underground toilet. He stood tall at the community centre, he rose above everyone else there, because of the death of a child he used to beat.

TWENTY

He was called as a witness four days later. Father and Mother sat in the courthouse and listened. Mathew Pit took the stand, staring out at the lawyers and the press who had come to hear. He was asked about his work and his life, and his hopes. He was asked about his little brother, Trenton, and he told of how he used to haul him in a wagon down to the river. He was asked about his mother's high blood pressure and the strain this had put on her heart. Twice he shook his head as if the terrible crime was beyond him.

At a very unspectacular moment the prosecution asked how Sydney treated the boy. Mathew's face moved quickly, like a picture gone slightly out of frame.

"Torment."

"You mean Sydney tormented the boy."

"Big torment — offered him what he couldn't give him. Offered me a job — didn't want nothin' to do with him — knew how he operated — torment — told him — didn't want him over botherin' the boy. Boy was scared of him."

"You told him — Trenton was frightened?"

"Told him — he run when I did."

Mathew's pale blue eyes stared with unabashed universal incivility at the world.

"And what did he bring over certain nights — when he was with the boy?"

"Bring over?"

"Yes. What did he have on him those nights in November and December?"

"That there book," Mathew said, and the prosecutor handed the book to him. He looked at it, too dignified to touch it. "It was this here he was reading to Trent, who wouldn't know no better a'tal the filthy filth, and then give him the wad a money to shut him up. That's why he stole the money from Leo McVicer good enough to give him a job in the first place I figure," Mathew said, not to the prosecutor or the coroner but to the audience, who nodded their heads.

"That's why he stole Leo McVicer's money," the prosecutor repeated in hopeless affirmation of the tragedy.

I have never found out what book it was. My father never told me, and could not bring himself to mention that time to me. It may have been *The Soft Machine* by Burroughs, or *The Naked Lunch*. It may have been one of a dozen books I came across over the years on his shelf; the books from America after Fitzgerald, but I do not exactly know which one.

Later that night my mother prepared our meal in silence. We had gotten back home that afternoon, Autumn and I — both unable to stand being away from them — thinking we could help when we couldn't; understanding the world was against us without knowing why, Autumn quoting poems and cracking jokes, and me wanting to fight the world.

Finally Mom asked Dad what kind of book it was. My father said it was a book that explored sexual mores, using explicit sex to describe it.

"Don't worry, Elly, it's just a book — we are still allowed to read in this country — as long as we are allowed to read." And he began to eat his macaroni and cheese in silence.

My mother did not know about this book. She had been a rural working girl brought up in the rather vicious circle of female bullies and pious nuns, and now she must defend a book she herself might never understand or want to read and a book that perhaps made light of her entire life. Yet it seemed the world had been turned upside down — she was defending someone who was looked upon as immoral, and Mat Pit and Cynthia scorning us and looked upon as being chaste.

But let me also say this — like my own father, the book was condemned not because it was pornographic but because it was great ... the editorial in the paper, by our brilliant investigative reporter, quoted a passage from it, with the heading: "Did Mr. Henderson Quote This to the Child?"

And our university here — men who should have come out in defence at least of the right of my father to read this book were silent, frightened, and as usual their decision to say and do nothing was meaningless to everyone but themselves. I later learned that out of all the books I suspected, all had been taught and romanticized by Dr. David Scone.

Still, Elly saw that my father missed the obvious — as bright men often do. He had believed that people at the university would come through for him and tell everyone the book's worth. He had been awaiting this in silence. There was, I hesitate to say, a childlike vanity in this hope.

"Sydney, listen to me," my mother said that night. "I want you to listen to me. You are allowed anything in this life — except the luxury of being different — this is why you are being tried. This is perhaps the only reason. Don't think professors get away with being different, because they do not — they conform — is that the word? Yes, conform. Not one has come out to defend you. They have all hidden. When Miss Young knew the book was to be used against you last week — and you said it was a great book — she went to the university and not one English professor came forward to claim its greatness. They didn't want to be associated with you even though she said she saw it on at least three professors' shelves. You are not human to them; they don't want you to read what they do or come to the same conclusions they come to. So I now know what their learning is worth.

"I have lived only in Tabusintac, but I know learning is worthless to those who have no insight — and power can even turn Diedre against me, who I love. Besides, scared people will turn on you in a second. I can't bear to read the papers because they lie," she said, tears in her eyes. She sat at the end kitchen chair and put her hands on her lap.

"You do not understand — no accomplishment overcomes the stigma of being different. That's what Miss Young told me. I try not to think about it and cannot eat my supper or nothing. I didn't understand it at first. But now I do. You are not different in the way difference is acceptable but in another, bigger way. If you did something — well, like Dr. David Scone, who chained himself to the Department of Indian Affairs desk and wore Micmac clothes — perhaps they would look at you differently. But I think Dr. David Scone did that not for Dan Augustine but for himself. You are different."

"How?" Father asked.

"You don't fight — you don't protest — you say nothing. Miss Young says that comes because you saw so much violence when you were a child, you cannot imagine being violent yourself. That might be honourable — and certainly much more honourable than the men I grew up beside, who fought and rowed in their dooryards — like the Pits — still, it makes you different — and that is what Isabel Young is up against. She is up against them all alone — and my heart breaks for her when I think of it. She is a hero — not you, Sydney — *she* is."

Autumn looked at me in a scared way. I kept my head down, eating. It was somehow natural for Mom to want to hurt him at this time. We had all been through a lot. But he only nodded. It did not matter to him if he was called a hero or a coward. He had been called a coward all his life.

"If I ever leave you, I will leave you not over what I have suffered but over what Miss Isabel Young has suffered," Mother said, getting up from the table.

I don't think my father ever truly understood my mother's sacrifice. Perhaps he did not understand anyone's sacrifice. He finally kissed her, felt the little child kick in her belly.

"You do not understand," he said. "I know how my life will go — it is a mathematical certainty — as certain as any matter of calculus that I will be condemned. I do know that, so it doesn't matter if they condemn me now or later. They must do it, for they fear me."

"Aren't family fights fun?" Autumn quipped, but no one heard but me.

The other woman who sacrificed herself for my father at that time was Isabel Young. She is like one of the many women who sacrifice all their lives for a point of law or truth or faith. Brilliant, kind, and unforgiving about something in her own nature.

She has disappeared, like most people from my life. She went unmarried — and alone. She walked the courthouse that day and for years after. She never spoke to the press, or tried to sound radical. She knew true revelation had little to do with the radical thought of the sixties and seventies or eighties.

She appeared and was gone, wearing hats pulled down over her ears, a tissue-carrying hypochondriac who in her life never had a date. Yet when she appeared in court — ah, in court beyond anything else she was a master. I do not know if my father ever thought of her much later. I don't even know if he thanked her properly, because, you see, he did not believe in lawyers.

I know she loved him. A passionate love. At the end, she gave him a fleeting hug, and then kissed Elly on the cheek. She had been their only friend.

I do not know where she has gone. I hope for her and deny her nothing in life. You see, Dad and Mom weren't able to pay her, and I have money to give her now; as long as she doesn't mind where it is from.

She ate by herself at Polly's Restaurant and bore in silence the puritanical disdain of the patrons, the menace of the gloating waitress. Everyone except she believed in the guilt of Sydney Henderson. She worked long after the others had given up for the day, going over the stress level on the buckled steel span, the way the bolts were cut, the notes collected about my father's ability to use dynamite one summer to blow rocks compared to how it was thrown at the bridge.

TWENTY-ONE

When Mathew came to the stand the next day, Isabel asked him about his relationship with Trenton. He began to grit his teeth when she suggested it was he and not Sydney who tormented the child.

She was the kind of person Mathew hated, the kind of person he feared — a woman of 109 pounds, with a peaked face, who did not at all fear him. And he realized that she did not fear him in the truest sense of the word — not just because she was hiding behind the law or her ability to practise it. She did not fear him in some elemental way.

"You tormented the child many times, didn't you — and tormented his dog?"

"That's all made-up nonsense," he said.

"Is this the book," she said, taking it from the table and handing it to him, "that Mr. Henderson read to Trent? Did you hear a reading?"

"No, I didn't — but Cynthia did."

"Cynthia did. Well, how do you know what's in the book?"

"I got a good glance at the filth — I know."

"When —?"

"I picked it up — I looked it over — this was the book he was reading to the boy — I seen — and he tried to pay him off, then threw him down over the bridge — as if he weren't nothing at all." He shook his head, tapped his feet, and was stolid in his refusal to look her way. She handed him the book and he took it, looked at it, and quickly handed it back.

"That's her," he said.

"Are you sure?" she asked.

"It's the book," he said.

"No, it isn't," she said, and she handed it to the sheriff.

"It looks like the book," the sheriff said, partly as a question.

"It's my brother's book," Miss Young said, picking it up again. "His name is on the inside cover — he teaches it in Halifax — I had to send for it because no professor at Saint Michael's would pretend to have a copy. See — these notes were made by him — and here — this passage — this filthy filth — about sex — was underlined by me — at two this morning." She turned to the court and held up the book for all to see. "See here — at the back — by people like Edmund Wilson, Edith Sitwell, etc. — *'a great and profound novel'* — see? Even if this book *was* read to Trenton — which I assure you it wasn't — it would have done him no ill. He would not have had the least conception of what it was saying. The younger radical set at the university in Chatham teach it — they teach it as a great book, as a modern classic — to get back at the priests I suspect, oh yes, that's the height of their radicalism — but they have not come forward to say it's a great book. Well," she added, "they're from Chatham."

She closed it, put it down, turned away, and, suddenly turning back, said she had no more questions for Mathew Pit. Mathew had to be told three times to leave the stand. Cynthia glared at him — for mentioning her name. Above all Cynthia knew then and there that she must remain on the sidelines if she was to further any ambition she might entertain.

The truth is — if I can say this — Mathew was a bully, but in his heart of hearts he loved the boy as much as anyone ever did, and Isabel Young had the audacity to question this. And in a way this moment, after living the short and regal splendidness of acceptance, was the beginning of his downfall.

Later in the week Connie Devlin took the stand. He said he saw Sydney on the bridge, and swore to it. It seemed a breath of sanity had returned.

"And who was near the abutment when you made your rounds?"

"It was Syd," Connie said, pointing his finger, "driving the truck up there, and I said, 'Syd — don't do it, Syd — don't do it.' But did he listen? No, he didn't listen. I said, 'Sydney, you went and cut them bolts — that whole section is gonna go' — and he just says ta me, 'Well, so what!'"

I was in court for the first time that day. Connie gave a sad, whimsical twist to his head, as if he was reflecting upon this, and he glanced my way. I wanted to glare at him but could not.

"Why do you think he may have been there?" Isabel asked.

"Knock the span down — kerplunk."

"You were brave to stay there and not to report it."

"I was brave — but before I could report it everyone already knew."

"My, my — and why would Sydney do something so dangerous and destructive?"

"Complained to me at the house, he weren't going to be foreman

— said people was all against him. I said, to him, I said, 'Listen here, Sydney — ya don't join in nothin', ya always caused trouble — so how can we 'spect ya to belong?'

"His wife Elly, she come to me beggin' me to try and cover it up — like dirt in a hole, I s'pose — and said Constable Morris was on to her. I said, 'Well Elly — it's a good job, 'cause he might hopefully straighten you out — and get you way from that desperate man.'"

The spectators clapped. Connie then sniffed in satisfaction and looked my way again.

On Monday afternoon Connie came to the stand once more. Many of the community's women were in the room, sitting three rows behind my parents, with Cynthia; they being her constant companions at the hearing. That day, one was the waitress from Polly's.

Isabel smoothed her gown and went to the front of the desk.

She asked Connie if he had been fired for drinking. He denied that he was drinking. She asked who had gotten his job back for him.

"Sydney Henderson," he said. "He wanted me to let him destroy the bridge is why," Connie said with a loud retort.

"Oh, I thought that was Mathew who asked you that — because he was not hired on —"

This was objected to.

"Did you see him with the boy before that day — or only after?"

"I don't know — he walked the boy home."

"Home?"

"Yes."

"Why did he *walk* the boy home? Can you tell the court that? That company truck was always available for him. Why did he *walk* Trenton home?"

"I don't know."

"Oh, but you do know. Sydney does not know, nor has he ever learned, how to drive. He cannot drive an automatic let alone a stick shift."

"Ya, he is some stupid man," Connie sniffed.

"Then who manoeuvred the truck onto the bridge?" Isabel then turned her back on Connie Devlin and went to the table. She looked through her notes and then pointed out three things. The first was that Connie had not even been on the bridge at the time of the accident — that not only did he not punch his clock but he was still eating his supper. This could be verified by Jay Beard, who had walked by his house at that time.

"If he had been doing his job he may have feared being injured or killed himself when the dynamite blew. Someone told him to stay home because of that." She flipped a page.

The second point was the fact that Sydney could not drive and could never have manoeuvred that truck into that position. None of Sydney's fingerprints were on the steering wheel in the truck.

And the third was the time Connie said he saw Sydney on the night of Trenton's death. That was the exact time, no matter how they wished to hide it, that even the prosecution had registered that Sydney was talking to Alvina Pit on the phone.

Isabel turned to the women sitting with Cynthia and smiled.

TWENTY-TWO

A week later the sheriff and the coroner recommended that my father not be sent to trial. This came down on February 26, 1983. They gave a dozen reasons. The weak span was a company problem. The sabotage could not in any way — even the minutest way — be linked to Sydney.

Then the book. The book was considered a classic, and any man had a right to read what he wanted. The watchman was an unreliable source — his time clock, through his own fault or mechanical failure, was not useful to anyone, and his story was suspect. It was not clear if he was even on the bridge — at least reasonable doubt serviced in this regard.

Then the dynamite. Anyone who would know how to plant a charge as Sydney did when he was seventeen would know how to damage a structure better than that — and if he had time to drive onto the bridge and accost a boy in the truck, was he not frightened of the span collapsing before he himself could escape? These were serious unanswered questions.

And — *Sydney did not drive.*

The most damaging testimony against Father concerned the robbery. However, there were other ways the money could have ended up in Trenton's possession. The idea that anyone would give a retarded boy five hundred dollars for a sexual favour was highly unlikely. Find out where the money came from and you would find the person or persons responsible for the boy's death and the destruction of the span.

Sheriff Bulgar said this did not make him feel easy about letting Sydney go. It simply meant that the prosecution had failed to convince anyone beyond a reasonable doubt that what happened was more than an unfortunate accident or that other people were not involved. Everything was unconvincing. The trial would be as well.

My father had his own scenario worked out. He had hidden his thoughts from Isabel Young but took out a diagram later that week and showed it to my mother. For two hours he went over every point as we sat listening. He did not understand it completely, but he was certain he could reveal the hidden codes in such a way as to show who had taken the money. He said he would go to Leo McVicer and exonerate Elly, which was the only thing my father wanted.

"There must have been a small crime to allow the larger crime. The theft was done to *entrap* us — so as far as my thinking is, the robbery at the house must have been done as a coverup — again and again I come to the same conclusion — the same one. The robbing of money was secondary. Something terrible happened at the house *before* the robbery to make the robbery necessary, if it was to be blamed on you. The bridge is another matter altogether and came as a complete convenience to those who wish to discredit me." He paused.

"Still, *you* were the one they wanted to initially discredit — I wasn't a worry to them." He took Elly's hand. "It was you — it was not to protect Mathew. It had to be someone closer to McVicer — perhaps Rudy Bellanger. Is there something you are not telling me? Did you see Mr. Bellanger do something at the house or store which was unfortunate."

"Of course not, Sydney."

"Hm," he said. "Well, it must have something to do with him — they wanted you gone so Leo would not find out —" He looked at my mother gently and said, "Oh, I know you think I'm silly, but mathematically it works out — Mathew Pit took the money, and Trenton was not really attempting to give it back to me but to Leo — and Cynthia doesn't know, or want to know, that Mathew is guilty — she used to love me — now she hates me."

"Hates you," Autumn said. (I think she believed this to be all very romantic at the moment.)

"At any rate, Mathew Pit knows he has to make me culpable forever — that is why he hates me too — now they are both in turmoil. Strange how it will someday all come together."

"Sydney — I want you to do something," Mom said.

"What?"

"I want you to forget what you just said — we have another child coming — I want more than anything no more trouble —"

"Oh, I don't care about me — it is you I am thinking of."

"Then don't do or say another thing — *please!*"

Sydney shrugged. He continued eating his cooling soup. Finally he said:

"So I know — that's all I know."

"Please stop!" Mother shouted, wringing her hands. "Or I will leave you forever — I swear I will go away!"

We all went to bed that night in silence. The wind blew over our house. I could see the light from the stove. I could see my mother's knicknacks on the mantel. I bet I prayed for her, though I didn't believe in God. The next morning we went off to school, and Father, taking his smelt nets, went to work.

The new opinion (or the same opinion in a new form) was that my father was not a poor fool from some Bartibog swamp, but a rural Machiavellian, his books and his poor treatment of my mother used against him.

FURY

ONE

A few weeks later there was a full moon, and stars dotted the sky. The snow was hard, and even though the mercury was low, the first scent of spring could be felt in those dry tiny orbs of air. Constable Morris went to Polly's Restaurant to calm down Mathew Pit, who had just gotten into a fight with a trucker, a fight he attributed to his family's suffering.

Mathew sat with his hands on a bottle of beer, his jean jacket rolled up showing the sleeves of a frayed white sweater, and complained to Constable Morris about the inequality of the law. Why have a law if the law allowed this? What right did the law have to make his family suffer these indignities? Just because he once had legal troubles was it right for the law to persecute him?

Constable Morris agreed and apologized for the entire case. It was not handled properly at any level, and never since the murder of young Karrie Smith some years before had there been such a debacle.

"Good men suffer all the time because cases are not handled properly," Morris said. He blamed the prosecution for botching what was essentially an easy conviction.

"What if he confesses?" Mathew said.

"If he confesses, he confesses," Morris said. "An inquest isn't a trial — a confession would change it all."

Morris then whispered something to hearten Mathew. Morris said he was a tough boy himself and came from tough people but there was one thing he knew.

"And what is that?" Mathew asked.

"Murder is always open," Morris continued. "You think I have given up — I never give up. I won't give up until that bastard is behind bars — and his wife is free of the torment she has suffered. She shouldn't be made pregnant by that son of a bitch."

Mathew flinched at the line:

"Murder is always open."

He went home later that night and his mother called to him. She had heard about the fight at the bar from a neighbour who phoned. He went to her, kissed her forehead. She was sitting up, propped by two pillows. Her room had the oddly familiar style of faded flowers, and a lingering second scent of the aged within the fragrance of those flowers, caught in the warm pink walls, and the deep Maritime scent of midwinter thaw, which had turned to ice again in the night.

Alvina's teeth were on the nightstand beside her, along with a box of Kleenex. The television had been brought upstairs, and she kept pointing the remote at it like a gun, her arm straight and her lips pressed tight. She watched *Mass for Shut-ins*, and *The Billy Graham Crusades*, and reruns of *The Mary Tyler Moore Show*. But now her TV with its two-foot-long rabbit ears was off. She looked at her son, and he joked with her. But she was distressed and had prayed at church.

The day before she had asked him to swear to her on a Bible that he knew nothing of Trenton's death or of the truck driven onto the span or the bolts being cut. She had grown old in the last four months and looked at him tonight with eyes filled with disappointment.

"What is wrong?" he asked.

"Why won't you swear on the Bible for me? If you have not committed a sin, then why not do this? For Trenton's sake."

"It's not my kind of book," he said. "Beside, I have bigger fish to fry —" He sniffed. "Talking to a constable tonight an' everything else."

She looked at him and plucked the quilt with her fingers. "I could not stand it if you did it. Kiss Saint Jude." She nervously reached about her neck and held the medallion up with her trembling fingers toward his mouth, in bright hope and expectation. He turned away.

"No, I don't kiss Saint Jude — I used to — but lately I don't like him — I used to pray to him when I hunted, and I never had no luck.

I used to pray to him when I trapped, and coyotes took the catch. Saint Jude cares more for coyotes than he does for me, I figure."

She knew Mathew had said in December that he would do exactly what had been done: sabotage the bridge and stop work on it. Now Alvina had to convince herself, as Mathew's old mother who loved him, that he had not done what was in his mind to do, but that for some insane reason *Sydney*, who had never bothered her before, *had*.

Alvina also knew, the moment she had accused Sydney on the bridge, with the boy's body lying in front of her, the implications of what she was saying: that the mother of a dead child could cause the rancour she did. It was in her heart to wound him. But now she could not take any of it back. She had become, like Rudy and Connie Devlin, an unwilling conspirator in her son's commission of a horrible crime.

Mathew kissed her cheek as she put the medal of Saint Jude back under her nightdress.

"I love you, Mom," he said, "and I loved Trenton too."

Mathew went downstairs and into the back room where Trenton had spent much of his time. Cynthia was sitting alone with a blanket over her considering many things this night.

She looked at Mathew and returned to her binoculars to watch our house. She was aware that there was an immense grace allowed the Pits because of the death of this child, and she and Mathew wanted more.

Still, as Mathew looked at her he worried. Because he could see a future where this grace would not be so easily attained. As each day passed, the suffering of Elly and Sydney would be considered monstrous if the truth came to light.

Worse, every day for the last three weeks Connie was at the house asking for his money. The four thousand dollars that Mathew had promised him. He had to do something about that.

Still, Connie was discreet enough never to mention the truth. It was in a way *unconscionable* that someone would be mean enough to mention the truth to Mathew, after all he'd been through.

Mathew's thinking was simply the logical progression from illogical circumstance. The truth was an aberration to everyone in our community who believed in my father's guilt. To tell this truth would be a genuine inconvenience.

For more than two months everyone on the river had believed Mathew was a hero. People from far and wide wrote him letters, sent cards and money. They drew nooses on these cards and letters and called radio programs to talk about the reinstatement of the death penalty.

He received money from Maritimers and Miramichers as far away as Calgary and Edmonton. And many wanted action against my father. Many said they would gladly come home for target practice. My father's death would be seen as a legitimate form of reprisal. I had heard this myself, and in some terrible way believed it.

But Mathew was not doing as well as he could have. He feared Rudy would break under the pressure very soon. Worse, Connie Devlin could blackmail him.

And recently he had made a fundamental mistake, the same mistake he had been making since he was sixteen. He had taken three gallons of gas without paying for it. The news about this had spread, and people heard that he had used his favourable position to act as his old self. He had tried to make up for it, but the manager of the gas bar wouldn't take money for the gas and looked disappointed. Both he and Cynthia had felt a coolness toward them since the three gallons of gas.

TWO

Mathew sat on a hard-backed kitchen chair and spoke to his sister. He told her he was preparing to file suit against the McVicer construction company. He said this was suggested to him as a possible avenue to justice by a number of people, and he knew a lawyer to handle it. It was the best thing to do to receive compensation. But what he actually wanted more than anything else was to be talked into it, not only by the lawyer but by Cynthia as well. For if she did not go for it, it would be because she sensed too much danger.

"What kind of compensation would change Trenton's death?" Cynthia asked quickly. She wanted to hear from his lips the amount he might be seeking.

"I know nothing will ever change his death — as I told Mom — still, we have a good case —" Then he added, "No, never mind it — I'm not going to cheapen his death by no fuckin' money." He looked at her under his eyebrows, with his pale blue eyes. Then he shifted his gaze minutely, staring into the corner. Finally she lighted a cigarette, inhaled deeply, and turning her head to blow away the smoke, said: "When?"

"When what?"

"When did you speak to the lawyer?"

"In the bar yesterday — told us to go and see him. But never mind it. I'm done with it. I decided. I want no more to do with it. I decided. I will go and kill Sydney and have done with it. They can take me away in handcuffs." As he said this, he glanced at the window sill. He rubbed his nose and looked away.

For the last month Mathew had been conferring with Connie Devlin in the hope that Connie would shoot Sydney for him. Mathew's hope was that it would be looked upon as an internal dispute, that Connie as night watchman would be considered culpable in Sydney's schemes and was willing to shoot him to keep him silent. That would put Mathew in the clear.

Cynthia looked at him with her clear and brilliant eyes. He glanced at her and glanced away.

"When does he want us to go and see him?" she asked.

"Who?" he said as if distracted.

"The fuckin' lawyer," Cynthia said.

"Tomorrow," he said, as if the very nature of the word "tomorrow" was tormenting him because of its endless pettiness. He looked at the knuckle of his left hand and rubbed it against the fabric of the couch.

But Cynthia, like him in so many ways, understood him better than he knew. She knew they were running out of options. They must sue now or forget the whole thing, and to kill Sydney would prove to the people how tormented her brother was.

In a way it was completely logical. In a way Cynthia realized she must play the cards remaining to her in perfect order. Not to sue or attempt to injure Sydney would be a subtle admission, and people would begin to view them as fraudulent. But what she realized more than anything was Connie Devlin's reticence in helping them any more; that he wanted payment for everything now, the four thousand he somehow believed he was owed. She told Mathew he had one option.

"To shoot through Sydney's door and hit the fucker —"

He hesitated. "I know — but still everyone will know it was me."

"That's the point," Cynthia said. "Don't you turn into a gutless puke on me — he won't even get the cops — and people will hear about it. More important, Connie Devlin will *fear* you again — he doesn't now. And the lawyer will hear of it too, and treat you with more respect. All of this will be in your general favour."

This plan to Cynthia was both brilliant and ruefully truthful.

"I'm not questioning it," he said, "but things might get tricky."

"Of course they'll get tricky — so tricky — but you don't really have a choice — damned if you do, maybe, but damned if you don't. If Devlin ever says he saw you, or that he knew of what you were doing — or if the robbery at Leo's is investigated and Rudy cracks — it's all over. You can't tell me for certain that no one saw you," Cynthia said, "but if we can keep our cool, things can still turn out. It will get tricky if you kill Sydney — but not if you wound him —"

He realized she was right.

Then she said, "Connie Devlin is a danger to us, so we will have to think of him as well. If he's lumped in with the company in our lawsuit, he won't be on our side — he'll turn against us. The best thing to do is to make it very clear how you feel about him."

Mathew sat down again. "What do you mean?"

"I mean this. We have a window of opportunity, but it could backfire.

The company might sue Connie Devlin for breach of responsibility —
he should have reported the truck on the span — the lousy rebar pulled
up, the bolts hacked off! He will then turn on us in'a second."

Mathew blanched white. "I don't want to do it then," he said.

"You silly fuck — you have no choice now," she said. "You have to
act this out in one way or the other. Fear is a good keeper-quieter.
And Connie will fear you if you are ruthless."

The fact that lies had forced him into this was apparent to them both.

Again they were silent. The night was still, and cars passed on the
highway. The moon sat over the house, and its light flooded the yard.

Cynthia knew he had robbed Leo McVicer — she had watched him
go into the house through the back door. But more worrisome was the
possibility that others had seen him near the house that night.

More importantly she knew he had loosened the bolts on the buckled steel. Though she did not see him pull the truck up to the abutment,
she knew he had three sticks of dynamite, and now there were two.

But if this information came out, it would break her mother's
heart — and Cynthia had much to lose as well. So she played out her
remaining options. One was to take definite action against Connie
Devlin — which would tie him and Sydney together.

The other worry was Rudy Bellanger.

She had told Rudy when he came to see her last week that unless
he kept quiet, he would lose everything, every hope and dream he
ever had entertained in the last ten years. He had smiled and said,
"You're crazy — I want no more to do with either of you — I can go
to the police and take my chances with them."

But then she played her ace. And he realized in her sullen face
that she had kept it for just such a moment.

"Why am I crazy?" she said, looking through him. "Remember that
night near Christmas when you visited Mat, and I came downstairs
after my bath in my nightie — well, you had to have me, didn't you.
I struggled. I tried to protest, remember? And I couldn't resist. Well,
I'm knocked up, and I need payment for the child."

"It can't be mine," Rudy said, his lower lip trembling.

"What do you take me for — can't be mine? Who in hell's is it? Some goddamn Indian's from Burnt Church? Can be mine will land you in court — can't be mine will land you in prison — ha! You blew your load in ten seconds — can't be mine, try it — just try it. What will little Gladys think of that!"

Now that Rudy was vulnerable and in too deep to find an avenue to escape she allowed him none. None of this was done with conscious malice. It simply happened, suddenly — like her pregnancy. She would see an opening and dive in. There always came a moment when she thought it better not to continue, but then her eyes would burn like brilliant dark stars, her beauty would turn suddenly vulgar and wanton, and she would tell people to *dare* her.

She was not overly brave, nor fatalistically ambitious. Yet she played her cards at opportune times and believed that everything she did was thought out beforehand.

Now with Rudy's ill and sad wife she felt as a woman does who has just made a four non trump bid against an opponent who once ridiculed her play. She remembered how Gladys condescended to her as a girl. Now, she had been *knocked up* by Gladys's husband. This gave her a leverage with the rich. She felt powerful. The machinations and worry of men had always given her power.

Because of this pregnancy, she felt equal to every person in town, to self-appointed professor Scone who spoke in the papers and, most important and ominous of all, to Leopold McVicer. The thing that neither Diedre nor Dr. Scone seemed to understand was that *anyone* could be self-appointed. And Cynthia had thought of grander things than her brother; or even of Diedre and David Scone. Both those people were slaves of public opinion, which in a way was a greater impediment than moral law. The vast number of self-appointed archangels were usually slaves of public opinion. Cynthia did not necessarily have that problem.

Once last summer Leo was putting some flowers in his back yard beds, and she, being bored, had wandered through the back woods, beyond those huge enclosed fields and out along his dusty back lane.

She passed some of his graders and tractors, a few of his gravel trucks. The smell of mud gave her a slightly erotic sensation. She was wearing a loose halter top and tight shorts. He smiled upon her, wearing an old hat and khaki pants. She walked straight up to him, but realized his daughter, Gladys, was inside the porch on one of the old wicker chairs, painting, in her straw hat and heavy print dress. So she did not stay, even though he asked her to come into the house for a drink of lemonade.

"No, not today," she had said, clicking her tongue. She knew he would remember her, would remember the clicking of her tongue, because she wanted him, too.

Still, this did not make her loyal to him if money could come through a lawsuit against him. But also it did not make her loyal to Mathew if the lawsuit were to fail and Leo showed interest again.

Though she was sorry her poor innocent brother was dead (and she was very sorry), she was left daily indications that life would be much better for her because of it. Cynthia knew the one way to prove outrage was action, and she had to prod Mathew into taking it.

"It is Connie we have to get — you should never have allowed him to know *anything* about you," she now said. "You cannot trust a man. I am very different from you — I have already planned my life, and I will do something every bit as big as anyone on the river." She smiled at this, like a slave might.

The fact was, far from being free, Cynthia had always been institutional in her thoughts.

Cynthia knew and used the same language as Diedre did, the language of a social contract that mattered so little in true human affairs. That is, Cynthia could easily talk about dispossessed, and marginal, and traumatized, and underprivileged, and emancipation, and victims, and family unit in the jargon of the social worker whenever it was to her advantage. And she could drop it in a second when it wasn't.

Cynthia knew how the police worked, how the social services worked, because she had been a product of them. She knew about welfare, and she knew how to make these programs work in her favour. She had always been able to get money for her mother when others failed.

Tonight she did not like to admit that the death of her brother had become a game in which she was deciding how to dupe those authorities who had taken an interest in her, yet she could not deny its appeal. Her conversation with Mathew never suggested this, even though both of them felt the same sensation; this would allow them to *prosper*. No matter that she did not want to recognize this internal and provocative truth, she was stuck within the core of its veracity.

"First we go to the lawyer," Mathew said. He did not look at her when he said this. "There is a chance at a good deal of money. The lawyer said it wouldn't even have to go to trial — that Leo is vulnerable now and would be willing to settle. It's not for us, it's for Mom," he added. "It's for Trenton's memory."

"For how much?" Cynthia asked, rolling a toke and looking at him, hands on her knees, and her knees spread.

"Anywhere from fifty to a hundred thousand."

"Trenton was worth more than that," she said. "That's the first thing."

But $100,000 was an enormous amount for her.

Cynthia sat up, threw the blanket off, and asked him to hand her her jeans. She asked him again what money would be worth the child's life. He said, his voice genuinely breaking, that he didn't know.

THREE

The next morning Mathew dressed in the frigid air of his bedroom, and covered himself with his best clothes. His best clothes were five years out of date, a button was split, and he wore a pair of cowboy boots that gave his pants a ridge at the calf.

Cynthia knew lawyers fascinated Mathew Pit because they allowed him entrance into a world of jurisprudence where everyone was supposedly equal. More than that, that world allowed him in a legal way to be superior to those who had condescended to him, and allowed him to show a regal bearing that the law granted the "margin-alized." Although he hadn't considered including Cynthia or his mother in his quest for money, he realized he must now. That he relied on Cynthia day in and day out was something both of them knew.

Therefore he and Cynthia went to a lawyer, as representatives from their family. They were going to sue the construction company and Leo McVicer himself. This is what pleased Cynthia — the idea that she could sue "Leo McVicer himself."

Both Mathew and Cynthia realized that the law, like their entire lives, was a game where truth did not matter, but the appearance of truth mattered.

Even their lawyer didn't care if he was called ethical. In fact it was *better* if he was called unethical. The more stories about him, the greater his notoriety, the more hilarious it all was. It was much better if he was called *shrewd*, and he could show this shrewdness in a grand way in a small town, and bring in elements of manoeuvring that other lawyers might not try. This is why Mathew was drawn to him.

And there was a story this lawyer often told about Roy Henderson, my grandfather, trying to pay his lawyer with one- and two-dollar bills on the court steps after he was found guilty, and how this money blew out of his hand and got wet in the rain. To him this was profoundly comical. When it was once mentioned to him that my grandfather was an illiterate man who had nothing and died in jail with nothing but an address in his wallet, he answered stiffly and morally by saying, "Law is the law."

The lawyer's name was Frederick Snook. And he liked to be called Frederick. He had watched Newcastle grow — the paper mills got larger, the bars spread with the town, video games, cable, and satellite dishes brought the world to our door — the great empire to our south. We drove American cars, played American music, dressed in American clothes, danced American dances under the glitter globes, and yet there was a glass partition that kept us on the far side of the American experience. The Pits he considered outsiders because they had in some ways failed to keep up with that experience, and Snook, who had been to both Hawaii and Atlantic City, considered them unknowledgeable because of this. More significant, *his* experience was the only experience important to them. They coveted it, like some teenage girls covet makeup — that is, it is what they believed would prove them real. The Experience of my father who read Plato and Kant was not viable for Cynthia. And one true way to show it was to be included into the world that radiated somewhere else, wherever that somewhere was, the world that for this one moment had stopped pissing in their face.

Mathew came to Snook's office wearing a pale yellow shirt open at the neck, a grey sports jacket, which was too tight, and black slacks, with a pair of high-heel cowboy boots. Cynthia dressed in a tight black dress, with a stain on the left shoulder, and black high heels with fishnet stockings. Her pregnancy showed in this dress as a small mound. She had a diamond stud in her nose. The impression they made on the lawyer, who had defended Mathew two times, for poaching, and Cynthia once, for assaulting a bride at a wedding, was that of two wild creatures come to town.

Mathew's hair was receding. But he still wore it in the ducktail he had a few years ago when he was last charged. His eyes were still mirror blue. Cynthia's eyes bore through the lawyer and made him uncomfortable. He offered coffee, but they were downriver people and asked for tea. The tea he gave them, a scented Indian flavour he kept for widows whose trust funds he managed, and at times syphoned, Cynthia pushed away with one hand and sat back in a motion of complete revulsion.

"It's not the kind of tea you are used to," he said sadly.

"No," she said. "Faggot fuckin' tea." Then she laughed aloud, not

at what she said, but because of the startled expression on his face
after she said it.

The lawyer often told other lawyers she was crazy. And other
lawyers would say, "Yes — but I'd let her wrap her crazy legs around
my head," to which Frederick would caution, "The crazy quiff would
eat you alive."

However, he now showed he had an immense regard for her. He
nodded and assured them he had heard all about the case, that he
felt sickened by it, that it was a terrible injustice to hard-working,
decent people. Mathew's former crimes seemed to elicit more sympathy from him and qualify the Pits for a bigger payout.

"That's how they treated you," he said. "They never let you off though
your crimes were minor. Then very likely because of your former jail
time, they withhold a job for you on the bridge where you could have
provided for Trenton. But they hire a man whose past actions are ques-
tionable, and a man who openly obsesses about your brother."

"Openly what?" Cynthia asked quickly, inhaling cigarette smoke
and holding it in.

"Obsesses — dreams about — I'm sorry, but it's true. Worse, they
have no command over their worker's dereliction of duty. Wait and
you'll see the company squirm," he said.

"We don't want to blame Connie Devlin," Mathew said suddenly.

"You don't?"

"Well — he's a cousin —"

Mathew stopped speaking and looked with fear at Cynthia.

"But if he's in on it, he's in on it," Cynthia said.

"That's right" Mathew said, though his face turned white in the dry
midwinter air.

"I know it's hard — I know you are both grieving — I am not a
priest, but I do perform a similar service — not for the other world
but for this one." Freddy Snook wore his loud checked three-piece
suit with a bright orange silk tie. He looked at them and sighed,
tapping a pencil on his desk, in a manner that seemed to authenti-
cate what he had just said about these two exceptional human beings.

"And what about Sydney — how will he pay?" Cynthia said, crossing her legs slowly. She still had never forgotten that her beauty, her immense sexuality, had been no match for my poor mother's genteel grace. She also realized that her sexual freedom had offered her not my father but the world of failed men who had squandered their lives in sin.

"We will take Sydney for everything," Frederick said, and he gave a gleeful squeal and shook his head. Then he added piously, "Although it will never be enough."

Cynthia nodded, and Mathew felt overwhelmed by a sense of righteous anger. What he and Cynthia did not know, as Snook put his arms about their shoulders and walked them to the door, was that Snook had been Leo McVicer's lawyer for years — was on a retainer, and had defended him successfully in five lawsuits.

He would not easily give McVicer up to them, but he would keep McVicer informed in a casual way, so as not to damage his ethical sensibility.

FOUR

Two nights later, in a heavy March rain that was once again turning to snow, my father came home drunk. I glanced out the window and my father was crawling on his hands and knees. He got up and staggered badly and fell against one of the slick spruce trees on the dark side of our yard, and started yelling at it. I had never seen him take a drink before, let alone be drunk. He looked hideous, his jacket soaking and his hair beaten flat upon his head. Right in front of our little shoebox of a house, he looked as if he had lost his way; he looked like a cowering drenched dog.

Mother and I rushed out to get him. He was singing and crying. He did not seem to know who my mother was.

He had drank rum coming back from his last day on the smelt field. Someone had taken his sled, but he had managed to put a few smelts in his coat, some sticking tail up, some with their frozen heads looking out his pockets. He had then staggered to the road, ashamed of his drunkenness, and walked to the gas bar and asked for help.

"You are beyond help," the man at the gas bar reportedly said. "You're drunk now because you have guilt right through your stinking pores."

"That is so," my father said. "I am guilty about Trenton — I am deeply sorry — I wish I had not acted the way I did. I want some more to drink." (The gas bar was known far and wide as a bootleggers'.)

"Confess and I'll give you some. What you just said to me say to Constable Morris!"

"Confess," said a woman who had come for gas.

"Confess," another man said, and then another. And soon they were taunting him. "Confess confess — and you can have a bottle of wine."

Father looked about at everyone, and tried to walk into the back room to get the wine. The manager followed him and opened the back door to the harsh blue evening air. My father had not smelled such air — which was mixed by every breath he took with alcohol — since he was a boy of seventeen. He picked up a bottle of wine. No other man dared go near him.

He stumbled across the road in the grainy winter twilight filled with spotted snow and rain, and was almost hit by a transport. He heard the air brakes shriek, and the blow horn sound. Then after two hours in the cold night he found his way home.

Before the night was over people went to Mathew and told him that my father was drunk — and had said he was sorry he hadn't treated Trenton differently — which proved his guilt. They stood in the kitchen, eager to disclose this information, for whatever suspicion they had had of Mathew was suddenly and irrevocably proven wrong.

"How can you ever stay so calm?" he was asked by Danny Sheppard, the man who had touched my shoulder the month before — the reputed father of the stillborn child.

"I stay calm because I have a clean conscience," Mathew said.

The Pit house was filled with visitors all the next day; they came and went paying their respects all over again. Even Jay Beard went to Pit's house. He asked to see Alvina. She was sitting in a rocking chair staring at the road as if longing to see someone walk along it just once more. He asked her please as a favour to a man she had grown up with — a man who once had thoughts of interest in her — not to listen to gossip, but to wait and see. But Alvina felt exactly the opposite now. She must believe what comforted her. It comforted her to know that Sydney had confessed, and that various people told her they were not going to let him get away with it. Not this time! They would take matters into their own hands! The police had done nothing. Six or seven people had told her as much. And even though in her heart she felt something was wrong, even though in her heart she did not trust her own children, how could she turn away from this confession of Sydney's, a confession that exonerated her boy? She stared at Jay with a sadness he had never seen before in anyone, and he was shaken.

When he went back downstairs, Mathew was sitting with some friends. Bennie Sheppard was standing by the sink. You were dealing with the most corrupt people on the river when dealing with the Sheppards. Everyone knew this. But now, in the smell of hash and wine, that did not matter at all.

Mathew did not look at Jay Beard. All his life he had been given raw deals, and this is what showed on his face. And the proof of the terrible things Jay Beard had once believed about him was excised.

"Whatd'ya say now?" Bennie Sheppard said. "Proved wrong, ain'cha — proved wrong."

Jay stood at the door hat in hand and simply said he did not feel in his heart that Sydney Henderson had done anything.

"I know it looks bad," he said.

"Looks bad — looks bad! Yer so good at levelling charges at Mat

Pit," Danny Sheppard said, "'bout a lobster, about a moose, about a pound of pot — but this is 'bout a child."

In their faces at this moment was seen the hilarious certainty of Mat's proclamation, and even Jay Beard felt that they might be right. He too had begun to lose hope.

"I'm very sorry about Trenton," he said to Mat. Mat looked at him with a terrible sadness.

"Ya know — we are just ordinary people, Jay," Cynthia chimed in. "We don't have much — or ever had much — my father worked his guts out and died — Mat has had his trouble — but they wouldn't even hire him on that bridge — for a few stinkin' dollars —"

"I know," Jay said, "I know."

They both looked hurt and said nothing. He went back to his trailer. He had known my father since he was a child. But how could he continue to support him after this? He was not very fond of the Pits, but they did have a point. He just did not know. Why had his own life been so hard? He did not know — but this was the most terrible trial he had yet to endure. And he was a man approaching sixty-five.

All the river knew about Father by the next evening. Sydney Henderson got drunk and confessed! Sydney Henderson had made a fool of the courts. Constable Morris, who had tried his damnedest to get the child molester off the street, heard about this as well.

Mathew was seen driving his car up and down the road crying and carrying a rifle. He stopped on a level stretch and opened the door and was seen with his head in his hands. The sky was lenten and foreboding. There was a smell of raw ice in flurries of bitter snow. Finally some people stopped to speak to him. The man and woman who operated our gas bar, from where Mathew had stolen the gas and Dad had taken the wine, told him to keep a stiff upper lip, that everyone had sympathy for him.

"He's a drunken pig now," the woman said, "so he'll confess yet again — and you won't have to do a thing." She touched his hand.

A wail went up from Mathew like the cry to God that Cain himself may have made. It was not that he did not believe what was being said; he believed it absolutely to be true. People had to do something about Sydney Henderson *now!*

This couple, happy to help him because they had always feared him, stayed beside him, worried he would injure himself. He liked to hear them implore him not to act violently because it gave him a thrill of standing above others and being marked as special. But there was a moment, when taking out a Buck knife, he cut his finger in torment.

"Please, Mat," the man said. "How long has I known ya, boy — these bastards don't get away with it —"

"I feel I have to kill Connie Devlin," Mat told them. "Connie — you know he shoulda looked out for Trenton, but he wasn't even there — he wasn't even there! And them floodlights was off. Why was they off? He must be in league with Sydney all along. They pulled it off together. Connie and that bastard." He looked from one to the other with a look of stupefied revelation.

"I know, but you have to think of your mom," the woman said. "What will that do to her, a good woman like that? Everyone admires you — you just have to be strong. There are people here on this road — who have decided that they won't let that man leave his house again. They will stand guard outside the house waiting for him —"

"They want me to sue — a whole bunch of lawyers is after me to sue Leo McVicer. But I don't even want the money and if I get a million dollars I might just burn it all up in a pile on the bridge." He then took five dollars from his pocket and burned it, and saw that it had the effect Cynthia told him it would.

Late the next day Devlin went to the Pit house and asked to see Mathew. He was ushered into the back room, a room with spotted red wallpaper and deep leather chairs, where Mathew had a small office and kept things that had been stolen. Devlin came in certain he had the upper hand, and remained certain until he stared at Mathew's face. Suddenly his nerve failed, and he began to tremble.

"Why did you say that I deserved to die?" he asked, fidgeting. "People are saying the Sheppards are going to get me — what did I do?"

"Why weren't you there to protect Trenton," Mathew said, "like I begged you to be when I knew Sydney was trying to lure him away? Why didn't you protect him — why did you leave those lights off!"

"But you told me to stay at home — you promised me four thousand dollars if I left the lights off."

"Four thousand dollars! Stay at home! I told you?" Mathew said, jumping to his feet and slapping Connie's face. "I told you? That's a lie! I already got one confession — I'll get yours too — if you don't watch it."

Connie stared at Mat and then at Cynthia.

"Yer right," he said finally. "I'm not thinkin' good."

"Not one penny —" Cynthia said. "Yer our cousin, we take care of you — but if we find you and Sydney were in this together — to make money — stinkin' money on a child's death — you understand — it would break Alvina's heart even more to know that her brother's son was in on this!"

Connie, realizing the precariousness of his position, smiled like a hurt child. "I'm on yer side, Alvina knows," he whispered. "You know that too — you do — Cynthia — I'm not asking for nothing." He smiled again, his face white, and asked if there was anything they needed, or what errand he could run, and when he left them he looked as though he was walking on eggs.

FIVE

My father was put to bed and sweated off the drunk like he used to do as a young man. He asked me to take his clothes away and bind his wrists to the headboard, and I did what he asked. I hid his clothes in the hole behind my bed, all of them.

His eyes were black. I thought he had been beaten after he got drunk. I did not know he had been beaten so they could set him drunk. But he had not died — and those who had beaten him took this as proof of how evil he was.

Father called me to him. It was important to him that I know he did not drink intentionally or in any way confess to hurting Trenton, as was now being said by everyone. He only confessed to his *conceit* — that he should not have tried to help the boy. But what kind of weakness in a man would make him confess to such a conceit as that?

His mouth was cut by the bottle because he had broken it with his teeth when he had tried to stop them. He told me he had left the ice field about three that afternoon. He was met by a man who said he wanted to speak to him about a job. My father was not gullible, but we were in desperate need of money.

"Come with me," the man said. "We'll give you forty bucks for piling on some eight-foot for us today. We know you can pile it as well as anyone on the river."

Dad was like a child. Forty dollars for loading a truck. Even though he knew he might be in danger, he also needed the money for Autumn, who needed new glasses.

They walked along the path together. Not Father's usual path, but one that skirted below the Pits' property. Father was again suspicious about walking down this way (where would the truck be here?) and he slowed down and looked back over his shoulder. And then two other men came out of the woods behind him.

"Was Mathew one?" I asked.

"No," he said firmly.

They held him down, pried open his mouth, and poured alcohol down his throat. He bit and swallowed the glass. He asked me if I was ashamed of him. I said of course not, but for minutes I did not look his way. His big thick glasses had been broken, the lenses lost in the snow, and he couldn't read his books without them.

We did not tell Mother what had happened. He told her he had a relapse. It would be terrible for Mom to know that men, actual living breathing men, had done this to him; yet it was as bad for me *not* to believe him. He remained in bed and asked for Jay Beard. Jay came, and went in to see my father for an hour.

When Jay came out I had a chance to talk to him. I see myself now as a skinny kid in a dirty white shirt and a pair of dress pants too large for me.

"Is he telling the truth?" I asked. I looked up at him with such expectation I started to shiver.

Jay just shook his head. He held Dad's broken glasses. He had found the lenses. He would take them home and try to repair them.

"I don't know if he is or isn't," he said. "Perhaps that is what having faith means — I just don't know, boy. But there is one thing — the Sheppard boys are gone away — they're hiding from something — that means something is not right."

I got bandages and gauze and wrapped Dad's hands. I bathed his mouth every few hours with a swab.

I was numb and could not think. And for days I could not go outside or attend school. Here is the list I managed to write down at this time. I called it the Seven Deadly Sins, and though I kept it out of sight, both Mom and Autumn knew about it.

1) Refuses blood test and denies he is father of Cynthia's child — child dies while in Father's arms.
2) Mother works at McVicer's — Father and Mother accused of robbery.
3) Job on the bridge — bridge collapses.
4) Says wants to take care of Trenton — Trenton dies.
5) Says he didn't influence or harm boy — boy's body covered with stolen money.
6) Trenton dies at night — Father predicts as much.
7) Father doesn't drink — Father gets drunk and confesses.

SIX

Our house was silent. The days were once again frigid sharp and clear, and our small house sat out in this brilliant cold surrounded by empty air and snow. We could hear the boards creak when night fell, and we could hear men, one or two and then more sneaking up to our place and throwing objects at the door. They were the shadows of my youth. We did not go out. We were silent. We did not contact the police.

Four or five days after Dad came home drunk, Autumn and I were finally sent to the gas bar for a loaf of bread, for there was no longer food to eat. But the woman (the woman who had spoken to Mathew) said the store was closed. The air smelled of ash and grey cloud. I banged on the door until her husband came out and chased us away with a certain amount of weary duty. Because of his look, I then made up my mind. To protect my family, by any means. My father read Aristotle and spoke of civility and equality — but Aristotle was the teacher of Alexander the Great — there were other options —

We walked back from the store, without our bread, in the last echoes of daylight, and watched the sun linger down over the hard tamarack trees. Both of us were famished and felt emptiness gnaw at the pit of our stomachs. I took Autumn's hand, and she looked up at me and blinked, and smiled.

I had been thinking since the trial that there was a far greater need and reason for revenge. Simply put, Autumn had been happy to see her picture in the paper during the inquest, but we as a family never spoke of it. Her picture was in the paper because she was a delicate little creature with white skin and white hair. She did not understand then that they were using her looks against us. The picture on its own pleased her. I thought of this as we walked home and as she held my hand.

When we got home our mother was lying on the cot near the stove. She was now four or five months' pregnant. My father was pacing back and forth, his face pale, lips trembling. He asked us if we got the bread. I said no. He asked us if anyone was outside. I said I didn't think there was. He nodded, and looked at Mother. His mouth was healing. His face was calm, the injuries, so I thought, were mending. Then he sat down.

Neither said anything, about the bullet hole through the side wall that had busted through Dad's library and smashed a picture of Saint Thérèse of the child Jesus in the opposite room and caused a flesh wound on his arm that dripped blood like a tap. I think I was angrier at *them* than at whoever shot the rifle.

"What are you going to do?" I said to Dad. "Phone the police?"

"No," Father said, and his logic here was as strangely sane as Mat Pit's. "It can't be proven who shot what. Everyone saw me drunk for the first time in fifteen years. Morris is now on a rampage against me again — and so too is Diedre Whyne and our compassionate Dr. David Scone. Worse than anything, it is taking me everything *not* to drink. I could not go to the police and start an investigation again *without* drinking! If I drink again I swear to Christ I will drink until I die. *They* will win.

"You do not know what your mom and I went through before with Constable Morris. And that would be your mother's ruin. I have to think of her! Everyone on the river thinks I drank because of guilt — everyone believes that people tried to take the bottle *from* me and that's why I got a black eye. Even our only friend, Jay Beard, has said it looks bad for me now."

He laughed suddenly, and Autumn laughed as well. Autumn's laugh was almost insane.

"It was them!" I yelled. "I will kill them — like they tried to do to you and Mommie."

My father looked at me, startled at my rage. Then he spoke sternly.

"I will not tell you this again. But do you understand? They cannot do this and *not* destroy themselves. This will lead to their destruction.

It is not that I want it — it is so, no matter what I want. What do *you* want me to do — shoot at them? I won't. I can't and I won't."

"Yes," I said. "Shoot holes through the whole bunch of them — kill the cunts!" I roared — using the word I could not imagine saying two months before.

"Leave it be — and wait. The Pits are not people to fool with," Autumn said.

"Even if he set everything in motion?" I yelled at her.

"Men don't set things like this in motion," Father said, "it always spirals out of control. That's why the men are outside. And it is out of control because men do not control themselves. I don't want to see you become involved and then lose yourself too."

"At least we have tea," Autumn said. "That's better than nothing."

When she passed by me, her face took on an urgent expression. "We're sitting ducks," she said. "You be Donald, I be fuckin' Daffy." And she burst out laughing again.

Mother (and for the only time in my life did I think she *was* an imbecile) suddenly asked me to go to church. "It is nearing seven o'clock," she advised. "Please go for me — please, I cannot go tonight."

"I am not going to church tonight," I said, more astonished at her than at my father's wound. "Jesus Christ, there are men standing right outside the door —"

"Please," Mother said. "For your brother's sake — everything will turn out if you go and pray for your brother's sake, please. Pray for deliverance from evil."

"I have no brother," I said.

But Autumn whispered to me, "She's talking about the little unseen lad."

Just to get away from the insanity of the house, I left for church, along the old path Dad took to the smelt nets. By now there was a moon in the sky lighting the snow, and the soft smell of ashes. Halfway along this path, in a small copse of trees, I looked back and could see the light shining through the hole the bullet had made in the back tin. And just as I saw this and looked down, I spied the shell from a thirty-thirty and the tracks from a pair of boots. I picked the shell up, holding it with my shirt sleeve, and placed it in my pocket, thinking I had the evidence I needed. Then I continued to church in giddy confidence.

But coming to the oak doors, I balked. I turned and cursed. I waited outside. I promised myself I would not go to church again, for anyone.

"Let my fuckin' brother die," I said aloud. "The Virgin Mary don't love us nohow — my mother is cursed by her." And I spit. I spit, and looked about hoping people had seen me, and then up at the sky, which seemed to be pulsating slowly.

After eight o'clock the doors opened, and a small collection of stragglers and country-born parishioners came out after mass. I approached Rudy Bellanger. I knew him as a man everyone respected. I showed him the thirty-thirty jacket.

"That's what the Pits fired at us," I said excitedly. "Someone got to help us soon — they are the ones who did all this. I think they robbed your father-in-law's house — yes I do." I said this so quickly spit came from my mouth. "So it isn't right for my mother — they wounded Dad — they did."

I was shaking all over. I do not know how often you have been in the position where you had to beg the truth, but it is a horrible feeling. You get a glimpse into the ages — into Cassandra's hopeless moments.

Rudy looked at me. There was a gasp when he breathed air. "Please," he said, as if he were in pain. "That isn't true?"

"It was fired at our house — it could have killed Mommie," I said. "My mom — you must remember Mom?"

"God," he said. He shut his eyes, and his knees buckled just slightly.

"I'm taking it to the police," I said. "And the police will help us — if you drive me — they might have a reward." (I felt so small.) "I'll pay," I said, smiling timidly. Just then the church doors closed behind us.

He took out money and handed it to me.

"Keep this between you and me — until I can help you," he said. "Let me keep this for a while — please, take the money, take it home to your mom — please —"

He put the shell in his pocket. It was dark, so I went under the street-light to count his money and could still smell the gunpowder. There was forty dollars. I walked along the shore for three miles in the splendid night and came out above Gordon's wharf to go to a store where they didn't know me, to buy us bread and milk and bologna and cheese. More strange than anything else, I longed to be drunk.

SEVEN

Autumn and I weren't allowed out very much, so we stayed near each other. On Saturday afternoons we made taffy and fudge, or we went in back of the house to small frozen puddles and played hockey, with Autumn in the net, wearing magazines as goalie pads. We made up names and had jokes for the people allied against us; and there were many of them — every kid on the road, except for Cheryl Voteur.

"We won't let them bother us," Autumn would say when boys called her names. Still, Valentine's Day, I saw her standing under a tree at the top of our lane crying.

That did not dampen her spirits. Boyfriends were a dime a dozen, she said. She liked a boy the next day, and then another, until she had worked her way down to the very last boy on a list. Oh, I knew she had a list — I saw it on the window sill of her small room. Tom and Ted and Ralph and Bill all crossed off. I also saw her try to engage goofy boys in conversation. It would start like this:

"Don't you think that's exactly like *The Mayor of Casterbridge* — hmm —?" Then she would quote a passage to them from the rather obscure Matthew Arnold poem *Stanzas in Memory of the Author of "Obermann."*

"The white mists rolling like a sea!
I hear the torrents roar.
— Yes, Obermann, all speaks of thee;
I feel thee near once more!
A fever in these pages burns
Beneath the calm they feign;
A wounded human spirit turns,
Here, on its bed of pain."

With these lines spoken to him by a tiny albino girl breathing on her pink glasses, the poor youngster would flee into the school parking lot.

Once that spring I went into her room. There she sat, deathly still on her chair, with rouge on her cheeks and a wig on her head. She never spoke, never moved, never batted an eye. Finally, not able to get her to speak, I turned to leave.

"I am a porcelain doll," she whispered, "worth much money — I am kind of a Pinocchio — I do not lie."

"Ah, they can do nothing to us," she would tell me with a great love, "and soon they will tire of it all." But often she snuck along the ditches in the dark, and hid from the boys who teased her, trying to put snow down her pants.

At this time I asked Autumn's advice on how to approach Penny Porier.

"Wear a dress —"

"What?"

"Wait for Sadie Hawkins Day — the end of March — the girls ask the boys out, and I'm sure she will ask you."

"I can't wear a dress —"

"Ah, but you must — most of the clothes you have on are Griffin's — you cannot be sure she is seeing you or her brother — wait until Sadie Hawkins Day."

Autumn told me she liked a boy as well, Darren Voteur. She smiled clumsily. I said nothing. I realized that she had picked the most miserable boy in school to like, because she had worked her way down the entire list.

Out of class the days were always dark and black, and Penny's father picked her up in his half-ton truck so she wouldn't have to walk home, because she often caught colds. Griffin kept me away from her at school.

I turned more bitter than Autumn. I cursed my clothes and my name — my name especially.

At night I thought of Penny lying in bed in white pyjamas on a white pillow, and sadness like electric shock passed through me. I had never felt, or had never been allowed to feel, like this before.

"I will love her to the end of time," I told myself one day as I walked the river after school. The ice had a brilliant blue charm to it, and on the ice I could see who was coming behind me. I had stopped going down our lane, just as Autumn had hidden in the ditches.

People said if it wasn't for Jay Beard, already an old man, with his hands pained with arthritis, who constantly looked out for us, Father would be dead, our house and possessions burned to the ground. It was Jay Beard, using his old .38 revolver, that kept people away from us. I waited for my father, for once in his life, to stand by a friend and help *him*.

But when my father heard that there was an oath some men had sworn to kill Jay Beard for helping us, he simply went back to mending his smelt nets for the next year and building a new shelf for Mom. I told Autumn that Father seemed too gullible to protect anyone. And all my worries were focussed on my mother and sister and Jay Beard. My hope was also — if for self-preservation or honour I do not know — that my father would die, and Jay Beard would become my father.

Autumn told me that the men had broken a window in his trailer and smashed his television set when he was down protecting Dad and Mom.

"He has no money to replace that," Autumn said, "so we should raise the money — you and I."

But I had no idea how to raise the money, and neither did Autumn. Worst of all, my father didn't seem to understand all that he owed this man.

"When I get older I'm going to be like you," I said.

"Boy," Jay said, "be like your dad. They will not bother you or Elly — as long as you don't wander too far from home by yerselves — you have to take time to have this peter out — after a while people will come to their senses."

"My father will get them," I said, looking first at Dad and then at Autumn. "He is planning it now — no one knows what he is planning. He will take care of those lads," I said. The urgency in my voice almost caused me tears.

EIGHT

It was Sadie Hawkins Day. I walked into the corridor in a long dress, with an old purse, while my sister dressed as an outrageously well-mannered albino Huckleberry Finn, with a straw hat. We were such outcasts, we had to try during these contrived events to make ourselves belong. And in the weak-lighted corridor both of us sensed this too late.

We were standing alone in the hallway when Penny's brother, Griffin, approached.

Ah — she has enlisted her brother, I thought. I actually thought like that then.

Griffin was large for his age, with insolent, unhappy eyes. He had the eyes of most boys of fourteen and fifteen, at times haughty and haunted with impure thoughts boys can neither control nor advance and go to confession to relate. He wore loose jeans, a shirt with the tail hanging down, and new sneakers. He was famous for stealing pens and trying to talk like his father.

As he passed by that day he turned and suddenly thrust a compass point deep into my arm. I hollered in pain as he fled down the corridor shouting, "Scum as you has no right to bother me sister!"

Penny, wearing a sweater tied by its arms over her shoulder, walked quickly into her room, as if she were trying to escape me. Blood bubbled up and out of the dress sleeve, leaving a wider and wider spot. Autumn tried to get me to sit down so she could get the principal.

"No," I shouted. "No principal — a lot of good principals do for us!"

I went to get a paper towel from the boys' washroom. I had never fought or thrown a punch at anyone. It was an aberration to my father, and he had instilled in me this idea of physical violence as an aberration. I put the paper towel under the dress sleeve and pressed against my arm, which had turned numb. I felt nauseous.

When I left the washroom it seemed the entire school had gathered to watch what I would do.

I went into class and kept my head down. I believed what had happened to be my father's fault. I did not go to the principal, for I assumed he would not help (just as my father did not go to the police). I tore off my dress — I wore my own clothes under it. I remembered the sadness after my mother and father had taken the letters to Constable Morris. I now recognized that I and Autumn were looked upon like they. Griffin Porier stared at me, gave my clothes that he once owned a knowing frown, and sat two rows over.

My family was doubly reproached. This begged my silence.

I was in a no man's land made palpable by the smell of the old school itself, wherein lay a thousand forgotten moments, wherein sheltered a thousand callow children and urged them onward into pointless and mediocre lives. In that school years before I was there, there was our Rhodes scholar, Gerald Dove, groomed by Leo McVicer, and the year after I left, another Rhodes scholar. The schoolboard and principal were ecstatic. But is that not as miserable and as pointless a future as any other I have spoken about?

Yes, it is even more pointless — for these Rhodes scholars go off to their destiny in middle management of petroleum companies and computer chains — brilliant in their civic-mindedness and their slavish willingness to belong, and leave us, the *unsatisfied ones*, as Yeats might call us — the Devlins, Voteurs Pits, Poriers, and Hendersons — in the sweet aftermath of embittered winter storms, to our bloodied selves. Our lives were not the lives of Rhodes scholars, even if Autumn was brighter than one. We were instead people with a *true* destiny, recognizable only in our universal lunacy under the winter skies.

I stood after school in the schoolyard, awaiting my sister, watching the yellow buses turn toward the frozen bay, carrying my mother's dress under my arm. Autumn still in her Huck Finn costume walked up to me. The schoolyard had the smell of pulp and sulphur, the building was silent, and snow whispered from the pointed corners while the circular ventilators clattered from the centre of its roof and threw wisps of snow into the stark sky.

That weekend we did not go outside. Jay Beard came down to our house with a box of groceries. The night was stony and cold, and yet on the television I listened to the closing stock reports from Toronto and New York as if our world was that world. For the first time I became cognizant of the idea of people living in different centuries — none more content than the other.

In my little house, the nineteenth-century supper had taken place while on the television the twentieth-century stocks had just closed. The vigilantes, I suppose, could have been in any time, any place.

Autumn said she would not allow her life to be held hostage by them outside. I told her she had no choice.

"I have a choice — of course I do — everyone does." She smiled gaily and tossed a copy of *David Copperfield* my way. "Now that's your choice — once you enter it you will be free of Mat Pit."

NINE

I went to school the next morning without a coat. I did this because my father was often impermeable to cold and I wished to prove myself to him. His rumoured excommunication had done nothing to him or Mom to keep them out of the grip of churches.

I went to my desk and became distracted by work. I was behind in everything, yet still believed at this time that it would make a difference, that I would be a great doctor or lawyer or engineer; or, better yet, that I would build buildings to house people whom I had heard were homeless in the cities; I would do all of this and they would see that my father and my family were good. That is the only thing I dreamed of then.

I was working on an essay about the reshaping of power in industrialized England in the 1840s and the burgeoning middle classes, and comparing this phenomenon to the reshaping of power in the information age, the age of the computer, where we had newly arrived. In reality the essay was a way to level a charge against the authorities who tormented people who could be easily bullied and humiliated. So this was the information age! The information of Constable Morris was no more true just because it had now been placed in a computer.

It was an essay I had written in a flood of anger on small scraps of notepaper because I no longer had a scribbler. The notepaper was arranged in meticulous order later that morning, and I had reserved a time to copy it into the new library computer that afternoon. The last line on the last page of the notepaper said: "For my father has been treated unfairly, and has never hurt or bullied my sister or me, for he is a man of God." It was a line I crossed out, not because it wasn't true, but because Father said one should never beg the truth.

Our high school catered to busloads of kids from all of rural downriver, the sons and daughters of miners and fishermen; a school made up of children whose fathers knew what it was like to work hard, and knew injury or death on the job, thrust forward slowly but surely into our tattered new age; a millennium waiting to burst forth upon us in all its pith.

When I came back after lunch, the pages of my essay, all of them, had been thrown as paper airplanes out the window. The sky still hung black over the schoolyard, and four buses waited in the dreary lot.

I could not now type my essay into the new computer and I was forced after school to go out and try to find as much of it as I could in the parking lot. Boys and girls gathered about and watched me as I struggled to collect the drab ink-marked papers. When I came back to the front doors I saw Autumn amid the disenchanted youthful stares.

Griffin Porier leaned his heavy arm across my sister's head, as if she were a post. I saw her knees buckle under the weight as she once again tried to make a joke of it.

As cowardly as I was, I suddenly felt obligated to defend the idea of her life being as sacred as Griffin Porier's.

I remembered what Leo McVicer had told me. "Someday you will box — like me you will have no choice." Why had that made Leo happy? I was now terrified.

I put my hands up. I held them about two feet apart. I had never in my life put my hands up and I stared at them, in front of me, as if they were in themselves two enemies. Behind me stretched the walls of ice and the silent bay where small dark inland islands sat in a meticulous cold and glassy dusk waiting for the warm winds of the southwest to come.

Griffin walked around me, throwing left hooks and staggering me until I went down. I looked up at the crowd, seeing no kindly face except my sister's.

Then, rolling over, I pressed my fingers on the snow and by that rose again to my feet. My tie flapped, and the air was harsh against my lungs as I tasted my blood. My forehead had swollen from a punch, my nose was broken, and blood scattered like red ribbons along my shirt and pants and over the desolate parking lot, indented by a thousand forgotten winter footprints where pages of my essay were caught on specks of swollen ice or disappeared into the last winter light, one with the words "McVicer's company monopolizes all our life" written in a scrawl. The crowd pulsated in and out about us, driving Griffin on with its shouts and palpitations.

I turned my head away when I was hit a fourth time and saw many faces looking at me, and Autumn's face transfixed by my suffering — even though the punches never really hurt at that moment. Then as Autumn ran to protect me, Griffin threw out a left. Before I could stop her the blow glanced off her chin, and she fell. Everyone was silent.

Griffin laughed, turned against me again, and threw a hard right hand. This time I stepped into it and grabbed his fist in my palm. Suddenly and quite strangely I realized a most terrible secret for me to know. I was twice as strong as he. His fist withered in my grip, and he let out a yell and dropped to his knees as if begging me to stop. I hauled him to his feet with my hand, but the pain on his face was unbearable to look at.

So I knew first-hand that what my father had said was right — that every injury done to someone is done again to the perpetrator of that injury; and the only way to lessen its effect is to cultivate "a hardness of heart" against other living beings.

I picked up Autumn, put my arm around her, and turned along the snow path, the snow dotted with specks of my bright red blood.

"I'll get you, you cowardly bastard," Griffin Porier yelled, but the crowd looked at him differently than they had two minutes before.

I went home. Later that night I heard some commotion outside, and someone tossing a bottle. My father lay in bed listening to men as they questioned his courage and asked him to come out and face them and have a drink. It went on for an unbearable length of time.

A man would yell, "Come on out and have a drink," be silent for a moment and then shout again, "Come on out and have a drink!"

Then they advanced on the house, but a pistol shot rang out. Reeling in drunkenness, they ran away. They didn't even stop to pretend they were brave. Another shot was fired from old Jay Beard's pistol. We heard them yelling and a truck driving off.

I began to cry. I wanted to go out and help him. But I did not.

My tie lay in the sink. My mother got up early and dried it, and resewed my pants. My boots, once my father's, eight years old, were shined by Autumn in the morning. And in some dreadful way I knew, because of my strength, what it was like to be the men outside.

TEN

The next night it started to snow, and the snow came down over our small house and the yellow yard, and I thought of my rabbit snares I would check in the morning. I had to kill them because my father refused welfare and we needed to eat. It was always worse when the rabbit was alive because then I would have to find a stick of wood to club it.

My face was bruised and swollen, and Autumn and I sat in the far back room of the house, where the one chaise longue and our few summer things were kept. I looked at her for a long time, and then I said:

"Things will be different from now on — we will never be bothered from now on — I will not allow anything to happen to you from now on. Not a tear from your face will flow —"

At first she said nothing — stupefied, I suppose, at what I was whispering. It was like Adam talking to Eve — I had left my mother and father, left the valley of the Saints, and had been thrust forward into the thorns. There was a sense of myself apart from the wishes of my family.

"Do you believe in hell?" I said.

"Yes."

"Do you believe in heaven?"

"Yes — but not as much as hell," she said, smiling.

"Do you think good people go to church?"

"Yes."

"Does Jay Beard go to church?"

"No! He hates church — he hates the priest. You know that."

"Does the priest protect our family — has he been down to offer comfort? Has he ever said a kind thing about us at mass? Has he ever spoken to us when we went to catechism? Or has he told people to leave Mommie and Daddie alone?"

"No — of course not — he wouldn't come near us!"

"Does Jay Beard protect our family?"

"Yes — with his life, it seems."

"Is that a good thing?"

"Well, I might have self-interest — but I would say offhand yes."

"What do you think of him?" I said.

She thought a moment. Then, "I think he is wise," she said.

"But is he as wise and brave as Dad?" I said, almost trembling.

"I suppose."

"Would you like *me* to become more like Jay Beard?"

"No — like Dad," she said.

"Do you think I could become like Jay Beard?"

"I'm not sure."

I lighted a cigarette. She stared dumbfounded at me. Then I handed it to her. She inhaled and coughed and clutched at her throat in a mocking death throe. I lighted another for myself, and blew the smoke out slowly.

I stood — exercising my grand sense of morality — and I took out of my back jean pocket the heavy Bowie-shaped bone-handled knife with its seven-inch stainless steel blade. I had bought it with the money Rudy Bellanger gave me. I smiled at her when she looked at it.

"Oh," she said. "Will that gut a rabbit?"

"I would someday like to become like Jay Beard — I have to!"

Autumn was silent. Yet I think the thought of freedom suddenly seemed promising to her. I took out a small ring with a small stone and put it on her finger.

"I was going to give this to Penny — well, a girlfriend — but I have no girl — so I will give it to you — this will be our marriage."

"I finally have a boyfriend," she said.

I asked her what she wanted to do. She wanted to be a veterinarian and win the McVicer scholarship and — she blushed — write a book. The McVicer scholarship was worth fifteen thousand dollars.

"McVicer will never give you that scholarship," I said, "but I will pay him back."

Autumn admitted she was scared and stayed in her room whenever she was alone.

"You will never have to do that again," I said. "You will never have to worry anymore — I will go to jail before you are teased again."

The next morning I got up in the cold and went to check my snares as my father set out for mass.

"You go pray — and I'll find us something to eat," I yelled, my breath floating in front of my face.

I found the snow had covered most of the snares but there was a rabbit in one, buried up to his back. The trees were still, and in the hedges I could smell smoke from fires burning in wood stoves up the inlet.

I walked out of the woods, skinned the rabbit, and left it hanging on the back clothesline. I woke Autumn and told her I would find potatoes and carrots and we would have a rabbit stew.

Then I went off to school. I walked into the boys' washroom and saw Griffin Porier there. I stood still, my heart beating a mile a minute — just like the heart of the poor rabbit before I had killed it that morning.

"You touch me again, I will crush your head," I said. "I will kill you — no matter who your uncle is, no matter if I am excommunicated, no matter what happens to me — you will be dead."

He looked at me, smiled weakly, and said, "Oh, sure."

But as I approached him he backed away. It was the first time anyone had ever backed away from me.

Griffin ran from the washroom.

In his run I felt seared into my brain the horrible dishonesty of the universe dressed up in a moral accusation against my father. And I now realized that everything my father trusted — the church, hard work, the saints, the Poriers themselves — was bogus. And in a real way it didn't matter that my father had caused nothing. I should not be so quick to forgive him just because he had caused nothing. Because in another way, his inaction had caused it all — all the misery forced upon us was caused because he elected to be passive. What if he had taken action sooner? If he had fought years before, he would not have left it up to me — or worse, to poor half-crippled Jay Beard. I smelled the pungent hide of the rabbit on my hands — what other child on the river this day, with microwave ovens and video games Autumn and I had never played, had to gut a rabbit for dinner that night? No, those I sat beside, shared my noon hours with, had been a part of the twentieth century for a long while; and would soon become a part of the twenty-first.

We had our stew that night, for I stole both the carrots and the potatoes from the gas bar.

The winter moon bathed the houses in light and the wind was gentle. Spring was coming, a month after it came to most other places. Easter was here. My mom had not lost the child in her belly. I could smell water in the snow and the houses were dim and dark, and the lives in those houses warm and cosy. These were houses of men who had worked for McVicer for years. Their sons and daughters had ordinary ambitions, became lawyers and engineers. There was laughter from those houses, and rock music played from an open window.

What, I asked, had my father ever given my mother? I cursed him. I wanted to fight him. I remembered how Mom told me he walked the highway and back to visit his father in prison without complaint. Had I ever done anything close to that? But, then, rebellion is such a savage against itself, in youth and all men of no consequence.

ELEVEN

On Easter Sunday we went to church. The pane-glass windows shone brightly and the pebbles were bare on the shore. A stiff breeze blew all morning, and our clothes were clean and pressed. After we got home a bit of snow fell, and as happens sometimes in spring, the day turned cold, the ditches froze. Mom brought our clothes in from the line. The wood my father had cut was dwindling.

I went for a walk before dinner. The sky was pale, with floating clouds; and the ditches held forlorn trappings of early spring — bent grasses, bottle labels, used condoms in the field above home, and other signs of the winter ending. The bay was brown and choppy now that the ice was gone, and as I went toward it, feeling somewhat lost under the opening salvo of spring, I found myself in Pit's back field. I was suddenly filled with a fancy — I would have to call it fancy more than an urge or a craving — a fancy to confront Mathew Pit, to boldly go up to him and slap his face. Which with my size and strength at the time might be suicidal. But then, if considering the Machiavellian proposal to be daring rather than cautious, to entice fortune to your side, it could be done, I thought. I always knew that daring was not beyond me. And since we had tried it my father's way, now perhaps we might try it mine. I believed Mat was guilty of blasting the bridge, though I could not prove it. But why in God's name did I have to prove it? They had proved nothing about us. How could anyone think my father a bad man and Mr. Pit a good one? Yet they did.

The day grew colder, and the sound of faraway traffic petered out. It was the day Christ was resurrected into the clouds, or appeared to Mary Magdalene in a form she did not know. It could be *my* resurrection as well if I did this right.

I walked through the short spruce stands, past the dog house, with dog hair caught on a nail, and into their back yard sunken with half-melted ice, the flurries of falling snow making the ground like black pencil streaks on a white scribbler page. I thought of my essay I had never been able to redo, and my almost certain failure this year at school.

I had never been into Pit's yard before, and was surprised at how solitary and unattended the place was. I had expected their lives to be much fuller and happier than ours. Yet their house looked shabbier and more desolate than any I had ever seen, except perhaps for the Voteurs'.

I looked through the hallway window and saw an open door to the dining room, with a bit of light coming from it, and just the edge of a tablecloth on a wood table. This was where Trenton had spent his life, I thought. The last thing he might have done was look from this window at the setting sun.

Right beside me — I touched it with my hand — was a double-bladed axe, old and rusted but still with a strong handle, which was covered in snow. I clutched it as I stood there feeling the snow burn my bare hand. Then Mathew Pit himself came out of the dining room and walked toward the window I crouched under, with his shirt off, his chest and arms tattooed and heavily muscled. He who had destroyed our life stopped, near this window, and looked across to our house. He who had beaten my father, had forced him to drink alcohol (though I could not prove it), laughed at my beautiful sister and coveted my mother.

Easily I could have killed him. (I was strong enough to put the axe through his chest.) He had called my father a coward, but he would never call me the same, I thought. I held the axe. I gulped air and felt dizzy.

The air was turning more bitter and darkness was falling over the trees. I could hear the coyotes begin to yap and round each other up. I tried to think of Mathew with hatred; at what he had said to my mom and my sister and how he had treated my dad. But I could do nothing.

He closed the drapes, and I heard him say, "Cynthia? Is someone here? Why am I alone today?" I realized that though it was Easter Sunday he *was* alone; the resurrection never mattered to him, and his house bore the oppression of that disinterest. I realized that to kill him now would be the most appropriate time. No one was home; and if I covered my tracks, it might be thought to be someone else.

To kill him would betray my father. But not to kill him would be to betray my father. I have deliberated on this moment for years. It has been my life's deliberation. My life would have forever changed if I had had resolve at that moment. My action might have saved us all — Autumn, and my little brother, Percy, about to be born in a shack off Highway 11.

I held the axe, and I counted. I said to myself that if I closed my eyes and saw red spots, as one sometimes does, I would stand up and thrust the axe through the pane. I closed my eyes. There were no red spots. After another long wait, with me shivering and shaking, I heard Mathew walk away. I was angry that I had missed my chance. It was the same as if I had a dangerous bear in my sights and chose not to fire, and watched him waddle away over a hill, knowing that bear might come back to maul my sister.

I stood and ran across the field toward the brook, laughing my head off. If power was so easily attained, there must be something fundamentally the matter with it. One swipe of that axe, powerful or not, would certainly have made my mother's life tolerable, my sister no longer pee the bed, and me happy for the first time. Even my father's appendix might stop acting up.

I came home, and my father and mother and Autumn were at the table with a pink ham. The house was warm. There was a window near the kitchen table, and a window much higher on the far side of the opened room. Under that window was a mantel where Mom placed her knicknacks, and a picture of Autumn at her First Communion (I had taken mine down). Next to the stove was the cot Mom lay upon. Next to that was the back door. Next to the back door was the bathroom door. Dad's books were on shelves everywhere in this room.

To the left of the kitchen table were five small steps to the "upstairs," where our three bedrooms were, not much more than cubbyholes really, which Dad had built on as we grew.

My father was saying grace, and he stopped and looked at me. I smiled and he smiled also. But there was something in his look that said he knew where I had been. The smile, mild and kind, said he knew what I had not done.

I lived in that torment for three weeks. It was coming on to May, and I was lucky enough to earn some money by cleaning the yard about McVicer's store. Perhaps he felt guilty about something. Each time I came home, I saw Mathew in the distance and had a strange desire to kill him. But something happened that prevented it, showing there had been an ongoing conference about us in places we did not know.

Ms. Whyne, receiving much support from altruistic groups, came to "the children's rescue." Jay Beard came to our house to tell us this might come about, a few weeks after Easter, and for Mother to prepare herself for the worst; and that he would act as a character witness whenever he could.

So one night Diedre Whyne came with Constable Morris, who always looked appropriately grave and somewhat put out when he faced my mother, as if her character had let him down. The paperwork was in order; another RCMP officer stood outside with a shotgun in case my father returned some kind of fire.

We were taken. A dozen or more people waited at the top of our lane to watch us leave, and as we were being driven slowly away, they clapped their hands. Autumn went in one direction and I in the other. Mom was six or seven months' pregnant.

Mother went to court and sat listening to Ms. Whyne describe her as semi-literate and our family as poverty-stricken, her husband suspected in a series of crimes that, when drinking, he freely admitted to.

From the transcript of these hearings I learned what officialdom thought of us:

"Their mother is a woman who has lived with a violent-prone individual named Sydney Henderson, who himself has come from an abusive home. He has seen a life of violence and has often been violent himself. Elly is pregnant again, and has no means to take care of her other two children. She is childlike in her ideas, kind in her attitude, and has endured one terrible pregnancy after the other because of her husband's religious belief, suffering miscarriage and hemorrhage.

"There is a bullet hole in the wall of their house, and they live in constant fear since the death of Trenton Pit, a boy Sydney Henderson was influencing. Lyle is fourteen, just the age when children need strong parental guidance. His sister, Autumn Lynn, is an albino child of thirteen who is tormented at school. She has started her menses and is easily led. If we do not rescue them now they will not be rescued."

Christ, even I could believe that.

I was sent to live with Hanny Brown and his wife, and Autumn stayed in Chatham with Ms. Whyne in Covenant House, a place Ms. Whyne ran with government funds. The Voteur girls had stayed there, and relatives of theirs from down river. It was called a safe house for female children who have been abused. That Autumn Lynn had not been abused did not seem to matter, because she seemed a prime candidate for abuse.

Just the amount of stuff I was given by my foster parents induced a surreal feeling of the betrayal of my parents. Hanny Brown took me to movies, and with Autumn and Ms. Whyne we went to the Atlantic Exhibition, rode the Tilt-a-Whirl and the Octopus, ate candy apples and cotton candy — while my father in his old blue suit pants and Mother in her maternity dress suffered in silence in the scorching summer heat, with the black woods and chirping frogs all around them.

I hated myself for a candy apple, but I could not stop eating it. In Hanny Brown's house, I found an old fishing knapsack. I stole what I could to take home — baking soda, salt, ketchup, sugar, coffee, tea. I hid the knapsack in my room. One day, checking the sack, I found a bag of flour placed there, and going down to supper that evening could not look my hosts in the face.

Ms. Whyne shared the duties of Covenant House with her friend Dawn Fleager, and they were subsidized by government money. Their relationship was incorporated as strange celebration into small-town civility toward non-conformism at that time. That is, Diedre was at the height of her power, and I had none at all. Her mistake, as well as mine, was to think her power would last. That those very conformists who now hated my father would not someday in some way, seeing their chance, turn their turret tanks on her.

What Diedre wanted was to help Mother in some kind of self-aware-ness course. The idea that Diedre was self-aware and my mother was not has often struck me as hilarious. My mother, however, said she would travel once a week to the Bowie school to learn about nutrition and health care for herself and her children. I know this was not really what Diedre had intended, but it did work in my mother's favour.

On September 7 I came back to Hanny Brown's house after fish-ing. I walked into the porch at four o'clock. Two men and a woman were standing in the front room. I didn't know who the men were; they both wore suits and had beaming faces with startled eyes, and rather fine rings on their fingers. They were from the provincial office of the Department of Social Services. They were Ms. Whyne's bosses and oversaw all her affairs at Covenant House.

Ms. Whyne was with them. She had a striking face, a pronounced jaw. She had the type of face that as she got older its traits of social cruelty became more pronounced; traits always hidden in our culture just under the surface like the effects of sin on a picture of Dorian Gray. She smiled at me, with a kind of unfelt affection, and asked me to go pack my things. I came down without the knapsack filled with stolen staples, but Hanny Brown went up and got it for me. And as I was leaving, bright tears burned in his wife's eyes.

Ms. Whyne took my hand as I walked to the car. I said nothing against Ms. Whyne, and I held her hand. Part of me was by now a social slave. I would squeeze the slave out of myself, as Chekhov said, but not for a while. They had made me love cookies and cakes and wanting to belong, and to lie to myself, to believe they were brighter than me or Autumn or my father, to accept reprimand without question. No — I had always wanted to belong; and my father had prevented it. By belonging I betrayed him; and so too did Autumn.

Still, my mother had come through. Thirty-three and exhausted, she had cleaned and scrubbed. Dad had redone two rooms and had taken a job the unemployment department had found for him — a job picking up garbage. They bought a new crib. They swallowed all the little pride they had left. But we were going home.

Four or five months later Diedre Whyne found work in another department. She had given her all to our case, had worked on us for fourteen years. She pulled back her divisions and retreated into the hills. We felt we would never see her again.

Percy, our brother, whom I had told the Virgin Mary I did not care lived, was born. I came home to find an infant in the crib, covered in a blue coverlet, with a sudden burst of sunlight falling on his bald head. His eyes were closed, his little fists were clenched.

I ran to find Autumn. She was sitting out back on our one lawn-chair, near the fir trees smoking a cigarette — her face, I realized, suddenly beautiful, and her life, as far as most people were concerned, already damned.

TWELVE

Well over two years passed with Dad collecting garbage for Elliot Pearson. When I came from school I would see him hanging on to the back of the five-ton truck, or throwing garbage up into the box. He did this methodically and like an artist, his tie flying back over his shoulder. He wore his suit. I tell you this not because I think it unnatural for a man who lived like my father to wear a suit collecting garbage; it was as frayed and worn as the garbage he collected, so at some level it was appropriate.

Dad would hold on to the side of the truck with one arm, allowing his other arm and his leg to lean out over the pavement as the truck moved along in the drizzle of snow. And the snow fell. Our river was dredged and opened by ice breakers all winter, and huge paper ships came into port, from Europe and the States.

However, with us, it was as always. And it didn't seem to matter to Dad or to anyone at the unemployment office that Isabel Young had told Mom that Sydney's I.Q. might be near 170. God, if it took that I.Q. to get a job as a garbage collector for Elliot Pearson, I was in trouble.

I fought every day and I stole. When I fought, my father was never again mentioned to me. And people knew I carried a knife. When I stole from McVicer's store, I was respected and feared by those my age. I would steal diapers for little Percy and nylons for my mom. McVicer knew this, for later that year he offered me a job sorting work pants and shirts two days a week.

"You'll be able to buy something for yer family — who knows — diapers, maybe — or who knows — nylons for yer mom —"

What I did buy — what I ran to buy, what I rejoiced in buying — was contacts and a wig for Autumn Lynn.

One day I saw in a small field hidden from our house two older boys with my sister. She was laughing, and smoking a joint, and one kissed her — and one put his hand between her legs.

I did nothing, because those boys had given me my first bottle of wine. So in this time of our acceptance, the other way to be a slave reared its head. I, and Autumn, were considered "one of them." Others made "allowances" for my father. And as long as I made these same allowances (which didn't seem like much) I would be included.

I accepted the allowances, which said my father was guilty. One day I overheard a remark intended for me to overhear: "He's not responsible for what his old man did — his old man's a pervert — he's a good lad —"

It was a profound moment, one that told me that I — and Autumn — no longer had to own up to who they thought my father was, and that I could disown him like a fleck of lint on the new shirt he had bought me with his last paycheque. I tried to fight this moment, to go to my father and beg forgiveness, to go to my mother and ask for her blessing, but I saw how easy it would be for me now if I went along with them. This is why Autumn lay in the field with her panties off.

I knew this now. I told Autumn what I was thinking.

"I love Dad. But look what Dad did to us," I said, "and why we are in these scrapes. But we don't have to be — you and I will bolt above all of that — now people think you're pretty — well you are, Autumn — but you use it to *your* advantage, not theirs — if you know what I say." I could not look at her when I said this.

I had bought Autumn things to make her look pretty, because I was secretly ashamed of her, and she knew this as well, and this is why her body meant nothing to her. So that very week I gave them to her. I bought her a black wig, and I had her go to the optometrist the next Tuesday and be fitted for contacts. I paid for both of these things by working for McVicer on the weekend and by trapping martin and mink. There was a good spot for mink farther up Arron Brook, and I tell you I had discovered it by myself.

By Wednesday she looked prettier than I could have imagined. This was what the world continually asked us to do. To betray my father, my mother, to leave their side, to let them die alone.

195

THIRTEEN

It was February of 1986 when the letter came. I brought it to the house, thinking to myself that it might be a letter of glad tidings, something to do with Dad's complete exoneration.

All of us gathered about the table, and I postured my indifference to what the letter would say (while my heart raced). But exoneration of any kind was not the case. It was a letter saying that my father and mother owed some seventeen thousand dollars in back taxes plus interest, from the time he was in business digging wells. My father had not filed taxes because he had in his entire life earned so little he had no idea about taxes, no matter how well read he was. He was now penalized for not filing his income taxes during a three- or four-year period. It was done, as all things are done today, by computer from Ottawa. The local tax department had not even handled the case.

Father had to travel back and forth to town seeing people about his taxes. Jay Beard drove him. The clerk told Dad to write a letter to the senior collection officer, which he did. He waited four weeks. The letter he received verified that they had put a lien on his house, and they would expect payment within the year or they would determine the reason for non-compliance. That they would obtain securities, monitor his accounts to ensure commitments were maintained; they would also liaise with Sheriff Bulgar, and other parties if need be, and maintain the *integrity* of the tax legislation.

Neither my mother nor I understood this language, nor did my father understand it well. He only told me that he did not have a bank account, so what would they monitor? I knew that for him this was a staggering amount of money. A Ms. Hardwicke at the local tax office told my mother and father that if it were up to her, she would relieve them of this burden.

"I thought it *was* up to you," my father said.

"It was computed," Ms. Hardwicke said. "The charge came out of the new profiling we do by computer. The computer found your earnings, evaluated a fine, and compounded it because of penalty. It is up to the senior officer to dismiss the burden."

"Well, can the senior officer do so?" Mother asked.

"No. I have your file — it was sent to me. I can only encourage you to pay it. But as I say, it is up to the senior officer — do you understand? She has many backlogged cases and is new to the department."

Dad came back from visiting Ms. Hardwicke one day in March and told us that in spite of him conveying how little we had, the lien was not only on our home but had been extended to the few scrub acres we owned, so that our mature stand of wood, which he had hoped to cut, could be taken if we cut it.

"Will we be forced to sell the house?" my mother asked (as if anyone would buy our house).

"No — I won't sell what I have — but if I cut the wood and sold it, they would claim the profit."

We sat around the table. For the first time I felt that their eyes were on me, as if they were looking to me for an answer. And so I gave them one.

"Move everything out of the house — and take your chainsaw to it — cut the walls down — cut the wood, burn it — leave this place for somewhere else — for some other country —"

Autumn looked at me and grinned.

My father gave me a startled, remarkable look. Then he smiled at Mother. He had another scenario. Oh boys, his was a great plan, let me tell you!

My father's ingenious plan was not to fight anyone, not to chop the house up, but to *comply* with the tax department's wishes.

"I will leave for the powerline they are putting through up north of the province. I will live there and earn my way out of this debt — I've lived in camps before, and I can again. There is good money."

He went on to say it would take him two or three years to free us of this burden but he was physically and mentally fit. He told me he would send half of his pay to us, keep a little, and send the rest to the tax department.

"I've always enjoyed a spartan life. When I grew up I had very little — but I did not lack for anything. I fished trout and kept a chicken or two. When my father couldn't find steady work, he hunted. I spent extra money on books. At seventeen I was reading Euripides."

"Who's Euripides?" Autumn asked, for she was reading everything she could, and wanted to be a writer.

"An American," my mother answered. Father looked at me cautiously. In her gentle heart Mother always thought everyone important was an American. My father once said, "Well so do they — so there is no harm."

"I will pay it all," he said now. And he told me I would have to become the head of the house. I already felt that I was.

His plan was absurd, I told him. Still, I knew that his going would leave me freer and relieve our family of any more serious trouble.

"It's Mathew Pit's fault," I blurted. "If it takes forever I will crush him and Connie Devlin under me!"

Autumn looked at me, and her eyes closed shyly because she did not believe what I was saying. Besides, she always felt I was bringing her bad luck when I spoke this way.

My father only sighed.

"You're right about one thing," he said. "It is strange how my life has turned out. It is strange the power that has been used against me. It is strange that save for Isabel Young and Jay Beard no one has helped us. But if you saw what I saw in my childhood, you would know why I do and say as I do."

This was the first indication that there ever was a reason behind his logic. Though I believed he was using his childhood to shirk his responsibility to *our* childhood. Though I had found out that indifference to him was the safest way for Autumn and me, I was still determined to kill someone in revenge. I told him he did not have the right to mention Jay Beard's name, because Jay Beard was brave and stood his ground. I told him that Jay Beard often came to check on us in the middle of the winter.

"I know that, son," Sydney said.

"Then you should be ashamed of yourself," I yelled.

The next afternoon I went to see Mr. McVicer. He was sitting in his office at the rear of his house. There were two phones on his desk. This impressed me more than anything else. Behind him was a topographical map of our region — Arron Brook, of our woodlots, his land, his mill, and all the families that worked for him. I stood before him, in an old pair of miner's boots and torn winter coat and a toque with a hole in the top.

"I need a loan," I said. My legs were trembling.

He stared at me. He didn't say a thing. In a glass case on his left were four or five rifles. On his right was a picture of him in a canoe, flyfishing at the Arron Brook Forks — the place of destitution for our family. He stared at me so long I began to hang my head, but I managed not to.

"I need a loan," I said.

"I heard you," he said, biting on his pipe and talking through his teeth. The phone rang but he didn't answer it. He stared at me instead. "What do you need — I've been thinking — I pay you twenty-five on the weekends — you haven't bought a thing for yerself yet — you have taken good care of Autumn. So I'm thinking you want something — a rifle — a fishing rod — how much?"

"Seventeen thousand dollars," I said.

The phone rang again and still looking at me he picked it up. He listened, then said, without raising his voice:

"I don't give a fiddler's fuck how you get that road opened, Abby, the plows are there, and you open the cocksucker by tomorrow — I want in there by tomorrow night. I have equipment in there."

He slammed down the phone. And turned his gaze on me again.

"That's a lot of money," he said.

"Yes," I said.

"How could you pay it back?"

"I would go to work —"

"Where?"

I held my breath and then I said, "I bet I could open up that road for you."

He smiled, finally.

"Oh, I know you could — in ten years — but not now. I'll tell you what I will do — you get through high school, and you come to see me — and you will never have to worry about a job again. Now I'm no Prof. David Scone or any of his ilk — *they who teach and don't know* — I don't care for learning — but I care for knowledge. You give me the knowledge that you can get through school — that you can be more than your dad — who I never disliked, mind you — and I'll pay you thirty thousand dollars the first year you work for me — that's thirty thousand dollars when you are eighteen. More than that, I will see to Autumn's university."

I stared. I could say nothing. I saw on the map behind his head the small thick wood where I trapped my mink marked in red with my name and the number 15. That's how many mink I had taken that year. He knew everything!

"Best I can do," he said, kindly. "Best anyone will ever do for you."

FOURTEEN

The next morning I walked to school with the ambition to graduate, and struck a teacher, Mr. Neile from Chatham, who had just suspended Cheryl Voteur. She had come to me for help. No one else would have done it. It was the only thing my conscience allowed. My punch grazed his face, and he half-dragged me to the door of the principal's office. I saw blood on his mouth. I truly felt ashamed. But when the principal mentioned my father as the root of this problem, I told them I would never ever go back.

That night my father tried to speak to me, but I would not listen.

"At least I'm not gutless — at least I fight back — but you — everyone still thinks you done it." My eyes blurred with tears, as Percy watched me.

"I think Trenton's death was preordained," my father said.

"Christ almighty — for what?"

"To set in motion my test and to in the end be blessed. I am far the better for it now — and I don't want to be the better for it on the back of some poor child's death. But there are multiple factors involved in someone's life — and it had to be. I have been tempered by fire — just like I knew I would be that day on the church roof. I know what is owed us and what has been paid, and I say to you, Lyle, that much is owed us and little has been paid. That is far better than the other way around. Have much owing you, instead of owing much!"

For the first time, I did not want my father in the house. A wind was blowing from the bay; the temperature had dropped. Autumn had gone out to her school play rehearsal. It was time to state my case.

"Take this," I said, showing him the hunting knife I had bought with the money Rudy Bellanger gave me, having hidden it under my bed and in my sweater for over two years, "and protect yourself — instead of getting Jay Beard to do it."

"No —" He laughed. I couldn't stand that he laughed at me, but now I realize he laughed not at me but at himself and the terrible way he had failed me.

"Do you really think that the truth matters?" I asked. "They know *nothing* about you. They care nothing about you. But they would kill you." I was shaking.

"You'll get up to the powerline, they will find out who you are, and the men won't want to help you. You'll get in trouble and die! Christ!"

"I will die no matter." Father smiled. "And so will they. There is nothing I can do. I cannot change anyone. For me to go to McVicer and say, 'Mr. McVicer, you have treated my father immorally — for he scouted this land for you in 1938 — you once tried to escape paying for the clean-up of the Oyster River fire — and have balked at your duty toward my family and fought the environmental study. You hired Gerald Dove to use him, and do not want him to tell you the truth. Elly did not rob you, and I could no more harm a child than destroy a bridge I took pride in working on.' What if I did say that? It is what I know, yet I have no right to force others to feel it."

"Because of Trenton's death you have turned in one direction, Mathew and Cynthia in the other," I said. "They are getting more and more powerful and you are getting weaker and weaker. Mat hangs about with the Sheppards, who are as bad as he is."

"Well, that has nothing to do with me," Sydney said. "It has to do with Mathew himself. He has set out on a course quite different from mine. What do you want, son? For me to join them in order to be safe — or perhaps with that knife you intend something? If they destroy us they destroy themselves — not one breath of air comes against us that does not harm them as well — if you have read *The Forged Coupon* by Tolstoy you know this."

"You are a fool!" I shouted.

He nodded like an accused criminal told to stand on scales next to the sandbags that would snap his neck in the morning. I think my calling him a fool hurt him that much. He had a right not to expect that from me.

I told him he was mean to my mother, and he had done nothing for us, and people were right to suspect him. He may as well have fucked Cynthia and have beaten my mother for the good he was! I told him I could take care of the house. I asked him to leave to go up north to put up the powerline like he said he would.

"Why shouldn't you go? As long as you're here there is trouble — as soon as you go everything will be fine — I get along with everyone. And your books — what good do they do — nothing," I yelled, "not a damn thing. But look, if someone hurts us again — look what I got for them." I flashed my knife again, and he tried to grab it from me. I yanked it away and blood spurted from his palm.

"You don't understand," I cried. "Mom will die, I know. Autumn is alone, she tries to be brave but still she is frightened — and she is already getting finger fucked by boys because she doesn't think she is pretty enough to have a real date. People make fun of her. Why do you think they used her picture in the paper — to show we were *inbred*, to have everyone laughing at us — and she knows this — she does. And it's McVicer's fault she is a squinty-eyed albino!"

My father shook his head as if pleading with me to stop speaking, while he wrapped a cloth around his hand. But I did not. I could not. I believed I had to tell him the truth.

"She's a damn albino — that's why her picture was used — and I have to lug her about everywhere and try to keep the fingers off her pussy, do you understand?"

Father shook his head again, shyly, blood seeping through the cloth. His eyes were shining. But he was not looking at me — but behind me. I turned and saw Autumn. Autumn, who I thought had left for her school play practice, had heard what I had said. Autumn, whom I loved. Autumn, whom I would die for!

She began to smile and then her face crumpled into a picture of sorrow like I have never seen in my life again. She turned away from us and went into her room. I saw how her body flinched horribly under her costume, as if her very body was desperately trying to regain its lost dignity.

We looked over and Mom was crying. She kept telling me to stop fighting or they would take us away again. It seemed she cried because of what I had said about Autumn. Her face crumbled too. But my father knew about Autumn, and had kept it silent; not only because of Mom's feelings but because of Autumn herself, who he felt was afflicted. Even as her father he did not judge her. Yet the world — the goddamn world was tearing us apart.

"Ask him," I said. "Ask him what he did on the bridge — maybe it is all true — maybe they are right. Maybe me being crazy and Autumn being easy comes because he is nuts."

I left the house. I walked in circles most of the night, and the longer I walked, the sadder I became. I could not get Autumn's smile out of my mind, or my mother's crying. What did it matter what Autumn had done? Who was I? My father, beset by problems and as good a man as I have met, did not judge.

With the red dawn over the tin roof of our shack, the smell of heavy smoke in the air, I went back inside. Autumn was in her small room asleep in her play costume. Mother was asleep in her bed. On the table there was a note:

> "Dear Lyle:
> "You are right of course. All my life I have been a burden to those who see things more clearly than I. I was a burden to my father, and now I am a burden to you and little Autumn. I think I can find work — I will stay and work until our debt is paid. Then things might get better. Take care of yourself and Autumn and Percy, and be kind to whoever comes to our door. Love, Dad."

My father left just before dawn and walked to Ferry Road, and got a drive in a truck with Bliss Hanrahan, the trucker Mathew Pit had punched that night long ago. It was the first time Bliss spoke to my father about things that bothered him. He told my father that the only person who might have turned off the security lights the night of Trenton's death was Connie Devlin. This had bothered Bliss Hanrahan now for two years.

My father said nothing.

The second thing Hanrahan spoke about was the letters written to Mom and Dad. A group of people at Polly's Restaurant had done this as a joke, he told my father, for they were sure my father was guilty.

"They meant nothing by it — you know what they can get up to for a joke around here," Bliss said. But now after all this time, it seemed that my father might not have been responsible, and the joke should be exposed for what it was.

Bliss was an average man. He kept looking at my father trying to devise some idea. And he wished to be cautious, and did not want to be overly sympathetic. Still, he knew Connie and Mat, and he also knew that the letters were written by others. That he had not come forward with either piece of information made him now less reticent about my father's innocence; and a guilt tugged at him.

My father was let off in late afternoon, north of Campbellton along a stretch of interconnecting woods roads, and walked until dark. There he found the camp and the foreman, and was hired the next day.

Later, Hanrahan spoke to an RCMP officer, just in passing, about these strange things. This officer's name was John Delano. He had been following the events from afar, interested in them because all did not seem right. He placed a phone call that night, and finally set in motion events that would change our life.

There were times after Dad left when our lane was frozen stiff, and we were all waiting for him to come home, and Christmas was nearing. I would then remember the sunlight on his glasses when he spoke to me and I would be transported into the land of his gentle sorrow — a sorrow like brilliant old wine, a sorrow that comes with knowledge and wisdom. That is the closest I've ever come to knowing my father. I do not think that when in happier times he spoke of a gentle life as we picked blueberries in the field — spoke about the ideas that encapsulated both him and my mother — that he had ever thought (and why in God's name should he?) he would be forced to literally live it with the excruciating balancing act of a man on a tightrope in the wind. But then again, in some way — don't we all? I found Tolstoy's *The Forged Coupon* he had taken out for me to read and placed it back on the shelves of books without opening it. I vowed not to ever read another book.

For an instant, a split second in the dawn air, I felt free to pursue my dreams. Yes, and they were so different from my father's I almost cried.

FIFTEEN

Dad left before Percy was three. I carry a picture of Percy on his third birthday; Dad's chair is empty, so he must have been gone.

I tried for a time to be Percy's father. I took him for walks, in his wagon, and we would stop along our lane to collect his bugs. Our lane was overgrown with green whip grass, and surrounded by high trees that waved above our heads in the summer breezes.

Percy had four jars filled with grasshoppers and crickets, caterpillars and snails. He'd wait for me to come home from fishing, jar in hand. He'd open the front door and run to give me a hug.

"You should not wander anywhere alone, Percy," I told him one day. "You might tumble in the brook."

I would bring the wagon around and Percy would tell me he needed his lucky bow tie. We would search the house for it. A red snap-on bow tie. Then, bow tie secured, jar in hand, he would sit in the wagon, his feet in red rubber boots.

My mother had almost lost her life giving birth to him. She had bled and her afterbirth was hard to issue. To the day three months later, Cynthia Pit's child, Teresa May, was born. She also was a child of sorrow, had a bad heart, and Mathew and Cynthia were at the hospital in Moncton many times while the little girl was examined and re-examined, always dressed impeccably and with pearl stud earrings. Most everyone, I think, except Gladys, knew Teresa to be

Rudy Bellanger's daughter. Or maybe she did know by the time the child had her third birthday.

Percy and Teresa, in spite of their family histories, were like brother and sister from the start. Nor could Autumn or I help but love the little girl Percy did.

I constantly worried about the way Percy would wander by himself. One day, fearing he had drowned, I went along the old smelt path and found him sitting on a stump, his hands folded, looking at the leaves budding on the trees above him, his mouth slightly opened as if he was speaking to himself, or singing.

Another day, when I was pulling him in the wagon, he asked me if I was going away.

"Of course not, Percy." I stopped the wagon. He looked up at me and shielded his eyes from the sunlight. His face was calm. Yet my answer did not convince him.

"I have a deep feeling in my heart that soon you are going away," he whispered.

I started pulling the wagon again. "Oh, Percy, that's not true — Daddy has gone away to work — but that's not so bad, he will come home again. You shouldn't worry about these things."

The wagon stopped with a sudden jerk and one of the back wheels began to wobble, so I bent down and hammered it back into place with a rock.

"I think I will go away some day, too," Percy sighed. "But don't tell Mom. It'll make her sad."

He rubbed his eyes, because sunlight was in them. The afternoon shadows lengthened, and at a dusty warm place on the lane between two large pines, sunlight filtered down, and there in that patch of sun stood Autumn with her plastic book bag, waiting for us.

"Hello," Percy called.

"Big Percy," Autumn shouted, and waved, and she walked out of the filtering light and became a visible part of us. That day was the first time I realized that she was or would be beautiful. I had never known that she could be. She walked with us to the house.

We had a comfortable house by then, with a small greenhouse off the kitchen that made it feel like summer, even when there was six feet of snow over our back-yard trees. Jay Beard had built this for Mom the spring Dad left. And beyond the upstairs window, there was a view of the bay and lower Arron Brook. There was wood panelling on the walls and checkered drapes my mother made in the den. The wood stove was new, and our little oil furnace heated the house well.

But more important, we were not bothered now by anyone, because my father was away.

Like Dad, I went fishing in Arron Brook. And as I explored this vast area of bog and forest I would take Percy and Autumn with me; but Autumn was frightened in the woods, having no sense of direction — so I was honourbound to stay with them when we went anywhere off the road.

One day Mom said in a strange tone I had never heard before — it seemed to no more come from her than it had from the wind: "Lyle, you have to take care of your brother — and sister — do you understand?"

"Of course, Mom."

"Your father is away, and we are alone — do you understand?"

"Yes, Mom."

"Good." She smiled and smoothed her dress, and went inside and closed the door. Her voice sounded like the trees waving over my head, or the clouds moving, and there was a moment when it seemed she was no longer there.

It was now June. The hollows were filled with old leaves, the sun was out, the lanes were filled with dry mud. At night the sky was like building blocks of eternity — the stars were everywhere. Up on the road McVicer's men were at work repaving a stretch, and every day I took Percy up the lane in the wagon to watch them on the rollers and await my father's return. (I knew Dad wasn't coming, but Percy was never convinced.) Then after a while Percy would sigh and say:

"I guess he isn't coming home today."

"No, not today."

One day in late June, Percy and I had a game of marbles in a dirt hole at the back of the house. It was Percy's marble pot, near a patch of grass called the lumpy ground. He would sit there whenever we were away and watch for us. Or he and Scupper Pit, Trenton's old dog, would lie side by side and stare at the sky, surrounded by dandelions and bees. Once he made his mom a daisy chain that she wore about her neck.

After that game I got my rod, and we walked to the field and down the road to the brook.

Percy carried his marbles and his picnic with him. We met Autumn coming down the lane, and she dropped her book bag and joined us. I kept walking farther up the brook, over windfalls and wild stingers, and they followed me. When I came to the place I was going to fish, I waited for them, and threw a small lean-to together for them.

"Where is the way back?" Autumn said.

"Up through the swale there," I said.

"Up there?" Autumn asked. I looked to where she was pointing.

"No — if you go up there you will get lost. I said there —" And I pointed again to my right. Autumn, whether she understood or not, said nothing more.

Percy was holding Autumn's hand, and she was covered in burdocks and kept swatting away flies. Percy sat down and unwrapped his sandwich. As long as Autumn and Percy were together and could see me, they would not be frightened.

Anyway, I don't know if it was some idea that I was through with them taking advantage of me, or that I was angry with my mom, but that day I moved away from both Percy and Autumn and crossed the roaring stream.

I crossed the stream. I left them alone.

There was a pool farther down, along a stretch of the stream that had a gravel bank, a doff of warm sun upon it. I knew there were big trout lying there. I had seen them at this time last year, at dusk one evening when I was coming home.

The earth was still damp. Birds were sitting on the branches flitting away — and I forgot about the time. I knew I was committing an act of dishonour by leaving my brother and sister. But it was like all acts in youth, both thoughtless and somewhat intentional.

For my thought might have been something like this: "What if I do go and leave them? It'll give them some spunk — that's what they need. I have spunk, surely they need some too. It is a hard world when you are born without protection."

And that made me feel not like their older brother but more like their master. They did not know that I felt that way. I was their older brother who loved them, and yet this was the game I was now playing. They did not know I was playing a game, exercising a moral thought or judgment upon them.

The day was hot, but the water cool, and the sun played on the refreshing rip of water just south of the gravel bar. Beyond that rip was an old log where I knew there were big trout. The trout of my youth. The trout of my youth are forever gone.

I had no waders. Waders at that time seemed to me to be for rich Americans — and even rich Canadian sports I called Americans at that time.

I stepped into the water, and with my line wearing the hook and bobbin, I waited. I was in a bad position to land a fish — I would have to cross again and try to haul it up on the beach. And as I was thinking this, I felt the pull — later on, when I was older, I could tell the difference instantly between a trout and a fish — by fish I mean salmon — by the way they pulled. The pull with a trout — even the ravenous ones are somewhat less intense. But it was on and it was a big trout. It wasn't a sea run but a beautiful big brown trout that rolled and rolled and sank my bobbin — I was too excited and I pulled — and pulled. And then perhaps the worst feeling that anyone is ever to have — the line went limp. It was as if I had been cheated out of pay.

Still and all — I had lost it but I knew at that moment I was a fisherman.

Also — I didn't mind losing that fish. In fact, there was always something strange about getting one trout. But it was more complex than that — it wasn't just the idea of one fish on a string making you look derelict, with your knees muddy and pants soaked. It was also the idea that I must pay observance to an apprenticeship — the apprenticeship of life that none had taught me.

I spent the rest of the day looking over my bobbin and line, setting them just right and casting into that rip, letting the bobbin move in the laconic deep current toward the log. But nothing more happened. No other fish attended me. And then it was falling dark, and I was way out upon a rather opulent log — I don't know how I had crossed the stream.

That was when I suddenly realized it — *the children.* I had been gone for hours. I had let my mother down.

In the dark I rushed back through the woods. If I move my hair I can show the remnant of a scar. It was dark and I could hardly see — I had my rod and tackle box with me. I also was secretly frightened of bears now. I had seen two before, and now it was dark.

The night held a soft warmth in the spruces. What sickened me was this — my response to the *feeling* I had had earlier in the day when, unknown to them, I *bullied* them into being alone by saying to myself that it would give them spunk. It was for this cringing feeling of power that I held the greatest anger now. It was the cringing feeling of power of people like Mathew Pit. So now I knew it. I began to understand what my father had been fighting all his life. Not that power was not in him, but that, like all mankind, it *was.* But he fought it!

I heard the slap of a beaver tail to my left. All was still, and then suddenly a great black shadow appeared in front of me, a huge animal moving just beyond my reach.

I went into the stream, at the worst place possible, and found myself up to my waist in high water with the moose no more than three feet away. I ran from it, so that I lost my balance and went under completely. I believed (for Arron Brook filled with fickle eddies and hidden undertows is a deadly brook) I would drown and never see my parents or my siblings again.

The moose ignored my ignorance, and just trying to stay out of my way went on across the bar, a great beast and was lost on the other side. The trees were in that warm gloom of a late-spring night.

I reached the little lean-to. But they were not there. Only silence and the pulse of my heart in my ears. I saw Percy's sneaker tracks alongside Autumn's leading directly into the swale. Inside that bog and tall grass they would soon lose sight of, and not be able to hear, the brook. It was the one place I did not want them to go.

I let the blackflies light upon me as if penance was needed, watched them suck at my sunburned arms, and then went up the warm and shadowy hill looking for a sign of my children (for this is how I thought of them). I searched the pathway that led to our small house, and then turned right, through the ghastly burned-over stumps, from where our area got its name, all looking like spectres from some terrible civil war battle. *The Wilderness*, perhaps. I called out to them, and every tree seemed to stare back dumb-founded at me.

"How did you let this happen — where are your children?"

I was sixteen years old, and I had done a disreputable thing that my father never would.

"All is madness without love." This is what I heard, in the gentle late-spring wind. It was exactly what my father said to me when he grabbed hold of the knife I had showed him that night. The blood was so red that had dripped on the floor. He looked up at me in terrible tenderness.

"Lyle," he said, his face white.

And what had I said?

"You fool — goddamn fool — cut your hand now, no-nothin' fool — I never —"

At that moment my father looked pleadingly at my mother.

"I have failed everyone," he said. "Constable Morris was right —
you are too beautiful to be stuck with me."

Elly, who still had her suitcase with things to take to Saint John on
a trip we never made. And too, why had she stayed with my father
when all others had cast him away — was it pride? Or stubbornness
or folly? I'll tell you what, it was worse than pride, folly, or duty. It was
done — it had to have been done — for love.

Until I was walking through the ghostly remnants above Arron
Brook I had forgotten those lines. I had simply remembered turning
and seeing Autumn. But now those moments returned to me.

"All is madness without love." And my father had not said it. *My
mother had.*

I had lost her Percy and I sat crying and cursing God. I told God
that I would kill myself if Percy died. If He didn't want a suicide on
His hands He had better shape up and give Percy back! I knew I had
told myself — no, told the Virgin Mary! — I didn't care if the child
was born — and now He had taken me up on it.

I turned back and walked toward home to tell Mother. When I got
home the porch light was on. Mother was out. *She must have heard and
gone to look for them.*

I panicked. I could not think clearly enough to grab a flashlight
and go into the woods again. I went into my father's room. What had
I ever accomplished in my life except to harm others? I held the knife
to my throat, closed my eyes. (It would be, you see, my sense of
honour. I pictured people crying over me, seeing finally my great
tragic scope.) I heard a cough upstairs. I turned almost hysterically
and climbed the stairs.

Autumn was asleep in her bed, her few dolls set up about the room
as if to protect her, her white dress hanging in the closet, her small
shoes covered in mud on the mat, a book by Turgenev lying face up
on the bed. Her nightgown was opened and her small left breast was
visible in the light. To me she would probably become the most beautiful woman on the river. It usually took her an extra forty minutes
to get home from school, because of Darren Voteur waiting to follow

her. Her excesses with other boys did not diminish his love for her, and there was no way to shake him unless she walked across the highway and travelled along the ditch so she would not be seen. This was a predicament issued by the decree of poverty. Her poverty. Poverty I could not cure, nor God want to. Darren himself was caught in it — he could have no one else — but he thought perhaps he could have her. Worse was the fact that there was a moment when he might have *had* her. The moment had passed, and he couldn't forget it. So he followed her, at a hundred yards, in the forlorn embrace of unrequited love, and waited near the mailbox until darkness and squalls of cold drove him home.

Sometimes he would come to the house, sit with Mom at the kitchen table, sometimes for hours.

Thinking of this I gently covered her breast, turned, and went into our room.

Percy was lying face down in his bed in our room, his fists clenched about some wild flowers he had picked. He coughed in his sleep again and, turning to me suddenly, smiled.

SIXTEEN

In the next eighteen months I got into three fights with those I accused of having partaken in the vigilantism against my dad.

I was brought to juvenile hall just before the Christmas break. Mom and Autumn and Percy came along, Autumn's face painted like rouge on a porcelain doll.

The day I was brought up I chanced to see Penny Porier. She was in town for a doctor's appointment with her father and mother. Her father gave me a glance, and in that glance the whole weight of the roadway's scorn was distributed on my shoulders. Her mother held me longer in her gaze, wearing her mink stole with the mink eyes embedded in it.

These looks infused me with the condemnation neighbours had for me. Autumn whispered in my ear that Penny's mother looked mortified to be seen with us, as if common decency should prevent us acknowledging them in front of decent town people.

"So let's not acknowledge them," Autumn whispered. Autumn saying that if Leo McVicer had told them to treat my mother with respect they would have fawned the ground, and, as Autumn said, "licked my real white bum."

I was at that moment ashamed of Autumn with her apple-painted cheeks and her hanging dress. I was more ashamed of my sports jacket with the pockets torn, and a bit of leather saver showing in the winter sun. Penny walked away, covering her face with her white rabbit muff.

Percy was bewildered when the prosecution called me a ruffian, and I realized for the first time how much both my brother and sister looked up to me; how both had come to support me.

Still, my family's lack of influence and power seemed a testimony of their *love* for me as we sat in that dreary place. I could not tell the court that my fights were in search of those men who had beaten my dad, those shadows that had formed about our house at night, with Jay Beard seated on a stump. Or that by my fights I had solved nothing.

The judge told me that he had no reason to dislike me but wondered if perhaps I did not dislike myself, and that I had become what was considered a nuisance to all decent people down river.

Isabel Young told the judge that these fights occurred because of my duty to protect my family; and as misguided as that might seem to him, she understood the events that had influenced them. I lived in a very different world from many — even many of my neighbours had not seen a night like I. Besides, my mother relied upon me and was not well.

This was the first public acknowledgement of my mother's illness. Also, now in the public forum was conversation pertaining to my I.Q., which I had no reason to hope was high. However, it being relayed that it was made me seem like my dad, another monster of his own making.

"God almighty," Autumn whispered, "another fucking genius in the family — how many is one family allowed?"

The judge told me I would have to clean our downriver community centre and help with the upkeep of the community rink, and that if I was brought up again I would be dealt with severely.

Because of my mother — because of how as she got to her feet she rested her hand on the shoulder of Autumn (who was now trying to look more and more like a woman) and how Autumn's dress, for all of Autumn's brilliance (and perhaps poignant because of such brilliance), hung lower on one side than the other — I hated myself when we went out into that January glare, into the snow that never had any more regard for us than anyone else.

There was always snow that winter. I read magazine articles on space shuttles. I read magazine articles on Chevy trucks, Motorola homes, dreamed of getting myself a job. I found it hard to keep the family warm, though I did the best I could. And in the middle of January, still doing community service, I realized we no longer had money for oil. I trekked through the woods every afternoon, when the sky was grey or purple, and began to rob wood from the piles up the back road that had been yarded but not moved. This was still the four-foot wood. Not the eight-foot lengths — which it is today.

I would lug this contraband through the woods along the iced-over Arron Brook on our old bobsled and put it with my pile, hoping my mom would not catch on. Once that winter she said to me, "It seems like a miracle."

"What does?"

"I have prayed often that we would not run out of wood, and every morning I look out the cord seems the same size. We burn wood — yet it doesn't diminish."

I was glad of my ability to keep her warm and guilty about the theft.

There was one thing I did not know. While I did my duty at the centre, Constable Morris, who always knew where I would be, came to visit my mother, pretending my delinquency was what he was there to address. He spoke in familiar terms with Autumn and brought Percy candy. On two occasions he brought my mother presents. It was another opportunity to make her feel that Dad was inadequate and had abandoned her. He spoke of cases where fathers left their children. Each time Morris heard of one of these cases he would bring it home to Mother.

Autumn would try her best to fend him off, but her brilliance was no match for his devotion. Her plan was to protect Mother from Morris and to spare me from knowing what was going on, sure I would get into more trouble if I did.

I stayed out after I flooded the community centre rink and drank. I drank because of the dirt in my hair and the cut of my clothes. I met Cheryl Voteur at the rink during this time. She too was doing community work because she had robbed Vachon cakes from the back of a truck to bring home to her brother and sister.

SEVENTEEN

I do not know who lived in a poorer house, Cheryl or I. But I suppose I would give the nod to her. For beyond anything else there was a scatological violence the likes of which were different from ours. About the house was a cluster of red and frozen alders, the windows were covered in heavy plastic, the house itself sank down toward the road, the road it hugged was unpaved and broken down. Inside the walls one could hear the rats nonchalantly gnawing after nine o'clock at night. A desperate tree clung by torn roots to the back field and above them ran a yellow white sky. Her younger brother, Darren, seemed sorrowful and strange, and I knew that he was himself being bullied. Besides, his loss of Autumn's love, which he thought he once had, bothered him. I spoke to him about this, and he shrugged as if it was nothing.

He kept to himself in a small attic room upstairs, listened to heavy rock music, grew his fingernails and hair long. He passed us by with a brooding look; his room was filled with posters of the band Megadeth. I realized that out of those airwaves of information that always tell the poor who they should be, he had chosen strange examples.

Cheryl had had a baby when she was fourteen she called Moo Moo. She had the same dreams of any girl her age from California, New York, or Toronto — she dreamed of being a model, of being like Madonna or Cyndi Lauper. She had her ears and nose pierced and read novels like *Love's Light Anew, The Weekend Romance, The Tall Dark Stranger, Love Island.* They filled the small crooked bookshelf in the living room of the dank drab house. She gave me some to take to Autumn, not knowing that Autumn was reading Malamud and Flannery O'Connor; nor I think knowing that books *could* be different than hers. Cynthia Pit was her mentor.

I did not understand then what I now believe. Cynthia and Cheryl were examples of how our family had failed the river. For the river was hurrying on, like the world, and had no time to stop to reflect on the greater ideas of where it was going. The music was new, the age was new, the idea of freedom for Cheryl *seemed* new as well. How could my father, who believed in the ancient quest of absolute truth, ever compete here? No wonder he was laughed at. His wisdom did not bring money, did not alleviate hardship, but caused a lack of one and a surplus of the other, and who would opt for that? Worst of all, his wisdom never told people they had no moral responsibility. It told them they had, and must at every waking moment be conscious of it. No wonder they hated him.

I found out, one cold winter night when I was seventeen, that Cheryl shared the same secrets of poverty as my sister, Autumn Lynn.

Her panties were faded and ripped when I took them off; and when she had her period she often used rags from the upstairs closet.

She asked me why I fought. I told her I wanted to get even with those people who had blamed my dad and beat him.

She smiled knowingly and said, "The Sheppards beat your dad."

The Sheppards kept their drugs at her house. So I had to be careful of her indictment. Samson, skinny and blacker looking than when my father brought him the groceries, was afraid of the Sheppards, of being caught, not only with the drugs but with whole sides of moose and deer meat the Sheppards stored in his back room and sold on the black market.

Cheryl feared the police as well, not only for her father's but for her daughter's sake. Too often they had been kept indentured because of what those they associated with had implicated them in. That was the secret in our world. Now moose and deer meat hung to their rafters out back.

Cheryl did not want to lose the child. And I began to realize, as she kissed me and stroked my hair (and other parts of me), this is why I was here. She wanted me to protect her family from the same shadows that had once plagued mine.

Strangely, the Sheppards were nice to me. That is because they knew where Morris was before I did. And Morris would never ruin his chances with my mom by raiding the place and implicating me in anything.

So my interest in Cheryl helped them. Being nice to me meant that they believed I either did not know they had beaten my father or, worse, I knew but did not hold it against them — which was closer to the truth.

Cheryl told me that after Dad's beating, someone gave the Sheppards runaway money. They had both left for Ontario; that they ran like rabbits.

"Someone has to be brave and put a stop to them," she said.

Her life, almost like Cynthia Pit's, had been pressed out and stamped. The dizzying mathematics, history, all the multiple questions on a sheet had been marked with an X to make her a failure. She had gone on, believing that leaving the torturous tests of the old school would make her a success. It had been just one more way to lose. All of a sudden her choices had lessened and she was scrambling in the dark. But her eyes were tender and the hope in her heart still soft.

"Of course I'll help," I said. But saying that and doing it were two different things, I knew.

Besides, Danny Sheppard had put his arm around me after I got community service work and hugged me, his harsh breath in my face as he asked me how I was.

"Keep a stiff pecker, boy," he had said. "You'll be a good lad someday."

Did I want to ruin that feeling? No, never — no one had treated me so kindly. At least none as tough as they. To gain their approval had made me self-deluded and vain. Powerful people had finally smiled on me. I was known as a tough boy. And this is what my father had feared and years ago had cautioned me against. But I had crossed the Rubicon — or another river, or Arron Brook.

Cheryl wanted me to descend into Dante's hell. I smiled at her, like my Beatrice, but, even after all my talk of revenge, was unsure whether I was ready for the plummet.

So one night when I left her house I made my way home by the back road. I came upon the Sheppards' house, a huge rambling place near the water and hidden by ragged, half-bare spruces. I stopped to look into the orange light of a downstairs window. I saw Bennie and Danny Sheppard handing a toke back and forth. Scrawny, muscled, tall, and dishevelled they stood before me. I knew these were the men of the shadows, the very men from my youth, the men who had defiled my mother with their talk. I had reason to hate.

Then Mathew Pit himself entered the room, with a platter of moose steaks, nodding at something one of them said.

All of a sudden Mat Pit, putting the steaks on the table, looked through the window and stared straight at me, his face as bold as it was inscrutable. His hands came up to his face and he continued to stare at the vagary of darkness outside. I did not know if he had seen me or not, or what I would do if he had. I knew at that moment that I had fought with young men I knew in my heart were not responsible for my dad's beating, but the much more dangerous Sheppards I did not seek out.

Perhaps it wasn't them, I thought. Yes, it would be hard to prove it was.

I went home that night, and saw Constable Morris's car in my yard. It was fortuitous for him, my trouble with the law. I went inside and saw Autumn playing checkers with Percy, long past his bedtime.

"Another cup of tea, Percy, dear," she said when I entered.

I began staying at home.

EIGHTEEN

For a long while I said nothing to him. I only listened to him. He came and went when he wanted.

"Now that he's gone, Elly, what are you to do with yourself?" Morris asked Mom one night, spying father's books, making a mechanical nod to my sister. We were in an awful state. We did not want to insult him, yet had our mother's honour to protect. Nor did I want him there for a lot of other reasons.

I had stolen the chalice from the church. One Sunday I had gone past the vestry and saw it sitting out of its dome. It was snowing and blowing and people were helping push cars out of the parking lot. I went into the vestry, picked up the chalice, and put it under my thin red jacket. I brought it home and hid it in my room, in the wall behind Dad's books. I believed I could get a lot for it — but I soon found out how hard it was to move. The theft was on the news, and my mother said the rosary and prayed for it to be returned.

Cheryl Voteur asked who I thought would have taken it. I knew that it would not be long before people found out — and when they did, all of what was thought about my father and family would be justified.

When Constable Morris came, he sat fifteen feet from a stolen chalice the entire river was looking for — even the Baptist minister had appealed for its return. The Knights of Columbus had put up a reward, and it was spoken about at mass. People were blaming the Sheppards, and Bennie had made a statement that he and his brother would find out who the real thief was.

After hearing that, I did not go outside. It was deep in winter; the nights were frozen silent, with stars gleaming over our tiny house, shaped like a worn old shoebox on its edge.

Mom sat in the bathroom with the door locked when Morris came in. I would end up entertaining him by playing chess. I always had to manoeuvre my queen and bishop, my rook and knight into being vulnerable enough for him to take, so he could win.

He would stay for an hour or two and boast to me about his time playing hockey. He spoke about the case against us, and how he had tried to help Mom by treating her as a human being. He also said he understood I had some difficulty with my father, and he assured me that he would guard anything I wanted to tell him. So one night, in the midst of all my other worries, I said:

"I have something to tell you about Dad."

"Oh? What?" he said.

"Do you remember when he and Mom went to visit you at the police station?"

"Of course," he said.

"Well — here it goes," I said. "It's from Shakespeare!"

"What is?"

"What my father quoted," I said, "It's from *King Lear* — he read it when he was sixteen by himself. After his father died he lived here. He redid the walls and added a room for Mom. Didn't he, Mom?" We were silent, listening to the wind. The bathroom door was closed and locked.

"Yes," Mom said from the bathroom. Autumn came over and sat down beside us with a shawl wrapped about her entire body and head, and only her completely white face visible. She blinked her tiny eyelashes. Her sitting beside him seemed to rattle Morris.

"Is that a good play — *King Lear*?" he asked.

"Yes," I said. "It's a great play — Orwell has written a wonderful defence of it, because Tolstoy attacked it so mercilessly."

"Tolstoy didn't know what he was talking about?" Morris asked.

"No," Autumn said quietly. "Tolstoy always knew — didn't he, Lyle? And he knew this — that as great as he was — and Tolstoy is very great indeed — Shakespeare is greater. This is what Mr. Leo Tolstoy knew — and can you imagine, not being satisfied with being Leo Tolstoy?" She smiled at me — not at Morris.

"Yes," mother answered from the bathroom, and then was silent.

Morris went red in the face. "Why didn't your father say so?" he complained, looking from me to Autumn. "If he had only said so — things may have been different."

"I don't know," Autumn answered. "But he never begs the truth in front of those who are contemptuous of him."

"He didn't want to hurt your feelings," Mother said from behind her shield.

We all looked at the bathroom door.

"I don't know much about plays — or things like Tolstoy," Morris said, apologetically.

"There is no shame in that," Autumn said, tender-heartedly, but looking only at me.

"No," I said, "except the lowest common denominator attacked my father — those who would have burned books attacked my father. You were part of that, Constable Morris. You know that too — deep down in your heart. But my father — you could take any book you wanted, and my dad could tell you about it."

"Shakespeare's plays?" Morris said, sadly contemplating the books. "You have read them?"

"Of course," I said, though I had read only *Hamlet* and *Lear*.

"You people seem to have loads of education," Morris said, with an inflection that meant, *Why do you live like you do?* and another hidden inflection that meant, *I am an enemy of that.*

"Yes. Our father taught us," Autumn answered calmly, "not to want anything, but to live just like we do." She reached out and took my hand — oh, staged treachery of the moment. I held her hand, as if we were always holding hands; and as if this was not the first time since school we did so.

"Do you think I've gotten your father wrong?"

"Oh yes," Mother said again from the bathroom.

"Completely," I said. "But that doesn't matter."

"Why?"

"The case will be reopened," Autumn said, "for we will not let it die."

"As long as there is a breath in my body I will not allow my father's name to be so besmirched," I said.

"Well — so much of the accusations seemed to fit at the time — I'm sorry, Elly — but isn't that so."

There was no sound from the bathroom.

"Sooner or later it will be solved," I said, eating a banana and looking at it. "They are saying that Constable John Delano is back on the river. He is known to be smart."

"I think it will be considered terrible that this ever happened to us, and many people will be sorry," Autumn said.

"Yes" I said. "Do you know, someone took rum and set my father drunk — and I had to tie him to the bed. Now, beyond the hilarity generated by that there is also profound indignity."

"I know that," Morris said, surprised that I and Autumn could speak with authority.

It was a night in late February months after Dad left. And Morris was troubled by these words. He was shocked — that all along his actions, and his motives, were easily seen through by my mom and dad. His face flushed at the name of John Delano.

"Who do you think set your father drunk?" he said.

"I know who, and I will get them," I said, but my voice was sad.

"You should tell me."

"I'll tell you everything I know someday," I said.

Morris did not come back to the house. I remember him now as a man who had no idea of the responsibility or maturity his vocation required.

Later, one night in March, when the wind was warming and I had come home from the Voteurs', I saw him skating with one of the women from Legaceville on our community's homemade rink, the one my community service kept flooded.

The night Morris left our house was perhaps the last happy night I spent with Autumn. She made taffy again, and we hollered and sang, and I held Percy as I danced about the floor, and Percy hugged us all and made up a song called "Mom and Me and Me and Mom."

Autumn said everything would turn out now, she felt it in her heart, and she hugged Mom and gave me a kiss.

Still, what was I? I tried to think of what I was, and came up with the answer.

I was nothing more than a thug with Tolstoy in my pocket.

NINETEEN

What happened to my soul because I stole the chalice? It began to shrink. Not because of the saints whose memories it housed in its circular hole, or not for any threat from the heavens. But because the Sheppards over time, a time when I was paralyzed about how to react, found out I had it. Now, along with everything else, I was terrified they would turn me in for the reward. I was slightly less worried that they would kill me, as they said they would. I had been outflanked, because having been suspected in my stead, they had attained a moral *power* over me that they would never have attained over my dad.

Worse, I had puffed myself up in front of Morris. How could I now go to him and beg his help by telling him I had stolen the chalice?

There are vague and cavernous reaches in Dante's hell where the worst sin is betrayal — but the hell I was in was not Dante's so much as Milton's, where Satan stood facing his son — Death.

I had descended to a place I did not believe in. A battle raged inside me, with grand marshals and winged regiments fighting over the contested ground of right and wrong. A battle almost everyone partakes in, and almost no one any longer believes.

A few weeks after I entered this hell, politely trading on Cheryl Voteur's warm legs and kisses, I was told by her (the only one I had confided in) that the Sheppards now knew I had stolen this chalice and were out to get me, and that she had put herself in danger by trying to stop them.

I felt I had to ask *their* forgiveness. That did me, carrying my seven-inch Bowie knife, a lot of good, didn't it?

That is when I began to see the nature of my crime; no matter *who* the Sheppards were, no matter whom they had harmed, it was *who I was* that counted. I realized it was part of the hidden decree in our natures that my father spoke about. And worse, Cheryl saw this. I was no longer her hero. And she was susceptible to heroes. She needed them. Yet here she was doing all she could to protect me!

Just like Rudy's sin against my mother, by this unthinking act of theft I had boxed myself into a corner. I had cursed my father's lack of action — to find at the end I had no moral stamina to do what I swore must be done by him. The moral stamina came from *not* doing it. Jay Beard was an exception — and his road had no guarantee.

"Bring the chalice here and I will sneak into their house and set the fuckers up," Cheryl said, sitting naked and facing me with her bum on my thighs. "You go tell Morris you saw them bring it to their house — when Morris comes I will have put the chalice somewhere it can be found! — and I'll fill the fuckin' thing with morphine and cocaine." She kissed me.

"That would be appalling to do," I said weakly.

"It would not at all be appalling to them," she said angrily. "They would do it to *you* in a second."

I saw the world as much more complex and internecine than I ever had before. I saw how comfortably the Sheppards fit in a world I did not. They fit as easily as Mat Pit, because everything was potentially viable to them from the beginning. And Mat Pit? Well, Mat Pit fit as easily as Leopold McVicer.

TWENTY

By early March the accusations Gerald Dove had made against McVicer's Works mounted. The incidences of allergy, cancer, and miscarriage among our community were eight times the provincial or national average.

There were weekly meetings at the one-room schoolhouse, and I went to them. The highway was dark, the stars out at seven. I walked across the new bridge and down the old Bowie Road to the school. It was well lighted, and you could see your breath even though it was crowded. People drank coffee in Tim Hortons cups. There were ice crystals inside the window, and everyone kept on their hats and gloves.

I saw Penny Porier for the first time since she had seen me in town. Did she know I still loved her? Did she know that at nights in summer when the breeze was gentle I made up stories to myself of how she would soon phone me, or come to see me? But I had lost my virginity to Cheryl Voteur. And Penny? She had watched as others ridiculed me.

She had left that past September for Mount Saint Vincent University in Halifax, but had been forced by illness to come home before Christmas; hence the visits to the doctors. She had always been sickly, I knew that.

She stood so close to me I could see her breath in the cool school-room. She told a friend near her that she had undergone many tests in Halifax. She felt she was very ill, but she didn't know why.

"You're only eighteen," I whispered hoarsely. "You'll be all right — they'll find out what it is! You have to be — you do." There were tears in my tough eyes. I don't know if she heard.

And then I got close enough to touch her — my fingers touched her coat as she passed by. I saw her turn and walk toward the front.

Mr. Porier had not wanted to blame her sickness on anything to do with McVicer. Her illness in his mind was only temporary, and a woman's thing. Anything else would make false his entire life.

Now his own daughter had gone over to the enemy camp. He had tried to threaten her. One morning he had broken into the bath-room when she was sitting on the flush and had shaken his belt in her face. Griffin had to rush in and step between them. Porier, his eyes blazing, his short thick arms furiously moving at his sides, threw the belt at his son and kicked the yellow bathroom wall. And now McVicer phoned every half hour, wanting to find out if there was anything he could do.

Her father had begged her not to go to the meetings. He went to her room and, looking distraught, he tried to cajole and coax her into staying home.

"I don't know what Leo's going to think," he kept saying.

Penny initially had few allies here. Certain people wanted to use her sickness against McVicer — and for them it would be good publicity if she died. I think Penny knew this; but she rode this wave as long as she could.

What McVicer feared came to pass. At the third meeting they put her on the stage with Dove and took a picture, his arm around her, protecting her from her own family. She told us about her symptoms. For years her period had not started, her weight was always low; she was forever tired. And in the mill — behind her back yard — dozens of barrels of herbicide and pesticide were stored when she was a baby girl. Ike Pit had worked there and he had died, and a dozen others as well.

The next day McVicer went to her and said he would pay for her education if she would not be part of these meetings. He told her that Dove was out to crush both him and her father. McVicer took her hand, patted it, and insisted he make her tea. He brought it over to her, along with tinned cookies from his store, and asked if she would like to see a specialist in Toronto. He looked at her, his eyes filled with the power her father feared. He told her about his war experiences — how he had fought at Caen. How he had been pinned down by a German machine gunner outside Antwerp. How he had put three hundred men to work in the woods. All the while he held her hand.

She had swallowed hard (for she could hardly eat) and told McVicer she mustn't take his kindness. "Oh," she had said. "What education will I need now? What specialist should I go to? When was the last time you came here to serve me tea? How often have you phoned my dad in the middle of the night to do some errand? How smartly he jumped to your tunes, how trite was his life, to feel important by waiting for you to make your Christmas visit! We lived our lives in a frugal house, without books or knowledge or even much love."

McVicer chuckled, and looked at her father with grave, penetrating eyes.

She climbed the stairs that night to go to bed and saw her father sitting in his room, everything in place, staring at the floor, while the clock ticked behind his broad, muscled back. The next day, he and her mother came into her room, with its pink bedspread and dried flowers in a green vase.

It was this visit to her room that hurt her more than anything else they did. She remembered their vacation to Prince Edward Island when she was a girl of seven, and how they had to leave three days early because McVicer needed Abby home. They never got back to that little cottage where she had collected red mud and seashells. It was this memory that made her fight back with tears in her eyes. Griffin, sitting in his own room, listened to the argument and, not being able to stand it, lay down on his bed, and bent a pillow to cover his ears. It was her eighteenth birthday.

"It's just a woman problem — girls have them — that's all —"
Porier said finally, in a loud but faltering voice. "Think a Mr. McVicer
— now ain't the time to desert him."

Penny didn't answer. She sat on the side of her bed, fumbling with
her bedspread and staring at the floor.

"You know, your father's been very good to you — think of that,"
Betty said to her, holding her head high.

"Listen," her father added, "yer mom says you always wanted to get
away for a shopping trip — say we do that — just me and yer mom
and you — how will that be? Wouldn't that be fun — away on a shopping trip — down to Boston on a shopping trip?"

In offering her this, he offered her *all* he ever had. But she went
to the meeting.

TWENTY-ONE

Gerald Dove was now forty. He was thin as a string, with large,
haunted eyes and the white skin that complements red hair.

I knew Leo's Machiavellian mind believed Dove was just the man
to prove these allegations against his mill false, even if he had to twist
a fact or two. Gerald had come home hoping to be able to help his
mentor in his time of need.

For a while the study went in Leo's favour; they had cleaned up,
they had taken the barrels away. But Gerald had left his mentor's
house ages ago, and had taken a small room in a motel. He had
complained to the police that his phone had been bugged, and his
room broken into, and that he was sure he was being followed.

A rumour surfaced that he had broken into his own motel room
and destroyed his own files because they went in McVicer's favour,

and that he only came back to ruin McVicer because McVicer had broken up his relationship with Gladys. (I am sure McVicer spread these rumours himself.)

I went to the schoolhouse and saw the letters PCDD and TCDD with arrows and circles attending them, and molecules drawn on the old blackboard, framed like stop signs and yield signs. Gerald talked to us about the reaction of toxins on menstruating women, and herbicides and pesticides on the respiratory faculties of northern children.

I felt unusually sorry for us all. Men with heavy beards and the huge hands of pulpcutters, their hands cut and gouged by years of work, with grade seven education, now saw for the first time a world far beyond tractor grease in minus-thirty weather, a world far removed from taking the hide from deer in November.

Now Dove drew his molecules on the blackboard, his thin hands covered in chalk dust, the eraser emitting the clouds of chalk dust.

It made those tired, kindly, heavy-handed men aware that the world had gone beyond them into another century. And really, here, on this black night, we were straddling three centuries. Woodcutters sat with university students who listened patiently to an explanation of toxic waste and the computer printout done at M.I.T.

So I smelled McVicer's nineteenth-century blood on Gerald Dove's thin twenty-first-century hands. I was sure McVicer would crumble. We all were sure.

The government quickly allied itself with the people, with the scientists, with Gerald Dove; and McVicer — whom it had championed for years — was alone. Many nights that winter, McVicer's house was locked.

I wanted him condemned. I laughed in the cold air under the sparkling stars with all my heart. Yet I still admired him. I don't know who else did. Maybe no one else, maybe everyone.

I was attracted to McVicer, to his solitude; an old man at the end of his life facing what his life had been without help, without explanation, and better yet, without apology. He slept with a shotgun beside his bed.

I waited and I watched, and I went to the meetings nodding my head at what others said. McVicer claimed he was now a scapegoat for a frightened uncaring government. He had not used these chemical scythes any more than anyone else, and he declared that he had protested his innocence in front of a governmental watchdog commit-tee years before — about the time of the robbery. He was prepared to make some restitution if the government would issue a statement clar-ifying certain relevant points. The government was silent.

His daughter, Gladys, watched the snow fall over the ground, over the bitter tar black wharf and under the distant highway lights, believ-ing in her father's goodness and her own worthlessness. Every day Leo blamed her. Every day he told her Gerald Dove had come home just to cause them pain because of her. She took an overdose of muscle relaxants and tried to sleep. Rudy found her and got her to the hospi-tal; Leo tried to keep it quiet. It was here Rudy realized his wife had always loved someone else. And some part of him was heartbroken.

In the next few weeks those on Dove's side made Penny Porier believe that all of this was being done exclusively for her. They took her away from her father, moved her into her own apartment in town, with a nurse. Her life in the northern part of the province, once so insignificant, now shone with tragedy, and she was inter-viewed and photographed and spoken about on national T.V.

I smelled McVicer's blood and waited, I suppose with the uncon-scionable human glee felt at others' disaster. No one spoke to McVicer coming and going from church after Penny Porier's inter-view, even though he released a statement about the money he was giving for the new stained-glass project there.

For years the provincial government had funded Gerald Dove, and paid for the lawyers who represented the five families who had launched the lawsuit. Doing this amounted to coercion. The government was deter-mined to get to the bottom of this case, and to be on the right side of the litigation. Yet the government also didn't wish to be investigated.

On March 19, Leo McVicer called a press conference. He said that not only had he used these herbicides but the government had reimbursed him throughout the sixties to the tune of thousands of dollars and had encouraged McVicer's Works and other mills, in letters and phone calls, to use these dangerous sprays. And why? Well, McVicer said, they had obligations to chemical companies in the States who supplied the herbicides and pesticides. And why? Well, said McVicer, so they could find buyers for the province's wood products, in competition with British Columbia and the northern states. And did the premier, who spoke increasingly about his awareness of the sacredness of our environment and the legacy left to us by the First Nations, know this? Why, of course, said McVicer. Can this be proven? Most definitely, said McVicer. He had the government's letters about subsidization to prove it. Where were they?

"Ah," said Mr. Leopold McVicer, shaking his head sadly. "They are locked away in my safe."

TWENTY-TWO

I could sell the chalice to no one. I had nowhere to put it except in the wall where I had once hidden Dad's clothes. There was a reward from the Knights of Columbus. Twice I had to hide from the Sheppards on the way home from the Bowie school, and threw up on the lane.

Finally, Mathew Pit took an interest. I was told to go and see him. I went to him with a great deal of trepidation. He had the power to save or destroy me depending on what he thought of me. It was he alone who could make it right with the Sheppards. So all my toughness had diminished.

Earlier that winter my trap lines ran parallel to his, and he had left me alone; so when I had some blond hash on me (given to me by Cheryl Voteur) I gave him a chunk.

He tolerated my presence on the trap line that ran above his. When I shot a coyote that had been robbing his beaver trap, I pelted it out for him and left it near his connabear trap.

Then I had started to lift weights. I went to the old gym at the school at six every second morning. And to my surprise Mat Pit was there. At first we never spoke. He lifted free weights and I worked the Universal, but one morning he was lifting heavy and needed a spotter. He lifted three hundred pounds for ten reps. Against my own best intentions, I suddenly felt obligated to help him out.

The Sheppards had gone to him first, asking him to help them. Instead, he met Autumn on the highway one afternoon and asked to see me. I went to his house and met him in the back room.

I sat and faced him. If he was prepared to do this favour it would be the most important thing he could do for me. It would free me from the Sheppards, who would have killed me. It indebted me to him and I would have to repay him sometime, or somewhere. I knew this.

I sat before him. He looked up from what he was doing and told me calmly not to trust anyone, especially the Sheppards.

"I don't trust them," I said. I was about to say "Nor do I trust you," but I checked myself.

"But how will we get rid of that chalice?" he said sadly. "It was a bad trick that — you should've known better — didn't your mom teach you to respect nothin' about religion?"

He said I had done it because of my ignorance and youth. But he knew nothing of the Christmas box years before.

"We don't touch the church here," he said, "and you have to be reasonable — leave the older people alone — leave kids alone — that's very important!" I fell under his gaze because of Trenton. No matter what I said, my father's guilt was still possible.

Then he placed a line of cocaine down for us to sniff, and bent over it with his huge forearms. I had never tried cocaine before and told him I didn't want it. He just handed me the twenty-dollar bill and nodded his head, so I did a line.

I told him I had no idea why I took the chalice. I also said I was sorry.

"Never be sorry — that's just what the Sheppards want from you — if they think you are sorry or scared you won't be able to behave like a man," he said calmly, looking down at the mirror and then rubbing some coke off his nose. "I never say sorry, never say please — I never say either to any man. Do you think McVicer is guilty?"

"Depends of what," I said.

He looked up and smirked.

"Of course he is — but will they get him?"

"I don't know."

"They won't get him — and that little girl — Porier — she will die broke — but my lawsuit will get him." He smiled self-indulgently, and a little crudely. He sniffed another line and looked at me carefully.

Then he said that taking the chalice was a *daring* thing to do. I said I did not feel daring and the best way to fence it might be to sell it to one of the Catholic sailors on one of the paper boats. He reached out and slapped my face.

"That's shit! That's the way to go to jail," he said, pointing a finger at me. "You listen to me, because I care for you, and don't go near the fuckin' Sheppards!"

I hesitated. Then I said, "You tell me how to fence this and I'll owe you." I did not rub my cheek though it stung like hell. Never once had my father hit me.

He grinned. There were specks of dirt in his straw-blond hair, and his eyes were red from drinking.

"Give it to me," he said, "and I'll get five hundred dollars for you."

That was half the reward the Knights of Columbus had offered.

That night I brought it over to him wrapped in the best blanket I could find, Percy's security blanket. It was a gold chalice, and when I had stolen it there were still some blessed hosts in it. They were still there when I handed it to him. He looked at it, took a few hosts to chew, dumped the rest on the ground, into the snow now soft with spring rain, poured some Napoleon wine in it and drank and handed it to me, and I drank. Then he took the cloth and wiped it out clean, and wiped the fingerprints off it, much like a priest might do after mass.

"Go home and wait. I'll call you," he said merrily.

Two days later he called. I went to see him, and he handed me five hundred dollars. He had taken the chalice to Rudy Bellanger, who took it to the Knights of Columbus, and they had cut the cheque for him without question. Mat could have kept all the money. I would have been in no position to challenge him if he had.

That long-ago night the bells rang out for the blessed event of the gold chalice being returned. The priest said the theft was a mystery that only God knew, but the return of the chalice was a miracle.

My mother came to me and asked me if I had heard the news.

"What news is that?" I asked.

"A miracle has happened today," she said timidly.

"Another miracle — what miracle?"

"Our chalice has been returned to Father Porier." Percy laughed and clapped. I said to myself I would not get into any more trouble. With the five hundred dollars I bought Mom and Percy and Autumn a new colour T.V.

I was disgusted with myself. I had relied on others to take care of me. I was unable to protect Cheryl. And I remembered how Jay Beard protected my father while his own house was under assault.

TWENTY-THREE

Gerald Dove sat with his lawyers the very night the bells rang for the return of the chalice. The lawyers for the five families wanted to sue the government and use the tape of McVicer's press conference to fuel the possibility of fresh litigation.

Dove himself did not know why he thought this was a trap if the lawyers did not. But everything he knew about McVicer pointed to one. He had cornered the one man he never wanted to fight against. The man who had come to the orphanage about something years ago, and saw him, a red-headed child, sitting in the middle of a crib-lined room. McVicer had picked the child up, asked about his parents — the father had died on one of McVicer's saws before the child was born, and the mother had died just a few months before. McVicer, in the grand way McVicer had, became his mentor.

Dove was exhausted. That night they were sitting in Penny Porier's small, freshly decorated apartment. There was light classical music playing from the radio beside her. Penny would listen to nothing else even though classical music troubled her quiet, beautiful face.

She turned this troubled face on her lawyers. She had a blanket over her and drank apple juice from a straw.

Dove knew that he had used her. Worse, he didn't know how much he had used her until that very moment. He told her that with those letters from McVicer's safe it might be proven that our government knew exactly what was going on. That Canadian companies were hand in glove with government funding; a government needing the approval of larger companies in the States; and that not only she but hundreds and hundreds of people were harmed. Yet *she* was their main client. He asked her if they should proceed. She felt a tickle in her throat from the apple juice — and blushed because she had a crush on Dove, and had learned in a month to say the things that would please him.

"Of course," she said.

In fact she did it only to please him — for nothing else mattered much.

The next day her lawyers filed suit against the very government that had been funding their research, alleging complicity and gross negligence.

Within three days they realized their mistake. Their research funding was immediately withdrawn.

Dove could no longer travel to investigate other cases on behalf of the lawyers or get corroborating testimony from stateside companies. To go to court was impossible, because the government and McVicer and the chemical companies in the States were willing to stall for years. Penny Porier might be dead in a matter of months.

On March 28 Dove tried to phone McVicer, but McVicer, when he heard Dove's name, broke a fly rod over his knee and would not take the call.

It became apparent Dove's lawyers could no longer fight the case on behalf of the families unless they did it out of their own pockets. An argument erupted in Penny's apartment, on the morning of April 1, while she lay on the couch.

"Oh," Penny said to them suddenly, lifting her head. "This is Bach — I think — yes."

By the next weekend only Gerald Dove and Griffin stood beside Penny, who was now seen as ridiculous and greedy and filled with schemes of betrayal.

Dove tried to keep her in an apartment and have the nurse. But he was finding it impossible to pay the bills. In desperation he wrote to Gladys McVicer, Penny's godmother. But Gladys, in terror of her father's rages against Dove, was helpless.

Finally Griffin, the only member of her family to speak to her, drove her back home.

The one remaining lawyer, as a favour to Dove, tried to subpoena the letters, but McVicer now asserted they were misplaced long ago, and the court, in the infuriating conceit of courts, smelling a blind weakness in Dove's case, refused a warrant for lack of probable cause.

In late April it was decided, for Penny Porier's sake (whom everyone from the government to McVicer himself said they loved), to settle out of court. The government offered Penny what it offered the other families in a gesture of good will: three thousand dollars.

McVicer also assured Abby that he was still the foreman, even though he had not called him in weeks. Abby had no pension, not a chance to be hired anywhere else. He was over fifty. He hung about the store, nervous and with a hopeful face. His wife made McVicer a pan of her famous date squares. It was rumoured Leo had thrown them to his horses.

People began to gossip about Penny, saying that her disease was from a condition of modern promiscuity and she had set everything up to blame McVicer because she didn't want it to reflect poorly on her strict Catholic family, her uncle being a modest and pious priest. Some men drove by in an old convertible and yelled insults at her house. Griffin ran outside and grabbed a rock, flung it impotently at the sky as the men taunted him and laughed.

After gossip about Penny travelled on the wires, McVicer published a statement refuting the rumours and pleaded with the public not to listen to hearsay.

Penny Porier, still with braces on her bottom teeth, died in the last week of April, at the age of eighteen. I did not go to her funeral.

TWENTY-FOUR

Three days later I was walking the old asphalt lane that led to McVicer's general store. I was happy the chalice scrape was over. The wind was soft and the night was sweet. I had my coat opened and my hands in my pockets. Lights were on in the houses and the snow was melting down in the dooryards.

I knew someone was in the woods hiding from me. I kept walking and then spun around. I saw someone running to the far side of the road, then cutting across the field toward the highway.

I went above him, through the woods, and met him as he came out just below the back field of the community centre. It was Griffin Porier.

"What's goin' on?" I said. "You following me? You want another punch in the fuckin' head?"

"No," he said. He was shaking like a leaf. He was carrying a canister of gas.

"What the hell are you doing, then?"

"Nothin'." Tears ran down his face. "I wanted to burn his old store — for lying and cheating us," he said. "Dad worked for him for thirty years — and now he is home alone — it's as if he *is* dead — and Penny — but I chickened out —"

"Give *me*," I said. "You don't have the fibre to do what you have to!"

I hauled the canister from him in fury, and the broken hockey stick with a rag tied about it he had in his belt.

It was one of those spring nights when the moonlight glints off fields full of receding snow and bathes the laneways in soft expectations of spring and summer. I approached the store from the back — and from the back it looked dilapidated, covered in tin and rivets and black tarpaper. It had stood for eighty years. I had worked in it. It was as if it belonged to me as well as anyone.

I smashed a window with the torch, then lighted it and threw it down on a shelf of work pants, and then I poured gas over it. It was as if the store had been waiting eighty years for me to come to do this. I was out of my body watching myself from a great height.

Two days later McVicer asked to see me. I went to his house, stood in his office, and looked at his great collection of fishing flies and the broken fly rod in the corner. He sat down and looked up at me. He was wearing Levi's jeans, which always look strange on a man in his sixties, no matter if he is youthful or not. He told me he had not slept since the fire. His face looked weary. He had been away all yesterday with the insurance adjuster. He told me that the insurance people believed that because his own highway, which skirted north of our little community, had made his store superfluous, he had had it torched himself. They were going to withhold payment. He stared at me.

He was an outcast.

"Didn't I give everyone turkey at Christmas? Who would burn my store, for cripes sake, Lyle — who?"

"I don't know, sir," I said.

"And I never paid minimum wage — I always paid a nickel more."

He opened up his glass fly box and, fastidiously peering over them, asked if I wanted to take a few. I took a Royal Coachman, for luck.

"Show me your hands," he said. I did so. He looked at them curiously and held them in his, close to his chest. His eyes flashed when he held them. He ran his thumb over my knuckles. It was on the tip of my tongue to confess. But then he said:

"Ah — I told you you would box." His rough old hands were shaking just slightly. "I have no store anymore," he said, releasing my hands and reaching out to pick up the remains of the fly rod he had snapped in two. "No — don't have no store no more. I want you to know I didn't hurt your father or mother — I liked them."

He didn't look at me, but continued to inspect his rod for a moment. I said nothing.

"Man can be defeated but not destroyed," he said, a line that finishes, "Man can be destroyed but not defeated."

I told him it was from Hemingway. He did not know that. He told me someone had said it to him once when he was in trouble.

I nodded and he let me go.

TWENTY-FIVE

It was summer of 1989. My father had been gone almost three years. Percy had no memory of him, and I was more content.

Dad sent us letters, with money, telling us how he prayed for us (not one of his prayers, which I called his praters, did I keep or return) and that what he was doing now would insure our future (a lie) and we would all be together again (I did not care).

Elly read these letters by holding the paper straight out in front of her because her eyes were growing weak. My mother loved him and was still lovely, her hair with just the first traces of grey would fall in front of her eyes in the old sunlight that came upon the kitchen table in the after-supper hours.

She and Percy kept a garden with some beans and peas — we were trying to get Percy to try a pea, and would put one on his plate every night for supper. Which he did not trouble himself to eat. He would, however, eat around it.

Elly and he would go to their garden each morning and look at the crop of carrots and beans and turnips, which Autumn informed us were rutabagas. Then in the afternoon as summer went along Mom would sit on the porch shelling the peas and Percy would lie out in the grass with Scupper Pit. Autumn, who had a job as a summer counsellor at school, would come home about two.

My mother had taken a catering job that spring for the McTavish woman whose house she used to board at. My mother, twice a week, had to deliver twenty-five sandwiches to those workers on the road, and the names of those she had to deliver sandwiches to were written out on a piece of notepaper on the kitchen table in her crooked hopeless handwriting. Often when I woke she was gone out to get those ingredients for those sandwiches.

My mother's little sandwich empire. She would walk up the road alone, a small woman with soft auburn hair, and a slight sad smile. Sometimes in the evening she would tell Percy and Autumn a story about how when Dad came home she wouldn't have to make sandwiches anymore, and she might take a course at a university.

"How wonderful it will be," Elly would say, folding her hands on her lap. Then she would sigh, and in a moment of vulnerability say again, "Yes, how wonderful it will all be."

————

Father wrote saying he would be home before Christmas. I do not know why but I defended him to others and hated him myself. But when Autumn asked me to pose with the rest of the family as Jay Beard snapped a picture to send to him, I would not.

Over the last few years, I took the money that Father sent us and with it paid the hydro and the oil and bought the groceries. I told Autumn I never spent it on myself. But I never showed her how much Dad sent. At first I spent just a little of it, and then a little more. Until his money obsessed me each time I went to town; I drank much of it away. I heard Father worked until his feet bled, in places that could bust you apart. So I knew I was obligated not to touch a cent. I tried to put this money back. I had trapped the winter before for muskrat and beaver and, setting up a bait using a poor deranged horse, shot ten coyotes with the old over-and-under .22/410 my father owned, and pelted them out and sold each for thirty bucks. I suppose I thought myself tough, and I had a reputation. But the money came and went and I still had nothing to show for it. I was going nowhere, neither to university nor to hell.

Autumn knew I was taking Dad's money for myself, so it was hard to look at her. It was hard to look at myself. Each time I took ten dollars I cut myself a small mark on my left arm with my knife, to remind me when I took off my shirt how much in blood I owed my dad. Then I started on my right arm. Then the cuts became deeper and longer. And one day somewhere up Arron Brook, far away on a windy bluff, I realized I had spent more than twelve hundred dollars of money that belonged rightly to the family, and that the marks criss-crossing my arms did nothing more than mock me for my weakness.

"Are you going to take Percy and me swimming up to Gordon's wharf?" Autumn asked one day, trying to make amends. I said I would.

But I had no time for them. Not even to take Percy to the circus that year. Though I promised, and promised again and then once more. And he waited to go. Every morning he got up and, brushing

Scupper Pit, would say: "This will be the day — Lyle will take me to the circus."

I stayed out near the brook for days at a time.

Even there, I sometimes heard of Father. I would hear of him from strangers I met fishing on the Bartibog in the reddish brown pools at twilight. I wore a knife on my hip and carried a knife in my boot.

One time a man asked me if he was still alive. The man told me he knew him and had always felt the accusations against him were lies.

"You know he is a great man," the fellow said.

"I don't know him at all — nor would I want to," I said, trying to control my voice, and the damn tears coming to my eyes. The man nodded and moved down the pool and disappeared in the grainy twilight.

Why in God's name could I not have peace from him? I would not spend another cent of his money, I told myself. And if he was a great man, so too would I be. That is, I did not know how much I envied him. But I envied him. He had made his life in spite of poverty, scorn, and intolerance. He had made it what it had to be. He had fashioned it as Marcus Aurelius advised. He had done what men all over the world *say* men should do. And in order to prove myself to him, what had I become?

TWENTY-SIX

Sometimes after fishing when I walked up Burnt Hill, I could see our small home on the flat in amongst the trees, and far, far away, a speck so small he was almost indiscernible, Percy hauling his wagon up the cool dusty lane to wait for me, with Trenton Pit's old dog, Scupper, hobbling along behind.

In the other direction, the Pit house would be steely quiet, with faint pink clouds far above it, and across the greenish blue bay, the indistinct houses of Bay du Vin, and behind me the ominous old house of Mr. Leo McVicer.

The Pit house was a house of sorrow because of baby Teresa's heart. The yard was filled with potholes, the house's siding was faded yellow and covered with ten years of dirt. The house itself seemed to sit unnaturally on the foundation Cynthia had procured. The swing set in the yard was new, an addition paid for by Rudy Bellanger, and made the house look more desolate. Often Teresa was down in Moncton or Halifax in intensive care. I remember how Cynthia looked uncomfortable in the skirts and dresses she wore to the hospital.

At least half of Rudy's pay went to protect himself and keep Cynthia quiet. Cynthia was frightened that the child would die, a fear that came from a delicate reason she could not admit to herself. How could she hold Rudy to blackmail if the child died? Now that the store was gone, Rudy had no steady employment. At the start of that year he had eight thousand dollars put away, because one day he wanted to go to university, so impressed was he by Gerald Dove, whom he knew Gladys once loved. He had talked about university to me one night, thinking he would impress me.

"Have you ever heard of a writer named — ah — James Joyce?" He squinted his sad eyes at me.

I told him I had, told him what Joyce wrote, and he shook his head.

"The more I learn, the less it is I know," he admitted sadly.

Yet he slowly gave that university money up to Cynthia over the next few months. He was still living in the huge house, still had certain duties to do for Leo, but every sharp wind from the bay reminded him that life was passing him by and he had done nothing. The same buoy he saw at ten was the buoy he saw now at forty.

One night, I came home drunk, a bottle of wine still in my hand. I woke everyone. I called my mother down to make me supper.

"Shh," Autumn said.

"Don't shh me," I said, raising my hand to strike her. I stopped.

"It's just you'll wake up Percy — and he's —"

"He's what?"

"He's going to go to first grade — Mom and I registered him for the fall — he is excited about it. He waited up to show you his pencil all day —"

When I went to bed Percy pretended to be asleep, with his caterpillar collection on his nightstand, his small sneakers beside the bed with his socks in them, and his bow tie hanging from one of the bedposts. His pencil was gripped in his hand. Now and then, as I staggered and sang, he would open an eye and look at me and then quickly close it again. He saw the cuts on my arms, and a tattoo on my left arm that I had gotten at the circus.

As I undressed I saw four dollars in an envelope on Percy's dresser, and a strange word written on the envelope: *Getir.*

The next morning I couldn't look at them. They sat stone-faced at the table. I ran outside in the rain.

I spent the rest of the summer dividing my time between fishing and cutting wood for the winter — the more wood I could cut, the less oil we would burn, the less money I would need. I found buyers for most of the things I had.

TWENTY-SEVEN

About twice a month my mother received a letter marked "URGENT" from the tax department indicating how much she and my father owed, the accumulated interest on the back taxes, and the urgency with which they must pay. One day, looking through the kitchen drawers for a file to sharpen the chainsaw blade, I found these letters stuffed in a plastic bag, hidden behind the cleaning rags. I took them out and read them. It was the disaster my father had brought upon her, by his one venture into business, which she could not fight or endure and so hid from her children, even though I considered myself the man of the house.

I took out my rage on my mother, who shook as I shouted at her. She had relied upon me so long that I was no longer her son. I remember hearing how Mathew Pit tormented Trenton. Well, I had become the same. Finally, after cursing her and Dad for an hour, spit coming to my mouth, I stopped, and sat down beside her in a stupor. She was shaking, her head down, her nose running, her left foot crooked over her right. She was staring at her shoes.

Autumn had grabbed me and I had thrown her and blackened her eye. Percy sat on the couch, watching us throughout, without a word. Now, wanting to make it up to them, I asked, "How can they take what little we have?"

But Mom did not respond. She knew that I myself had taken money. I myself had spent it on wine. She sat as she always did, hands on her apron, looking beyond me.

"Well, we will go up and see them!" I said. "I'll straighten this here out for you, Mom — I will."

Autumn would no longer speak to me. But my mother did what I said. Though she was ill and spent much of her time sitting on the porch now, she and I went to the tax department above the post office in Chatham and sat in the waiting room waiting for Ms. Hardwicke to see us.

That afternoon we discovered that Ms. Hardwicke had been taken from our case and another woman had been given our file. This woman was working as a supervisor. Her name was Whyne.

Diedre Whyne sat down at her desk, now and then glancing my mother's way but keeping her eyes off me. She cleared her throat.

She told us that the tax department had a plan of action. We could relieve ourselves of part of this burden if we sold the wood on the land we owned. She estimated that we could get ten thousand dollars. She had a topographical map of the area and it showed our property as lots 987–988 and 990. It was 988 where she focussed her attention.

I told her she had overestimated the wood's worth by about six thousand dollars. She asked me if I had cut any yet. I didn't answer her. I told her the tax burden was my father's. But this was not true. It was as much my mother's burden, and it was the property that could be used to alleviate it, for that belonged to both Mother and Father.

"I need that wood to cut," I said.

"You can cut it and sell it —" Ms. Whyne said.

"I need to burn it for winter wood."

"But not if you move out of the house," Ms. Whyne said. "If you moved into a low-rental in town — sold the property — the debt would be paid — I am not at all trying to harm you — you understand I am trying to help you. I have been racking my brain to find a way to get Elly out from under all of this. I have not slept because of it. I feel responsible for her —"

"But we are not going to move out of our house," my mother said. "We are waiting for my husband — he won't know where we are."

Ms. Whyne sighed. "How many times have I predicted this? Men running away after leaving the woman with a houseful of children."

Mother fidgeted and looked at me quickly, as if to warn me not to say anything.

"Fine —" Whyne said, "but if you cut the wood on your property, we would want you to sell it — for we do have a right to it, you see. I have looked at every angle here — and there is nothing I can do, besides offer you a two-bedroom low-rental on Margaret Street — I have it set aside for you."

"How did you know I was cutting wood on my property?" I asked.

"Are you cutting wood on your property?"

"For firewood for the winter."

"I'm sorry," she said, turning to Mother, "but you are obligated to sell it — you cannot just *use* it."

We went back home. Whyne's position was one of pointless and

limited provincial power. I learned years later that at any time someone either here or in Saint John could have, in what would be called
"an act of mercy," taken this burden away from us completely. This is
what Ms. Hardwicke knew, and why she was transferred from our case.

I sat in a kitchen chair in the dark and tried to think.

"They can't take everything away," I told my mother. But she simply
put her hands on her lap and sighed.

The next day I took Dad's old chainsaw, which he had used for
cutting the ice during smelting season. I cut a number of birch trees
in the morning. I cut them into four-foot lengths and hid them as
best I could under bushes and smelt netting. Then I took my rod,
with a few butt bugs, and proceeded to the water.

I got home late that evening. I saw the lawnchair sitting out in the
front yard, on a patch of grass and dirt. The house was dark, and a
bird or two still twittered. A piece of Percy's birthday cake was left out
for me on the table. I went upstairs. In the room I saw Percy's envelope, with the word *Getir* written on it and the few crumpled dollars
in it. I looked for a dollar in my pocket to give him, but my pockets
were as empty as my heart.

The next day I went to collect the wood I had cut. It was early in the
morning, with pearls of wet dew on the tall grass. I walked along Arron
Brook, smelling the rot of windfalls, and saw the sunlight meander
through the tops of the trees. A crow made a racket at me. I began to
look for my wood and thought I must have walked up too far.

But I hadn't. A truck had come in on the path that led from the
highway and had taken away my wood. There wasn't a stick left out
of my four cords. The chatter of a squirrel made me look up, high
above the trees, to curse.

I went to the tax department and waited for over an hour. I had
almost talked myself out of staying when Ms. Whyne said she would
see me. It was quarter after four in the afternoon. They worked until
four-thirty in the summer months.

I was ushered along the hallway toward her cubicle, past pictures
of streams and old spruce trees. The day had turned hot, and the air

conditioner was on in the office. Behind her cubicle stretched others in the half dark. Faraway sunlight pressed through the narrow window blinds.

She was wearing large earrings and a flowered blouse, and a plain light blue skirt. Her face was damp white and her eyes wide, a look prevalent among people in offices during the summer.

"My wood was taken," I said.

"Yes — we were able to get the truck right in," she said.

"That is my wood for the winter," I said. "We need it to heat our house."

"It belongs to Revenue Canada," she said. She cleared her throat and picked up a glass of water, shifted some papers and glanced up at me, with her eyes very wide and dry. Her lips touched the water in the glass, and she smiled slightly, as if to herself.

"I'll pay you back," I whispered.

"Pardon?"

"I'll pay you back," I whispered. "My father was ruined, over nothing at all. But I am not my father. I will not be."

"Oh — a threat." She said, "I've never had a threat."

I had no weapons to fight back. Not the weapons that are now allowed. So I turned and put my fist through the window.

I was taken to the hospital needing eleven stitches. The police came and questioned me at supper hour, as I sat on a gurney. Constable Morris came in.

"Lyle," he said, "think of Elly."

He questioned me as to whether or not I had threatened Ms. Whyne. I said I had not, and had no intention of it, nor did I mean to break the window. What I realized was this — my father had told him the truth and deserved to be believed, and he did not wish to believe my father, for my mother's sake. I told him a lie — and he desperately wished to believe me for my mother's sake.

He told me he did not know what I was into, or with who — but he wanted to tell me this.

"What?" I asked.

He told me the Sheppards were to be raided soon, and not to dare go near there or the Voteur house.

I told him Cheryl and her family should not be harmed, it wasn't their doing.

"If you mention a word of this I'll run *you* in," he said. "I'm doing this for your mom — for your mom — don't go near that fuckin' house. I'm doing this for Sydney," he said, "not for you. I don't want to see you in a scrape."

I was released at eight o'clock. There were conditions. I was not to go near Ms. Whyne or the tax department again or I would be charged with assault and I would have to go to jail.

The east wind reminded me of fall, and that my wood should be piled under its stable. My hand pained. I thought of how Dad had grabbed my knife — how utterly useless I thought his act. But what had mine garnered me? Nothing more or less than Dad's. And I saw my father's act as a proud and noble act of a man. An act selfless. My act was of a youth foolish. Besides, Father had no guilt. I could not walk past a mirror during the light of day.

Three days later, Danny Sheppard was picked up at his house. Knowing he was in for a prison sentence, he fired a rifle at a cop. The shot missed. This police officer was Constable Morris.

Danny came up for trial sometime later. And by chance Rudy Bellanger was on the jury. They had all kinds of evidence against him, and found Danny guilty of trafficking to children on the reserve. It was his fourth offence and everyone knew he was going away, even though with his hair cut short and a clean suit, one of the police officers could not pick him out in the courtroom.

Rudy was the jury foreman and pronounced the verdict with great relish. Rudy did not understand why Mathew was so quiet and alarmed. But I did.

As soon as the sentence of eleven years was imposed and the courtroom cleared, Danny told Constable John Delano that both he and

Bennie knew things about the bridge and the long-ago robbery at McVicer's house.

With Rudy boasting his part in their downfall, I became aware that when he helped sentence Danny Sheppard, he had sentenced Mathew and himself. He just did not know it yet. Mathew took two trips to visit his friend in Dorchester and came home glummer each time. Even Connie Devlin did not speak to him now.

Their world would crumble without my help, just as my father had said. They who lift a hand against you do so against themselves. If only I had believed him just a little I might still be free.

LOVE

ONE

Mathew and Cynthia had convinced themselves they would be able to retire after they won their lawsuit. Yet almost six years had gone by and they waited, as people of little knowledge wait, always thinking their lawyer had their best interests in mind, and that he was more than a lawyer, he was a friend. That is, they believed what Snook himself had cultivated, and understood legal procrastination only in the way he wanted them to. Until the entire community was tired of hearing about their legal battles. As for Snook, he had taken three thousand dollars from them and rarely, if ever, thought of their case.

A week after Danny Sheppard's sentencing, Frederick Snook came down from town. I watched as his car pulled into their yard. He got out in the twilight, wearing the same loud suit I had once seen him wear in court. He brushed some dust off his loafers and, looking unfavourably upon the large old house, went inside. He took little Teresa May's fingers in his and made faces and took a quarter from her ear and handed it to her. Though five years of age, she looked like she was three.

He asked about her condition and discovered how serious it was; that someday she may need a heart transplant. Then, feeling he had done a civic duty, he faced his clients and said what it was he had come to say.

"I've gotten an offer — an offer to put all of this behind us now."

Cynthia looked at Mathew and winked. Mathew sniffed.

The offer was a one-time lump sum payment of two thousand dollars.

There was silence at the bare metal table. They could not speak. The offer was a thousand dollars less than what they had already spent on the litigation.

Frederick listened with a pious blankness as they cursed everyone, as if his failure was *their* fault. They shouted at him about all the plans they had had and what they were led to believe. He left with a sense of heaviness and the injured merit that men of Snook's legal and business acumen often have at just these times.

They drove to his office two days later. He had not thought he would be seeing them again and looked startled when they came in. Cynthia held little Teresa May, who had a flowered hairband about her head and a long scar visible on her chest. But the lawyer did not feel it was the proper time to shake the child's fingers. She had become just a sickly kid whose mother this lawyer had always considered "white trash."

Snook took out two file folders and went to the desk. He extended his hand to two chairs.

He told them that the lawyers for McVicer had come up with what they thought was a reasonable offer.

"I wouldn't want to be rich in this parish," Snook said, as if Cynthia and Mat should empathize with their opponent's position.

That they did not take this offer was understandable but completely up to them. It was the words *reasonable offer* that cut to their souls.

Mathew wore the same sports jacket and the same cowboy boots he had worn all those years before; Cynthia the same dress, the one she also wore to hospital with baby Teresa. Snook shook his head sadly as he kept looking up from a dossier to one or the other as he spoke.

"What all the experts say is that the span that gave way wouldn't have if it had not been for sabotage. This would likely be in the company's favour at trial, and not I think in yours or Connie Devlin's. I have your interest at stake. It would be a very large expense to go on from here — he's a bastard, McVicer — but he has smart men working for him."

Both sighed and said they had decided to take the money. He closed the folders, stood, and walked to the filing cabinet.

"I wish you had decided that before," he said.

"Why?"

"Well, the offer has been withdrawn — it was a one-time offer —"

"Withdrawn?" Cynthia said.

He looked at them with numb blankness that for once showed him to be a tired middle-aged man.

"They can't withdraw it," Mathew said, his face completely white. "They offered it to us — they did — they offered it to us."

Cynthia exclaimed that it wasn't fair. It wasn't fair to her mother.

"I know it isn't fair," their lawyer said. "Nothing about McVicer is fair — you saw how he handled Penny Porier. He grew up in a gutter and he can fight like a dog over a piece of meat."

Then the lawyer asked Mathew if he would mind leaving the office for a second. Mathew didn't want to until Cynthia told him to. He went out, slamming the door. Snook then told the woman that they were in no position to proceed.

"Why not?" Cynthia said brazenly, as a person does whose confidence rests on never caring to know the facts.

"Because John Delano is now the officer heading the investigation — and he's not like Morris. He has a recent statement from the Sheppard brother — Danny — that trash in Dorchester — ready to give anyone up. From what I know — and I can't verify it yet — the statement implies that Connie Devlin was supposed to be paid four thousand dollars — that Mathew drove the truck the night Trenton died, and that Mathew robbed McVicer's house of five hundred dollars. You see, Devlin is terrified of going to jail — gutless weasel — because of the very lawsuit *you* filed. If you had not filed it, this new investigation might not have started. Connie will want immunity for what he will tell on your brother and Rudy Bellanger. If he gets it your brother faces a murder charge. This is why the offer was so minuscule and why it was withdrawn yesterday. Besides, the community — the river, the province — everyone who had an opinion on Sydney Henderson will want your brother's blood."

Cynthia stared at him.

"Personally I don't think they have a leg to stand on — not with hearsay evidence from someone like Danny Sheppard. Still, this is going to be hard on your mom, if Connie Devlin turns."

"I see," Cynthia said.

She did not understand everything, but she was not surprised by any of it.

Cynthia stood, feeling absurd in her dress, took her purse, opened it, and found a cigarette. She held her child in her left arm as she lighted the cigarette, blew the smoke out of the side of her mouth, almost as a warning, and prepared to leave the office.

"I share your outrage," Snook said, picking up the phone and asking, "Do you think Devlin is at home?"

"Not fuckin' likely," she said, closing the door.

TWO

They drove home along the empty road that evening. The stars were coming out over the bay, a buoy winked out, as if God still had everyone's best interest at heart. Mathew's gaze was vacant, his face thin and tired. He stared over fields he didn't own and houses he had never been invited into. For a moment he had loudly proclaimed himself a victim and by this had danced above those houses. Now the cloud upon which he walked had turned to ash.

Cynthia had told him exactly what the lawyer said about Connie. Told him the new officer, John Delano, knew, told him that both Connie and Mathew were culpable. Told him they wanted another fish — Rudy Bellanger.

Told him that this is what McVicer himself had been silently doing for months, ever since he had stopped the lawsuit over the groundwater and herbicides — he was closing a noose around the necks of those other few who had gone against him. Told him how long McVicer had felt Rudy and Mathew were involved. Since the day

Mathew took the stand at the inquest. She didn't tell him to strike a deal and give Rudy up. She wanted that card to play for herself.

Cynthia sighed. "How did everything get so wrong?" The child was asleep, the car engine droned, Black Sabbath played.

"Connie Devlin," Mathew said. "First he blames it all on Sydney Henderson and now he blames it all on me." His eyes moved to the right and left, as if he was trying to find a way out. He knew he needed money, and fast.

"Connie — 'member when Connie stole my smelts and had the 'dacity to blame it all on Sydney?"

Cynthia looked at him, startled by the complete switch, the complete falseness; and how easily he had attained it, and how easily she accepted it. But this made her aware of the terrible dilemma she was now cornered in.

"I always knew Connie was a son of a bitch," she said. "Poor damn Sydney, a lot of people hate him for no reason — I never hated him, I told them I never. I like his boy, Lyle — a strong, kind kid — and Elly too, and I never made fun of Autumn for being a pink-eyes al-been-o like others did." She blew out some smoke.

"I know I know I know," Mathew said. "You and I know he was not the one. It was Connie trying to kill people — Connie and Rudy — who was always dangerous. I was scared of them both, you ask me."

"Well, you didn't want to live like that — that's the problem —"

There was a dead silence, each one of them trying to think of a way to save themselves.

"It's time to change the water on the beans," Mathew said, gripping the steering wheel. Yet his heart was racing. He had no idea what to do.

Ontario, he was thinking. I will go to Ontario.

The house was quiet when they got home, and it was after dark.

Mathew went upstairs to his room and sat on the edge of the sagging bed, smoking and looking out the window. It was a room he had spent his entire life in, and he remembered himself here at various stages of his life. He remembered himself as a teenager looking out at the fire above Oyster River sand pile, seeing the black smoke funnel up and cover the sun and a hellish red haze meander over the road as McVicer, along with the other men, fought with axe and shovel to contain it. Mathew, ordered on by his father, Ike, had set the fire.

Now an owl flew through the trees in the slanted purple twilight and disappeared. Far away the remnants of the burned-over stumps stood out, with the new growth surrounding them.

Mathew got pains in his stomach if he was worried and smoked too much. But he couldn't get rid of the thought that Connie would betray him. What was more aggravating was the fact that part of him *knew* this day would come.

Yet having known this day would eventually come did not stop Mathew from pressing ahead. Or stop him from laughing and talking and buying Freddy Snook drinks. The idea that his lawyer was a con man had attracted Mathew, because Mathew could not be attracted to anyone else.

Constable Morris had been accused of bad police work and was taking antidepressants. It seemed strange to Mathew that this big hulking man with the thick neck muscles would be on antidepressants, but it was so.

I wish I had some antidepressants, Mathew thought suddenly.

The tone of the newspaper had changed as well. It had been changing for months. They asked for a new police investigation to be opened to clear my father, to pay him compensation — to take his case before the Human Rights Commission, where David Scone now sat.

A man like Mathew, who couldn't predict or, more important, *use* the shifts of fortune as well as his sister, was suddenly humiliated. He took the bottle of rum from his dresser and drank a large glass.

He felt it only a matter of time before he would be brought to trial. He thought fleetingly that it was all Rudy Bellanger's fault. Without Rudy Bellanger's attack on my mother, no robbery would have occurred, no money would have been stolen, and Trenton would be alive. He had forgotten the terrible part he had played.

Mathew stood, took off his suit jacket, and fumbled about for his jean jacket. He went into his mother's room, and kissed her, even though he was angry with her. She should have handled Sydney differently that night he came to ask about Trenton. (He didn't remember that he'd told her to say exactly what she had.)

He stared at her in both anger and pity. She had come home from mass and had fallen asleep in her clothes. On the mantel was a picture of the Virgin Mary, but Mathew could not look at it without thinking of Trenton. Once Trenton had upset Mathew's tools, and grabbed the picture of the Virgin so Mathew wouldn't hit him. Still, Mathew hit him, and kicked him. Mathew had always beaten him; just like their father had beaten Mathew. Mathew had taken those beatings to protect his mother and sister. Yet what had happened? He had turned into the same kind of man as his father.

Tonight the old lady's television was on, and *Wheel of Fortune* was playing, the wheel spinning when he closed the door.

He went to the closet and took the 12-gauge pump and walked downstairs, outside, and across the road.

The air smelled of fall, the scent of musk. On his left, close to the new bridge, with its large citified lights leaving a rarefied glow on the water, and across from our dark and muddy lane, sat the old beaten-up trailer of Jay Beard. Jay's trailer light shone on the shale rock foundation and made those rocks glisten to the sound of guitar music. His lot was surrounded by deep spruce and gnarled shrubs.

Mathew walked up his lane, walked toward the field behind, and ended up on the old Russell Road. After a few minutes he came to Connie Devlin's house, its white siding still warm and its small lawn decorations spinning and whirling in the wind. Mathew loaded the pump and walked to the door and opened it with his left hand, the shotgun in his right.

The closet had been cleaned out, and there were clothes all over the floor. A note on the table asked Devlin's sister to please turn off the water so the pipes wouldn't freeze that winter and put antifreeze in the toilet bowl.

Mathew went back outside and across the lawn. He turned and fired a brace of birdshot at the house, and kept on walking.

Back in the dark old house of his mother, he meticulously, with his black comb, combed his blond hair in a ducktail in front of the small kitchen mirror just like in a movie, even though he never had anywhere to go.

THREE

Cynthia knew that everything had changed for them, that the lawsuit showed their hidden contours of greed and self-interested pity.

She could see that something grander must propel her future now. Any idea that she cared for others was decimated once you studied her face and heard her laughter. Yet those who knew she did not care for them cared deeply for her. Her wild beauty had seduced many, some boys as young as eighteen.

Cynthia had been Mathew's most loyal adviser and friend, but it was time to loosen her tethers. Mathew was neither trusted nor liked. She saw this as a liability to herself. If he was to go to jail she must distance herself *now*. She must give Mathew up. It would be for the best. To escape prosecution herself, she would hand them Rudy Bellanger too. She was preparing to phone the police to test the ground.

But the next morning the telephone rang. It was Rudy Bellanger. He said he had to see her.

"I can't possibly," she said.

"It is urgent," he said and hung up.

Rudy came to her at ten on a quiet, bright day. She was sitting on a green chair in her bedroom. Her bedroom suite looked foreign to the house, as if it kept as its guest some countrified prima donna.

Many houses in the country have a room like this, done over by a sister or a daughter who could never leave home.

Before he could speak she told him she didn't want anything; that it was not in her nature to want, but that he was behind in payments for the child; and that she had never planned to become dependent on him.

"I have no more money," Rudy said. "Honest to God I don't have any — I've paid you, I've paid Mathew — both of you have come to me over the last five years —"

She looked closely at him. From the time of Teresa's birth until now she had received some nineteen thousand dollars from him. Could it be that even this pittance would run out?

"What do you mean, you have no more money?"

"My wife has a trust fund and a residual from the pulp mill from the years when Leo sublet his land to them — but it's not all that much, perhaps no more than forty thousand left. She needs care; she is in a wheelchair now more and more. And someone is telling lies about — us — to her — about — the child. She has not spoken to me in months — and neither has Leo."

"Well what about Teresa — should she suffer because of that!"

Rudy nodded glumly and waited patiently to tell her why he had come.

"I've suffered because of you," she said. "My God, it's my own fault for falling in love with a married man." Then she shed a tear, as easily as she did everything else.

He stared at her face, her dark hair and tight slacks, and wondered if this was true. He was vain enough to hope that it was. He smiled slightly, like a child.

Cynthia's eyes brightened. "You know I never meant to harm you, Rudy — I was the one that kept them away from you as best I could — it was Mathew — wasn't it. Connie and Mathew and you — all in this together. I have to go to the police. I mean, if *you* go to Dorchester — I don't want to go — really, I've been harbouring fugitives — Mathew, and you. Even though I love you this is very serious stuff. My love has made my head all wobbly."

"Your head wobbly —"

"Yes — and I've prayed to the Virgin — look." She pointed in regal fashion to an old picture of the Virgin Mary. "I prayed to her to get her act together and help me. The Virgin told me, in kind of a little voice, that I was blinded by love for you — and I think the Virgin Mary is telling me to turn you in — it would be for the best, wouldn't it?"

"God — no," Rudy said. "I kept quiet, now *you* have to."

"Why?" Cynthia asked innocently. "Hmm?"

"I — I could be *harmed*. If I go to jail, I mean — if you love me as you say — and I know — I mean, I've prayed to the Virgin as well — but, well — you can't take everything she says so seriously!"

Cynthia stared at him blankly.

"I would be culpable in everything — I'd get ten years in jail. I couldn't face that," Rudy whispered.

"What am I to do? I'm a nobody, just a little country girl who likes to listen to Dwight Yoakum and Steve Earle, but I refuse to go to jail as a nobody. It's high time I was a somebody, came forward and had a little article written about me. How's Gladys?" she said, lighting a cigarette.

Rudy didn't answer.

"Rudy, what do you do during the day? I never see you, so you must do something."

"I'm at the unemployment office looking for work. I was washing windows in town."

Cynthia burst out laughing, a coarse, self-indulgent, and provocative laugh. Rudy had started out washing windows at McVicer's store twenty-five years before.

"It doesn't do any good to laugh," Rudy whispered. He felt as if needles had been shoved through his body, and he remembered his own laughter at Elly when he showed her the gold money clip. "With Leo's store burned I can't do much — washing windows is a job — I don't know what else I'm going to do with myself."

"Where will all of Leo's money go?" Cynthia asked.

Rudy said nothing. He looked out the back window at the string of cottages below.

"If Connie changes his story — poor Mathew is in a mess —" Cynthia continued, "and you too. And you know they'd just as soon charge an innocent man as a guilty one. My worries are for my mother —" She took a drag of her cigarette and scrutinized him. "And your wife — if you have to go to jail as well."

Rudy felt the air on his skin, and realized that this was the moment he had been dreading for years. The moment when people he trusted would consider him expendable.

"But you were the one," Cynthia said. "In some ways you hired Mathew to do *everything*. How will Leo take that!"

There was a long pause. Then Rudy looked at her.

"Please — I've just come to do you another favour."

"What?" Cynthia said suspiciously.

"You asked me to introduce you to Leo McVicer."

"I never asked you that," Cynthia said, flushing. "I hope you didn't tell him I asked you that."

"I was told to tell you that he wants to see you — he told me to tell you to go to his house — I'm just bringing you a message. But please don't tell him anything — it's the only thing I ask. Please."

"He wants to see me — why, in God's name?" Cynthia said at the same moment he was begging.

Then they were both abruptly silent, and she looked at him with a certain gravity, and just as one might with an errand boy, she had nothing more to say to him at all.

FOUR

My mother was ill that day, and I was with her as I saw Cynthia leave, smelled smoke and early fall, heard far off the short huff of a young moose that I knew I would call and butcher. I did not know where Cynthia was going in her swaying way that seemed to squander so much, like the scent of late-summer flowers, the overripe apple bins of fall.

I saw her leave in a plain summer dress, the length of which was somewhere above her knee. After she left I saw Mathew Pit, looking sick, come into the yard and walk toward the brook. There he sat on an old chaise longe staring at the water, as he sometimes did when fighting off a binge. Cynthia left in the other direction.

I know what happened that day, just as I know what has happened all the days before. I wish I could have changed just one action; the reflection of that change might vastly have altered me.

Their back path led through the gravel pit and to the dark, worn path through the spruce grove that smelled so green to a hidden trampled field behind Leo McVicer's. I know how she must have moved, for I envisioned her. Hers was a remarkable journey — for it was a journey that would radically shift the balance of power and loyalty for myself and others.

She came to a tree, and paused in a moment of splendid isolation, a woman as proud as the world, living in solitude. She came to McVicer's back fence and tried to climb it, catching her leg on the wire and tearing the skin.

McVicer was sitting in the porch staring out at the bay and winging a red alder switch when she came to the front of the house. The water had taken on the look of desolation that water takes on in September, after the vacationers have again sought the comfort of the town or the cities of Toronto, Montreal, and Boston.

So our shore was now abandoned, and the water suspended for one second or two before the maelstrom. Leo, too, looked as if he had postponed his slide into old age. And flush with his recent victories — for he knew Mathew and Connie and Rudy would go under now — he was offering a laurel wreath to the one he wished to save. It was the same bestowal he had once given Gerald Dove, or a dozen others over the years. His power allowed him to pick and choose. He saw her walk through his back gate, knock on the door, and enter with a smile.

"Why, you are hurt," Leo said. He jumped up in a spry way and took her hand, which was large for a woman's. "Look — let me get something for you, girl —"

He pressed his hand against the small of her back and led her into the living room.

"Really, I'm fine," she said.

"Fine — nonsense altogether." He left, and she was alone to gaze about the room. He came back with cotton balls and iodine and kneeled before her. She let him take her leg in his hands and wash her cut, and she stared at the top of his white head, cropped close, with reddish wrinkled skin on the back of his neck, and his hair unkempt; not like a man with *so* much money. And when he stood she was suddenly surprised at how poorly fitted and unnatural looking his false teeth were. His life was in the woods, and though he might have thousands tucked away, he still called mathematics figures and men with education eggheads.

He took a seat beside her. He smelled of spruce gum and earth, of moments cast against the ice and snow that should never be a cause of disrespect. But now children thought him an old man and of no importance at all. They did not even care about the Second World War, let alone think it important that he exercised extreme courage in it.

"So, Miss Pit, how is your mom?"

"Please — call me Cynthia — she is okay —" And then her voice changed. "But Trenton's death took a lot out of her."

He was smiling when she said this, and his smile faded, first on the side of his face nearest her.

"That was terrible," he said, "but they get theirs back, you see, those people who cause those things, they never get away. They might think they get away for three or four years, and then suddenly new information comes forward, and the little boy is avenged — and new charges will be laid by Christmas or soon after!"

This startled her, and frightened her as well. He raised his finger and pointed to the ceiling as if it was in God's hands and he alone understood this. Then he glared down at the carpet and looked up suddenly.

He told her that he needed her advice about who might help look after his daughter.

"Oh my, what's wrong?" Cynthia asked, with feigned concern that she could not disguise, and he could not help but detect though he pretended he did not.

"She is an invalid more than ever," he said. "She is depressed too, and has no friends. She used to have a monkey when she was a girl — but he died. Rudy wouldn't allow her none." He paused, his brow furrowed.

"A monkey —?"

"No — friends — wouldn't allow her no friends."

"Oh yes," Cynthia said.

"She has a wheelchair — but it's very hard for her where the hallways are carpeted. And I've gotten her a hospital bed but it's still out in the garage. Rudy is completely useless — I don't know if you know him?"

"Rudy? Oh yes." Cynthia expressed a slight smile of disapproval that Leo welcomed. It seemed to make her feigned concern for Gladys more acceptable.

"And how is your little girl?" he said, eyeing her quickly.

"Teresa — she's okay — in fact, I was going to bring her today but thought against it — I'll bring her over some day maybe to see you."

"She was named after Mother Teresa, I bet," Leo said.

"Oh yes," Cynthia said, although this was the first she had heard of it.

He nodded. Then they were both silent. He felt attracted to her, and she let him be. She crossed her legs suddenly to look at her cut, which allowed him a slight view of her panties, and then she looked up at him with large brown eyes.

"I can do it any time," she said, without changing her position.

"Pardon me?"

"I could help your daughter —" she said, rubbing the scrape with her fingers. Her nails were painted purple. "I've taken a course in homecare because of Trenton. It was a while ago, and I don't have references — but I can help her in and out of the bath, take her for walks, cook a meal — you know, that kind of thing."

"That kind of thing," was said softly and coyly, as if it was a coded message or soft trap, and she looked again at the scrape.

Then she put her knee down and pressed her legs together shyly.

There was another long pause, and Leo McVicer scrutinized her. Then he smiled, once again showing the poor fit of his false teeth.

"Of course — that would be good —"

When she got up to leave he walked behind her. He suddenly felt the same man he was years ago, when he had walked into a dispute at his sawmill and taken a peavey out of the hand of the man who had promised to crush his skull.

But Cynthia had also gone through a metamorphosis. Suddenly she was not the Cynthia who had talked to Rudy that morning, but was concerned and tolerant of others, was not envious of Gladys's money but was her compatriot, who wished to help and protect her. When Cynthia turned at the door Leo was very close to her and her breasts pressed against him.

"Oh!" she said.

He laughed uncertainly and grabbed her shoulders to keep his balance.

"You come tomorrow afternoon and we will work out the money — and, well —"

"Of course," she said. "I'll be here at three o'clock."

She left the house along the walkway and disappeared, while he went outside and straightened gunnysacks over the newly planted pear trees. They never grew here, but nonetheless were planted every few years on a whim. He watched her walking away, saw her lilting sway, and his heart leapt in old fire and joy.

At this time Leo was sixty-five years of age, and reflecting on his life. After Cynthia left, Leo dressed and went to a Knights of Columbus meeting with his son-in-law.

In Rudy's pocket were the plans for the marina; in his mind was his sales pitch to his father-in-law. If he did not get this marina, he would be destitute.

In Rudy's soul was an unquenchable fear that he would as always be refused the money. In his heart was his hope that this marina would rekindle Cynthia's interest in him, if only to keep her from betraying him.

So, driving along the reserve with its small incomplete houses, and children sitting out on porches in the last hour of the day, the rays of sun falling on patches and slanted roofs, on shingles shining and dull, on empty dog tins, and the green grass at the back of the house, cool in the evening air, Rudy waited his moment.

Bellanger saw all of this, saw it all, and kept going over in his mind what he would say to Leo and when he would say it.

When we get to Carl Francis's house, he would tell himself. But the Francis house would be passed by; the porch, the dark second-storey window, the small speedboat with its fancy red flag.

Bellanger knew Leo McVicer was at the height of his power, even though, at sixty-five, he had almost ended his years of work. His decisions, always final, came quickly and without any thought. The car progressed, as well as the silence. But suddenly Leo moved in his seat, looked over at Rudy, and said:

"Son of a bitch, a goddamn marina!"

"What?" Rudy said.

"It's what the people up in town have almost finished — surprised you didn't know? Amalgamation is coming and they are going to make us into a city — so of course we must look like a city. Now we don't have scows or boats or working people like I grew up with, and you grew up with too, Rudy — we have pretty little sailboats —"

"Where did you hear this?"

"Just heard." Leo sniffed. "Just heard."

He did not tell Rudy that he had known of Rudy's plans for three years and had been quietly working to build a marina in town with a small consortium of trusted pals. That he had convinced himself that Rudy had stolen *his* idea; and that this marina, of which he owned

37 percent, and which he pretended he hated, would be opened officially next July first.

They passed the entrance to the church ground, the last place Rudy had reflected on before the old man had spoken.

FIVE

Only a few Knights made it to the meeting, and fewer stayed for mass.

Leopold's mind was not on church. It was on a variety of things men's minds are on when they go to church. Sports flitted to boxing, to ridicule in his youth, to the laughter he had had to endure as the son of a drunkard, to his mother's death, to his mistakes in business that resulted in an argument with his men and the collapse of his sawmill.

Saint Augustine wrote that men always believe they can con God into serving them, asking not for direction in their lives but for gain if they do right in service of Him, and he uses Cain's discussions with God to prove this. Though my father and I had read Saint Augustine, and perhaps Leopold McVicer had not, Leopold was a personification of this particular wry truth on this particular dusky fall evening.

He wanted to have a relationship with Cynthia, and he wanted God to believe that he was hoping for Gladys's well-being and thus sanction this relationship as being in the interests of his daughter. He also wanted the insurance money from his lost store and promised God a stained-glass window.

He wanted his sins forgiven, but sins he was not willing to admit to. Those sins he was not willing to admit to he wanted overlooked; they had to do with his mistress and the treatment of his three other children; and his mill, and the initial spill into the upper levels of Arron Brook.

People never knew how clever this old man really was. He had understood things for a long while now. He knew only Connie could have turned off the floodlights, only Mathew could have frightened him enough to do it; and Rudy was involved. Why? Because of the tag from the inside of Elly's skirt that had been left on the carpet that day, and the way the vacuuming had stopped, so that the creases on the floor were different. And Rudy's boots running down the road, which would never have been noticed, except the native boy Darcy Paul had helped Leo with his deer and had mentioned it peculiar; someone running with cowboy boots on the wrong feet. All of this had Leo suspicious, as did a speck of blood on the tile behind the carpet. He was sure there had been an attempt at an assault. It took him longer to decide Rudy was involved in the robbery, to cover his assault, and the bridge to cover up the robbery. He was still uncertain until a few months ago. But this is why he never gave Rudy the marina.

This week or the next he would tell Gladys what he had discovered, and let her decide how she wanted to proceed. Well, actually he would tell her how to proceed. And Rudy would be gone from their lives.

He stayed on his knees and prayed. He prayed for forgiveness and grace and peace of mind. And he prayed to get back at those who had sabotaged his bridge. He did not take communion.

SIX

After mass Leo went into the vestry to speak to Father Porier about Vicka, the girl from Yugoslavia who, along with five other children, claimed she had seen the Virgin Mary.

The week before, Leo had promised to write a cheque to help

cover Vicka's visit and he now wanted to know if Porier thought Vicka was a crook or was she on the up and up.

"Oh I think so," Porier said. "She is just a child who has had a wonderful gift and wishes to share it with the world."

Leo looked at one of the young altar boys who was leaving the room, and then looked back at Porier. He said he would help with her visit but he would be surprised if there was a miracle. Porier asked him if he believed in miracles.

"I don't know why God gives messages to Vicka and not to — oh, someone on T.V. like Regis and Kathie Lee — you know what I mean."

Porier nodded, and waited as Leo lit his pipe.

"You know, Leo, what you just said reminded me of something —"

Leopold, forever suspicious, suddenly felt he was being chastised.

"I was thinking of the little albino girl — the poet — what's her name?"

"Autumn Henderson?"

"Ah, Henderson — and how she came here with her little brother — yesterday — what's his name?"

"The little one — Percy."

"Ah yes — Percy — and that old dog of Trenton Pit — the little dog with the pointy ears and flat face — what's its name?"

"Scupper Pit," Leo said.

"Ah yes, Scupper Pit," Father Porier said. He smiled and went into some kind of reverie, and then looked at Leo.

"Well, what did they want?" Leo asked.

"Who?"

"The children — the children — not Scupper — I don't feel Scupper wanted much — except to follow the children — but what did the children want?"

"Well, the children. Autumn had the little girl with her too — what's her name — the little Pit girl?"

"Mother Teresa Pit."

"Ah yes, Mother Teresa Pit. Autumn asked for a blessing of her because of her heart. Then Percy wanted me to bless Scupper Pit. So

I blessed Scupper. Percy wanted to pray at the bones of our saint for Teresa Pit and for his mother, who is sick."

"Their mother is sick? Elly?"

"Very sick — very sick —" Porier said. "She has had numerous miscarriages, you see — and — well, with herbicides et cetera —"

Porier lowered his eyes sadly. He knew who McVicer's three children were, where they went and who baptized them as theirs — and this knowledge gave him a certain power over McVicer.

"Percy is wonderful, and he lifted Teresa up for me to bless her. I told him that there were no saint bones in the church. And the little boy said to me, 'But there are!'

"'Oh,' I said, 'are there saint bones in *my* church?" (Here he affected astonishment.) "And Leopold, do you know what Percy said?"

"No, I don't," Leo said. "I don't know what Percy said. How would I know what Percy said? Percy may have said anything."

"Percy said, 'If there are no saint bones, then there is no church — you cannot have one without the other.'"

Leo was exasperated. He was exasperated because he didn't know what the child had meant, didn't know why it was a great thing to say, yet was jealous of the little child for saying it, especially after he had written a cheque for the visit of Vicka. Could Percy do that? No, he could not. It was always up to him, McVicer.

"Children say all kinds of things," he said. "I have said similar things myself."

"You have?" Porier said.

"Of course I did — lots of smart things. Anyway," Leopold said, "I know Mathew Pit did it — the robbery."

"What — How —?"

"You know the five hundred dollars? I bet my pocket money Elly never confessed to it at your confessional. Why? Because she never did it."

"Oh —"

"Mathew Pit — he had me fooled for a day or two — no, not even that long!"

The light had gone from the room and only a few electric candles burned. The altar boys had all gone.

"You see, no matter how long, things get figured out."

"You are right," Porier said. "All things unseen will be seen."

This struck Leopold not as comforting as he left.

The autumn night was warm, and smelled of rain through the oak doors. In the autumn night Porier stood, turned out the lights, and locked the back church door, from where he could see the white marble altar glowing faintly. He could not admit to himself the sexual misdeeds he had committed on the two poorest children in his ward thirty-five years before — his one lapse in all this time — Sydney Henderson and Connie Devlin.

Sydney had survived in some fashion. But it had ruined Devlin's life, so that he became a cheat, a drunk, and a liar in the world. Porier saw in Devlin's weak mouth and small, deceitful eyes a vague yet discerning moment of himself, of his own sad soul. He was hoping for God's forgiveness, without wanting to bear any further cross.

He knew who McVicer's other children were.

He knew. He knew who had burned the store, and who asked to have it done. He probably knew my father was innocent of every crime ever bestowed upon him.

Leo went home. He sat and thought a long time. Now the natives were saying he had stolen their land and were demanding restitution. And Dr. David Scone, who had once sat at his table, had taken their side; and so too had Diedre Whyne. Perhaps he would lose it all. But not if he was smart. He took off his uniform and sat in a chair near his bed. All his friends were now dead; others whom he had fed and clothed had turned against him in their piss-arsed pants. The premier, a man he had helped get elected, had snubbed him last Christmas. David Scone was publishing a book on the injustices against the First Nations. It was being serialized in the local paper. Seven times in the first three chapters Leo's company was mentioned, the wood he had cut, the roads he had dug out. And Scone wrote his reports against him in an office building his lumber had built and on paper his softwood had supplied.

Whyne was dead, Ike Pit was dead; those who had once offered him a Senate seat in Ottawa were dead, their pictures stiffly hanging on the walls of the Legislature. Unfortunately he was not dead. He was old, and his time had gone.

He loaded his shotgun as he did now every night.

Man can be defeated but not destroyed, he thought, and took some comfort in this, as a freezing man takes comfort in a small patch of sunlight on the snow.

Yet he thought of Percy, helping lift Teresa Pit so Father Porier would bless her, and was sad. He gave a prayer that he would build the church roof as long as God left him in peace. But when he closed his eyes, he saw only Percy Henderson, hauling Scupper Pit in his wagon, up to the church to pray for sweet, gentle Elly McGowan.

SEVEN

Some nights Percy would sit by Mom, playing cards or checkers as she rested on the couch. She would tell him stories about long ago, when Autumn and I were children.

Often I was out, poaching, or drinking. If the poor rabbits knew I was selling their dead bodies for wine, they would be heartbroken.

Many nights I stood outside of a dance shivering because I didn't have the three bucks cover charge. I smelled of woodsmoke and iron, my eyes were deep brown, my skin the colour of poverty. I had colds that would not stop, I coughed night and day, or when I sat at the table in my thin shirt, sipping from a quart of smuggled-in wine, with a pack of Export "makins" sticking out of my pocket. Girls would pass my table and not look in my direction, frightened I would ask them over. Many times I could smell the balsam fir on me because I had loaded wood. Looking at old pictures, I realized that I resembled Roy Henderson, even to the clothes I wore. I had drifted back into the nineteenth century.

So what did it matter that I could quote Plato, or that my father had read to me as a child? I knew nothing about music. When once asked if I knew who the Beatles were, I said: a small armoured bug with mandible. I had fought back, I had learned. I had, like Autumn, taken certain courses in the frivolity of the world, only to sound ridiculous when I sang the lyrics coming from the age of yuppies, of *Bright Lights, Big City.*

On Thanksgiving Saturday there was a dance, and I came home drunk. Elly said that Dad had phoned. He had wanted to talk to me, and they had left the phone line open for a half hour. She told me he would be home for Christmas. She never told him she was sick — never that I was drunk. Mom asked me if I would go to church the next morning for her. She had never been drunk. I on the other hand had taken to being what my neighbours *thought* I was. For, once I became what they had delighted in saying I was, they feared me.

Still our old house belied my monstership. I wasn't even a thief in my heart. I sought not darkness but light. So such a rebellion as mine was a heartbroken one. And little Autumn knew this.

Whenever I saw the faded palm leaves from an old Palm Sunday behind a picture of Saint Bernadette of Lourdes, I would tremble. In the never-forgotten stories from my childlike mother I would remember that when our Virgin was speaking to Saint Bernadette, the voices from hell arose, and one look from the Virgin's quiet face sent them into howling submission and final silence. I would remember that Saint Bernadette's body in its glass resting spot had never corrupted. And I would realize that I had miserably failed these childhood stories, but I had never in my heart outgrown them. Never had I really disbelieved them.

More fool I to believe something I could not commit to and damn myself for my human weakness each and every day, when millions who mocked my belief never suffered a pang.

Mom believed. She believed in miracles just as she gave money she could ill afford to Save the Whales, Save the Seals, Save the Children. In this was her response to miracles in her life. So leave her to them. She believed in Saint Thérèse of the child Jesus, of little Saint Flora beheaded for her faith. There was in this, in the rains of autumn, or in the scent of the lilac of late spring, a feeling of quiet wonder and of peace.

Still, my mother had a peace beyond any I had experienced. She had a picture of a sperm whale that someone told her her money had helped keep alive. Christ, did they not know my mother had not a nickel?

I had just come from the dance. Our community centre was an old one-room school moved out on skids to the highway, and a bar and a dance floor put in. I went there, now looked upon as the failure I was.

And what had I done that very night to prove myself? I had attacked the fisherman Hanny Brown. And what was the reason? Well, he was six foot three and strong as a bear, but hadn't I proven to myself I could hit like a mule?

He had no idea why I attacked him, and I needed a reason. I yelled, so everyone would hear, that he had called my mother a whore.

"That is not true, son — I would say that to no woman."

I started to turn away but saw Cynthia Pit by the bar looking across at me. I threw a short right and I felt his legs buckle within the very vibration of my punch. He put his hand up to cover his mouth, and I came back with a left hook. And Hanny dropped. His wife started crying — his face was covered in blood, his shirt and tie spotted bright red, and he rolled over and pushed himself up.

"Son," he said, "I did nothing."

"Well there you go — I just did," I said, laughing. I walked out through the crowd, everyone looking at me until I looked at them.

Mathew followed me out. I will tell you this, I was under his spell. There was no question about it.

Mathew brought out a paper towel for me to wipe Hanny's blood from my hand. He smiled when he saw it, and handed me a smoke. He said I had done a good job, and told me he had more wood to steal.

"I want you to go somewhere with me."

"Where —?"

"Just somewhere — will you or not?"

I shrugged as if to say it made no difference. Then I went home. Once I was alone, my elation subsided, and I was left only with a picture of Hanny's kind dark face looking at me in confusion and in shame because I had hit him in front of his wife.

I needed my mother to hate me as I went into the house that night. So I began shouting at them, and Mom began to shake. Autumn glared at me and got up and left the house, so I yelled at her and called her a whore.

"Please," Mother said, reaching a hand toward me. "I am glad you can take care of yourself, but tomorrow go to church and recite the prayer of Saint Francis."

The air smelled of medicine and night, her nightgown was white with small blue flowers; her throat was bare and showed the strains of her coughing. Dr. Savard had come down once — only once — to tell her it was her nerves, and that she was going through early menopause. He left her pills that sat upon a table. It is almost indescribable, how his affluence and modern knowledge was so out of place in our shanty. Its faded walls and small rooms, which I had once delighted in. Now her hand trembled as she held it out.

It was the very first time I never took her hand. In my spitefulness — in my feelings of shame and anger and poverty — in the accumulated terror I had suffered and made others suffer I lashed out:

"The church has done a great shitload of good for you," I said. "A self-centred quiff for a priest."

I stumbled against Percy and the cup of tea he was carrying to Mom fell from his hand. He crouched down and began to pick up the pieces.

"I will get Mom another cup," he said.

"Never mind her goddamn tea!" I roared at him. He didn't look at me, and continued to pick up the pieces.

"Oh Percy, I'll get it," Mom said, and she tried to sit up. Ashamed, yet filled with newfound boldness and hate, and disgusted by their kindness, I fled. I sat on the old couch behind the house.

I had nowhere to go, and my head was reeling with the pointless drunkenness of youth. Mathew had told me things almost in code, and I was trying to understand them.

The code was this: A man — a true man — did what he wanted to. Society was fine for people who could profit by it, but the community had left the two of us, Mathew and me, out. So why be cowed by a community that spit in my face? Look it straight in the face and dare it to spit. The code also said, take care of the weak and never hurt the innocent. This was Mathew's secret code to me. And I firmly believed he practised it.

It was a grand code, I thought. And if I had this code I needed nothing. Besides, weren't the community and the towns along the river prepared to accept people who relied upon this code, and weren't they frightened of men who used it? And didn't those who used it have greater and more admirable souls than those who did not, and didn't I acknowledge this myself by secretly envying those men? If I envied their spunk and irreverence, so too did others.

"My father believed them," I said to Mathew. "Now he owes taxes and they spit in his face."

"What would you do if they did to you what they did to your father?" Mathew said to me one day.

I thought, and said: "They wouldn't dare."

Mathew smiled.

I felt power surge through my body. I had given the right answer. And this was why I had needed to prove myself by hitting Hanny Brown.

In back of the house on this cool October night I watched the stars and wondered how long it would take to travel to one if I went the speed of light. I held my hand over my eyes and watched the heavens, while inside I heard my mother and Percy speak.

She asked Percy if he thought I was angry at them, for they were left alone so often.

"Oh no," Percy said. "Lyle finds me bugs and caterpillars and took me fishing."

"But he hasn't taken you to do any of those things in a long time — it's well over a year. He hardly speaks to me. He always looks angry — I've never seen anyone so angry with the world. I know he has had a bad time in the world. But your father has had a worse time, and your father never looked angry. And Autumn too — she has been afflicted since childhood — she has no money, and boys have made fun of her — and used her — I know they have. She has come home from dances quietly and secretly crying. But she faces it, works to give us what she can — and she had a poem published, did you know —"

"Lyle cut the wood, and I watched him —"

"Autumn," Mother said, "poor little Autumn. I think we have failed our children — your father and I — they wanted so much more than us. Percy, do you understand — I saw boys and girls with money, at the church picnics, and looked in my purse and there was nothing to give them. It broke my heart."

"Scupper Pit has a sore paw — and he has to ride in my wagon."

"I'm sorry," my mother said, "but when your daddy comes home he can fix that — he is the bravest man you will ever meet — and see those books — you and I could not read them all, but your daddy could. I get so confused with books, and money — I get all mixed up — I think I have the money to pay something to keep the whales alive and then I don't — but not your dad — he is the only brave man I have met — well except for Mr. Beard. One night your dad was sitting here and I was standing in the doorway to the study. I was pregnant with you — which means you were in my tummy — and I turned and your father — Sydney, my husband — said, 'You have to come here and lie down now.' I don't know why he said this, but he did. He stood and made room for me to lie down, and walked by the study door. He stood there as if facing a test from God. He said nothing. He waited. There was a loud sharp noise and he held his arm. A man had shot through our house — you and I would have died. How did he know this? He is brave — good and kind, you will see."

"Lyle is brave," Percy said.

I waited, holding my breath, my hand still over my face looking at the stars. I wanted my mother to say, "Yes, he is very brave." I wanted her to acknowledge my bravery, because I had put my hand through a window, hit a big fisherman, and carried a knife. No one fucked with me. Even as far down as Tracadie they had heard of me by now, and when I looked into the mirror I saw the cold self-mesmerizing eyes of youthful disillusioned pain; the kind of eyes I had sought since seeing those eyes in Mathew Pit when I was ten years of age.

But my mother said something, and I did not catch what it was, which disappointed me. Perhaps she did say I was brave. That was all I wanted.

My mother told Percy his tea was delicious, and that she had at one picnic served eight hundred cups of tea. Again there was silence. The light went out in the house. The wind in the trees blew. Percy said softly:

"Mom — I am making a wish that you won't go away."

The evening was still sweet, even with the harsh aftertaste of wine.

EIGHT

The next morning Jay Beard asked to see me, so I went to his house. He came outside and sat on an old drum, looking at me with his craggy face covered in grey beard. He asked me what had happened at the dance.

"I'll backhand any son of a bitch who comes near me."

"Our river has enough bastards like that — but only a few brave men," Jay said quietly. "And you hanging around with Mathew will do you no good — or do you remember?"

This comment scalded me, and my regard for Mr. Beard allowed its truth to wound, while my respect for him disallowed any reprisal. I remember how he stood outside with a service revolver in midwinter protecting us. I owed him much, and he never asked for anything in return. Strangely I had thought I had become more like him, but he was here to tell me I had not.

The next Friday I was busy cutting some support staffs for our old back shed while Percy sat on a stump watching me. The day had a stiff wind across the bay, and from far away I could smell salt off the water. When I looked again Percy was gone.

After searching the house I went into the woods and crossed Arron Brook and went up the long crooked road toward the hill — the one where I could see both mine and Pit's property. I saw Percy far away, near the highway. Then he crossed the road, in cautious steps, and ran to Jay Beard's trailer. I walked back through the broken windfalls and made it to Arron Brook. Then I crossed onto Russell Road and walked into Beard's yard. It was now late Friday afternoon and there was a smell of fish somewhere along the old highway; the pointless fast that lingered in the spots of blue autumn heaven.

Inside Jay Beard's trailer was my small brother, listening as Jay played his guitar. Percy had his hands folded on his lap, his feet in red rubber boots still almost six inches from the kitchen floor, and his bow tie as always crooked. Suddenly he looked up at me through the window, and smiled a delightful smile in the late-afternoon sun. Then he went back to watching Mr. Beard's fingers, with Scupper waiting patiently at his feet.

On those days when I had thought he was going up the lane to wait for me he was actually going to hear the old country and western music of Mr. Beard. And I realized what the word *Getir* on the envelope was. Percy was saving for a guitar.

I turned and went home. I was sad, and a little envious, and I did not know why. Mathew met me at our front door. He had been waiting for me.

"Can you come?" he asked.

"Where?"

"I have somewhere to go."

"How long?"

"Just an hour or so."

I went inside and told Mom I had to go. She was lying with her eyes half-opened staring at the ceiling while Autumn was making her soup.

"Where are you going, love?" she said.

"Oh — I have things to do — people to see."

"I've been thinking of my life in the orphanage," my mother said, "all day — all those sad little children that I knew. It is very strange."

I never knew that her words, her movements, and her smile would haunt my every moment the rest of my life.

We travelled that day for fifteen miles, and then along a broken, winding road toward the bay. The trees' leaves were tinged and frost-bitten, the sun lingered on the dash, and there was a scent of fall on the car seat.

We were going to an old lot, down an overgrown road against the bald autumn shoreline, that once belonged to Leo McVicer. I saw a moose trail thrashed toward the dark spruce on the far side. In the air was a hawk circling like a bitter omen of winter. I saw ten or twelve tombstones, overgrown, twisted and mossy.

My heart stopped.

"These are others McVicer never spoke of — these are men who died working for him. Most of them was bachelors, lived alone — and had no one but each other. Here now," Mat said, walking along the old moose trail, "is ninety to a hundred barrels I buried — he was still using it up until ten year ago. This is what he didn't want Dove to know." He looked about at the gravestones. "These men worked with him in the forties and fifties after the war — this was their graveyard — but the community about here faded away. A few of them were married with kids and stuff — though the majority weren't. They all died of poison. This is my grandfather — and my father, Kyle Ike Pit — and here, Lyle, is your grandfather — Roy Henderson. Your mother is dying because of what these guys sprayed —"

We were very close to the bay. Chokecherry bushes lined the old fallen graveyard. The sound of a bird twittering and trailing the last of its stay here came to me through a cloud of cold.

"I helped me old man bury a ton of barrels. I know the government is happy to blame McVicer if they can or side with him if they have to. It is time to get him back!" Mathew said, and then with a soft hand on my shoulder he said, "Think of what he did to your father."

I took a drink and looked out past the trampled field to an old horse standing in thigh-high grass, to a cloth of some kind wrapped about a clothesline in a faroff yard of a bleak yellow house.

Mathew's eyes were steely blue now, his voice soothing.

"That's all been said and done," I answered, "said and done."

"But what if we find the letters as well? That would prove it — isn't that what we should do? There's probably money in it too — lots of it. But think of the government letters — it'll prove what I know — and if I do, everyone — the premier, his lawyers from Chatham, all of them — will pay."

"How do you know he has a safe?"

"Of course he has a safe — of course he has a safe. We have to get the money before the natives," Mathew said. "That's the next ones to go after it —"

"We will sue," I said, shivering. "Sue him again."

Mathew's face was calm, and filled with the light from the weak sun. Afternoon was drawing on its shadows, and some boat trailers rested along the roadside to the bay, ready for hauled-up speedboats. He spoke softly, almost without interest.

"Suing will keep us in court," he continued. "I don't know how much time your mother has — I know Teresa May has a year or less — if we got bogged down in court — I know that's more legal — but I tried it that way."

I realized at this moment that all my life and what I had done and my poverty and my reaction to it, and my solitude in school, and my love of Christmas until it came, and my yearning madness for Penny Porier, and the dreary spotted tablecloth in our kitchen or the perpetual sadness of our lane with Percy and his wagon, or my mother's smile when she was being bullied, or the circuses we could not go to or the foster parents where we sat, nay the very cough of my mother and the suffering of my father for unanswering Christ had caused this moment. I could say yes or no. I said nothing.

I realized that the money had mesmerized Mathew. He knew he would be in jail soon for Trenton's death, and he had to either face up to his crime or boldly assert himself and rob a safe and escape. And I liked him well enough then to help him. Well, he had helped me with the chalice. I owed him something.

I wondered just fleetingly if Mathew was even thinking of sharing the money with me. Then I smiled. I wanted revenge as much as he wanted money. I needed it to fulfill my basic thesis against the false doctrine of my father. Except I might say, where had my thesis taken me? Exactly where my dad said it would.

I stared at Roy Henderson's little stone with the date already invisible and stained.

I had become exactly as those who had hated us. And it had happened without my even trying. Mathew drove me back home. We didn't speak. I thought of nothing as I walked down the lane.

I had wanted nothing to do with this robbery, until I found Percy sitting by himself in the small kitchen in the dark. He told me Mommie was in the hospital. Percy had been waiting on his small kitchen chair for three hours in silence.

I had to dress the child. I found a white shirt faded almost to yellow, and a pair of dark dress pants, and an old pair of shoes that I shined. I washed and changed and we started up the road.

All along our lane Percy was looking and waiting for Autumn, but she was not here. Then he picked some leaves, to make into some kind of a bouquet for Mom. Then, as if distracted, he said:

"I went to the church and prayed so Mom would be better for her birthday."

"It's not your fault, Percy," I said, my voice breaking just a little.

"Lyle — it is not your fault either," he whispered.

NINE

We reached the hospital after nine o'clock. My mother was on the second floor, in a room with two other women. Her hair, I saw now, was almost grey at thirty-nine years of age. Her face was sunken. Percy gave her the bouquet of birch and maple leaves. She kissed him gently and then asked for Autumn.

"She wasn't home," I said, "but I will find her — and she can visit you tomorrow."

She said nothing.

"I will phone Dad," I said.

"Oh no," she said, waving her hand weakly, "don't bother him — wait until he comes back — then Percy and I and Dad are going to Reversing Falls."

She began to fuss with the yellow collar of Percy's white shirt, and patted his chest. Then she straightened his bow tie.

Percy grinned at me as if this proposed trip was unquestionably true. I walked out into the corridor. The nurses were going from room to room on a night check of patients. I asked one what had happened to my mother. She told me to wait a moment and disappeared.

I sat in the corridor for twenty minutes or more. Then just as I was about to look for the nurse I saw Constable Morris coming toward me with another police officer. Dr. Savard was with them also. The doctor told me that my mother was suffering an internal injury, and asked point-blank if she had been struck.

"Of course not," I said.

"Well, she has been bleeding very badly — we are trying now to stop it," Savard said.

Constable Morris introduced me to Constable John Delano. Delano had insisted he come to see me about the investigation.

"What investigation?" I asked.

He asked me into the waiting room, and we sat down. Morris stood at the door. I knew Morris had needed my father to be guilty to save his career. His superiors had finally sensed this, and because of McVicer's importance, had quietly asked for someone else to look into what had happened. And now everything pointed to other people. And Delano knew who they were but as yet could not find Connie Devlin to corroborate it.

"You believe my father did none of it?" I asked Delano.

"I believe there was a crime committed on the bridge," Delano said, "but I'm positive your father didn't do it. I believe it was done to set up your father — I believe the money was robbed from McVicer but not by your mother —"

Delano said he had met with my father twice.

"When?" I asked.

"At the camp," he said. "Do you want me to contact him about your mom?"

"No — not now, please." My voice sounded too eager suddenly.

"The trouble with suing," Delano said, quite off the cuff, "is that it takes so long — it may make people wary — and then they lose the lawsuit and get nothing — like the five families a few years ago — they end up with a few hundred dollars. Your father wanted nothing to do with that. He stood alone — always. His life was not a convenience for himself, was it. You have Percy to think of."

Delano got up, shook my hand, wished me luck. Clearly he was warning me not to do what I was planning to do. But how had he known?

I found Percy sitting by his sleeping mother and we went out. The streets were quiet, and the world still. Moths gathered under the streetlights in town and fell to the raining pools, bathing their powder in water. Percy picked one up, dried it with a touch, and released it into the night.

"There are millions of moths, Percy," I said scornfully as I watched it flutter in its zigzagged bafflement a few feet away.

"It doesn't know that, Lyle," Percy said, taking my hand to cross the highway.

288

I carried my little brother down the long road to home as he hugged my neck. With his head resting on my shoulder, I whispered: "I love you, Percy — I love you and Mommie and Autumn, and I love Daddy too."

He had fallen asleep and did not hear.

I went that night and sat by our river. The water of our great river makes us disappear — we become at twilight in the babble of water a symphony of ghosts. As spots on the river darken, and the shadows are gorged by night, we remember the ghosts of children, of ourselves as boys and girls at six and seven far up on the Bartibog or Arron Brook, turning to smile when a trout is hooked. Of our mother in a light-hearted moment fifteen years before. The moment passes, the water continues on, the boys and girls leave the trout stream for the uncertain stream of life, and become as I was now, sitting beside it.

But somewhere in a magical twinkling as you walk in the faraway future, you remember those children around a small blowdown in the middle of a faraway time and are filled with sweet sadness. I wanted to go back there, to that time; the time when I believed my father was a hero and took his offered hand.

TEN

Mother planned for Percy to go to First Communion, spoke to Autumn about him, all the while knowing that death was in the room with her, waiting.

Mom had arranged for a boy to come to take care of him in those forgotten afternoons after class. Darren Voteur. He was the only person available at that time. Since Autumn and I knew him, we felt comfortable having him there a few hours a day.

I did not know until later that things did not go well.

"What can you do, Percy," Darren asked one afternoon during a week of drizzle and storms, "about your mom? She will die soon — will you cry?"

Percy sighed. "I can pray when Autumn takes me."

"Prayer doesn't do much good —" Darren said.

"Mommie likes caramels," Percy said. "I could buy her caramels."

"It's more than caramels, Percy," Darren said. "She has a big tumour eating her away every day — and every day you go there your mom is littler."

The afternoon was pale and crisp and smelled of ice on fallen leaves.

"And you think you can just buy her caramels."

"I know, Darren," Percy whispered. "It's much more than caramels."

"Why am I here with you? Where is Lyle? Did you know, Percy — your brother and sister have left you — you'd better find me money or I won't stay." Darren wiped his hands across his mouth and looked over his shoulder.

"When Lyle comes he will give you the four dollars," Percy said.

"If it wasn't for me your mother would be dead now. Autumn and Lyle don't care about your mother. You think your mom likes caramels, do you? You know what I think? I think she is happy she is dying — to get away from you —"

When Percy looked up Darren smiled at him, his lips thin and his teeth white, and he had a small moustache, with two small moles on his cheek and two earrings in each ear. He had a Walkman he listened to, and he had cowboy boots, and he had a big wallet, and he liked Megadeth, and he said he had been to Toronto, where he had his tongue pierced.

"I heard your mom tell my mother last year she didn't like you."

Percy looked at Darren but said nothing.

"You know what Autumn likes, Percy?"

Percy smiled. "She likes to tickle me."

"She likes my big prick up her white cunt — that's what I think —

she wanted to go out with me, but she looks like a ghost," Darren said. "Have you ever seen Autumn's white cunt? I bet it's pretty. Have you? I know other boys have — they have all seen it — I told her I didn't want to go out with her — I told her." He was breathing strangely, excitedly as he spoke.

Percy kept his head down, ashamed of what had been said. Then he moved a checker. Percy's right shirt sleeve was busted through at the elbow. The autumn sun was faint and far away; the graders could be heard on the shore lifting timbers and rocks.

"I moved a checker," Percy said. "Now you move a checker."

"You moved a checker," Darren said, and he swiped the board clean. "I moved all the checkers."

Percy got down to pick the checkers up. When he stood up with the checkers, Darren struck him in the mouth.

The checkerboard went flying, and Percy fell. Blood trickled from his nose and lip. He got to his feet and sat on the couch where my mother had spent so much time when she was pregnant with him. He tried to get off the couch and go to the bathroom, but threw up on the floor. His bow tie was crooked, and he tried to straighten it. There was some blood on it, and his shoes were bent at the front and two sizes too large, so he looked like a little clown. He had waited for me to take him to the circus last summer. I never did.

"My head feels dizzy," Percy said.

"I'd better not have to hit you again, Percy," Darren said, walking about the room with his arms folded, "so you better clean that up — clean it up — go get the pail — go get the pail —"

The boy looked at him and tried to get up.

"I hope I don't have to hit you again," Darren said, and raised his hand.

But suddenly he was picked up by the scruff of the neck and thrown out the door. Darren stood up and came back in. And old Jay Beard, now nearing seventy, threw the boy outside once more, and kicked him in the behind, and Darren ran up the lane. Jay came back inside, washed my brother's face, rolled a cigarette and smoked it, and, holding Percy in his arms, told him that the boy didn't mean any harm. He was just not right in the head.

After a while the day got dark, and a breeze blew leaves across the lane, and neither turned on the lights.

ELEVEN

A few days later when I came home and walked down the lane, I saw Percy asleep in some ragweed, near his wagon. It was late in the day, the leaves had fallen and were being sucked along in the brook. There was a slight wind, yet most things were very still, and the ragweed branches carried the glow of the autumn sun. Jay Beard had gone to a meeting, and Autumn was in a school play, so he had been alone since he got home at three o'clock. Scupper Pit sat beside him, and I picked Percy up and carried him to the house with the old dog hobbling along behind us.

Percy told me that he had fallen asleep waiting for his father.

"What does your dad look like, Percy?" I asked.

"He is a kind man, and his face glows and he never says anything that isn't true. I saw him in the field."

"You saw him in the field when?"

"When Scupper Pit and I went to see Mr. Beard, he was standing looking at me. There was red sun on the branches, and he was there. He told me he would visit me again. He talked to Scupper and Scupper wagged his tail. Then he said I would go away with him when he came to visit me again."

"Who told you such a thing?"

"The man in the field!"

"Where did he say you would go?"

"He never said."

"Don't talk to him —" I said. "If you see him again come and get me — I will deal with him."

He screwed up his face in wonder and then gave me a smile.

"Don't be sad, Lyle," he said after a moment, touching my face with his hand. "Everyone is sad. Darren is so sad I told him not to come back — for whatever I do, I cannot make him happy anymore."

Tears flooded his eyes. His shoes were untied, his pink socks were wrinkled, his nose ran, and burdocks stuck to his shirt, and in his shirt pocket was a dog biscuit Jay Beard had given him for Scupper.

"I am not sad," I said, trembling suddenly. "Why did you say that?"

"I see into your heart," Percy whispered. "I see into everyone's heart. It is sad, just like Darren's heart, and Mathew Pit's heart. But the man in the field's heart doesn't beat — it glows."

He lay down on the couch with Scupper Pit and fell fast asleep. I sat with him all that night.

The next morning Diedre Whyne came to see me. She looked at me politely and held her purse with both hands. She wore a coat with padded shoulders and had a barrette in her hair that made her look younger than my mother had before she took ill. She told me she was looking for Autumn. I told her that Autumn was at school with Percy.

"We are dropping the charges against you," she said.

"What charges are those?" I said.

"The taxes," she said. "You should thank Ms. Hardwicke for this — she has been a tireless supporter of your cause. We just got the letter sent to us from Ottawa."

She took it out of her purse and handed it to me. I didn't take it, so she put it on the table.

"I see," I said. "Well, I'm glad."

"I was too strident — with my *concern*. Anyway, people did try to — *adjust* your life — I know you are angry about it. But if you knew the conditions in which your mom and dad grew up. The fifties and early sixties were much different than today — you couldn't imagine the poverty your father saw. It might seem to you that all we did was meddle — but that wasn't the case at all. Back then I had a duty to protect her. I knew your mother as a little girl — oh, she was so beautiful — I did not want to see her ruin her life — I was *against* the marriage — but perhaps I didn't help her, perhaps I tried things I shouldn't have — but I was young! It was the times we lived in — I got caught up like everyone. Do you think I was wrong?"

"How the hell should I know?" I said. "Certainly we've all paid for it." I added, "For your being young."

She gave a start, and cleared her throat. She asked for a glass of water, and I gave her one. She took a small drink and set it on the table.

Then she explained that three girls had come forward to say things against her, and one of the uncles, Bennie Sheppard, had come by to ask her for money. She told me she had not done anything like *that* to those girls, but people *might* believe them. She asked me if I knew them — the Voteur girls, and the Sheppard girl.

I told her I knew that they all stayed at Covenant House. She told me that Convenant House had been taken from her. She had worked tirelessly to start it — but an upstart, a younger, more volatile and self-righteous woman had come forward in the past little while with the accusations of the girls fresh on her lips.

"She is just out of Mount Saint Vincent and she thinks she knows everything. The girls all went to her to complain. None ever darkened my door with an allegation. None of it is true, but if people believe them — you know what might happen? Nothing has hit the papers yet — my family has managed to keep it out. But the damage is done, for once an idea is planted in someone's mind it is impossible to erase without — some kind of *help*." She took a breath as if our air was more valuable to her now than it had ever been before. She took another drink.

"I am in a very delicate situation — dealing as I did for twenty years with homeless or sexually abused girls and being —" She paused. "This was the reason I left social services and went to the tax department — I didn't go to the tax department to get you, as you suppose — it was only a coincidence."

I said nothing.

"There was an opening — I had training and my father had a few connections. I'm sorry also about the wood. But in reality it's what the tax department is forced to do. I was only doing what is required by law. I really thought I could get you somewhere else — some better place."

I didn't answer.

"I know what you might think of me, but I will swear on a Bible to my innocence," she said.

"A shitload of good that will do. My mother swore on a Bible in court — so did my father — and the whole river turned against them. You didn't believe in the worth of Bibles then. Nor did Mom and Dad have the comfort of keeping it out of the paper. You gave them a picture of Autumn so everyone would think the worst about us — if you know what I mean."

"I never wanted a child's picture in the paper!"

"Well it got in nonetheless."

"But couldn't you see how *we* would think — I mean how certain people *might* think? And then I believed you were being abused — how could I not think that —?"

But her own words confirmed the irony. I have always felt sad for women caught. Much more than men. Her private world — the world where she dreamed at night alone, of drowning in women's kisses — was now drowning her. Now Diedre needed our help, and the worst of it was, I wished I could help her.

Diedre stroked old Scupper Pit's hair, then brought her hand up with her fist closed and looked at me as if she had just thought of something that was agony to think.

"I'm not a bigot or a racist — but the new woman they have here is implying — because Cheryl's mother was Micmac — that I used them as easy targets — well, you know how they think," she said.

"I know that!" I yelled, tears brimming in my eyes. "I know that — but what in fuck does that matter now? Look at my muscles — why have I worked out for five years? Why? Why can I punch like a mule and yet why am I afraid? Why can I throw a man twice as big as me on his back in three seconds and why am I afraid? Why — why am I afraid! Why do I sleep with a knife? Why?" I paused and shrugged.

"I can take it, but it wasn't fair — not for Mommie," I said, almost like a child, "not for Autumn and Percy."

She smiled tenderly and reached out and took my hand. More than ever I felt her sadness and wanted to alleviate it. So would Autumn, that child who once smelled of poverty and icy silence and spruce and gave the world a crinkly hopeful smile it rarely gave her, who now, finally in her last year of high school, seemed no longer to be orphaned by the world but somehow striding above it.

"Take this," I said, and got from a drawer Isabel Young's card, and placed it on the table. "She is the best lawyer I know and the kindest person to ever deal with us — because that's all any of us want, Ms. Whyne — not revolution or doctrine but only kindness." I felt smug saying this, but I did not take it back.

She took the card and placed it in her purse.

I felt looking at her leaving that the old world was disappearing under our feet and another one was being born on the molten lava that our enemies' corpses created. Suddenly, quite unexpectedly and for the first time, I was beholden to no one in the world.

There is a moment in young people's lives when a fire erupts in the belly and a self-knowledge casts other knowledge aside. They strut like archangels though the caverns of both heaven and hell, yelling bons mots to each other from glittering tavern windows in the night. But even in my laughter I knew that revenge was futile and did nothing for the soul.

I looked at Autumn the next morning as she ate her cereal. For the first time I saw in her the epitomized elements of generous wit and kindness over adversity. The kind my father had prayed for me had been borne high in her — she was the dauntless *Roof Beam Carpenter*, the humorous undefeated champion of all our lives.

———

Constable Delano came to the house two days later. He had come down to look at the bullet hole, something that I thought everyone had forgotten. He paced out the area, and came back into the house and went over to the bookshelves. He picked up a book or two and mused over them, and then he said:

"What do people like Mathew ever get? He's got nothing. At this moment I guarantee you could start your life completely over. No more Mathew or Connie Devlin — or Constable Morris — or anyone. But it takes strength of character to just walk away. You feel you can't go into your future until you take care of the past. But, son, the past — and everything in the past — is gone. It is what Autumn knows — I spoke to her as well."

He then did something strange. He went to his car and brought back a small part of a hockey stick, tied a rag to it, dipped it in some gasoline, and handed it to me.

"Like this?" he asked.

I never spoke. I suppose I acted like my father had in front of Morris. Except he was innocent.

"Do you know how much currency you have?" he said, putting the stick down.

"What do you mean?"

"I mean things suddenly and unexpectedly change in your life. You are no longer the son of an outcast. I promise if I have a breath in my body, your father will never be an outcast again. And those who hated you? Well, all of them, including Diedre Whyne, are having their difficulties now. The truth does matter. There was a time I did not think it. All of a sudden falsehood just goes away."

Delano read a book for a moment and then put it back on the shelf.

"If you become involved, you won't get anything from it. Whatever it is will backfire. At the most critical moment he will turn against you, or you against him. It will *backfire*. When it happens you will *remember* I asked you to be careful."

With that he took his leave.

TWELVE

That night I went to the church because I had promised Mom I would register Percy for his First Communion. It was the first time I was near the church in years. The church was bare, if not barren. There were some faint flickering candles under the picture of Madonna and Child. I walked into the rectory and saw the chalice in the exact spot I had taken it from a few years before.

Porier was still here reading the paper. The church had the familiar smell of oak and wax. The wind blew outside.

I coughed gently and Porier took off his reading glasses and squinted at me. He was an old man now.

"You're the Henderson boy?" he said, peering forward so his wavy white hair fell over his forehead.

"Yes, I am."

I pulled up a chair and sat down.

"You have come to know when the mass is. Next Monday night at six o'clock," he said.

"What mass?"

"The mass Autumn and Percy have asked for your mother — look." He took out an envelope. It was Percy's envelope — I would not mistake it. It had fifteen dollars in it, saved by Percy for his guitar. He had given it away, like that. Neither Autumn nor he had told me.

"I didn't know they asked for a mass," I whispered.

He sat in front of me like an old gnome, with a paunch, and his pants hiked up over his ankles made his legs look withered. I told him that I had come to register Percy for First Communion. Then I said:

"I have to know what happened at the mill. My mind won't rest until I find this out — you must tell me."

I felt a strange peace after I spoke those words. The old man took out a cigarette and lighted it.

"It wasn't your grandfather," he said. "I am telling you this and no one else —"

"When did you know about my grandfather?" I asked.

"What is said to me in confession is said to me in confession. But your family is responsible for nothing. The papers have said as much now. I think I knew this for a while. But who can be sure? Anyway, those really responsible for the boy's death are facing long prison terms."

He had not flicked the ashes from his cigarette yet. It was another cold night and the corners of the church were dark.

"You are very loved," he said, "each one of you."

"By who?" I said.

"By God," he said.

This rather deflated me. I thought he might say by the head of the Human Rights Commission, Dr. David Scone, who has now heard about your case and is ready to instigate a lawsuit on your behalf. I too wanted to be heard by some commission somewhere. For some terrible ego I wanted Dr. David Scone to know of my father's innocence and his suffering.

But he could only say I was loved by God. I looked at Percy's small worn envelope, with the word "Getir" still legible in pencil. Then he told me my mother was loved.

"By who?" I said.

"Well, by everyone," he said. "By you, firstly — and of course by Autumn and Percy, and by your father, and by Hanny Brown, and by Jay Beard, and by many other people, especially her sisters. I know she is loved — since she was a little girl and adopted, just like her sisters were adopted — well, it was that age — they all were brought to the Orphanage of the Sisters of Charity. I carried them in my arms. We could not leave them where they were — there was no life for them way over there. I made a deal with Elly's mother. Maybe I owe you an apology. Your mom's sisters were adopted before she was — they were infants, and it was easier — but then she was adopted too — I saw to it — by Hanny Brown's father and mother, who, though they had eight children, took one more. I don't even remember who was older or younger — yer mom or her sisters — I have a difficult time remembering that."

"I don't have a clue what you are saying," I said. But a cold chill had come up my spine. I sat rigid like a man might who is tied to a chair and about to be shot.

Father Porier looked at me with tired red eyes.

"I thought you knew now. Everyone else on the river knows. It has all come out in the last few days. Isabel Young discovered it. Since she met your mother six years ago she has been trying to get information for her. First it was just on your mother's background — and on your mother's behalf. She was hoping she could get something *for* her. Then she discovered your mother was adopted by a poor man who owned a small fishing boat. But that her two sisters grew up in very different backgrounds, much better off. Private school. Both of them met at university without knowing who the other was. Both attended peace marches, both set out to help the world, and ran headlong into their sister, your mother, without knowing who she was. Isabel found out — and broke her silence three weeks ago — I was sure — I mean — you don't know? Diedre Whyne and Isabel Young are your mother's sisters. You must know that. They are McVicer's children."

I began to laugh so hard, tears blurred my fuckin' eyes.

THIRTEEN

I left the church, my hands thrust into my pockets, and through the glazed dark I saw another person going, I thought, away from me — but then I realized she was coming my way.

Autumn was wearing her white coat and boots. She wore no makeup, she had no contacts. She was like the little albino girl of six or seven, when we went to the church and she had won the flower for Dad at the fish tank.

"I have been trying to find you," she said. "I left Percy waiting for me. You have to come now," she whispered, tears sparkling in her eyes, "to say goodbye to our mommie."

She grabbed my arm to make me hurry as if we were going to catch a train and we started to run. As if it was all preordained, Father Porier drove by us and stopped his Pontiac at our lane. When we got to the car, Percy was already in the back seat wearing a safety belt that looked charmingly pessimistic on such a tiny child.

I can still smell after all these years the faint scent of holy water Autumn wore in this fall night. I wondered where she had gotten it, and wondered if she knew it labelled us rural Catholic of the worst order. Yet I also embraced it as authentically her. I recognized it again, like I did that night when Jay Beard drove us home from the picnic. To me it had the smell of diluted vinegar and made the clothes yellow.

Percy looked at me without speaking, as if my entering the car was a fact long known by him. His shirt was buttoned, but his bow tie was missing, and there was a brown spot on the collar. His shoes, though on the wrong feet, were carefully tied. He held in his hand a ribbon and a silver button. He never spoke to me, and he never cried. His eyes simply stared in front of him, the huge seatbelt like some grand inquisitor's cable that would stop his soul from rushing away to where it wanted to go; and maybe wanted to torture the child just a sweet while longer.

For the last three weeks he had sat beside Mom or stayed at home, or taken Scupper Pit in his wagon up the road to wait for his father. I had neglected him while every night he sat until dark waiting for her or Dad to come back. And as Mom's condition deteriorated he kept believing that every slip in her condition was temporary and that the doctors would perform a new treatment and she would recover.

And he would haul Scupper Pit down to the church. And sometimes thoughtless people would brush by him as they came out of church and ran off to their cars in the blowing snow. Once he was knocked down by some callow children running with a ball and Scupper started barking.

He did not understand that doctors could not help, no matter how much they wanted to, because something, time, intelligence, or the muddle of our lost millennium had stayed their hand.

When the car stopped, he waited for the seatbelt to be unsnapped, as if this was part of a ceremony. Autumn and I took his hand. Going up the steps he stumbled once, and said, "Excuse me," with grave solemnity, that sounded graver in the half-lighted hospital foyer. When we came into the foyer there was an unfortunate drunk at the door who was wailing. The drunk turned, looked at Percy with some hidden sullen hatred in his heart.

Percy stopped as if he recognized the fellow. Then he handed him his ribbon. The man took it, and held it in dumbfounded silence.

Percy clutched our hands tighter and looked at us both. We continued to walk, around the corner along the lighted hallways, while the drunk feebly called after him, the walls faint with the smell of sadness, urine, and love.

"She will wait for Dad," Percy said.

But Mom was unconscious. She had been for almost a week. Percy expected her to be awake now, and when we came in, he looked at us as if he had let us down, as if all his childlike optimism was proven wrong.

What had never happened in my mother's life happened at her death. The reunion of the sisters. Isabel was there when we came in. She stood and kissed me, and bending close kissed Autumn's white cheek and hugged Percy. A moment later, Diedre came to the door, which was half-closed, the room itself having the appearance of grey evening. She was all in a rush of purse and skirt and coat but stopped up, looked at us, at Mom, and hesitatingly came forward. She bent down and kissed her sister's pale forehead, and kissed it again, then rose up and smiled at us in a tragic way.

"She has suffered so much," she whispered to no one. Isabel quickly hugged her.

Father Porier performed the last rites. He gave Autumn communion, and then six months before he was supposed to, he gave Percy communion for the first time. I did not take it. I had no reason to.

As usual there were many little things that seemed of no consequence. Mom's notes for Percy's first grade she had written clumsily weeks before, reminding Autumn that she had provided money for his lunches, and to pick up a scribbler for him. (She did not know that Jay Beard had paid for these lunches and the scribbler because her money as usual was not nearly enough.) The phone number of Darren Voteur, the boy she had arranged to sit with Percy.

There was a folded note with *Sydney* scratched on the outside. There was a card from the Orphanage of the Sisters of Charity and two unopened letters from the Office of Mother Superior.

There were some other things: a pair of bedroom slippers I had bought her. And the basket of fruit brought to her by Hanny Brown, still under its plastic cover, and some new soap Autumn got her in Chatham. It was still wrapped in its decorative paper, sitting on the table, with the card. She died at 9:17 on the seventeenth of November 1989, thirty-nine years of age, leaving three children between the ages of eighteen and five, and a husband she had not seen in almost three years. She left her two dresses to Autumn, and five dollars to Percy. She left me the pure white stone Dad had thrown into her room the night he told her of his love.

Over the next couple of hours Diedre did nothing but speak to us about our trouble and how it was now all past. That we were the most recognized and suddenly loved family on the river. (Absurd as it was.) When she hugged me, her body felt like Mom's, and tears — goddamn tears — came to my eyes.

Autumn's face grew pensive and she took off the ring that I had given her when I told her no one would bother her ever again. She handed it to me.

"What's this for?" I asked, trying to sound calm.

"Please take it —"

"Why —?"

She looked at the ring. "I remember once Elly was trying to tell me a story — it was a story about Vincent Van Gogh — that Dad had told her, but she had no idea who he was. I was in a school play about a painter. That's why she wanted to tell it. Dad was not home and she felt it her duty. She kept getting more and more mixed up trying to tell it just like Dad. Let me tell you how she told this story."

"She sat with her hands on her lap," I said, "and smoothed her dress."

"Yes — exactly — and she tried to talk very sophisticated about him and his paintings. But she became more and more confused, and Dad wasn't at home to help her, and she seemed to look about the room for him. I couldn't help it, I burst out laughing. I know I hurt her feelings. She had worked her gumption up to tell me a story like Dad might, but she didn't remember the details — and I had laughed at her. So she stopped talking, and tried to remember something else about him, and couldn't. But I had hurt her heart, Lyle — I had hurt her tender heart. And do you know what it showed me?"

"What?"

"It showed me her incalculable beauty — I laughed at someone Van Gogh would have loved more than all the art dealers in the world, and I have yet to forgive myself. You see, she *never* in her life thought it necessary to laugh at *me*," Autumn said.

We were driven home. The house felt unnatural. Seeing the couch with the cushion at one end where Mom used to lie, and seeing my old suit she used to mend for me so I could go to school, made me choke back sobs, and I quickly went into the back room because I did not want Percy to see me cry.

It had been snowing up north all day and now it started here. The flakes came drifting into the small porch. Percy sat calmly on the couch. He never spoke, and his face was deathly white. A few people started to come to the door, people from both sides of the brook. Someone mentioned the funeral, and said Autumn and I should go to the undertakers. People sat about the house, bringing baskets of food, talking to Autumn about both Dad and Mom, while I couldn't stand still. Others came in and roughly assessed the place, wondered how anyone could spend winters here, let alone bring up children.

The next day in a heavy snowfall Jay Beard took us to the funeral parlour. We were to pick out a coffin — for about fifteen hundred dollars — but the young undertaker very solemnly told us that McVicer had picked one out for nine thousand.

"No," Autumn said, "she will not mind this coffin — she would mind the expensive one — she would say, 'No, that's too dear!'"

A day later the funeral mass was said by the Monsignor from Newcastle. He in his rather opulent church attire spoke of Mom's gentle heart and her yearning for Christ. That was true, but how in Christ would he ever know?

After the funeral mass the Monsignor sat Percy on his knee, and both looked very uncomfortable.

Everyone told Percy how brave he was.

When my mother was buried the day was solid and white. Wisps of snow energized the graveyard, and the stones rose solidly from furrows of snow. It was strange how few people actually knew her compared to those who knew *of* her. It was as if she had never existed, as if her whole life here — from her church picnic duties to her little sandwich-making empire — had caused not a ripple on the surface of our land.

So I want people to know that at her death she weighed 103 pounds, was thirty-nine years of age, had read three books, had travelled from Tabusintac to Newcastle on six occasions, had knitted her husband a new sweater for Christmas that very year. Her favourite birthday was her twenty-seventh. Her favourite girlfriend was Diedre Whyne. Her favourite person besides my father was Jay Beard. Her favourite television program, the one she watched with Percy, was *Lassie*, her favourite colour was blue, the colour of Percy's eyes. Of the three books she had read her favourite was *The Adventures of Huckleberry Finn*. I want people to know — I loved her.

I bent to the ground and kissed where she lay, and have not been back to it since.

REDEMPTION

ONE

My father heard of Mom being sick two weeks before she died. He gave his notice and prepared at that moment to come home.

The nights had turned cold, the bit of light during the day was extinguished by about four-thirty, and the earth had become still, puddles froze, old tractor ruts turned as hard as iron, and the blades of saws and graders whined a protest to humanity when they were started at dawn.

He had helped put the powerline through new green forest, through bog and cedar swamp, and it stretched from clearcut to clearcut, over rivers and beaver dam and brook. It lighted homes where they did not know him, computers of young women who would look at his life in dismissal, the main computer in the office of Dr. David Scone, the champion of human rights. And embedded deep in that computer was the file on my father, which my father had never seen.

Men and women certain of the new world and their right to be entitled would not have known my father's world, or known so little about it — never known the miles of trackless barrens the tons of rock moved. And what if anything would it matter?

Sydney Henderson had not read a paper in a year, knew nothing of current events. His hair was grey, his weight a solid 185. The men who had one time tormented him because he was different now held a place for him in their hearts.

"Why did you learn all of that, and read all of those books?" a glad-faced youngster named Alcide Dorion asked Dad three weeks before he went home. "What good is it for Sydney? What good did it do!"

"It is good in itself, and reason enough in itself," my father answered.

"What should I get from books?" Alcide asked in French.

"That you are not alone — even along this broken tractor road. You need to know nothing else," my father answered in French.

There were a few men who did not like him, never had any use for him. They were sardonic men, hard working with limited futures, and bitter at Sydney, whose ideas had spawned new and glorious concepts. One of these men was called Terrible Jon Driver. Once he had thrown Sydney's meatloaf in the fire and on many occasions he had made jokes about Sydney's manliness. Like ignorant men everywhere, Driver was self-righteous, egotistical, and petty. Two weeks before Sydney left camp, Driver hit the young boy for asking all those many questions.

"What do you need to know that tripe for?" he had said. He sat on his bunk with his arms folded.

Sydney jumped from his bunk and pulled Alcide to his feet. Driver looked at him with a contemptuous certainty that cold and barren work like his was given only to good men.

The next morning few men spoke with Dad, and Alcide Dorion, in here because his own father was dead and he had little brothers and sisters at home, embarrassed at having had my father protect him, could not go near him again. There were many ways for men like Jon Driver to win battles. One was understanding the supercilious contempt weak men always had for strong.

When Sydney sat upon his bunk in the half-lighted room, in the dark days of fall slipping now into winter, his body was solid muscle. He had twenty-five thousand dollars in his leather bag inside his canvas backpack. And he was ready to go home. He would walk nine miles out to the highway and catch the bus back to the Miramichi. Tomorrow night he would be with Elly again. He would hold and kiss Percy. He thought of the miles ahead of him and they seemed an insult; he wanted them to be gone in a second. After all this time, after three years, he had broken the great fetters of his self-imposed exile and was anxious to live. To live like other men, but by his own rules.

In his last letter home, which came to us after Mom was taken to the hospital, he had sketched out his future with bright hope and light blue ink. With hard work, he would finish a B.Ed. by the age of forty-three, and he would teach children like Percy. Life would be indeed different for us, he wrote.

"Lyle, you have suffered the most, I realize this. Even more than Autumn. Your mom and I remember you in faded and torn pants and shirt, alone while other children played. And I know your struggle has been harder than mine, but think of your abilities, the rainbow in our future."

He did not know how I had fallen from that great rainbow height in his heart.

And his trial was yet to come. The one he always knew would come. The one he had been awaiting ever since he made his pact with God when he was a child shovelling snow from the roof of the church. He knew it would come with snow.

Like Gerald Dove's trial over the molecule, Dad's trial was with his own human heart. Both were Old Testament trials, which people pretend no longer exist, or have forgotten in their world of internal clocks and self-assertion. In the book of Proverbs one might believe that all wrongs are rectified, justice measured equally, and to the good the triumph of the good — this is what we hope is true.

My father's trial came from another book — a stronger, more brilliant, more penetrating, and more painful book. He had forgotten about it now for a while, so content he was. He had saved his money — he could pay back his debt, he was finally free of everyone; John Delano in his visit to the camp some months before had told him he would not only be exonerated but get an award, perhaps as much as a million dollars.

But my father knew by heart the book of Job, where the world is not a certain place, where anything man has can be taken from him, leaving him to sit in stunned acceptance of the horrible Word of God. Only the young think there is freedom from that book — wise men and kings know it is the greatest and truest book in the world — and my father was nothing if not both of those.

Present at the camp was one Connie Devlin. He had slipped away from our river in panic, knowing his past of dishonour had now caught up to him. He by accident had found himself here and had been hired on as cook's help.

Soon, my father was plagued again by his youth. All over again his promise clutched his throat like a viper. All over again his miserable youth, his allergy to horses, his furious father, his blemished adolescence where he drank in his house to forget who he was, came back to him, and he saw himself at eleven years of age. All over again, behind him, sat Connie Devlin waiting to torment.

At camp Connie was implicated in a theft of some cassette tapes, and he ran to Sydney for protection. Two men came after him. One held a wrench in his hand ready to swing it until my father stepped between them. My father said nothing. He just stood where he was, his chest bare and his arms muscled. He made no move when the man lifted his wrench, like some old slave who has been hit too many times to ever flinch again.

Sydney was tempted to turn his back on him. If he did he would be safe, and he knew this. Connie was there for a reason Connie himself did not understand.

Sydney awkwardly asked the other men to be kind to Connie, for he had had a hard life. The other men, who had a reservoir of questions about Sydney himself, now saw in him a weakness, a crack full scale up his soul. Soon his defence of Connie embittered them, and he was shunned.

Dad said goodbye to the young boy Alcide, but the boy did not look at him. He had heard stories now, about Dad on the Miramichi, whispered against him by Connie. Father again had become an outcast, and the boy was only protecting himself.

Dad packed his duffle bag, dressed in his coat and boots and hat, and prepared to walk to the main road. He left a note for Alcide with a list of authors both French and English to read.

The day was bitterly cold. He walked out on the creaking steps at dawn, where just one part of a tin roof of a bunkhouse across the makeshift tractor road showed a patch of sunlight.

Connie hurried toward him, packed to go. He looked like a forlorn gnome, a patchwork of a dozen different fabrics to keep him warm, and a pair of old heavy leaden rubber boots, the kind that miners wear.

"I can't stay here without you," he pleaded. "I can't — you have to take me with you. Please, you have to — what will I do —"

"You have hurt me all my life," my father said quietly. "I should not have made my pact. I made my pact and knew the Sheppard boys forced me to drink and said nothing — it is a hard pact."

"I don't care about your pact — it's probably a stupid pact — but I did nothing to *you* — I haven't. It was Mathew — he robbed McVicer. I'll go to the police for you — as soon as we get home — he did it for Rudy, because Rudy tried to rape Elly — he did it, I swear. It was a set-up to take the heat off Rudy. Later he sabotaged the bridge. I was scared, let me tell you. Trenton just happened to be there looking for you at that time. Everyone soon thought it was you. I was scared to tell — haven't you ever been scared? I was so scared."

My father looked at Connie's small red ears and the tuft of hair on top of his forehead. How could his life have been so infused with treachery?

"Please please please give me one more chance — please just one more! — I'll tell everyone as soon as we get home."

My father said nothing, only nodded.

So Connie fell in behind Sydney, and disappeared with him around the corner of the waving frigid trees, talking as was his habit a mile a minute, so happy that he still had a friend.

It was dawn of November 17, 1989, the day of Elly's death. After a while snow began to fall, bitterly, as sharp as wire.

TWO

It was a few days after Mom's funeral before anyone knew Dad was missing. I had to go to Campbellton and try to find him. But no one knew what had happened to him, or even if he was alone or with someone. Jon Driver spent all his spare time searching the ravines to the north of the powerline. I searched to the southeast of Otter Brook until my feet bled in their boots. I stayed a month. Every day I looked at a map, and every day I waited for my father to come walking out of the trees toward me. I know as the search petered out and as men drifted away that I was looked upon as mad. In the end only Jon Driver and I remained. Jon Driver would not leave me.

There were too many storms, too many ways to turn. It was in Campbellton that I met Bliss Hanrahan, who had once given my father a drive. He stopped me on the street and spoke to me about Dad, and asked after Mom, not knowing she was dead.

"Where are you sleeping?" he asked.

"On the street."

He offered me a place to stay and I told him I did not need one.

"Why not?" he asked, grabbing my shoulder.

"Where were you?" I shrugged, tossing his hand away. "Where the fuck were you?"

The search coordinator between our Department of Forestry and Search and Rescue wanted to lock me up. I kept phoning him in the middle of the night from a phone booth, cursing him for not doing enough and not keeping the helicopters in the air. I told him that Autumn and Percy had just lost their mother, and now their father.

"I cannot help that, son — I am sorry."

And once he said: "Son, you are destroying yourself with guilt — it is you who have abandoned them, not your father and mother —"

"How — how have I abandoned them?"

"In your heart, son," he said, sobbing, "in your heart."

———

I came back home in January 1990. I got off the train at noon hour and made my way back down river. I waited at the little schoolhouse.

Then Percy appeared on the steps, Autumn holding his hand. Under his dark blue winter coat he wore a small suit jacket and old bow tie, just as his mother would have wanted. He looked down, and his face lighted and he ran into my arms.

The snow was reddened by the sun, the tamaracks as hard as steel, and the sky still with cold. We held Percy's hands as he walked between us.

"Do you know what Mother and Father meant to this world?"

I told them that Mom and Dad meant greatness. I told them that McVicer did not mean greatness, nor did Dr. David Scone, nor those men who wrote about native rights without spending one night with Cheryl Voteur. I told Autumn that did not matter. Everything in our world was backwards. I told her I had hurt my mother and father.

"Percy, when your birthday comes, we will go to Saint John," Autumn said. She told Percy all the things he would do. "How wonderful it will be," Autumn said.

THREE

Peace? It was that very week that Connie Devlin came home. I saw him walk past my mailbox at nine one evening. He wore a beautiful new coat and a pair of sheepskin boots. He was interviewed by police and said he knew nothing of my father's disappearance. But he was soon under their protection and within three days people said he had told them everything. A rumour started that I was looking for him and wanted to kill him. I came to believe this rumour. It caused in me a kind of anxious desperation that I loved. It was then that Mat Pit came to me. His face was sunken. I saw the look of a hunted man, a man who feared daylight and other people. Of all the people he had maimed, harmed, or influenced in his entire life, only Rudy Bellanger and myself still listened to him. Rudy, kicked out of his house long before Christmas, and under an investigation his own father-in-law had started, was also a broken man. Rudy still made plans, but no one listened to him now. Gladys had returned to her father's house, lived in the old doll room off the kitchen, and her large ranch-style house was up for sale, desolate as empty brick houses tend to be.

Pit came to me alone. The far-flung plans for empire, his parasitical hopes of inventing himself in the style of Leo or anyone else, had been snuffed away, like a candle snuffed by a finger. It left only the erupted blister of malcontent. Angrily he told me this, in violent, almost virulent language. And Cynthia? Cynthia he hated. For she wanted nothing more to do with him, ensconced as she was in the huge house on the bay. Did I know that she was engaged to McVicer? I nodded. How dare she be engaged, he ranted. Did I know she had a two-thousand-dollar diamond engagement ring? Again I nodded. How dare she!

He told me he no longer existed for her. The gravel drive, the old house she grew up in, the sunken yard, the desolate windows, the men she had given herself to — bullies and punks — had been swept away by a wave of her hand. To Leo she was a woman who had suffered at the hand of a brother now demonized — a victim he had rescued from some wild horror. Leo would not believe anything about Cynthia except what he wanted to. Leo had taken to wearing clothes Cynthia had picked out for him, and had his hair cut in a new style. It was obvious he was senile, Mat said. I nodded. It was rumoured that he had slapped his own daughter when she mentioned he was being silly.

"Ah yes — that's what Cynthia is like —" Mathew said. "I can't bear to think of my sister like that — but there you go."

I might have taken some pleasure in this, but I did not. It was not so peculiar to rural men suffering the new age. His jacket was torn, his boots were frayed, his hands blistered with cold. He was sick, and trying to find work. He also needed, more than anything else, to get away.

"How can you let Connie Devlin get away with this?" he said, after we drank wine and did two lines of cocaine. "You have to take him down — for your dad's honour. Remember we spoke so often about honour?" He put his hand on my shoulder.

"Police patrol his road every hour and he orders them about — he is in his glory," I answered. I was now sickened by everything, and Mat saw this and became desperate.

"Well that's easy — wait for a storm," Mat said, "when the patrol cars are off the road — when no one is around. I'm not thinking of myself," Mat said, "I know you have no reason to trust me — but Connie — rumour is he threw poor Sydney down a cliff — I'm shamed to think he's my cousin — he turned the floodlights off — he was the one who got Trenton — I know that now in my heart when it is too late. If I could bring yer dad back I'd soon trade places with him — yer dad suffered 'cause of what Connie did — me own cousin actin' like that there — Connie was the one who made me think yer dad hurt Trenton. I was beside myself, and for one time I didn't think clear. When a storm comes, that's yer best chance — he'll be alone — I'm not saying this for myself. I've got to go because I'll be blamed for a crime I never done — no one should have to suffer that! To be blamed for a crime they never done."

Every time he spoke my father's name, my eyes blurred, and seeing this he shook his head sadly, and after a time, he took his leave. For the first time in his life, I think, he may have been frightened of me.

FOUR

With Cynthia's arrival at Leo's house, with his wife moving into that house, and with his own house up for sale, Rudy had been suddenly thrust into hell. And if one did not believe in hell one had only to look at Rudy, see his eyes and his frayed windbreaker, and realize that in his pocket he carried a ticket stub to a room at the YMCA.

He could not stand for this. He would not and live. Yet he waited for Gladys to help him, and hung about his father-in-law's back yard, watching Cynthia eat cinnamon buns and coming and going in the Cadillac.

He had paid a terrible price for his infatuation. This is all he thought of now. Some days he would go up to the Pits' and wait for Mathew to talk to him. He would stand on the hill in back of their house and see the window of the room where he had had sex with Cynthia that fateful night. The window was often open, and darkness lay within.

When he was a child he was so frightened of failure and people. Now, too late, he realized his fear of life had crippled him. He might have done anything in his life, even have been a great man, and he had done nothing. When a child he had prayed to be safe, to be happy, to be loved. And now too late he realized that he had been given what he had prayed for. By the time he was twenty-one he had been safe and happy and loved. But it wasn't enough for him. And did he give anything in return? No. He had not been kind to Elly because of conceit and lust. He had not been good to Gladys because of greed. And he had not loved because of fear.

What had Leo McVicer ever done to him but say, "No, this won't do — you will not use me just because you married my child — I will not be fooled!" Rudy could not hate the old man for doing what he did.

Could he not even take his own life? This thought was often fleeting in his mind. No — he could not. But then, why not? What was the point of this — for eventually all his actions would be known. Still he had to stay alive. He would get money somehow and go away, to the place he had always wanted to go — Australia.

Rudy knew he would break under questioning. No escape hatch was in fact opened to him, except the truth. And the truth was that he had assaulted my mother and had had an affair lasting some seven years with Cynthia. That he had become a coward because of this — not in spite of this. That this type of weakness turned against a man and made a woman mean.

That because of cowardice he had relied upon Mathew Pit, as a friend and an adviser. And Mathew had robbed a house, and sabotaged a bridge. That the sabotaging of the bridge had cast Sydney Henderson into hell — but now, after all this time, after years, the man was about to be resurrected, and Rudy himself was cast into hell. And if one did not believe in hell, well, one had only to look at him.

The only time he had spoken to Constable Delano, at a party the summer before, he kept his eyes lowered. John Delano spoke to him kindly, even light-heartedly, but Rudy could not relax. And Delano whispered:

"The death of a boy is a terrible burden to place on an innocent man — you know that, Mr. Bellanger."

And Rudy felt his nose starting to run, and his eyes water. He was not more than a millisecond away from saying "I did it" when Delano changed the subject completely and asked after Gladys's heath.

Yet there was one solution. He had a child, Teresa. And he would go to Leo and claim this child in front of Cynthia. Perhaps in doing this, he could still save himself!

Rudy crept into his father-in-law's house by the same door he had taken the hour he had accosted my mother. He did this the Wednesday Mathew came to visit me.

He knew there would be no marina. The day after the Knights of Columbus meeting everything in his life had simply stopped. That was the day Leo had phoned Gladys, told her what he had suspected, and without Rudy being allowed to explain, to speak or say a thing, the marriage was over and he was no longer allowed on the property.

However, for Cynthia Pit it was all a natural progression in her life. She had had Danny Sheppard when she was a teenager and he was a big talker; then she had Rudy when she was a woman and he was the manager of his wife's store and had plans for a grand marina. Now she was the caregiver for a woman whose rich father was enamoured of her and had asked for her hand in marriage. She had not done a thing toward this end, it had just happened, as if it had all been preordained. Nor did she ever consider that she had betrayed almost everyone to gain this position.

Rudy waited for her in the very room my own mother had been interrogated in so long ago, hat in hand, staring at the carpet. When Cynthia finally came to see him, her beauty as wanton as ever, he said he wanted to speak to Leo. She told him it was impossible. He stammered and tried to think. Then he told her he still had plans to do something. That he would someday have a bar, with VLT machines, and it would cater mainly to younger kids.

"What does that sound like?" he asked her, his lips trembling and his hand shaking as he touched her face.

"It sounds just like you," Cynthia said coolly. "Everyone already has that — besides, I don't like those gambling machines, they hook young mothers with little children."

"I took care of Leo's business for years — I want something out of it," Rudy said. "I want to see him — to tell him — about — *us!*"

"Oh — well, I've been talking to your father-in-law about you, Rudy — and — well, let's say I have a different opinion of you," she said with a great air of disappointment.

"But he stoled my idea —" Rudy said loudly. "Leo stoled my idea for a marina." He slapped his hat on his leg.

He said he wanted to take Gladys out of her father's house, but

Cynthia would not allow this. He asked again to see Leo, and again she said no, and told him that if he did not leave she would call Constable Morris, who was a good friend of hers.

"Don't you think I don't know what's going on here?" he said.

Cynthia smiled. "Rudy, what are you saying?"

"I know you're in league with them and have turned your back on me and are trying to push me out of what is rightfully mine."

She looked at him piously. Then she picked up the phone.

"I will have to phone the police!"

"Please —" he said.

She paused and looked at him.

"You have come into this house uninvited — I hardly know you —" she said.

"What do you mean, into this house uninvited — who are you — and what do you mean, you hardly know me — how did we have a child together if you hardly know me! And if that comes out, what will Leo say to you then! And I am willing for it to all come out!" he shouted. "I will — it will all come out!"

But she remained perfectly calm — because she had told Leo and Gladys that Rudy would say all these things to discredit her.

"I just wanted things for us," he said after a moment.

"Is that why you stole Leo's idea?"

"What?"

"Leo's idea for a marina — the one he helped build in Newcastle. A decent, kind, wonderful man like Mr. Leo McVicer?" She looked at him, again with the resilience of one accustomed to the fabric of lies. He had to turn away from her deceitful look. It made her look, at the moment, truly ugly.

When turning, he saw his wife's legs as she sat in her room, holding the cane and listening to this horrible argument.

"Go — before you upset Gladys," Cynthia said, pointing. "She is in my care now."

"I — will not — I — I — Gladys — you know — you must know!"

Then seeing Leo in the room, he began to back away.

"Gladys?" he said once more, noticing her feet beyond the door, noticing the cane, remembering how helpless she was without him. "Gladys — you must know — you must!"

"Didn't I tell you?" Cynthia whispered to Leo with a forlorn smile. "This is what he's been like for years."

Hearing her say this Rudy yelled a half-hearted threat, pulled his boots on, and walked away from the house. He stared back over his shoulder at the frozen lane, the dark squall of embedded trees. He was terrified. How could people be so cruel to him? How could Cynthia just invent things about him? What would happen to him now? He would go to jail — and what would happen there? Nor did it matter that in any real way he had done almost nothing —

He had not walked one hundred yards when he saw Mathew Pit, waiting for him by the very tree Rudy had leaned against after he had assaulted my mother.

"How much do you think the bastard has in that house?" Mathew said. "A hundred thousand — a million or more?"

"I don't know — I don't."

"Well, you know one thing — the comb-ee-na-tion to his safe. That's one thing more than that bitch of my sister knows. Stick with me and we'll still get out of this scrape together."

Mathew turned his broad back on Rudy and hobbled ahead of him along the frozen road, his stomach in pain; and Rudy, crying, followed. Both soon covered in snow and shadows.

FIVE

That night as the wind howled against our house, Autumn told me that the police would arrest Connie and Mathew and Rudy. They would all be taken into custody and charged with manslaughter, perhaps on Friday, certainly no later than Monday. The whole road-way was whispering this in a gleeful clatter, as if a wicked spell against my family had been broken. There would be a string of other charges against Mathew.

"It looks like years in prison," Autumn said. "But let's just you and I stay out of it — for Mom and Dad's sake, please?"

"What about Dad?" I said.

"Connie Devlin knows — but he will always await the best deal he can get — he is in a position to trade one crime off the other. He sits in his house and has the police patrol it — orders pizzas — but all that will come to an end," Autumn said. "Just for Percy's sake, don't you get involved — they won't get away — there is nowhere for any of them to go except into a jail cell in Dorchester. Remember you said everything would change for us? Please?" She reached out and squeezed my hand.

I stayed awake all that night, and all Thursday drinking. Percy was staying home from school trying to help the old dog, Scupper Pit, who was at its end and lay near our wood stove feebly wagging its tail.

I believe that the beating Percy had taken had broken something in him, so near was it to his mother's death. He kept trying to do all the things he believed he needed to do. As if someone was watching him. Every day he tried to give me a present — sometimes it was nothing more than Father's socks.

"Look what I got you, Lyle," he would say, coming out from a closet.

Sometimes he phoned the Pits to ask after Teresa May, who was at the hospital in Halifax, and if he could send her a letter because he had two jokes. So I helped him write his letter. But though I had told him I would mail it, I didn't. It sat in the little jar on the table waiting to go.

Once, listening to the radio, he phoned in to answer a quiz that would win him a hundred dollars. I still remember him standing with the phone in his hand and waiting his turn to speak. But he spoke so softly and got the answer wrong. He hung up, turned to me, and smiled.

"Oh, Lyle," he said, "I almost got it —"

I would wake up periodically because Scupper, who lay on a mat near the stove, would begin to whine.

I finally told him I would take Scupper to the veterinarian on Friday. Autumn had to do a run-through that day of the play she had written with her drama teacher. But the more I thought of Connie Devlin the more insane I became. I was driven forward by the idea that my father's life would be nothing if I did not act.

I sat in my room brooding. I frightened myself when I saw my reflection in the mirror. And Thursday night Autumn opened the door when I was getting out of the tub. She saw the slashes all across my arms and chest from the knife I carried. It had taken me a good three years to make those marks. She gave a start, and then with a feeble smile said:

"Ah yes, Love — the death of a thousand cuts. I know it well."

That Friday morning I woke after Autumn had gone. The wind had turned cold. A blizzard was starting and snow was seeping through the back wall. We needed a new wall, but even Autumn didn't seem to care anymore.

I had a feeling that Connie Devlin would get away again. This blizzard on the very day Autumn had told me they were going to arrest the three of them was a trick by God, it was God's punishment against my family. He loved Connie Devlin more than He loved me. I thought of Mathew escaping. Mathew would always escape.

In my mind's eye I saw Devlin packing his clothes. How stupid the police were!

I would kill Devlin. It didn't matter to me if he had killed Dad or not. Nothing mattered except to act. I would go to prison. And there I would one day kill Mathew and Rudy and Danny Sheppard.

"You want to hear a joke?" Percy asked me as I was thinking this and peeling the label off a quart of Napoleon wine.

"What," I said.

"What do you say to a shy turtle?"

"I don't know, Percy, I don't know."

324

"You say to a shy turtle — come out of your shell," Percy said. He giggled, and I didn't answer.

"I heard that joke — I heard that joke — last week," Percy said.

His chest heaved and he coughed again. He had problems with his lungs, the smoke from our wood stove got to him. He blinked at me and tried to think of another joke but got confused. He fidgeted, trying to think of something to say. As I started for the door he tried to tell me the first joke again. Then he ran back to the dog.

It had started to snow long before I left the house.

SIX

Mathew was right. Cynthia and Leo had become engaged a short two weeks before. But in seeing him that day, Rudy had missed what was evident to others in the house; and what Cynthia wanted to keep secret as long as she could. Leo had had a stroke, and Cynthia had been put into the position of a nurse. This had happened the very night of their engagement as he opened a bottle of champagne. He stood, to get a bucket of ice, laughed about something, turned to speak, felt weak, and fell in front of her.

She got him to a chair where he shook violently. He refused to go to the hospital, and stayed mainly in his room, suspicious of everyone and angry when she made sounds or tried to help him. He kept asking for certain papers, and notes, and she was kept running trying to find them for him, frightened to death of his temper.

A week ago she telephoned Freddy Snook, asking him to come down and help. He appeared with an unsigned will, made up without clear beneficiary, telling her the old man had left no power of attorney. The estate was in limbo because Leo had that Irish suspicion of wills.

"What do you mean," Cynthia said, lighting a cigarette and pausing just slightly to blow out the match, "power of attorney?"

"No one to take care of his bills — or handle the finances of his estate — so when it is probated it may all return to the government. I told him and he said —"

"Poor Leo," she said. "What did he say?"

"He said he was going to give everything to — you — after you were married. He had no one else, except supposedly his other daughters; Gladys herself being so ill." Snook said this in a way that showed how little he believed in those other daughters.

"How much would all this stuff be worth?" Cynthia asked, sniffing, and looking about with the petulant curiosity of a child.

"I don't know — he lost a terrible amount — his mill is gone, he had to clean up the spill and pay restitution, his store is gone at a big loss, he has not received the bulk of his insurance, and he lost the construction job on the bridge because of — circumstances beyond his control — so."

Cynthia nodded. "So — how much?" she sniffed.

"Well — he'd have close to 250,000 in cash in the bank — and with his property, his construction equipment — his holdings in the new marina in Newcastle — probably 2.5 to 3 million."

Snook told her that since her claim might be contested at probate, if she had power of attorney she could at least control the funds — that is, the quarter-million dollars — and keep it away from Percy, Lyle, and Autumn, his "fraudulent" grandchildren. He was prepared to act on her behalf — so far no *real* grandchildren came forward. He was worried just slightly about Isabel Young, who had taken up their cause before. He said they must get Leopold to sign because he feared another will, probably tucked away in the safe upstairs.

"Then that's what we will have to do," she said.

It was done by wearing Leo down — because he wasn't sure what they wanted. He was afraid of Cynthia going away and leaving Gladys. He was also terrified of going to the hospital. Cynthia, sensing this, spoke about her daughter, Teresa May, who had gone to Halifax.

"I want to stay here — I want to stay with you — but I might have to go —"

Leo looked at her and kept trying to tell her something.

Cynthia, hearing Leo struggle to speak, ran from the room and sat in the alcove on the second floor, looking over the bay, crying, her knees shaking so much she could hear them knocking together. Back in the room Fred Snook faced Leo and began to lecture him about the greed of the Hendersons — the *flight* of Sydney Henderson at the time of Elly's death. It was time to sign the will, he said.

"She might be going," Freddy said, looking over his shoulder toward the door. "God, you don't want to lose her! We better do this while we can. I mean at least power of attorney — hmm?"

Snook's back was sticky with sweat, his gestures suddenly coarse. The air smelled of sickness and an aging man. Leo, cheeks sucked in, teeth in a jar, looked hopelessly after his fiancée — whom he had recently held for the first time.

Freddy, kneeling by Leo, kept the paper straight, the pen in his hand. It was one of those bright, glassy January days.

"Cripes," Snook said at that moment, jumping up, when he realized that Cynthia's leaving had caused Leo to wet himself, and it had doused his leg. Leopold McVicer, once the terror of the river, was now feeble and old.

Freddy went to the door and called to her. Then he went to the bookshelf and came back with a thick history book, with "Gladys McVicer, Grade 8, Netherwood School for Girls, 1961" on the inside cover to place under the paper. Cynthia came back. She stood at the door watching, remembering she had studied that book in school so long ago, and had liked the picture of the mountains and the clear blue lake.

Freddy was thinking he could not go through with it, but Leo, trying to wave Cynthia in, looked at them with sudden sharp glittering eyes, the kind that invalids have in a moment of crisis, and he signed his name legibly and in duplicate.

Cynthia went weak. Her legs buckled. She did not know why God had shone His bounty and love on her. But she could not let on, in any way, that He had. She had done this for *Leo's* peace of mind. Just as Leo wet himself when he thought she was leaving, Cynthia peed herself on seeing him sign, too excited to care.

Once Cynthia had in her possession the greatest weapon of her life, power of attorney for Leopold McVicer's estate, she no longer needed Mr. Snook. She did not answer his phone calls. She needed her family or her friends no longer.

She believed her security depended on her finding the other will and destroying it. She knew she had very little time. Everything had to be done soon. The gossip about Leo having suffered a stroke and her being nothing but a gold digger was spreading out like the ripples from a pebble thrown into a pool. This ripple grew wider and could not stop, for if it did, other, larger ripples would overtake it. Freddy would use this against her if he could.

The Thursday I stayed at home drinking, Cynthia went to Leo's room, closed the door, and dressed him. Folding her hands in front of her, wearing a loose top over black leotards and small ballet-shaped slippers, she told him that people wanted her gone, and were out to destroy her.

"Never," he managed.

"Well, they don't want me here — and I might have to leave —"

"Why —?"

"Why — jealousy," she said. "I never seen such a bunch of jealous leeches as those I used to know."

She was suspicious of this word *probate* and what it may signify when Leo died. She asked him about his other will. She told Leo that he must trust no one but her, or Gladys would have to be sent to a *mental institution*.

"What would anyone try?" he managed.

"To take control of your money and estate so you can't get at it — Freddy Snook been telling everyone you're incompetent. He wants to freeze your accounts. That's why I put him out of the house — he wanted me in on it. Imagine! Well, none of this is up to me, is it? So I am planning to leave tonight. The last thing I need is suspicion cast upon me! I'll just take you to the hospital — it's all I can do to keep from crying — I've done nothing in my life but shed tears!"

Leo's eyes sharpened. He kept pointing to the notepad by his bed. She handed it to him, and he scrawled, almost illegibly, "Take money out," tore the sheet off, and handed it to her.

She sighed. More power suddenly thrust into her hands.

It was not yet noon when Cynthia took the cell phone, took Gladys's Cadillac, and drove Leo into Chatham. She persuaded him to stop at the Peking Palace Restaurant. They had sweet-and-sour chicken balls in a dining room of empty tables with heavy silver utensils, white tablecloths, and a Chinese waiter in a spotted red blazer.

The day smelled of gravel and sanded sidewalks, and winter sky, with its white traces of clouds. There was very little sun to be found.

Then she helped him across the main street in the middle of the day, with sidewalks shaped like bobsled runs. She stopped the traffic by waving his heavy rubber-tipped cane, leading him by the hand past heavy dark wooden stores and shops separated by empty and lonely lots strewn with used Christmas trees, their icicles caught in the small breeze; the wild crazy Cynthia Pit and the last great lumber baron of our river.

They went to each bank, and each one smelled of sterile winter and artifacts of business swiftly moving into the computer age. He had always mistrusted banks, since he was a child and his mother was home dying of tuberculosis. Leo never entered a bank without remembering this. And he never forgot that *his* people were more like Cynthia than Dr. David Scone or Diedre Whyne. His people had the country on their backs. His people came from the Hill or Injuntown. His people were the ones betrayed, laughed at, scorned as much as the natives and blamed for being bigots. His people were like Elly McGowan (McGowan the name Leo gave her — because it was his mother's maiden name: all was hidden, you see, by wily Father Porier).

His eyes glanced from one teller to the other, trying to decipher their thoughts, knowing them to be *the others* — those who did not know, and did not understand, neither boldness nor power, nor goodness. No, they were not the ones who could ever make a decision on a man's life by themselves. He hated them, and he took Cynthia's hand.

"Mathew," he whispered, "is better than the lot of them —" And he waved his cane in a high arc and then dropped it quickly.

"We are here to do some business," Cynthia Pit loudly declared.

She followed his instructions implicitly. She kept open the main account for his construction company. She emptied the other accounts, some of them untouched for years, in four different branches. One was an account opened in 1954 that held money from the cut above Russell Road — that is a cut a quarter of a century old, and most of the men who worked it dead.

At each branch there was a conference. They had to verify who he was (two of the banks had not seen him in years). They had to verify her identity and signature. But once this was done, she was looked upon with the respect, artificial or not, that the monied are always given. And it was given her.

She brought his money back home with her in one large heavy paper shopping bag. She did not count it, and hadn't an idea where to put it, but was confident that as long as she remained calm and organized she would be able to keep it.

After Leo fell asleep that afternoon, she took the bag into the upstairs bathroom with its black and white tile, its tidy porcelain sink and flush. She sat on the side of the bathtub, and in the flat white light that lingered on the plastic curtains, she counted each bill. Her lips trembled in excitement, her eyes clouded with tears. She had to quell the urge to rush home and tell Mathew what she had gotten away with. She held $247,000 in her hand.

Now everyone would try to stop her, perhaps the other will would be found. Certainly Snook would feel cheated. Perhaps the Henderson kids would hire him. How she hated them. Or worse — a robbery. Yes, there would be a robbery sooner or later!

But before that — she had to find the other will and destroy it. Like Percy's moth, she should concentrate on being herself.

She went to see Gladys.

"I want to see Gerald," Gladys said. "I have a bit of money. We can live on that until he gets his grant — take me over to him. You don't need me here no more. I know he has phoned here for me — I heard you talking to him — I know he wants to see me! I know he applied for a grant — it was in the paper." And she picked up a recent newspaper and read what Dove had said in his application:

"'A look into the problems of regeneration after the defoliate years in the upper stretches of New Brunswick's Arron Brook, principally at McVicer's Works, and the question of applied reconstruction.'" She smiled after she read this, for it was so much like Gerald Dove.

But Cynthia suspected Dove; he would change Gladys in some way and make her want the money. Make her greedy. And there was of course something pathetic about an invalid being greedy. So Cynthia told her that she thought Gerald Dove had gone.

"Gone," Gladys said, "oh no." She smiled. "He is still here — still working toward his grant — still hoping to do something brave."

Cynthia looked out at the sky. It had turned mild and a snow had started. After Gladys went to sleep she went upstairs and took the money into her own room, with its small single bed. But she could not sleep. She kept looking down at the yard. Once she thought she saw Mathew's shadow outside. It would be nothing for him to kill her. In fact, if he robbed the place he might kill her just to keep her quiet.

She kept staring at the bag, trying not to think about it. She needed the other will. Finally she got up again.

She woke Leo. He came awake with a terrible start. And she whispered; "I have to help you upstairs —" She kissed him and placed her warm hand on his. "We have to put the money in the safe," she whispered.

He nodded, and she brought the walker over for him.

"I don't need it," he managed, and he stood.

She helped him along the hallway, and with his good right arm he firmly held the bannister, and she held his left arm. In this way, they made it upstairs. On the landing he stopped and waited. He was sure he'd heard a noise. Cynthia, who was brazen but never brave, felt her heart jump. If it was Mathew *now* she would never be able to stop him.

"What what what what?" Cynthia said.

Leo waved it off after a minute, saying it was the elm behind the house tapping on the ice. They continued.

The third-floor stairs were crooked and endlessly narrowing into the dank walls. At the top of these stairs there was a door, with a Robin Hood flour logo faded with time on its front. This door was locked. But searching the brick on each side, she found the key.

Far above even the second-floor rooms with their autumnal pictures of deer at streams and partridge on birch woods roads, she could feel the wind blowing and a kind of haunted feeling of time that had not passed. Some of the third floor was unfinished, and at each end, the exposed red brick chimneys were still bright orange all these many years, while their outsides were crumbling and black with soot. There were furnishings in the three rooms up here, dressers and old rugs and wall hangings and kids' games like Monopoly and Clue. There were pictures too, pitiless in their lost meaning. A picture of Arron Brook at twilight before the mill was built — when the water was crystal clear. An older picture of nuns at the Lazaretto in Tracadie in their underbibs taking care of three old women, obviously lepers, circa 1924.

And another picture of five woodsmen stripped almost naked washing their stockings. It was taken perhaps forty years before on an autumn afternoon in a batch house, and one of these men, stern as fire, was Leo McVicer. The man behind him was Roy Henderson — and staring at her with the dull lazy eyes that he always had was her own father, Kyle Ike Pit. She trembled when she looked at him now, as she had when she was a little girl. Often when he went to beat her Mathew would step in and take the beating for her. She remembered that now, and also how much she loved her father, and that one day he bought her the largest sucker in McVicer's store.

She wanted the other will. Once that will was destroyed, she would be free of McVicer, and of us all.

Cynthia handed him the bag of money. He looked in it, jostled the bag up and down, and they went over to the safe.

He blew on his right hand as if for luck and turned the combination; 12 left, 3 right, 20 left, and then back to the centre. With a jolt, the safe door opened.

He took the bag of money and tossed it in and closed the door.

She kept whispering the combination of the safe. It was his birthday. The twelfth of March, 1920.

She sat in the kitchen drinking a gin. She had to do something. There were not many options. She could call the police and give Mathew up and say she knew of the sabotage on the bridge and that he was planning a robbery — but if she did that, she would no longer have a free hand with the money. Secondly, if she left the old man and his daughter, they might get hurt when Mathew did come.

She decided she would leave, take the money and the old man and his daughter with her. She would leave them somewhere safe. Then she would go and get her daughter in Halifax. If ever caught she would say she was an abused woman who had to take her daughter because Rudy had threatened her. And wasn't that the case? Of course it was. No one would blame her for that. She knew also there was an underground railway for women running from abusive relationships. No one would ever find her.

She drank another gin and thought, sitting forward like a man, with her arms on her knees and a cigarette dangling in her mouth. Yes, it was the only way. But where could she leave Leo and Gladys? She thought of dozens of possibilities and dismissed them all. If she left them at anyone's house they would be suspicious and telephone the police. No, it had to be some place public — yet, still private? And where in God's name could that be? She thought of the Chinese restaurant — food waiters — but that would rouse suspicion as well.

Finally she butted her cigarette. At the back of her mind, Mathew's eyes were looking at her. He knew she had betrayed him. She was as good as dead. But so was the old man if he came in between Mathew and the money.

She heard Gladys and went to her room. The woman was lying on her side in a housecoat. She needed help to turn. Cynthia tried to make her comfortable again, and took a facecloth and washed her face.

Out of the blue, Gladys mentioned Medjugorje.

"What is that?" Cynthia asked.

"It is a place in Yugoslavia," Gladys said. "The Virgin is appearing to six children there — and has been for some years now." She reached into a stack of papers and found the latest *Catholic Bulletin*.

"But isn't it at war?" Cynthia said.

"There is no need to go *there* — one of the young women is coming here, Friday — maybe Leo and I can go. Leo helped finance her trip. Now he might benefit if he were to go see her. I don't care for myself, but it might help him. We can drive up to town and see her — her name is Vicka — and they are having a special mass — with the priests from town."

"Where — ?" Cynthia asked without any emotion.

"At the civic centre. It's been on the radio half the week."

Cynthia did not believe the Virgin did appear — at least to people like us. She scratched her nose as she read the *Bulletin*.

So Cynthia thought, take them to Vicka, leave them safe and sound with the Virgin Mother, and take the money and go. Leo would be expected there if he'd paid money to bring her, and what would be more natural than wheeling the ailing Gladys Bellanger and the elderly Mr. McVicer right to the front row!

"I will go," Gladys said, "because I think I was meant to go. I will ask forgiveness for poor Rudy, and having betrayed Gerald Dove. I will ask forgiveness because of my sisters."

"Yes yes — of course," Cynthia said. She smiled because of her continued good fortune, and leaving the woman went to bed.

She fell into a fitful sleep in her room. She saw everyone coming into her room to try to steal the money. Then she was naked and being washed over her breasts and face by a strange young woman. And this aroused her. Then someone was running away with a bag of money and she ran after them. She saw Mathew and a bear running down a hill toward Connie Devlin. The bear was telling Mathew that she had stolen the money — and had betrayed Mathew many times, not just this once. Cynthia fought with the bear and rolled down the hill. At the very bottom of the hill the bear became my father and began kissing her. She was naked because the young woman had washed her. She waited for my father to make love to her but he did not.

"Take care of your little girl," my father whispered. "She is more important than Leo's money."

Cynthia woke in a sweat. She stared at the ceiling. She stood and went back to the gloomy third floor that made her think of ghosts.

She opened the safe and took out the money. She reached deeper inside and found a brightly new manila envelope; it contained the first will, dated and signed by Leo McVicer, Diedre Whyne, and Isabel Young. Most of his estate was to go to Elly McGowan's children.

She stuffed it inside her blouse. She took Autumn and Percy's future — like that, without a qualm — and left the second will, the one Snook brought her, in its place. She took the money for her own little girl and walked as soundlessly as she could back down the stairs.

She started to leave the house, got to the door and opened it. The wind off the bay had turned cold, the whole road was a slick of heavy black ice, and snow fell.

"Cynthia?" Gladys called. "My legs won't stop aching!"

She hesitated, cursed, and closing the door, went back to Gladys.

Cynthia did not know that when she opened the safe an alarm went off near Leo's bed. He had set it the time they went upstairs together. He opened his eyes, listened to the wind in the willows, heard her creaking steps going downstairs, heard Gladys sneezing, remembered fleetingly Cynthia washing his chest, them making love, and then went back to sleep. Cynthia herself slept soundly until Friday morning.

SEVEN

Snow fell, cold, monotonous, and wondrous snow.

Leo McVicer woke. He saw a thoughtless parade of years, and was haunted by Penny Porier's body in her coffin. He was also haunted by years ago when he had to cross the bay in a storm, on a scow, alone. His mistress was having a child. He arrived late in the night. He remembered how he had disliked the feel of that child in his arms. Now that child, whom he too late loved, was dead.

He sat on the edge of the bed and looked into the morning air. Cynthia came in.

"It is snowing," she said.

"Fine," he said. "Will you give me a kiss?"

"Of course," she said.

She came over and kissed him. He realized at this moment the health of her body and the weakness of his. He tried not to be frightened of it.

"I don't want you out of my sight today — I want to plan for our wedding," he said.

"Our wedding?" She smiled uncertainly.

"I want to phone Fred Snook and talk to him."

"Not Fred — not today — you and Gladys are coming up to town with me," she said.

"What for?"

"To see Vicka — the woman who speaks to our Lady —" There was an urgency in her voice not there before.

"Do *you* believe that?" he said. He said *you* as if to say "Do you of all people believe that?"

"Your daughter wants to believe it," Cynthia said meekly, "so I'm doing it for her. And you helped bring Vicka here. I think it's appropriate to go there to pay our respects. She might be a blessing to you." She smiled again and turned on her heels.

"Hey," he said.

"What, love?"

"Once when I was robbed of five hundred dollars — it took me six years but I know who did it — I know everything that happened that day — I know what happened in the living room, and later that night. It will all come out."

She nodded and left the room quickly.

Lyle, he thought. The young man who is my grandson, who I want to run the McVicer Works!

I was told this is what my grandfather thought. I must come to help him. He now had no one else. But it was too late.

The wind came sharp, and the roadways were icy — the wires heavy, the bay frozen.

"It will get dark early — we should head up early — besides, we want a good seat — to see her," Leo heard Cynthia say nervously as she mixed pancakes. "People will be coming for miles and miles. Bishops, seminarians, and all that fuckin' crew!"

Leo made it down the stairs slowly — it took twenty minutes — and walked across the living room and opened the door to his daughter's room.

"Oh, Daddy," Gladys said, trying to sit up in bed, "you should not walk on your own."

The wind howled and snow battered the walls of the house. Both of them sat in Gladys's small doll room off the back of the kitchen, invalid, and alone.

Cynthia set the table carefully, spoon and fork and knife and plate and coffee cup, and tried to remain calm.

Mathew went to wake Rudy, who had stayed that Thursday night at Pit's house. He was a loud talker the night before, but now he tried to get out of going to his father-in-law's. He said he didn't know the combination to the safe, but he had told so many lies Mathew did not believe him.

"You and I are in this together —" Mathew said. "After all I did for you, you owe me this. You have robbed me — you owe me! We have no choice — do you understand, Rudy? Just as you said last night — we have no choice — we should have done this two months ago — I kept thinking Cynthia would help — but we have no choice now! Connie has told — do you understand me?"

Rudy began to shake spasmodically and then got sick to his stomach. Mathew stood over him with a facecloth and paper towels and looked far away across the road. It snowed over the great country of ice, over the bogs of cedar and spruce; the wails of coyotes in the fields; the windows and houses crusted with frost.

Cars were few and far between on the highway, and people were stuck in their houses. Schools were closed and locked, and the snow wisped silently against their small alcoves and worn steps.

Rudy stood before the mirror in a pink suit with cowboy boots. There was a sudden snap. And Mathew brought the 12-gauge pump action up to his face.

"We'll have no problem," Mathew said.

"But that's Gladys and Leo," Rudy said in astonishment. "We can't hurt them! And what about your own sister — I mean —"

"Yes — Cynthia," Mathew spit. "Trying to sneak away with my money. And they really treated *you* well. They lied to you, they stole your ideas — and Gladys is having an affair with Gerald Dove."

Rudy felt hot pins cover his entire body.

"We will go and do it — and go — to Australia," Rudy said, a smile of regret on his face. But his arms were limp and his legs were shaking.

EIGHT

I too waited for the snow to start falling heavily, and left Percy alone. I had to, even though I promised Autumn I would be with him. I told him I would be back home soon and help take Scupper to the vet. He waved with three fingers of his right hand as if, I believe now, he was waving goodbye.

"Lock the door after I'm gone," I said.

I walked outside and waited, and knocked on the door. Percy opened it. He looked up at me and smiled. I have never seen such a smile before or since.

"Lock the door," I told him angrily.

I closed the door and waited until I heard it lock. Then I turned into the storm and followed Autumn's half-obliterated tracks up the road. I reached the house after an hour of circling.

Devlin's house was closed, the blinds drawn, and it seemed so peaceful and sleepy in the snow. I knew that he had police now and again coming by, but they wouldn't be down here today; nine out of ten squad cars would be off the road, and the only calls that would be answered would be emergencies. I pulled out my knife and slipped in the back door.

The house was dark; the snow smelled metallic and wind whispered in the porch. Didn't I tell my father I would kill him? And should I?

I searched the house. I heard a noise and went into the basement. It was dark, the windows were small and green. There was a clothes-basket filled with laundry. I waited, and watched. I heard a squeak on the floorboards upstairs.

Upstairs, I thought. I will go and get him now. I looked at my watch. It was quarter past one in the afternoon. By quarter past two he would be dead.

I had had many arguments with my father about the nature of

goodness. About pacifism I quoted George Orwell against him, who in his essay on the Spanish Civil War said that foolish people believe that not resisting evil will put an end to it. It never did, I told my father proudly. It is best to take up the fight.

To both him and my mother I spoke of the Christian Brothers at Mount Cashel, the buggery of boys by priests, the cruelty of convents by stupid and inflexible nuns, the crawling of popes, like fiendish Pope Pius XII, after worldly power. Still nothing could convince them. Worse is that Mother shortly before she died said to me:

"So what if that *is* true? That does not make *me* less true — it does not make your father less good, or his bravery less real. Nor does it make a mockery of Saint Thérèse of the child Jesus."

But did it make me less true to be holding my knife? I walked back up the stairs, silently moving toward my destiny.

There was another creak, far down the hall.

"I'm coming for you," I said. There was only silence. I opened the cellar door and turned to my left, and proceeded down the orange carpeted hallway, with January light oozing through the one petty window. I took my gloved hand and lifted the phone. The lines were down. I heard a monotonous crash of icicles from the back roof. In the small living room with its new heavy leather chair, I smelled what I had always smelled from Connie Devlin — the leftover staleness of cigarettes and Kraft Dinner burned in a pot on the stove and eaten in front of the television.

Perhaps he has not had time to digest his food yet — and I will kill him, I thought. Well, that's too bad for him — he never thought of anything when he killed my father and left him somewhere to die."

The snow was falling hushed along Russell Road; the highway was down to one lane, hobbling along. I turned slowly and saw his bedroom door. I could see myself as I walked, feel every fibre of the carpet. Suddenly I was inside the bedroom. I looked at the bed, the phone beside it, the clock ticking.

Near the corner on the floor was Dad's black bag. I knew it from the time I was three. The last time I had seen it, Dad had it at the kitchen table, the day before he went away.

The window was dark blue, the room was grey and cold. I heard a soft clawing from the closet, a little like a cat. I held the knife and slid the door open.

At first I thought Connie was doing some sort of dance. He was staring straight at me, and I at him. His eyes were large, his cheeks huge, and the tuft of hair stuck straight out like a unicorn horn. He was swaying slightly back and forth, like he was doing a slow twist at the community centre on a Saturday night, his expression getting more and more serious, his eyes staring at me more and more fixedly.

I realized in a delayed way that he was in the process of hanging himself. The rope was tied to a rafter far above the closet proper. The squeaks I had heard were from his efforts in trying to accomplish this. But he had given up his squeaking and was looking at me in almost a reflective manner, his feet dangling a foot from the floor as I held the knife.

I cut him down.

He fell, sprawling in front of me on the floor, choking and spitting. I picked him up and sat him on the bed. Then, and I don't know why, I found myself running to get him water.

"Tea would be nice," he said politely.

I boiled the kettle, made tea, and brought it to him, in a cup. He took a drink.

"Water's too hot — tea hasn't *steeped*," he said, with an effeminate emphasis on the word *steeped*. He looked at me contemptuously, and shook his head. He knew his tea. Then he took another slurp and put the tea on the night table.

"Baby biscuits," he said. "Up in the cupboard."

I ran and got him the biscuits. He looked into the box, reached his hand in carefully, and took one. He picked up his tea and dunked his baby biscuit into it, and then, munching on it carefully, he began to tap his feet, the rope still around his neck.

341

I picked up my father's bag and held it close to me, smelled it.

"I'm afraid I spent most of it," he said.

"How much?" I asked in a whisper.

"Twenty-five thousand."

"God almighty, Connie."

"I was tempted," he said.

"What did you do with it?"

"Ordered a car." He handed me a brochure from the night table. "Power everything — power brakes, windows, airbags, seats — leather interior. Oh, I know I won't get it now — but —"

Then he lifted a venetian blind and looked out the window.

One could not see a foot because of the macabre swirling snow.

"Is the heat off?" he said.

"Might be."

"Go and check."

I went to the thermostat and got the furnace running. I had a strange feeling that I was ordained to be here by my father. I looked at the knife and it was foreign to me, just as Mathew and Rudy and Cynthia were now.

"It was snowing," Connie said as I walked back to his room. I could not go in to him, but stood sideways leaning against the wall to listen.

"Your dad had to stop for me many times. He got us turned around twice, and I blamed him for it. But both times he got us back out on the upper side of Otter Brook, going toward the road. My, the wind was cold, my mitts were freezing. I told him he didn't care for me — I asked him to wait up — and of course you know your father — he stopped and waited for me. I told him he shouldn't take such big steps because I only had little feet. Finally I just sat on a spruce stump and cursed him. I yelled at him, told him my toes were bleeding. How would you like it if your toes were bleeding, I said to him." Connie cleared his throat, munched a cookie, and continued.

"Syd told me the day would get neither longer nor warmer. But I told him I would not go until he made me a fire. So Sydney looked off toward the powerlines and then, sighing, set his knapsack down and lighted a fire for me. It was a nice fire. I liked it. I stretched my feet toward it, so steam came off my boots, and lighted a cigarette and watched how Sydney ran about for me. 'Collect some boughs,' I would say, and he would run and get them. 'How bout a snack?' I would say, and he opened his knapsack and gave me some doughnuts. It was when he opened his knapsack I saw his black bag stuffed way down in there. I asked him what he had in it, and he didn't answer. He went off to get more wood. It was when he was gone I looked into the bag and saw the money. So I put it inside my jacket. I could always tell him it had fallen out of his sack. I was contemplating how much money it was, and my boots caught on fire.

"I jumped up and began to run around in the snow trying to put them out. I started to run, and ran right over a cliff. We were still miles and miles from help of any kind. I fell to a ledge and lay there. I couldn't get back up — so after a long while, your father had no choice but to try and get me. But he had fallen over a stump in the woods and was in pain. I could see that. He was sweating yet the day had gotten colder. I knew he was in pain. It was his appendix.

"Of course he came down after me. He had to, it was as if we were on the church roof years ago. Did you know, Lyle, that when I went to the church picnics I used to pretend that Elly was my wife and we were at a big dinner? Elly was the only woman who was ever kind to me.

"Your father kept trying to get us out of the woods. He was so determined, Lyle — he fought like an animal inside himself to get rid of the pain and get us home. It was snowing so much we couldn't see ten feet in front of us. It reminded me of us as children shovelling the church roof years ago. How it seemed that nothing and everything had happened to us since that moment. When he got down to me, I knew he wasn't going to get back up, so I took his boots. I told him to give me his boots and I would make it to the highway and get help. It was all I could do. Your father tried to stand, and fell. I put his socks and boots on my feet, so he was in bare feet — and the bag of money was in my jacket. I told him I would be back — but perhaps he didn't think I would be. I left him on the ledge and was able to use the rope to get up.

"I couldn't wait for your father. I knew he was in pain, but I would not last two hours, certainly not the night, if I stayed there. Your father had carried me a mile that afternoon. But something was wrong with him. I'm not a doctor, Lyle. I wish I could have helped him. It was his appendix. He had them acting up since he was a child of eleven. Please look at it from my point of view. I wish people would look at things from my point of view for a change — things might go easier for me then. It's not been easy for me, you know — your dad knew that. That's why he let me take his boots.

"When I got to the top, I could hear him crying and calling out to someone. I realized he was talking to Elly.

"I don't know why I didn't step off that cliff and leave your dad in peace. Your dad would have made it out without me — and I would have had my problems solved. But it was I who made it!

"Let me tell you, I was in a terrible spot. Still, it's strange the things he said. He was speaking to you all. But the pain had gotten to him. He spoke about his poems too. He asked me to take them out of his knapsack and bring them home with me, and take the money to Elly. He didn't know I had the money on me, I guess. Well that's what I sensed. But then I figured Elly wouldn't miss the money — what she never had, she'd never miss. And then, well, who could blame me — thinking of that car — like I said, power everything.

"He lay on the ledge. He was lying on his left side speaking to me. I begged him to get up and to try it again. But he said he could not stand anymore. I kept looking at my watch, the hands turned green in the night, and yelling to him to get up. I called him names to get him to move. But I felt the black bag in my jacket, with his twenty-five thousand dollars.

"I knew he would not be found right away. Lyle, I asked him if he was in pain, and finally he told me that he wasn't in pain any longer. And then after five minutes he said:

"'I know, Elly — yes — I know — it was always right here — right here — you and me and the children —'

"I waited, and after a while when the snow got very deep, he stopped speaking. I went to his knapsack and found the poems. But I thought who would want his stupid poems? So I left them there.

"When the young students travelling down to Moncton found me walking on the side of the road, I had been up for thirty hours. I couldn't face going back to find him. I know I had promised, but they would know I had taken his boots — perhaps they would think I had pushed him over. At the end I couldn't help him. I've never been able to do those things like help people," Connie Devlin said. "But your dad was a good man that way, don't you think?"

NINE

At about this time Cynthia had the car running. But she could not convince the old man to go to it. He believed she was going to take him to Mathew, who would hit him over the head.

"I can't see anything," Cynthia said as she ran back to get them. (She had been running about for three quarters of an hour.) "Why in fuck does Canada have storms anyway?"

It was now almost two o'clock. They sat in the doll room, and Gladys tried to get her father to move.

"I'm not going anywhere," Leo said.

Cynthia's mind was still on the thousands upon thousands in the bag sitting on the kitchen table.

She felt she would have to make her escape by dressing like a man, and to that effect she was going to bring a bag with her, with a pair of Leo's corduroy pants and work shirt, and boots, and an old hat. Like many truly beautiful women, she could look like a man if she had to.

They would be looking for a woman in a car. She would abandon the car, take the train as a man. She would go to Halifax, wait for her child to have the operation, and then spirit her away.

"Get in the car," Cynthia said, "you stupid crippled old cocksucker — who I love."

She attempted to pull him to his feet. The old man sat where he was, his hair, in spite of his new hair style, slightly messed up.

"Please, Daddy, let's go," Gladys said.

Cynthia went upstairs. Upstairs there were almost a dozen rooms she had not entered before. Suddenly she sat down and put on Leo's clothes, shirt, pants, and sweater. She would run away by herself. But then, zippering his pants, she saw two figures far away, dots coming toward the house.

No one would get her money! She ran throughout the house to lock the doors. Then she went into the doll room to hide, forgetting the money on the kitchen table, in the paper bag.

Mathew walked toward the house in the gloomy snow, and Rudy trudged in front of him, turning around now and again and prodded on by Mathew's look. Rudy was talking, trying to get out of doing this horrible thing. But it was to no avail now. Every time he looked back over his shoulder, there was Mathew's implacable expression. Rudy's pants got caught on barbed wire and tore, and his knees were cold and shaking. They came to the woods in back of the house. Here Mathew loaded the shotgun.

"There's big money in there," Mathew said. "Big top dog money — that the McVicers stole from me." (This was Mathew's latest claim.)

"There is?" Rudy said.

"Thirty or forty thousand," Mathew said, sniffing. The shotgun fell into the snow and he had to pick it up and wipe the barrel. All in all, he said, he liked shotguns much better than rifles.

"A shotgun will blast a man in two," he said.

"Oh, I see," Rudy said.

Rudy was trying to make the moment seem natural to himself, but vomited once more.

"Why are you puking?" Mathew asked, astonished. "Something you eat?"

"Yes," Rudy said. Rudy said he would like to sit in the snow. His face looked pleading, like a little boy's. But Mathew prodded him with the shotgun, and Rudy went over the fence and into the field, marching before Mathew like a prisoner.

"After this I'm gettin' myself a pizza," Mathew said, but the gale, the trees filled with ice battered by this gale, drowned out his voice.

TEN

Though the school was closed that day, the run-through of the play Autumn had written on the Escuminac disaster took place. In the pivotal scene, a fisherman whose life was the centrepiece of her work, facing death in waves ninety feet high, managed to tie his own son to the mast before he was swept into the water and lost.

The scene she wrote was part of the true historical events of that night of June 29, 1959, which she could not have recreated unless she knew and held them in her soul.

From ten that morning they had gone over this pivotal scene, she changing lines and blocks for two actors, and her drama teacher — a young man of twenty-two, a writer just like she wanted to be — became more and more silent and respectful.

They rehearsed until two that afternoon. Behind the stage, where other students were still working on the props, she could see the snowfall covering the whole world outside. But she felt cosy in here, and flushed and excited by work, by the true nature of her work. She was secretly in love as well.

Her drama teacher came over to her, and took her hand in his and whispered, "What are you going to do with such large talent?"

"I am going home and make little Percy his supper," she whispered in his ear, standing on her tiptoes.

She told me later that as soon as she said this, the drama teacher looked strangely at her, and she felt ice cold.

ELEVEN

Mathew smashed the window at the back door — the door Rudy had entered when he believed he loved my mother. He reached in and unfastened the lock, and he bullied Rudy through the door. There was no more pretense that he or anyone else was a partner with Mat Pit. Mat Pit who had begun his struggle against the world when he was sixteen.

Cynthia was sitting in the doll room with her two invalids. The heat and lights were out — the power was off. Mat and Rudy moved through the kitchen, never looking in the bag that sat on the table, and right past the doll room.

Leo realized too late why Cynthia wanted them out of the house. Far above them they heard footsteps. They heard the two men walking, now and then they heard the crash and bang of furniture as both hunted for the safe. Not even Rudy had been up to the third floor before. Cynthia was only the fourth person to have seen the safe.

"Shhh," Cynthia said. "They'll not find us — just be still."

Gladys sat where she was, tears running down her face, not so much because of fear but because she could not help.

"My cell phone," she whispered. "It's in my purse — we can call Gerald."

"Where?" Cynthia whispered.

"In the living room — in my purse."

"I can't go out there," Cynthia said after a moment.

"Why not?" the old man said.

"I'm frightened," she admitted.

The wind blew. They were silent again. Leo stood.

"Well, I'm not frightened," he said.

There was no sound from upstairs. But Mathew and Rudy were two floors above; the door had been kicked in, and Mathew had come face to face with the picture of his father. Even he shuddered at this. If Rudy had been able to open the safe, and if they had found nothing in it but those letters from the government of years gone by, they would have simply left the house.

But Rudy could not open it. Mathew began to chide and hit him, causing a cut on his ear much like my mother had suffered in this house years before.

"Damn you," Mathew said. "You promised me riches — it's been fifteen years!"

Rudy had never had the combination to the safe, and he had never been hit since he was a child. He had simply lied. He had told everyone he handled money, hundreds of thousands, had paid cash for his Monte Carlo when it really belonged to the family business, as did his empty house. Nothing at all was in his name. Mathew, who all his life believed to be true what at the moment he wanted to be true, had fallen again and again for these lies, because the man had something Mathew had never enjoyed — wealthy connections.

Rudy hunched over, listening to the gale wind shake, felt his ear bleeding.

"Come," Mathew said, "open it."

Rudy tried again and again and again. "Don't hurt me," he pleaded, "I'm trying, you know."

"Trying," Mathew said, "trying — if you think *I* hurt you, wait until you see Danny Sheppard and the boys in Dorchester prison."

Rudy looked back over his shoulder at him and nodded like a little boy.

"Move," Mathew said. Rudy scrambled out of the way. Mathew fired point-blank at the safe. Some pellets ricocheted back and hit his leg. He roared in anger.

Mathew went to the rectangular window overlooking the side yard and smashed it open with the butt of the shotgun. He came back and began to haul the safe to the window. It was not easy and he roared to give himself strength. He believed the fall from the window would break the safe and all the money would tumble into the snow.

"If you can't help me lift it onto the ledge I just won't give you any," Mathew said. Mathew's pants were torn and both his legs were bleeding, and what was stranger still, smoke was coming from his skin.

Leo heard the shot. The fury of the gale told him he might have one chance and one punch left, and the way he dragged his left leg in his new white sneakers told him he would probably die after he threw it. But his life as a boy coming to manhood, the memory of his mother's agony, told him it did not matter, that he had lived his life as best he could, and was resourceful and brave when he needed to be. And now as much as any time, he needed to be.

He waited for those upstairs to come down. But they did not. He reached the purse, and began to carry it to the room.

Suddenly he saw his safe fall through the air and land on his pear tree outside the bay window. It landed with a dull thud, which did nothing at all to it, and all was silent again, with snow from the roof whispering down over it. Leo smiled, and walked toward the doll room.

Unfortunately the purse was upside down. Behind him, ten one-dollar coins Gladys used when she played the poker machines at the new marina that one time fell one after the other onto the carpet my mother had once fussed over, all the way to the door.

"You're not getting a sniff of my money," Mathew said to Rudy, "after I did all the work."

He turned and started down the stairs, his footsteps falling in brutal fashion toward the main floor, mindless of the blood running down his legs. Inside the doll room behind the kitchen, Leo was preparing for a final battle. He would wait, as if waiting for a fighter to move laterally, and then he would throw his right cross — a punch he well knew how to double up. Then he would see how tough Mathew Pit was.

The phone was not in the purse, though Gladys kept looking for it. Cynthia remembered that she had taken it to the Cadillac. Now she could not admit to this. Leo stared at her, not in anger but in pity, remembered her fascinating body not in lust but in sadness, and shook his head at his own folly.

Rudy could not bring himself to move, knowing that if he remained where he was, he would be safe. All his life he had asked whomever it was people pray to, to be safe. But it was his own life that manoeuvred him here at this time. He thought, If he finds them he will kill them.

Mathew was mesmerized by his own nature, by his own self-aggrandized viciousness, the immense fear he instilled with his bellowing.

He almost missed it in the gloom of the house as he went to leave. But something made him turn and go back to the living room again, past that old paper bag on the kitchen table. He saw the coins leading to the small door of the doll room. Perhaps, he thought, those coins fell from the safe. Yes, that was it, and he picked them up, one at a time, thinking them a great treasure. He followed them to the door.

If Leo had not gone for the purse, nothing would have happened besides a botched robbery. Rudy was now on the lower stairs.

Mathew began to feel about for the door handle.

The first thing Cynthia said when she saw him was, "Go away — and nothing will happen." The three of them tried to bar the door. They were all like children, I suppose. At the end I think almost everyone is.

Rudy walked downstairs shaking, standing at the very spot where my mother had stood declaring her innocence. The great old house was cold and silent.

"Where's the money?" Mathew kept shouting. "Come and open the safe for me and no one will get hurt."

351

"You may's well go — for I will not open the safe," Leo said.

Mathew kept lifting the rifle butt to hit the old man. But the old man stood his ground.

"Come and open it or I'll smash yer face in," Mathew said. "All of this is your fault, Leo, all of it — every stinkin' bit!"

"Leave us be."

At first Rudy did not know who had said this. Then he realized it was the sound of a feeble old man. Rudy went closer and stood outside the door, listening to what was going on.

At that exact moment Mathew slapped Cynthia as hard as he could, "for cheating him," and Leo threw his right hand. Mathew sprawled backwards. When Leo threw the punch — the hardest punch he had thrown in forty-five years — he himself fell to his knees. When he fell to his knees Rudy instinctively ran to pick him up. But he stopped, because of fear, and the sight of the shotgun. He looked at it, and it paralyzed him. Leo and Mathew began to fight for the shotgun, and Leo was kicked in the face. A spurt of blood from the old man shot straight into the air like a geyser.

"Help him, Rudy," Cynthia pleaded after Mathew threw her back the second time against the wall, her own nose bleeding.

"God," Rudy said, trembling.

Mathew kicked Leo again.

"Rudy, dear — you have to now," Gladys begged.

Mathew wrestled the gun away from the old man.

Still, Leo managed to throw his right once again and send Mathew reeling, so that one shelf of dolls, immaculate in their dresses, and perhaps worth thousands of dollars, came tumbling onto Mathew's head.

Mathew turned the shotgun toward Leo.

He hesitated. In that second the world seemed to stop for all of them. In that second there might have still been time to put everything back in its place.

As Mathew turned the gun, Rudy held his arms up over his face and jumped as if jumping into a pool of cold water, coming down between Mathew and Leo. Mathew saw this at the very instant he pulled the trigger. He had intended to fire over Leo's head, to make him stop. Rudy's smile was pleading and hopeful when he jumped, just as it had been most of his life.

No one heard the shot until Rudy fell backwards. Another shelf of dolls crashed down, and Rudy could see his own hands falling, and it was as if he was holding little Teresa May who was hugging him, and she was smiling as he picked her up one summer day when he was wearing Bermuda shorts. But that was all; there was someone else in the room, talking to him now, telling him to come away quickly, to hurry, for they had to go; and he was dead before he hit the ground, the plans for his marina sticking out of his jacket pocket, his eyes wide open.

Mathew grabbed Cynthia by the hair and dragged her toward the car.

"You fuckin' fuckin' fuckin' cunt, you'll open the safe," he said as he passed the paper bag on the kitchen table. "Think the likes of you could fuckin' trick me!"

In the afternoon twilight, he hauled the safe into the back seat, pushed his sister into the front seat, and drove through the heavy snow, veering right and left in a trance of his own making.

Cynthia's face was spotted with Rudy's blood, which ran from her eyes like tears. She was dressed much like the man who had told Percy that he would someday have to go away.

TWELVE

Percy was waiting for me to come home. He had set the clock before him on the kitchen table, and had made himself a glass of Quik and a peanut butter sandwich — half for him and half for Scupper.

I did not come home, just as I had not come home many days. Just as I had not taken him to the circus. Finally he went to the phone and dialled Jay Beard's number. He waited. There was no sound, but he did not know why. He went and sat beside Scupper again.

"Scupper Pit," he said, biting into his peanut butter sandwich, "what do cows do on Saturday night?"

He waited.

"They go to the MOOO-vies!" He laughed. "That's a joke Mommie told me — when I was little."

He looked inquisitively at his sandwich and took one more bite. Then he put it down on the plate carefully, and looked about the room. Everything he had ever known was here, waiting within forty yards of his house. The birds he fed, the daisy chain he had made for his mom one summer day.

He sighed, and clasped his hands together and waited as the clock ticked. Then he stood and went quietly to the telephone again and dialled Jay Beard's number. And he waited. There was no sound at all. He did not understand that the phone lines were down. He went back and sat on the chair. Again he listened to the clock ticking.

"Scupper — I'm sorry," he said finally. The dog was, at fifteen years, unable to walk, and over the last week was unable to eat. It could not go outside to urinate, and Percy cleaned its fur of pee every day. Percy believed that the vet would make it all better again.

He looked out the window. The sandwich sat on his plate, and his Quik was half-finished. He put on his boots and coat. He did this, and sat in the seat again waiting for me.

"When Lyle comes back, Scupper," he said, and the wind blew, and far above him the clouds moved. But then, as if something finally prevented him, and went out of his spirit, he stopped saying I would be home. I had never been home for him in a long time.

He put Scupper in his old security blanket and picked him up.

He should not have had to carry the dog. Nor did he know he was putting the dog in more distress. He opened the door, stepped into the blinding snow, and tried to make it to the road five hundred yards away. He fell three times and the dog fell with him. Each time Percy struggled to catch his breath in the gale-force wind.

Each time he fell he would pick the dog up again, and cross from one side of our lane to the other, staggering and seeing places where I used to help him collect his bugs; the thing he remembered about me, I guess.

He talked to the dog and told him things he told no one else. They would all be happy and go for a picnic. And Lyle had a funny story, and Autumn showed him how to dance, when we all got in our sock feet to wax the floor; and his mommie showed him how to make muffins one afternoon. He stopped in the middle of the lane, snow falling on his orange hat, and thought of Elly, and how she smoothed her hands on her dress the day he made her the daisy chain — the only thing he remembered of her now. He looked behind him, as if he might see her sitting on the porch, smoothing the dress with her hands and saying, "Oh, Percy darling, how are you?"

But there was no one there anymore. And she would not be there ever again. And suddenly for the very first time he was aware of it.

He was not even sure if he was on the lane, for the drifts were so high and the snow so blinding. He did not know where the road was, because of the storm. It was almost impossible for him to breathe. But he kept struggling with the dog. Everything was white and the trees were blotted out and shrouded in twilight. Our mailbox too was covered now — his last indicator of where the lane stopped and Highway 11 began was under snow.

He kept walking to the trailer, where Jay Beard often gave him cookies and played the guitar.

"Scupper," he said, turning his face away from the wind, "I hope Lyle doesn't know that my heart is broken."

He stumbled again slightly, the snow past his thighs. He sat down, not knowing he was in the middle of the highway.

"I am tired, Scupper Pit," he whispered.

Looking up he saw too late the car lights and the man who once told him he would have to go away.

Jay Beard saw it all from his trailer and ran outside in his bare feet. Autumn ran from the corner of the bridge, and someone shouted for Jay to get an ambulance.

Scupper was still lying across his master, and licking Percy's face. I have heard that Percy's nose was bloody, his blond hair wisped in the wind. I have heard his eyes were open and filled with tears.

I once told God I did not want that child to live. So just to prove to me what life was really worth, and what I in fury had cursed, God allowed me him six years.

Mathew did not stop. Cynthia tried to pull the car over but couldn't. Mathew looked once in the rearview mirror and kept going.

"This is my chance," Mathew said, sniffing. And he hit her.

"Shut up," he yelled. "Shut up or I'll send you straight to hell — I'll send you straight to hell!"

Even though she did not say a thing he kept yelling shut up and hitting her for a long time.

She lay against the front door, with her feet tucked under her to make herself as small as possible, as the wipers clacked against the frozen window. For fifteen minutes she said nothing as he beat her.

Finally, in the middle of town, right near an old cement wall, in front of one of our three-storey 1920 wooden houses, she opened the door and jumped, and rolled, and the Cadillac kept going.

She stood. Her back was bare and the wind lashed it. Her breasts and ribs and face were bruised. Little had she thought last night, or any night previous, that it would all somehow end here at the civic centre. She could not get the little boy's face out of her mind, and she staggered forward in a daze.

It was already after three. The door opened and she was swept in by others. Her fingers were red raw, her hands bent like claws. She was dressed like a man.

The place was filled. Waiting most of the day were nine thousand people. She was just one more as puny and insignificant as anyone else. The money had been left behind on the kitchen table, the legitimate will had fallen from her clothes when she was changing and lay in the upstairs room of that faraway house to tell the world that I and Autumn and Percy were the beneficiaries of three-quarters of Leo's estate.

She stood looking at the makeshift altar, with a few candles fluttering and people lining up at confessionals with beads in their hands — people in wheelchairs, on crutches, people with cameras, journalists who had come as critics, boys of nineteen scoffing and drinking at the back, babies crying, and thousands of men and women dressed in their best winter clothes all craning their necks.

Then there was a sound from an anteroom behind her, and an RCMP officer tried to move her out of the way. She looked and saw Constable Morris, given these civic duties now more and more. She nodded and tried to step aside, and stepped instead into the path of Vicka, the child visionary from Medjugorje.

Cynthia looked at this young woman and went numb. It was a rather blunt and rural face, not unpretty but far from sophisticated; she was dressed extremely plainly, and wore no makeup. Still, never had Cynthia seen such a face — it was filled with joy.

Vicka was just a foot from her and passing her by, seeming not to notice her at all. In her presence Cynthia could not control her emotions, and began to shake, and she lowered her head.

Suddenly Vicka stopped dead, turned to her, smiled, touched her shoulder softly, and whispered something in Yugoslavian, making the sign of the cross on Cynthia's forehead. When Cynthia looked up, the young woman had passed on, forever. Yet the message Cynthia Pit always maintained she felt through to her soul was this:

Holy Mother has asked you, her daughter, here today, and now wishes you to change your life.

Yet how could the Holy Mother (if there even was) know that a tough independent woman such as she was would come here today,

Cynthia thought? And how could she know, being dressed as a man, Cynthia was her *daughter?*

THIRTEEN

I did not go to Percy's funeral. No one could find me. He was waked in our living room for a few days and was buried near the house. It was where Autumn wanted him to be, since he had spent all his time there, near what was called his lumpy ground, where we played marbles. I felt I was unworthy to attend. I did not go to my father's funeral either — that spring he was found by Jon Driver, who brought the body out, and he was interred beside Mom. I was away, looking for Mathew Pit.

After a while I came home. It was a long and dry spring, the brook was low, and the bay was calm and serene. There were dried-out grasses and condoms in the field above. Autumn's play won first runner-up at the provincial drama festival. People were in swimming by June.

I walked down to the beach often. Poor sad Rudy Bellanger was dead and Mathew had disappeared. The Bellanger place was empty and was up for sale — and I would walk about it now and then, watching brown leaves drift over the patio. I could have easily bought it if I wanted. In fact, Gladys told Autumn and me we could have it without paying a cent. But we didn't want it.

Cynthia spent time in jail, but not much, a few months, and came back home to be with her mother and take care of her.

Leo lived another four years. He never got better, but he did not get any worse. He learned to play backgammon and would have men come in for a game all hours. He was present at Gladys and Gerald Dove's wedding, and lived with them later.

After a time Dove began to teach at the high school, and Gladys's health improved enough so she could walk with a cane. MS is a disease that can go into remission, and hers did.

Dove re-established McVicer's Works on our river and in our province to the tune of some millions. Some of those millions now belong to me.

I sometimes long for Penny Porier. At night I speak to her and make plans. Once I visited her grave and sat down and cried. But as Camus has informed us, I was only crying over something that no longer exists — is putrid and dead.

One day when I woke, Autumn was gone. It was not that she could not forgive me. I could not forgive myself. So she had to go. I didn't even know where.

I was sitting upstairs in the bedroom, the room I had shared with Percy. It was Easter Sunday. Percy's bow tie and shoes were still near his bed, as was the church bulletin we had received about his First Communion that he had kept on his mantel.

"Autumn," I said.

But she had left for somewhere I was not wanted.

I had all the money I ever wanted, I suppose hundreds of thousands of dollars, and could go anywhere I chose. So I chose to look for Mathew. That was as good a life as any. To prepare myself for this, I called him every name under the sun that I had learned growing up where I had, whatever name I had come across in the lexicon of pain and fury. But there were never enough names.

I packed Percy's clothes into a box, and found the five dollars Mom had left him. I left it with his clothes. I also found some dog biscuits in the pockets of a pair of his pants. Deep in the pocket of his suit jacket I found a picture of Mom sitting on the veranda. I left it where it was. I had not known greatness at all, had I?

I closed up the house, left the tiny little home and the obscure New Brunswick river. I found myself in Halifax. Walking along one night, to my great comfort I saw him. He stared at me, and ran, and

I ran, chased him into an alley, and he jumped me. I broke my hand punching the top of his head, and he flattened my nose — but he was gone. I followed him to Toronto.

Here no one knew what destruction I had caused. If I thought people were getting close to me, I would leave instantly. In that way I'm sure I was like Mathew Pit. We had both been created out of the same soil of the damned, the same wide empire of the poor. I slept on the streets just like he must have, haunted by voices as much as he was. Not because I could not afford a room — there was a trust account opened for me — but because I deserved no better.

"You're nothing but a gutless fuckin' punk," one of the officers said to me one night after I was picked up drunk. "I'd love to get you out on the street — how about I take off my uniform and we go outside."

"How about we do that right now?" I said. I took my sweater off, and he stared at the scars on my body and my arms, and said nothing more about our contest.

I carried no pictures, had no good memories, chose no occupation. I conspired to forget everything I had ever learned or known except for Mathew Pit. But I could not drink the pain away, or even keep it down. The hand I had broken on his head did not heal right — I went to no doctor because none had the kindness to visit my mom during her miscarriages. My hand pained in the dampness in the middle of winter.

FOURTEEN

In February, three years after I left home, I looked up and Gerald Dove was standing in front of me. He had placed a loonie into my hand as I sat near Maple Leaf Gardens.

"Lyle," he said, at first unsure and then kindly. He told me he was in Toronto taking some high-school children to a Leafs game against the Montreal Canadiens. He made me promise I would meet him for breakfast the next day; not only did I have part of a large estate to manage — and he wanted me home, for the decisions were mine and not his — but I had a compensation package to be settled with the provincial government, and David Scone and Diedre Whyne were both interested in seeing me to make headway in that regard.

Dove and his students gathered around me. Everyone wanted to shake my hand. I became emotional and self-conscious.

"You see how much your family is now honoured — because of your father and sister," Dove said.

"Autumn?" I said. I had not even known if she was alive. So many had left me.

"All these kids have *read* her — this is their reward for passing their mid-terms — to come to the game."

"What do you mean?"

"Her novel — and your father's poems — you didn't know? I can take you to any bookstore here and you can find Autumn's novel — can't he, kids?"

I started to shake violently. I was ashamed of representing my family to them. I turned and ran away, clutching myself; into the dark bowels of Toronto's midwinter.

I walked in the dark toward the lake, hoping to drown. But I couldn't even do that.

I left that night. I went to Europe. I wandered through Oslo on sunny winter afternoons. On the trains and in the bars I spoke to people who had their lives ordered, fastidious and kind-hearted, used to being punctual and correct.

I asked one young man I drank with if there was a Catholic church where I could go and light a candle. It was my mom's birthday. He looked at me with alarm, and whispered that there was, but he would not be sure where. That here Catholicism was looked upon as a sect, and its observers looked upon as imbeciles.

"Let us drink to my mother."

"Skoal," he said.

That night I went to the Oslo airport, a huge empty place filled with cement and glass and a few desks for security. The lights cast a cold glow on this ugly chamber while outside it was almost dark. In this grey northern darkness, much like our own, with people dour and alone, their lives seemingly as transient and as unfulfilled as mine, I was walking by a news kiosk when I stopped dead. I turned and went back, to a book section called, "New Voices for the Millennium."

She was looking out at me, wearing her contacts, but her hair was white, with just a small yellow streak at one side. The jacket said she lived in Toronto and was married, with one son. Sydney.

So she had raised herself above the torment of our youth. Unlike me she had crossed into a realm where her affliction did not matter anymore. I could see that her affliction was now a part of her grandeur and looked upon as a quality of artistic bravery.

She had a translucent beauty and a wilful Henderson look. Her phoenix could not be otherwise. Where were those boys who had tormented her now, took down her panties for candy — those girls who did not let her join? I remembered her clothes were almost rags doused with holy water, and the pink glasses she wore always folded on the window sill at night.

Now her white hair was the hair of an oracle, her eyes were the eyes of mercy. I too had once been ashamed of her, and couldn't protect her from the vileness of our youth.

I could see that the picture of her in our provincial paper, taken to expose us, had not succeeded in destroying our family. I bought her novel, though I could never bring myself to actually read it. It was dedicated to Percy.

Often I would go to airports hours before my flight and would sit and watch and wait and hope. What was I watching for? I did not know. Not for the longest time.

I knew that very few of these humans dressed impeccably and hauling their indispensable luggage would have seen moose and coyote blood, have stolen wood to survive a blast from winter, have carried a knife into a strange house in order to perpetrate a murder, or have seen a father almost beaten to death. I knew I was free of my past as long as I remained in transition from one place to the other, travelling with these newer, more organized, and more modern humans. Humankind that I could never really join. Not even if I tried. My gaze whenever I wanted told people to stay away.

I arrived in Paris this past spring. I visited Napoleon's tomb, walked by the Place de la Concorde, and went to the Montparnasse graveyard where Colette and Sarah Bernhardt, Oscar Wilde and Jim Morrison are buried. In the middle of this vast city graveyard I could not stop crying.

I had a room on the rue St. Denis and went back to it late on that cloudy afternoon. I lay on the bed, and wept.

You see, those tombs and mausoleums where all those grand people lay are larger and better built than the house Percy lived in, the place where he waited for his mother to come home — for me to take him to the circus — and I thought of his grave by the lumpy ground.

So I ended my travels. I came back home two months ago. But everything had changed in my house. It wasn't the same as it was when Autumn and I had slid across the new wax job in our sock feet or I had taken Percy for walks in his wagon. I just got lost in my house as small as it was. I would sit in a chair for a while, and then, remembering some painful incident, I would jump up and move to some other chair. This happened until I had nowhere to sit or stand. I couldn't even cook supper, because Mom and Percy had made tea there.

The Sheppard boys came, telling me lies about Mathew — how they had found him and had beaten him for me. They each wanted five hundred dollars. So I gave them money. They were quite fond of me now.

But when they came back the third time, giggling and laughing about how well they had managed things, I locked my door and went at them. I beat the teeth out of both of them. I smashed Danny's nose and cut Bennie's tongue when I punched him with my ringed finger. I'm sure they didn't think I could. They fled into the late-afternoon drizzle with a smell of balsam in the air. I never saw either of them again.

I went to visit Cheryl Voteur. I had bought a diamond for her. I started to propose. She smiled, and took my hand, and told me she was getting married to Griffin Porier. He was working now for Gerald Dove.

I stayed at home after that. I pawed through Dad's bookshelves, flipping books open and closing them. I would stand for hours at a time doing this.

I picked up Tolstoy's *The Forged Coupon*. I flipped it opened and saw words underlined and notations made not only by Dad but by Autumn. The pink carnation Autumn had won for Dad at the Christmas fish tank had been placed in it for safekeeping before Father went away. Age had faded it to a peach colour. I carefully put the book away and went outside.

Outside at every instant I would see Percy turning toward me, and smiling, with his hand to his mouth to stifle a cough, or his shirt out and his bow tie askew. I would talk to these ghosts, to all of them lingering here now. I would wake and sleep with them. Why not join them?

Three weeks ago, I placed my sister's novel and my dad's poems together on the kitchen table, along with Percy's First Communion bulletin, took the rifle from under the bed, loaded it, and sat in my chair with the barrel at my head.

I was wondering how long it would take for them to find my body, since no one, not even old Jay Beard, would come here now. He could not stand to walk the lane that Percy had, or play his guitar anymore.

I stared at the T.V., too lazy to go and shut it off. And the program was interrupted by a breaking news story.

A large fire was burning on the south end in Saint John. The residents of several buildings were forced outside in the cold. There were firemen and water tankers fighting the blaze — and far in the background at the doorway of this very place — this Empire Hotel — someone was sitting on a chair. It was Mathew Pit, a blanket around him, shivering and shaking.

He had come full circle — back to you — to this very building where you live, Mr. Terrieux. I saw his head and put the rifle down.

I came to Saint John the next day. I took a room in the tavern for the night and waited without sleep. The next morning I walked along the street in the cold and fog.

Mathew seemed to know I was coming. He was destitute, living in this rooming house three floors beneath you. He was lying on a mattress, staring at the water marks on the ceiling. He turned his head toward me and pointed his finger. I did not look at what he was pointing to. But the daylight came in through the window and made red spots on his bed. There was also a smell of flowers; the place was heavy with it. I reached over, right across his bed, and turned on the lamp. Perhaps this is what he had wanted me to do. I moved the lamp so I could study his face. He looked almost sixty now, and his hair was much thinner. His freckles had turned to blotches. His mouth was sunken. He lay above the covers, in long underwear, and was thin and gaunt. Here was Mathew Pit who had once bench pressed three hundred pounds and caused terror on our road.

Next to his bed he had some Chiclets, a few straws, a lime drink — I remembered how he liked lime drinks.

He was the last casualty of McVicer's Works. He had struggled in that fight in Halifax because he was in pain. But he had never admitted this, had never given up.

I couldn't kill him — I knew that, Mr. Terrieux. Just as you could not let a child drown. I couldn't kill anyone. That was my tragedy. I had failed everyone.

"He is trying to tell you something," I heard. "But he can no longer talk very good — he is trying to ask you something."

It was a soft voice.

I turned around. Sitting in the far corner, keeping a vigil with the dying, was a child of twelve or thirteen looking at me, with black curly hair and a stud in her nose, wearing jeans and sneakers and a blue leather jacket.

"Do you know him?" she asked.

"Yes," I said.

"He is my uncle —"

I could not see her well, and she did not come out of the shadows.

"Are you Teresa?" I asked.

"Yes. We're here to take him to the hospital, but he keeps fighting it. He thinks the policeman will come and get him. But they won't. It is over now." She had a sweet grown-up voice, clever and penetrating.

"Your mother is here?"

"Oh yes — she's just gone out for coffee. Do you know my mom?"

"Yes —" I said. "But it has been so long now."

I looked down at him again, and in a moment Cynthia opened the door. A light bathed the young girl until Cynthia closed the door. When Cynthia realized who I was she gave a gasp.

Cynthia had aged too. She had short grey hair, her body had rounded, and she had the beginnings of a double chin. In fact she looked like Alvina. She wore a silver cross about her neck, and no makeup.

"Hello, Lyle," she said. Her voice was huskier than before.

"You're Lyle *Henderson*?" Teresa said.

I nodded.

"I read your sister's book — it's about you and her and Percy — isn't it, Mom — I mean, it's a grown-up book, but I could read it. She made me laugh about waxing the floor, and collecting Percy's bugs."

Everything was in slow motion. I wanted so badly to die.

I saw Teresa May stand, put her hand on the table near the bed. I became aware of a very strange sensation looking at this young girl's hand.

"He wants to tell you he is sorry — for it all," Teresa said. There was a pause.

She came farther out of the shadows and smiled at me — the autumn light touched her olive cheek softly.

"You are little Teresa May," I said, almost in joy. "So everything turned out — for you — I know Percy lighted a candle for you — oh, on a dozen occasions. I remember that."

Her eyes were soft and kind.

I realized at this moment, with Teresa watching me, that he had *never* been out of my thoughts. It was not Mathew Pit I had been even searching for, Mr. Terrieux; not since that fight in Halifax.

I had been trying to find *him*.

I had gone to airports early and then earlier and then earlier still, thinking that I could *find* him. But he was not at the restaurants or in the airports or feeding the pigeons in the parks, though I some-times followed children home until their parents became concerned. It was him I was seeking. And last year I had gone to the circus insane enough to think I could find him and take him on all the rides.

Cynthia sat down near me. She told me Mathew had bone cancer, and that she had informed John Delano where he was two weeks ago; and Delano advised her to leave him be, for it was too late for retri-bution. So he would go to the hospital and be treated for the pain.

"But not the real pain," she added.

Teresa was standing beside the bed. Finally she said, "Mommie, tell him."

Cynthia put her hand on my shoulder and tears streamed from her eyes. In a way all of us were joined at that moment. I am not much for displays of emotion but I said nothing. I looked at her and her face was burning with tears. I stared at the cross on her neck, as if I was ashamed of everything in my life. It was what I had to focus on to keep from rushing away. Cynthia squeezed my hand as she spoke.

"Teresa May — has your Percy's heart," she whispered. "She would be dead now if she had not gotten it. There was no way for her or little Percy to know how it would come about — was there?"

Teresa took my hand and placed it under her blouse, so I could feel his heart. I kept my hand there and listened and felt a pain throughout my body, for Percy's unfathomable love and sadness.

I left them and went back home. John Delano told me about you, Mr. Terrieux, how you left the police force because you almost drowned that child. I was compelled to see you. I did not know you lived in the same building as our Mathew Pit until two nights ago.

But I want you to know you did the right thing. That if you had to walk along that brook and save that man a thousand times, or tens of thousands, you would do it. It was a universal duty given to you. I want you to know that, overall, it has been a life of joy. Of joy unending. Of Autumn and Percy and Elly McGowan. Who am I to ask for any of it over?

AFTERWORD

Lyle, sitting before him, speaking for the last nine or ten hours, was dressed in a blue sports jacket and a pair of blue dress pants; as was mentioned, having the appearance of a tavern bouncer. He wore a ring on the index finger of his right hand, which could be used in any street fight. Terrieux had met many people who looked like him all his life; and yet not one like him. Not one with that brilliance and that compassion.

Terrieux had interrupted a few times in the several hours. Once to clarify a point about the fire at Oyster River bar, and the amount of herbicide dumped, for it was Terrieux who had arrested Lyle's grandfather. It was Terrieux's patrol car Roy Henderson had crawled into that fateful day to fall asleep.

After everything had been said, Lyle's face exhibited a tenderness. Saying even more that tenderness is a commodity of valiant people.

The boy had come at noon. Now it was the middle of the night. Snow fell down over the grey streets and covered every side house and roof in a bath of white.

Lyle went to sleep at the table. And left the next morning without saying another word.

Terrieux slept most of the next day. Then he got up, and for the first time in ten years did not go to the tavern. A week later, still without a drink, he drove north to visit the Henderson house.

The lane was rocky and overgrown, and the little house was even smaller than he had imagined. The door was unlocked, though no one was home. Snow hugged the ditches and the spaces between the rocks and trees. He could not help going inside. Here he saw the books, just as they had been described to him, and the cot where Elly had lain.

How could anyone live through winter here?

After a while he went upstairs and into Autumn's bedroom. There was a chair with a faded white dress lying across it. A pair of worn black leather shoes were sitting in the closet. On the corner window sill with its chipped paint sat a pair of girl's pink glasses from another age.

He walked across the short hallway and opened the boys' bedroom door. Percy's bed was made; a picture of Scupper Pit sat on his mantel. In Lyle's corner was a recent newspaper account of McVicer's Works paying restitution; and that the company was worth some nineteen million. Terrieux stayed in the room for more than ten minutes, and a feeling of being in a sacred place overcame him. He quietly left the house.

Arron Brook gurgled away below the sloping ledge. There was a smell of snow in the low grey sky. There was not a sound of a bird. Behind the house, enclosed by a small, weathered fence, was Percy's grave. He had brought flowers for it. As he rose, he had the uncomfortable feeling that Lyle was watching him.

He left the small house, the yard, the remnants of Elly's garden. He drove to the church, where Mathew Pit's funeral was taking place that afternoon. He went inside, and sat in a pew, staring at the oak coffin. He noticed a woman with her back to him. He realized it was Cynthia Pit. He stared at the stained-glass window showing the ascension of an angel into the sky.

He left before the service finished and sat for a while in his car, smoking and watching the snow fall over the gravestones.

Then he drove on, toward Tabusintac, where his ex-wife lived with her second husband. He felt he must visit her again before it was too late. Though divorced for years, he tried to make amends that day by telling her about Percy and Autumn. He smiled a great gullible smile and kissed her cheek. But his wife was lonely, living in a large house overlooking the bay. Her husband was often away in Montreal because of company duties. There was talk of a secretary. She spoke of arthritis, and asked why God had been so cruel.

"It's *you* who destroyed my life — I won't *forgive* you that," she said in spite.

He said nothing more. He drove back to Saint John later that night. He still lives in the Empire Hotel, and drinks too much in the tavern across the street.

In June, Lyle was seen walking the hills looking down at the faraway road. In July, children ran from him if they saw the knife marks across his arms and chest. Some nights Griffin Porier found him along the highway drinking, and would drive him to the top of his lane. Lyle would not allow him to drive down it.

After a while he lived as a hermit and was never seen except far up the river, on occasion, with a fly rod and a small butt bug, seeking the trout he remembered from his childhood.

In early October he boarded up the house and disappeared with a few possessions. And though there is great interest, no one can find out where it is he has gone.

ACKNOWLEDGEMENTS

I would like to thank my editors, Maya Mavjee, and Martha Kanya-Forstner.

I would especially like to thank my agent, Anne McDermid, my wife, Peggy, and our children, John Thomas and Anton.